Letters to Olive

E. L. WALL

For the ones that are still searching.
You don't always have to put on a brave face –
in these pages you are safe and you are home.

Playlist

Spin You Around - Morgan Wallen

Weeping Willow - Warren Zeiders

Tennessee Whiskey - Chris Stapleton

Silver Springs (Live) - Fleetwood Mac

Falling - Joshua Radin

The Painter - Cody Johnson

Love You Anyway - Luke Combs

Makin' Me Look Good Again - Drake White

Watermelon Moonshine   Lainey Wilson

Simply the Best - Noah Reid

Babe I'm Gonna Leave You - Led Zeppelin

Where It Ends - Bailey Zimmerman

23 - Chayce Beckham

I Remember Everything (feat. Kacey Musgraves) - Zach Bryan

Come Back Home (Stripped) - Sofia Carson

No One's Gonna Love You - Band of Horses

Time in a Bottle - Jim Croce

I and Love and You - The Avett Brothers

Beautiful Things - Benson Boone

Worth the Wait - Spencer Crandall

1

Olive

The smell of fresh cut grass and blooming flowers wafts in the air around me. As I ride my bike down the gravel road, wind blowing my long auburn hair, I can't help but think, this is my favorite time of year. When everything comes alive. The days are hotter and longer, and the sun heats my skin giving it a deep glow. This is the first summer in a long time that I feel good, hopeful.

Just down the road is the Murphy's Pond, a secluded spot away from the rest of the town where I can rinse off the sheen of sweat building in my hairline. Ever since three summers ago when I tried to sneak in without anyone noticing, safe to say they noticed, I've been coming here to cool off. Once Mrs. Murphy saw me sneak in for the third or fourth time, she kindly informed me I was welcome here anytime but that I shouldn't sneak around like a field mouse. Embarrassment heated my cheeks and I apologized profusely, but she just clicked her tongue and said nonsense, I was a neighbor and welcomed.

It did a world of good for everyone involved, because ever since then the Murphy's have become Gran and Pop's new wheat supplier for the bakery. Pop was fed up with their previous supplier and the rising prices each season, so he sat down with Mr. Murphy and formed a partnership. He'll never admit that a sneaky sixteen-year-old is the reason they formed a friendship and business relationship with the Murphy's, but I knew it was true.

Their farm is only two miles from our house, so on hot days like this, I ride my bike over to the pond and relax. I always bring a book and a lunch to enjoy under the white oak, a huge tree on the banks of the pond, complete with a tire swing.

As I'm riding down the narrow path of thin trees, I hear a noise coming from the pond. It's private property so I never expect to see anyone else, aside from Mr. or Mrs. Murphy, and they hardly come here. They're always busy on the farm, so I usually have the benefit of being alone.

Rounding the corner to rest my bike against a tree, I see a boy swinging from the tire swing. Boy likely isn't the right term, because he looks to be older, more built and tanner too. I've never seen him before, but Mrs. Murphy told me she has two sons, so I assume this is one of them.

With a big splash, he lands in the water and resurfaces with a shake of his head before wiping the water off his face. "Can I help you?" he asks with a tilt of his head. Clearly, he wasn't expecting to have company as much as I wasn't.

"Hi." I wave awkwardly, suddenly unsure of how to socialize normally. He makes his way out of the water and strides over to me. Oh yeah, he's not a boy at all. He towers over me by at least half a foot and is covered in toned muscles.

I can feel my face flush because I've never been this close to a guy as handsome as the one before me. His skin is a creamy tan, he has shaggy dark blonde hair and the most amazing dark green eyes.

He clears his throat and I'm brought back to reality. The realization of being caught staring hits me and I stare down at my feet embarrassed.

"I'm Mitchell Murphy, but please, call me Mitch. Only my mom is allowed to call me by my full name." He speaks with a deep stern voice, with just a touch of rudeness. My face is probably redder than a tomato, but I lift my gaze to meet him and shake his hand firmly.

Something Pop taught me long ago is to always provide a firm handshake. He used to say, "there's no worse first impression than shaking the hand of a limp fish." My grasp throws him off because he raises his eyebrows and looks to our joined hands.

"I'm Olive. Olive Fournier. Well, technically my last name is Parker but I don't go by that name anymore, I live with my grandparents down the road. Usually no one is here so I just came by to cool off, but I'll give you some privacy." Wow, I am rambling like a lunatic, and suddenly I wish I had just said 'Hi, my name is Olive'. He releases my hand and I start to turn around and head for my bike.

"You can stay." he says with a shrug of his shoulders. Something tells me he doesn't really want my company, but his manners dictate otherwise. My head is telling me I should just go, maybe Gran could use some help at the bakery.

I'm not set to work until this afternoon, but I try to help

as much as I can. The louder part of my brain is urging me to join him. As if he can sense my hesitation he adds, "I promise I don't bite." He flashes me this coy smirk, his dimple coming into view before diving into the water.

Rivulets ripple as Mitch makes his way to the middle of the pond before coming up for air. I suppose there's nothing wrong with staying for a little while. Since graduation, most of my friends have dispersed off to college or trade schools leaving me behind. It might be nice to make a new friend, especially since I already like his parents.

I slip off my sandals and make my way to the water's edge, taking the spot I usually occupy when I'm here alone. I lay my blanket down and settle my feet into the water watching Mitch swim about. I'm hot from my ride over here, but suddenly I'm nervous to join him in the water. It's such an awkward thing to remove clothes before getting in the water, even more so now.

He dives under the water again and I take that moment to quickly pull my cotton white dress over my head and toss it on my blanket. I slink into the water up to my waist before he reemerges.

Mitch swims closer to me and floats on his back looking up at the trees surrounding the pond. "So, Olive. What's your story?" He asks so casually as though he isn't expecting me to blurt out that my parents died a few years ago in a car crash, all my friends left for college while I'm still here, and I have no idea what my future holds.

The words are on the tip of my tongue, desperately trying to come out. But I'm not trying to scare off the one person

I could become friends with this summer. So instead, I just reply,

"No story, really. I live here with my grandparents and help at the bakery."

He sits up and looks at me, "your grandparents are Joan and Henry?" I nod my head and wait for him to continue. "They're the sweetest people I've met since being back home. Joan makes the best oatmeal chocolate chip cookies I've ever had." He's smiling so big and so genuinely that I can't help the smile that spreads across my face. As soon as he registers his reaction, the smile fades and his face goes back to an indifferent scowl. I wonder who peed in his corn flakes this morning.

Gran does make the best cookies, though, I always assumed that was a biased opinion. "You said moved back, where were you before you came home?" I ask as I alternate between swimming in small circles and floating on my back, trying not to let his gruff exterior scare me off. With each passing minute I become more unsure around him, we just met and already I've gotten multiple different sides from him.

"I was studying agriculture at Cornell University, I just graduated." Shit, that stunned me into silence. That's an amazing school and a far cry from the small town we live in outside of Wichita. I can't imagine what it must have been like living in New York the last four years.

"Wow. That's impressive. It must have been amazing living in New York. I've never been anywhere but here so I have nothing to compare it to." He nods his head as if he understands exactly what I mean.

"You could say it was a culture shock." He's back to floating in the water, looking up at the treetops hanging overhead. The way the limbs hang low, with their overflowing leaves reminds me of the scene from The Little Mermaid in the boat. It's quiet in here, set away from the rest of the world in its own way. Probably why I come here so often.

I want to ask him more about school, but he's back to being guarded. If I push him too far or ask too many questions, he'll probably brush me off and leave. Can't decide which way I'd prefer that to go.

Floating on my back, I close my eyes and listen to everything around me, completely tuned in. The water ripples around my ears and I can feel little bubbles brushing my legs each time I kick. There's a sweetness to the air mixed with an earthy floral smell. Like nothing else around here. In the dead of summer, you can mostly smell the tar melting in the streets, it gets so hot.

But here, in the shade tucked back in a corner of the Murphy's land, it feels nothing like Kansas. Sometimes I think about getting out of here, moving to a different place where I don't know anyone and can start fresh. Not like here where I walk around, and people give me that look.

The pity look that is a constant reminder I'm the girl whose parents died in a car crash.

I wonder if Mitch knows about the accident. It happened years ago, and we didn't even know the Murphy's yet. He was probably too busy being a hotshot high school student to even care. I want to ask how old he is, given his appearance I'd definitely say a few years my senior, at least.

Good looking, obviously smart and likely raised well. I'm trying to coax my body into chilling out, but it's taken on a mind of its own. "So, how old are you?" I blurt out before I can even register my mouth is open and words are tumbling out.

A blush creeps across my face when I look up to see Mitch glaring at me. I can't tell if he's mad that I asked how old he is or what? But the look on his face has goosebumps erupting all over my body. I don't have much experience when it comes to guys, not that Mitch would even be interested in someone like me, but it does make me wonder.

He spent four years at a University, I'm sure he's had plenty of experience and would laugh if he knew how little I did. I'm suddenly hyper aware of my body, like he can see any flaws, especially with the look that is still on his face like I kicked his dog or something.

I've always had an olive complexion, which made me wonder if that's why my parents named me Olive, and long legs. When I was younger, they were gangly and thin, something that didn't attract the opposite sex too often. I never got big boobs like some of my friends, either. Another thing to add to my growing list of insecurities. Mitch is tall and strong, broad shoulders and tan skin, to him I must look like such a teenager still.

Whatever, I'm getting ahead of myself here, again. I barely know this guy and for all I know, he has a girlfriend already. Someone who looks that good surely has a line of women waiting to date him.

After what feels like forever, which was likely only a mere

few seconds, he flashes that smirk again and says, "I'm twenty-two." Okay, so I guess I didn't offend him, he just likes to tease the canary before he pounces and devours it whole. Me being the tiny and fragile canary, wouldn't stand a chance.

Mitch is eyeing me, waiting for me to respond, presumably with my own age, but I won't give him that satisfaction so easily. He made me wait, so it's only fair I play the game too. I take in a lungful of air and dip beneath the surface. I run my hands through my hair and enjoy the moment of quiet and tranquility that comes with submerging yourself underwater. The only problem is the moment always ends too quickly. Feeling my breath run out, I resurface and breathe in the humid summer air.

Water drips from my hair and face, and I use both hands to ring out the excess liquid before wiping my face as well. Clearing my eyes, I glance up and see Mitch glaring at me once again. Man, someone needs to tell this guy to eat a cookie or something, his mood swings remind me that time of the month when I PMS.

"Something wrong?" I finally ask with my eyebrows raised in his direction. If he wants to go hot and cold on me every five seconds, I'm happy to play along. I spend so much time being respectful living with Pop and Gran, I don't have this playful banter all that often.

"Just figured you'd tell me your age in return." Mitch says with a shrug as he shakes the water from his hair. We both make our way out and I reach for a towel. I wrap mine around my waist and gather my clothes and lunch. Mitch eyes me carefully as I pull my bag up over my shoulder with a confused look. I give him a big smile and just as I turn to leave, I say with a shrug, "you never asked." With a wink I walk away leaving behind a guy who more than likely is scowling at me…again.

My grandparents' house sits on a decent plot of land. Not like the Murphy's surely, but still bigger than most families in the area. The house itself has a rambling Victorian vibe to it and sits in front of a large field. Tall grass and wildflowers grow erratically there and as a kid I would often explore it. I would pretend I was lost in the jungle and roam the fields looking for salvation. The only negative was coming home with a dozen ticks on me.

Over the years the house has maintained its charm with the help of my grandparents and father before he passed away. Tall and white with black framed windows and a wraparound porch. Planters hang from each opening around the porch and Gran set it up with wicker furniture and pillows. In the left corner there's a bench swing that I like to sit on at night when the air isn't as heavy. Fireflies dance all around the fields and crickets play a tune that can only be described as mother nature's music.

I rest my bike against the railing and climb the steps to the screen door. We never lock the doors around here, in a small town such as this, there's never anything to worry about. Even though I lived with my parents, I still consider this the place where I grew up.

Hell, I'm still growing up.

When my parents died, I moved in permanently and even though I spent so much time here and it felt like home, it was still an adjustment. Coming here was always a treat, my favorite place in the world, when I moved in it was directly because of tragedy. That was a difficult feeling to overcome. I was only thirteen when they died, just coming up on my pivotal teen years. To make things worse, I got my first period the week after they died. I was devastated and mortified to have to ask Gran what to do.

Losing them so young made them miss a lot of things, like prom and graduation. I don't think about it too often, but one day I hope to get married and I'm always acutely aware that my father won't be there to walk me down the aisle.

No one is home so I take the steps two at a time upstairs to shower and dress for work. When I have the house to myself like this, I like to blare the radio and sing at the top of my lungs knowing no one can hear me. Our nearest neighbors are two miles down the road, and neither Mr. nor Mrs. Murphy has ever commented on hearing me sing.

Even if they had, they'd never tell me in fear of embarrassing me.

I dry my hair quickly and throw on a white t-shirt and jeans. I don't usually wear much makeup, but I like to apply a little mascara to highlight my eyelashes against my deep hazel eyes. Pulling my hair into a ponytail I grab my bike and head off into town.

Fournier Bakery sits on a corner spot in town, right across the street from the main restaurant. Gives people the perfect excuse to stop in for dessert once they're done with dinner.

The red and white striped awnings above the windows give it a candy stripe look and the tall green topiaries add an extra punch of color. Last year I talked Pop into setting up outdoor seating for people who want to enjoy the weather and people watch. At first, he was reluctant, but seeing how frequently people sit there, he realized it was a smart idea.

Gran patted my arm sweetly one afternoon when every table was occupied. Her way of kindly acknowledging my idea to better the bakery's business.

Fournier is our last name, and literally translates as 'baker' in French. Hence why the sign above the door simply says Fournier in scrawling cursive. If Pop had decided to put bakery after it, it would have translated as Baker Bakery. The idea always made me laugh.

The bell above the door chimes when I make my way inside and immediately, I'm struck with the smell of oatmeal. Instantly knowing Gran is making her signature oatmeal chocolate chip cookies. They're a crowd pleaser around here and she likely makes several dozen batches a week.

I round the counter and clock in before grabbing an apron to lay over my clothes. Gran smiles at me from the stool she's perched on rolling dough into balls. Before I can even ask what made her decide to go with oatmeal chocolate chip cookies today, the door to the office opens. I don't turn around immediately, assuming it's Pop, but when I do, I'm taken aback to see Mitch with that smirk and one dimple looking at me. Pop follows him out with a stack of papers he begins stuffing into a manilla envelope. But before I can say anything, Pop is speaking.

"Just let your parents know how grateful we are, again. We'll set something up this week to have dinner together at the house." He claps Mitch on the back and gives him a tight shoulder squeeze.

"What are you doing here?" I ask a little abruptly before I can think better of it. Gran gives me a disapproving look and I already know I'm going to get a refresh lesson on manners once he leaves.

"Mitch here is just grabbing some paperwork to give to his parents." Pop replies, clearly unaware of the tension between myself and Mitch.

"Well, that, and I just had to grab one of Joan's famous cookies here." Mitch winks at Gran causing a light blush to cover her cheeks. Maybe I need to give her a refresh of not flirting with customers. In front of her husband, no less.

"You're just sweet talking me, Mitchell." Gran smiles as she continues rolling dough into balls. "I'm sure you tell everyone that." She tries to sound convincing, but I can tell there's a part of her that knows he's telling the truth.

"I am many things Ms. Joan, but a liar is not one of them." He leans in to grab a fresh from the oven cookie and places a sweet kiss on her cheek. The gesture has her blushing again and something about it makes me smile despite my feelings just ten seconds ago. Mitch appears rough around the edges, but that sweet gesture to a well-aged woman goes a long way.

"Your mama raised you well I see." She pats his back before he pulls away and diverts her attention back to me. "Olive, I take it you met Mitchell here." I chuckle lightly remembering Mitch telling me not three hours ago, that only his mom calls him by his full name. Even if it bothered him that Gran did it too, which is doesn't appear to, something tells me he wouldn't correct her.

"Yes, we met this afternoon by the pond. I went up there like I usually do expecting to be alone when I heard him splash into the water. Scared me half to death." I add the last part with a little dramatic flair as I rest my palm across my chest. Mitch doesn't laugh, just nods his head in mock humor.

"I wasn't expecting any company, you're just lucky I had my pants on." He says flatly, but the thought still has a flush creeping up my neck. I try hurrying off to my work, but not before Mitch caught a glimpse of my blush. Dammit, I don't want to give him any inclination that he affects me in any way.

I'm working on condensing the shelves and moving leftover pastries to a sheet pan to be wrapped up and donated. At the end of each day, whatever is leftover gets wrapped up and delivered to the shelter just outside town. Gran never wants food to go to waste, so ever since I can remember, she or my mom would drive outside town and hand deliver the pastries to a homeless shelter. Along with any bread that wasn't purchased that day.

Gran always tries to include some extra sweets in there too. Hence why she's making oatmeal chocolate chip cookies. I assumed she was doing it for Mitch, but she informed me she had already begun making them by the time he showed up.

He's not as special as he thinks.

Usually, I offer to deliver to the shelter, I like the drive and it gives me a chance to check up on some of the locals there. Last week I went in and found out Sarah, a local woman who was living in the shelter with her daughter, had found a job and was already saving up for a place. Seeing these people struggle but still do their best to maintain a positive outlook makes me grateful for everything I have.

During my teenage years I was so bitter and depressed about my parents, I focused all my energy into being mad at the world. It took going to the shelter several times a week to see that I still had so much to be thankful for.

As I finish loading everything up Mitch emerges from the office with Pop. I was so wrapped up in my task, I didn't realize he was still here.

"Mitch, thanks again for hanging around with an old grump like me. You're a fine young man." He slaps him on the back to make light, but I can hear in his voice the true sincerity behind it. Pop isn't one to get touchy feely and express his emotions, so that gesture there means more than Mitch probably realizes.

"The pleasure is all mine, sir. Let me know if you need any more help and I'd be happy to come by. That is if Ms. Joan is willing to make more of those oatmeal cookies in exchange." He winks at her over the counter as she counts receipts. She doesn't look up, still focused on her task, but smiles big.

"Anytime, Mitchell. Hey, maybe you can take a ride with Olive to the shelter. I usually go with her to keep her company, but I'm dead tired."

My eyes bulge out of my head. Did she seriously just back him into a corner and make him feel obligated to go with me?

Add this to the list of mortifying moments in my life.

"Gran, please. I don't mind going by myself. I've done the drive a thousand times, and I'm sure Mitch has better things to do with his time." I'm clearly giving him an out, but instead of taking it he just smirks at me with a shrug of his shoulders.

"Anything for you, Ms. Joan. Besides, I wouldn't mind going for the drive. I haven't been to the shelter since high school when I volunteered."

I grab a stack of crates filled with pastries and baked goods while nodding my head towards the other stack for Mitch to grab. As we make our way out to the car I notice Mitch walk right past Gran's little sedan and in the direction of a pickup truck.

"We can take my truck. I need to pick something up anyways." His light and airy tone used for Gran and Pop is gone, replaced by the gruff man I met this afternoon.

"You know, you don't have to do this. You can duck out and Gran will assume you still came with me to help. I won't tell." I'm still just trying to give this guy an out. Surely, he doesn't want to spend the next hour with me, alone in the car.

He doesn't say anything, just opens the side door of his truck and slides the first box in before taking the one from my hands and placing it next to the first. Our fingers graze and an electric current radiates through me. Must be static electricity from the seat. But one look from Mitch tells me he felt it too. He furrows his brows and scowls at me like I disgust him and now my cheeks redden for a whole other reason.

I try to shrug it off and walk around him to hop in the passenger seat. The truck revs to life and Mitch backs out of the lot. The first fifteen minutes we drive in total silence. Mitch finally turns the radio on fiddling with the dials before some old country flows from the speakers.

"I was trying to give you an easy out since Gran kind of cornered you back there." I say out of the blue. Mitch glances in my direction slightly before focusing back on the road. Still, he says nothing. God, I desperately want to ask this guy what his deal is. Did I somehow offend him in the short amount of time we've spent together?

The tension is killing me.

We continue driving and I glance out the window at the storefronts rolling by. This time of night the roads are quiet and practically empty. Most shops around here close at five, except for the restaurant and the liquor store.

Mitch fiddles with the dials again, passing over radio stations with too much static, before stopping. He pulls out his phone and connects it into an aux cord. A slow song starts playing and for what reason I can't say, the hairs on my body rise. Something about this song is giving me chills, like I've heard it before. But I know that I haven't.

"What song is this?" I ask keeping my eyes trained on the road. Right now, I'm finding it difficult to breathe, so I try to focus on the trees whizzing by us. Very few times I hear a song that gives me the chills, and right now in the car with a stranger isn't one of those times I feel like getting deeply affected by a song.

Sensing my discomfort, Mitch goes to turn it off. "No, keep it on. I'm sorry, I know this is weird." I laugh nervously, fully aware of how crazy I must seem to him right now. I guess I'm hoping that hearing more of it will make a memory come into focus, or that I'll remember hearing it somewhere.

Gran always has music playing in the bakery, maybe I heard it at the shop. Not sure why my body would react to it this way though if that were the case.

"It's Fleetwood Mac." Mitch answers gruffly. "Not a fan?" he asks. I pause and look down at my hands resting in my lap and nervously start fidgeting with them. The thing is, I know I haven't heard this song before. Gran usually opts for old school country and occasionally Creedence Clearwater Revival for Pop. This is nothing like what they listen to.

"No, I just feel like I've heard it before, that's all." I can't give him an explanation anymore, because frankly, I don't understand it either. So, I go back to look out the window focusing on the landscape we pass on the way to the shelter. This ride feels longer than ever, and I'm practically jumping out of my seat the second we pull into the gravel lot.

Mitch opens the door and I hop out so he can grab the crates. He hands me the smaller, lighter box of treats. As we make our way up the steps, he looks at me, and I feel all the air in my lungs rush out. No, no, no, I really don't need this right now. It's not in my plan to fall for some brooding country guy when I have so many other things on my mind. I step ahead of him and shake the thought from my head. I'm just frazzled from the car ride, that's all this is. There is absolutely no other reason my heart rate picks up when he scowls at me like he does. I'm beginning to think he's incapable of making a genuine face.

Gwen spots me right away and comes rushing over to

help with the crate I'm carrying. "Hey sweetie, how are ya?" she says in her southern twang. Gwen is one of those people you can't help but love the moment you meet them. She runs the shelter, which is likely incredibly stressful, and yet she's always so light-hearted and smiling.

"I'm well, Gwen. How's everything here?" I ask while I place the second crate on the receiving table in the corner of the hall. All the people in the shelter gather in the large hall to eat their meals together. A few recognize me as I walk in and shuffle over to see what kind of treats Fournier bakery has donated this week.

"Same as always." She shrugs with a smile. That might sound like a bad thing, but consistency is key around here. Without the structure and planning Gwen goes to great lengths to keep in place, this place could easily fall apart.

"Mitchell Murphy, is that you?" Gwen says as she peers around me. Mitch has two cases in his hands and quickly sets them down to give Gwen a hug. So he's cordial with everyone except me. Got it.

"Gwen, it's been too long. The place looks great!" He replies easily as she gives him a firm hug. This is one of those moments where I wonder if my demeanor came off the wrong way earlier. My own insecurities are my problem, I know that, but I must have been projecting something negative to have Mitch dismiss me so easily.

The two of them chat for several minutes as I begin to unload the pastries, setting them up the way I always do. I don't realize that Gwen and Mitch are gone until after I finish my setup. I knew he volunteered here in high school, but I didn't realize how well the two of them knew each other.

It's not like I could ask Mitch. He'd probably just scowl at me again.

We spent thirty minutes at the shelter loading up trays of treats and chatting with some of the occupants there. Mitch rejoined me after talking with Gwen privately. He was a natural though, talking to the young kids about sports and farming. Every so often he would sneak a peek at me, and I wondered if that was his way of saying let's get the hell out of here. He said he used to volunteer here back in high school and it's as if he never left for college. There's something about his demeanor and attitude, it's warm and inviting.

Nothing like what I've received from him.

After we said our goodbyes, and promised to come back again next week, we headed out to the truck. It's warm, but a lot of the humidity from the day has lifted, leaving us with a soft breeze. It's still early and the sun is just now beginning to set, casting a warm glow across the fields. Just as I'm about to open the passenger door, Mitch stops me. He reaches past me and opens the door, waiting for me to hop in.

He runs so hot and cold, one minute he's scowling at me and the next he's opening the car door for me. I can tell his parents raised him with manners, but the facial expressions could use some work. Earlier this evening, I was thinking he felt trapped in having to spend time with me, but here he is being a gentleman.

It's confusing.

A few minutes into the drive I break the silence. "So, how often did you volunteer there?" I ask referring to Raising Hope shelter.

"A couple times a week, I guess." He says while keeping his eyes trained on the road. I want to ask more questions, but Mitch hasn't been one to open up that much, so I just nod my head in acknowledgement.

"Why do you ask?" he finally says once he realizes I'm not asking any follow up questions. I take this opportunity to make him wait a little, like he's been doing with me all day. I glance over to see him glaring at me again and it makes me want to laugh. Something he probably wouldn't find too funny.

"I don't know, you just seemed so at ease there. Gwen never mentioned she knew you and she's been running the place for as long as I can remember." He's back to watching the road and for some reason it feels like I've struck a nerve. Mitch doesn't strike me as the type of person to divulge in their feelings often, so I decide it's best not to push him.

While we were there he kept looking around as if he was searching for someone. I want to ask him about it but the air is thick right now, and not from the humidity. "When was the last time you were there?" I ask quietly, hoping I'm not pushing my luck.

He's quiet for several minutes again, thinking, when he finally says, "not since before I left for college." Four years is a long time to go without seeing someone he clearly cares about. That has to be the reason he quickly volunteered to come with me considering every other interaction we've had has led me to believe he doesn't particularly enjoy my company.

I decide not to ask any other questions and stay quiet in the seat next to him. The windows are down, allowing a soft breeze to filter in around us. My hair starts whipping around messily and I try my best to pull it up into a messy bun. The skin on my neck prickles, suddenly aware of two eyes on me, and I glance over to see Mitch watching me lift my long tresses off my shoulders.

He turns away again looking back to the road with a grumpy expression. Someone really needs to tell this guy to practice his facial expressions in a mirror. I roll my eyes and spend the next fifteen minutes of the way home watching the streets lights pop on.

We make it back to the bakery and Mitch pulls into the lot next to where I left my bike. The lights inside are all off so I know Gran and Pop have left for the night. I hop out of the truck before Mitch can come around and awkwardly open the door for me again. I reach for my bike when I notice him looking at me with a puzzled look.

"What are you doing?" he asks like he's annoyed.

"Um, I'm getting my bike…" I say, also slightly confused by why he's looking at me like that.

"Didn't you drive here? You can't ride home in the dark on a bike, Olive."

"Why not?" I ask with a little annoyance of my own. "I do it all the time with no issues." I cross my arms to rub some of the goosebumps away. It's not the least bit cold, but once again my body is a traitor and reacts to Mitch in a way my mind does not agree with.

Without so much as another word, Mitch grabs my bike and is hefting it into the bed of his truck. I go to protest when he turns, fixing me with a don't push it glare, and points to the seat I was sitting in not two minutes ago. When I make no move to get back in his truck, Mitch sighs and rubs a hand over his face. Why does it feel like he's looking at me like the annoying little sister he never wanted?

"Olive. Get in the truck." He's looking at me, waiting for me to oblige when I just cross my arms again and pop a hip out with dramatic flair. "Please." He adds a moment later.

"Ugh, fine." I throw my hands up and jump back up into the truck. This guy is unbelievable. I wonder if he's bipolar or something. Maybe I could ask Gran if she's ever heard Mrs. Murphy mention the roller coaster emotions of her son.

Back on the road I'm still pouting for being treated like a little kid. "You know I'm more than capable of getting myself home. I'm not a little kid." I say.

"Clearly." Mitch responds with sarcasm. I usually don't go around judging people I just met, but something about him makes my blood boil. The arrogance that practically oozes from his lips every second he talks makes me want to scream. Something I obviously can't do because that would just show him I do in fact act like a little kid.

"Olive, it's dark out and you only live down the road from me. If my mom knew I let you ride your bike home alone, she'd have my head." I let the silence drone on not wanting to say anything just yet when Mitch continues. "I'm just getting her off my back for spilling paint all over the rug." He laughs a little like the memory brings him some kind of twisted joy.

"How long ago was that?" I ask before thinking, clearly throwing out my previous thoughts of ignoring him.

"Seventh grade." He says flatly.

"Wow." Is all I can muster. "You must have been fun to raise." I roll my eyes and unbuckle my seat belt as Mitch pulls up in front of my house.

He gets out faster than me this time and grabs my bike from the back before I can do it myself. I really wanted to prove that I don't need his assistance, but I guess he would have taken it from me even if I had gotten to it first.

"Thanks." I say dryly as I grab my bike and head for the porch steps. I don't intend on saying goodnight or giving him any satisfaction with pleasantries.

I'm halfway across the porch when he says, "Hey Olive?" I turn around to see him smirk in my direction. "See you around." He winks and starts backing down the driveway. I'm left standing there just as confused as I have been all day around him. I guess I was right. Something about this summer already feels different.

2
Olive

The house is dark and still, so I make my way upstairs quietly, not to wake Pop and Gran. Once I've showered and gotten ready for bed, I feel restless even though it's nearly midnight. My body is tired, and I fall into bed lazily wrapping myself in blankets. But my mind is running in circles, reliving everything from today. I glance out my window to see the dark night sky blanketing the field.

One of my favorite things about living out here is the sky and all the stars visible without the flood of city lights. My bed has the perfect view of the field, and I can see dozens of fireflies dancing in the tall grass.

My eyes begin to feel heavy, and I nuzzle into my blankets enjoying the cool air filtering in through my window. Some nights around here are too humid to bear, while others are like this, cool and relaxing. The last thing I remember before everything goes black, is the scowl on Mitch's face. New hobby, find more ways to piss him off and make him scowl.

I fall asleep with a smile on my face.

Morning comes too fast, the bright sun shining through the windows because I forgot to shut the blackout curtains. I'm used to waking up and going through the motions of my day, but today I woke up with a smile. I jump out of bed and head downstairs to make breakfast. It's only six, Pop and Gran don't need to be at the bakery for a little while since they had Maureen open.

I pull everything I need to make waffles from the fridge and pantry and get to work. As I'm whisking the ingredients, waiting for the waffle iron to heat, I realize I don't do this as often as I should. It makes me feel guilty for not stepping up more to help my grandparents.

They sacrificed a lot to take in the depressed teenager who lost her parents. Not an easy task for two people in their sixties, especially when they're mourning the loss of their daughter on top of everything. I'm finishing up when Gran comes into the kitchen wrapped in her bathrobe.

"Good morning, Olive, to what do I owe this pleasant surprise?" she asks as she rubs the sleep from her eyes. A jab of guilt works its way through my chest, just another reminder I need to do this more often.

"I just wanted to do something nice for you and Pop. You both work so hard, and I wish I did more for you guys." I start plating the waffles and pull the syrup down from the cabinet and gesture Gran to take a seat.

She sits down with a sigh, "Sweetheart, you do plenty. Don't work yourself up."

I appreciate her graciousness, but we both know I haven't always been a peach to be around. I pour her a glass of orange juice and head back to make more waffles for when Pop comes down.

"These are wonderful, dear. You're learning a lot from working in the shop, I see. Pop will be impressed." She smiles with a forkful of waffles in her mouth, causing us both to laugh.

A moment goes by before Gran asks, "So, how did it go yesterday with Mitchell? I'm telling you, what a gentleman that boy is." She winks at me as she takes a sip of orange juice. That look on her face has me wondering if she and Mrs. Murphy plotted us getting together. I wouldn't be surprised. It would probably crush her to learn how closed off he actually is.

"It was good. Some of the people at the shelter still remembered Mitch, which seemed to please him. Then he drove me home so I didn't have to ride my bike in the dark." She doesn't say anything, but the raise of her eyebrows says plenty. Gran has always tried to gage where I'm at with boys and suggested setting me up with her friends' grandsons. I know she cares, but I usually brush off her requests. To her, we're a match made in heaven, and she doesn't even know he can barely stand being around me.

Just glares at me with distaste.

"Gran don't look at me like that. We just met *yesterday*." I say with a mock roll of my eyes.

"I didn't say anything, dear."

"You didn't have to. I can see it all over your face what you're thinking." I finish up the last round of waffles and set them on a plate for Pop. He comes down a moment later and

I know I'm safe from continuing this conversation, at least for now. Gran may like to pry, but she respects my privacy when it comes to talking about boys in front of Pop. To him, I'm still the six-year-old who dropped a bag of flour resulting in a huge mess and everything covered in white powder. We still laugh about that incident.

It's hard for him to see me growing up, especially since I didn't have any other siblings. They only had my mom so it's a hard pill for them to swallow. Truthfully, I think that's why Gran wants me to find someone so young. I think she's hoping I'll settle down and have kids that can grow up around her and Pop. The thought that they might not be around to see it happen, makes my chest heavy with grief. Something that hasn't even happened yet, but it's still on my mind constantly.

I guess that's part of the deal when you lose your parents at a young age, the fear you'll lose the only family you have left just as young.

"Well, well, what do we have here?" Pop shuffles into the kitchen, dressed for the day, unlike Gran. Pop isn't one to sleep in, so he's likely been up for at least an hour reading. Aging has been difficult for him, he's a hard worker and a go getter, so the slowing of his body has been hard for him.

In his mind he's still a young man capable of anything, but his body just isn't the same. He gets frustrated when he can't do the things he used to, and even more frustrated when he needs help. He never asks for it, but if someone offers, it's a battle he fights.

Knowing he needs the help, but not really wanting it. That's why it meant so much to see Mitch lend him a hand in the office yesterday. Pop will never admit he needed it, but I know he was silently grateful for it.

"Olive here decided to make us breakfast, Hen. They're damn good, she's come a long way from dropping that bag of flour." She and Pop chuckle, and I roll my eyes at the mention of that incident, *again*. I'm convinced on my tombstone it'll read, *"Olive Fournier – she once dropped a bag of flour when she was six – may she rest in peace."*

Pop takes a seat across from Gran and digs in. I don't even realize I'm holding my breath at first, but his opinion matters to me. Gran and I are eying him, waiting for a reaction, but he just chews the first mouthful and slugs down some orange juice. By the third mouthful I'm nearly heaving with anxiety, I just need him to say *something*.

"Henry, you're going to give the poor girl a panic attack." Gran nudges him playfully and gives me a look of understanding. The look that says, *"hon, I've been dealing with this man for years, I get it."*

He looks over at me and just smiles. I release the breath I've been holding, feeling all the blood rushing from my face. "They're great Olive, truly. I can taste the vanilla you added, and a touch of cinnamon sugar. They're perfect."

I smile and sit down beside him; I knew he'd catch the addition of cinnamon. "Thanks, Pop. I was hoping you'd notice that." He pats my hand and starts talking about the list of things he and Gran need to do today. I offer to come in early to help, but Gran says my regular shift is fine. Maureen will be there, so they're covered out front.

After breakfast, I wash all the dishes and clean up the

kitchen. My grandparents looked at me like I wasn't really Olive. As if some other entity entered my body and took over. I must admit, I like this version of me better. I don't want to say this change is directly because of meeting Mitch, because it definitely is not, I keep reminding myself that his presence is aloof at best.

But for so long I was just getting by, doing what needed to be done each day, I've missed *living*, I've missed that playful side of myself. Something that feels has long gone and died.

As irritating as Mitch can be, something about him lit a fire in me yesterday. Made me speak up instead of just going with the everyday flow of politeness. Interacting with customers keeps me on my best behavior, and after everything my grandparents have done for me, I couldn't bear to give them a hard time like when I was younger.

Gran and Pop head off to work a little while later and once again I have the house to myself. The humidity is rising, and I can feel the sweat beading on my forehead. I change into my two-piece black bathing suit, grab a towel, the current book I'm reading, and head to the pond.

The chances of running into Mitch here two days in a row feels unlikely. Probably why I convinced myself it was no big deal I wore my more revealing suit, rather than the simple dark green one-piece.

I lay my towel out along the edge of the water and start reading my book. After re-reading the same sentence four times, I close it feeling frustrated with my lack of focus right now. You cannot find a more peaceful place in town than right here. I sit up and look at the trees surrounding the pond and head over to the tall beautiful white oak tree with the tire swing attached to it.

I take a seat, swaying slowly as I lean my head back and close my eyes. This little patch of land feels like a private place separate from the rest of the surrounding area. Wichita has a lot of farmland, open spaces, and flat fields. But here, it's different, special.

I get lost in thought for a moment and don't realize I'm no longer alone. My body realizes it before I do, hyper aware of his presence across the pond. My eyes snap open to find Mitch standing there shirtless and glistening with sweat, my mouth goes dry, and I have to clear my throat before I choke on air.

As if I did something so profound, Mitch grunts in my direction before glancing down to remove his well-worn boots covered in dirt. Next, he strips his pants off and I look away. My brain is trying to remind my body that we don't like this guy, but my body doesn't seem to care.

I nervously cross my legs and wait for Mitch to jump into the water, while also trying to control my breathing. He strides up to the water's edge looking hot as hell, my mouth dries up again instantly at the sight of him. Tan skin glistening under a sheen of sweat, and a little dirt mixed into his hairline. I never thought the farmer look was hot, probably because most farmers I know are older, but damn was I wrong.

"Hello beautiful." He says, continuing towards the water and for a moment, I think he's talking to me. I start to blush and look down at my hands clasped together in my lap when reality slaps me in the face. He dives in and swims underwater for several seconds before poking his head back up. Once he resurfaces, he leans his body back to float on the water with his eyes closed.

This side of him seems so gentle and peaceful, no scowling or grunting, just relaxed and quiet. I don't realize I'm watching him so intently until I hear him clear his throat and I glance up to meet his eyes searing into me like two hot pokers.

Suddenly, I feel overheated and start to remove my shorts and shirt, aware of his eyes on me the whole time, as I make my way into the water. I don't look up at him as I wade in, for fear of what expression he's wearing now. Instead, I slowly dip down in the water and relish the way it covers my skin like a cool blanket.

I dunk my head under to cool my face down a bit, and when I resurface, Mitch is gone. I look around for him, but he's nowhere on the banks and I don't see any movement of water from beneath. Just as I begin to think he's left; I hear the water behind me ripple.

I turn around and let out a shriek. He's much closer than I expected and the air between us feels tight. My face is flushed again and he just laughs, amused with startling me. I desperately want to ask him if he feels the tension I feel, but I'd rather stick my hand in an open flame.

I need some space from him because being this close is setting my skin ablaze, and I desperately want to appear unfazed. I sink back underwater trying to cool the blush on my face when I feel the water move around me as he does the same.

In the quiet space beneath the surface, I feel a feather

light hand swipe across my leg. My brain knows it was either accidental, or likely a fish swimming by, but my body reacts anyways.

We resurface together and I wipe the water from my face, pulling in a deep breath before turning to face him. The look he's wearing is unreadable, and truthfully, he looks mad. I'm about to ask him what's wrong when he turns away from me and starts heading for the banks.

He climbs out, uses his t-shirt to wipe his face and grabs all his stuff. I'm watching him from the water wondering what the hell just happened, when he starts to walk away without saying a word.

"Hey!" I yell at his back, watching his steps falter slightly. "What's your problem?" I ask, obviously rudely, but I've had enough of this weird attitude and tension. Mitch stands there for a moment, then turns to me with a shrug of his shoulders.

"I don't know what you mean." That's all he says before sauntering off in the direction of the farm. Leaving me standing waist deep in the water more confused than ever. I am going to figure this guy out, one way or another. Thinking of his mood changes reminds me of the part in Shrek when he says ogres are like onions. Well, clearly Mitch is the same, and it looks like I've got a lot of layers to uncover.

3

MITCH

This girl is going to be the death of me. I had every intention of coming home and focusing on what needed to be done, working on the farm to help my parents. All was going to plan when Olive had to come into the picture. With her long tan legs and hazel eyes that have stories behind them. Stories I want to hear. But I shouldn't be getting this distracted by a girl.

I didn't spend four years getting a degree in agriculture in hopes to help my family, just to be sidetracked by a piece of ass. A nice piece of ass, I might add. I grip the rake in my hands so tight my knuckles go white. "Dammit." I mutter, as I wipe a hand through the sweat dripping in my hair. I need to stay focused. I can't let myself get wrapped up in a relationship right now.

But every time Olive looks at me with those hazel eyes and full pouty lips, I have to actively control my dick from getting hard. I know she sees the looks I give her; probably thinks I hate her. I know I would if someone scowled at me as much as I have. I can't help it though, if I look at her any other way, I'll practically undress her with my eyes. I bet she looks good undressed... "Fuck!"

I drop the rake and head to the barn to grab a Gatorade from the fridge. It's hot as hell out here already without fantasizing about my neighbor.

I take a long drink from the bottle enjoying the feel of the cold liquid gliding down my throat. Next to me, Rally nudges my shoulder with his nose. I drop the Gatorade bottle and turn my attention to the horse I've loved since I was a kid.

"Hey pal, feeling needy today?" I joke as I scratch his ears. He neighs at me, almost in agreement, and leans his head even farther into my palm. "You're a little slut for attention, you know that?" I joke. I give him a couple more scratches before grabbing the rake and getting back to work. Focus on work and do what needs to be done. Everything else can wait until a much-needed shower later.

There I can let my mind wander to the brunette a couple miles away.

After four hours distracting myself cleaning up around the barn, I'm officially drenched in sweat and starving for a hot meal. My mom has always been an exceptional cook, one thing I missed while away at college.

I make my way to the main house, ditch my dirty boots by the door and head for the shower. Once my body hits the steady stream of water, I feel the tension in my shoulders release a bit. I stand there for several minutes washing off a day of sweat and dirt, and watch it swirl down the drain.

After washing my hair and body I know it's time to get out, but thoughts from earlier start swirling in my mind.

Being so close to Olive in the pond today, I nearly grabbed her just to feel those soft lips against mine. My quick departure looked rude, that much I knew, especially when she accused me of having a problem. If only she knew the real problem I had been having at that moment.

Don't get a hard on.

Can't deny I would have enjoyed watching the color drain from her face as I told her what I wanted to do to her body in that water. But I'm not a college student anymore. I can't just go around fucking whoever I want, it's about time I grew up. I had responsibilities now more than ever, and sleeping with some girl I just met is the number one way to fuck up everything I've worked for the last four years.

The best option was to leave before I said something that would likely embarrass me and scare her. I've been nothing but short with her since we met, and I can tell the mixed signals I've been giving her is confusing. If I just grabbed her and kissed her in the middle of the pond with no explanation or lead-up, yeah, I probably would have gotten slapped.

There's a fire buried in her though, I can feel it. And I surely got a taste of it when she yelled at me this afternoon. I want to bring that fire to the surface and burn in it, let it brand me from the inside out. Her smell was intoxicating too, twice now I have been close enough to catch it and she smells like a literal paradise. Like coconuts and vanilla, the sweetest scent I could imagine.

What she must taste like...I slap a hand to the tiled wall in the shower and groan against it. God, what is wrong with me? I just told myself I can't get wrapped up in some romance right now and instead I have my hand wrapped up in something else.

I feel like I'm thirteen again, jerking off in the shower. I turn the water off and wrap myself in a towel, I need to get out of this bathroom and put on some clothes. It'll be much easier to keep my mind distracted at dinner with my parents, and not on how good Olive looks.

The delicious aroma of garlic rises to my room and the little boy in me is excited at the thought of spaghetti and meatballs waiting for me downstairs. Of course, paired with my mom's garlic bread and dipping oil. I run a hand through my wet hair and head downstairs, mouth watering all the while.

As I turn the corner, anticipating seeing my parents at the table, I'm stopped dead in my tracks when I see Olive next to my mom. "What the fuck?" I mumble when all heads, including Joan and Henry, turn in my direction.

"Mitchell! Language!" Mom scolds me before turning to our guests to apologize on my behalf. "Clearly his hosting skills could use a tune up." Mom jokes but I don't miss the look she gives me before turning back to Olive with a smile.

"Sorry, I just wasn't expecting company." I shrug and go to take a seat at the table, which coincidentally happens to be right next to Olive. It's like the universe wants to test me. As I take my seat that sweet scent strikes me again, and I breathe her in. Yup, I was right, if paradise was a person, it would smell exactly like Olive Fournier.

She fidgets in her seat uncomfortably and I realize I'm likely the one making her uncomfortable. I don't try to be an asshole; it just comes out that way.

Dad passes the bowls of food around the table, and we all fill our plates up before Mom leads our prayer. It hasn't changed since I was a kid, so I brace myself for what she's about to say.

"Let's take the hand of our neighbor and bless this meal before us." Mom says with her eyes closed reaching for Joan's hand on her left, and Olive's hand on her right. I sigh loudly and reach over to grasp Olive's other hand. The static I feel in my hand from her touch radiates down my body, but I try to brush it off acting unaffected.

Olive has these tiny soft hands and as hard as I try not to picture it, all I can think about is those hands splayed across my chest while she rides me. I have a problem, serious brain damage, clearly. My mom is currently saying a prayer blessing the food before us, and I'm sitting here holding hands with the bombshell that is my neighbor picturing her riding me into oblivion.

As soon as Mom finishes, I drop Olive's hand like it's a bomb about to go off. I eat my food as quickly as possible and excuse myself before dessert. Not sure how I'll be able to explain my way out of this later, but right now I need air. I rock in the chair on the porch and watch the fireflies dance around me. Wishing I could stop thinking about Olive, and failing, miserably. I haven't been so affected by a girl in *years*, not since early college days. I feel bad for being a jerk around her, but if I wasn't I would probably maul her. Both actions come off a bit strong.

So, here I sit contemplating how to be around her without

acting like an asshole and without touching her.

Both seem unlikely.

I take a slow sip of my whiskey and close my eyes. A moment later I hear the porch door creak open and the presence of someone coming closer. I don't open my eyes because I already know who it is. Mom would have announced herself immediately, and Dad walks like his feet have boulders attached to them.

The porch swing groans under the weight of her sitting down, and the unmistakable squeak begins as she swings. "I take it we weren't welcome company tonight. I would have warned you had I known." Her voice is so soft, so sweet, it makes me feel worse for being a dick to her all day. "I tried to get out of it, but Gran insisted, and I can't say no to her."

I grunt in acknowledgement and can almost hear how hard she rolls her eyes. "I like your grandparents," I say flatly, "they're good people." She laughs, though I detect she finds no humor in my statement.

"Ah, thank you for clearing that up. It's just *me* you have the problem with." I open my eyes to see her standing up from the swing and moving to the stairs of the porch. "Tell my grandparents I walked home." Before I can get a word out, she's down the steps and crossing the gravel driveway towards their property. Fuck, I really am a dick.

"Olive, wait." I jog after her, not wanting her to be upset by something I didn't say. "I never said I had a problem with you." I confess.

"No, maybe not in so many words, but the implication is there. Goodnight, Mitch." She stalks ahead of me with those long legs of hers. I can picture them wrapped around my waist while I…Christ. I slap my forehead feeling like a horny teenager. I want to chase after her, but sometimes it's best to cut your losses. She's better off anyways.

I turn around and head back to the rocking chair on the porch and take another sip of whiskey. Two minutes go by, and I can't help but worry about her getting home alone in the dark. She didn't ride her bike here, so a two mile walk in the dark isn't a short distance. In the house my parents are sending off Joan and Henry with leftovers and thanking them for coming. I should tell them Olive left so they can pick her up before she falls in a ditch along the way.

Joan smiles at me as I enter the front hall. "Mitchell, so nice to have dinner all together. We can't wait to host you all next week!" She leans in to kiss my cheek and I get the feeling this is going to be a regular occurrence. I smile at her before letting her know Olive left five minutes ago and should probably get picked up since it's so dark out. I sound like her concerned father.

Once they leave, my mother wastes no time in asking what my problem was at dinner and the Fournier's being here. I don't even know how to explain what my reaction was, so I just shrug my shoulders and tell her I'm tired. Thankfully she doesn't push any further, so I head up to my room. I get the feeling I'm going to be tired a lot these days.

I wake up around two in the morning, not something unusual for me, and head outside for some air. I like to take walks in the middle of the night, helps me clear my head. As a bonus, I never run into a single person. In this city, there are always people around.

As if my body willed me to, I walk past the Fournier's house and see a light on upstairs. My curiosity is piqued, and I walk closer to the house without thinking. Rounding the corner, I see the silhouette of a person perched on the roof over the front porch. In the moonlight it's impossible to miss the long wavy hair and slim legs. Olive is gazing up at the sky studying the stars.

I have never wanted to be seen so badly in my life, but I know how this will look if she catches me here in the middle of the night watching her watch the sky.

Creepy.

Quietly, I turn around and head back in the direction of the farm. This torn feeling is only going to grow more intense, and I don't know how ready I am to face those feelings. On one hand, I am desperate to get to know her, know her story. But the more rational side of me says I should back off. Mom told me years ago about Olive losing her parents in a car accident, the last thing she needs is a guy like me poking around her life.

As I climb back into bed, I keep picturing her on the roof illuminated by the moon. Her skin glowed like some ethereal angel and the image is forever imprinted on my brain. I try to relax my mind and get some sleep since I need to be up in three hours to bring my parents to the airport. They're only going to be gone for a few days, but that means the farm is on my shoulders.

Something I've never done before.

The staff here is great so I don't anticipate any problems, but this is my chance to show my parents I can shoulder the responsibility that comes with running the farm.

As soon as I close my eyes to finally get some sleep, my alarm blares from the bedside table. So much for a good night's sleep.

4

Olive

Last night was weird and eye-opening. Mitch doesn't care for me and at this rate, I don't care for him either. The guy clearly has something against me, and though he likes my grandparents, he doesn't see the need to be friends with me. Or even friendly, for that matter. Whatever, it's not like I need the approval of some college graduate with an insanely hot body.

Like, *really* hot.

I hate that I notice how good he looks, his tan skin and all those muscles…Ugh! What is wrong with me? I never thought I'd be the kind of girl to fall for the jerk, yet I can't stop thinking about him. It's ridiculous. I almost feel like his appeal would lessen if he were nice to me. There's something about feeling unwanted that makes a person desperate for approval.

If only my mom were here to give me some guidance. Knowing her, she'd probably encourage me to get to know him, remind me that you can't judge a book by its cover kind of thing. I roll my eyes but also sigh at how badly I'd love to hear that speech right now. The number of speeches I'm missing out on makes me want to cry. Most kids get frustrated hearing life lessons and lectures, but I'd kill for just one more.

Gran and Pop are already at the bakery, so I'm left alone to stew on the matter at hand. I can brush off his attitude and just ignore him or play nice in front of our families. Or I can give him shit for being a dick and demand an explanation. I wish I could say it wasn't the latter, but before I acknowledge what I'm doing, I'm on my bike racing over to Murphy's farm.

It's lunch time and the sky looks a little ominous right now so I doubt he's down by the pond. I walk around the front of their house when I see him wrangling a herd of sheep in the barn. Suddenly the wind picks up and goosebumps cover my arms. Before I can call out to him, I hear the sirens. The warning is loud and clear. A storm is coming and judging by how quickly the sky is going black, with a tint of green, it's a big one.

Just as Mitch closes and latches the barn door, he notices me. "Olive! What the fuck are you doing out here? Didn't you hear the storm warning?" He's shouting as he jogs over to me.

"Oh, you mean the storm warning that is currently blowing my eardrums out. No, I hadn't heard." I roll my eyes as he grabs my arm and yanks me towards a cellar door.

"Now is not the time for your sarcastic bullshit. Get in." He nudges me down the steps into a storm cellar fifty feet from their house. I was too busy being annoyed by him to grasp the reality of the situation.

"Wait! My grandparents, I need to call them! I need to make sure they get to their shelter at the bakery!" I'm a second away from panicking when Mitch grabs both of my shoulders and gives me a shake so that I look at him.

"The phone lines are likely down, Olive. I'm sure they'll be okay. Like you said, the sirens are loud enough to blow someone's eardrums." He holds my shoulders for another few seconds before frowning and dropping his arms by his side. Guess the second of comforting he was giving me is gone.

I need to try and distract myself from the impending disaster above us, so I turn around to take in our surroundings. There's a worn couch and two armchairs on one side of the room next to a mini fridge stocked with water bottles. Across from the seating area is a shelf with books and board games, covered in a thick layer of dust. The idea is sweet, but I don't know how I could relax enough to play a game of Yahtzee or read a book.

Without realizing, I begin pacing the small space feeling the body tremors come on. When I'm nervous or scared, I shake and shiver like I'm cold, when I'm just terrified. I don't expect Mitch to notice, or care, but some kind of comfort or distraction would go a long way right now.

I'm about to turn and pace the small space again when Mitch stops me and stands in my path. "You're going to wear a hole in the rug with all this nervous pacing." Ugh, what an ass.

"Oh, my apologies, truly. God forbid I wear down an ancient carpet sitting in a stuffy storm cellar! I'm not internally freaking out or anything!" I throw my hands up and let them slap at my sides when I drop them. "Have you ever heard of empathy? You should google it." I add sarcastically.

"Sit." Mitch says with a bit of bite to his tone. I want

to defy him and keep pacing but honestly, I'm so jittery I'm starting to feel light-headed. I take a seat on the couch expecting him to sit on one of the armchairs across from me, but instead he sits beside me. "I'm not trying to be a jerk. I'm just anxious as well, okay?"

I peek up at him and notice the crease in his brow, something I didn't notice a few minutes ago, being too scared for myself. I have reasons to be worried, but so does he, I realize. "Do you think the animals will be okay?" I ask just as a loud screeching sound from the wind erupts above us. I jump and scoot closer to Mitch.

His hand reaches out and grasps mine. This time it's different than it was at dinner last night. This time it feels comforting. I hold his hand in return hoping it eases some of the tension in his shoulders like it did for me.

"They'll be alright." He says finally but looks down at the hand holding mine. "This is just the first time my parents put me in charge of the farm and a storm hits. Feels like the universe is testing me in so many ways lately."

I want to ask him what other ways he means, but I'm trying to stay focused on what is clearly his main concern. "I'm sure you did all you could, considering. There's no way you could be held responsible for any damage or mistakes during the storm." I'm trying to be understanding but the look he fixes me with says I shouldn't have said anything.

"It is my responsibility, Olive. I was left in charge, and I need to be prepared for anything." He gets up and now he's the one pacing. Watching him pace makes me giggle realizing I probably looked just as ridiculous when I was doing the same thing a few minutes ago.

Mitch looks up at me with his infamous scowl and that only makes me laugh more. "Is something funny, Olive?" He asks with a touch of annoyance in his tone. I shake my head as my giggles rack my body. "No, really. Tell me, Olive, what about this shit show situation is funny to you?!" Now I've made him genuinely mad, and it only adds fuel to my already building fire.

I laugh uncontrollably until I feel a pillow whack me in the face. Instantly my body freezes and I look at him in mock horror. He seriously just threw a pillow at my face. I'm watching him to gage what kind of reaction that just got out of him when he cracks a smile. It's small, but it's there. "Did you seriously just throw a pillow at me?" I shriek even though I'm well on my way to laughing again.

"I believe I did, Miss Fournier." He places his hands on his hips and lifts his head in the air to give himself some kind of leverage. I jump from the couch, grabbing a pillow with me as I do, ready to throttle him with it when a hand clamps around the wrist holding the pillow. "Think about what you're about to do, Olive." His tone is warning, and it sends a thrill through me.

Why do I want to egg him on right now, in a storm cellar during a tornado? I'm not thinking rationally, and I don't care. If not here and now, then when?

I reach down for another pillow in ninja fashion and launch it right at Mitch's head. He drops my wrist and gives me a look of pure evil that has me scared and turned on. Before I can even think, I'm being pushed down to the couch in one swift movement. I'm laughing hysterically when Mitch lands on top of me holding both hands above my head as he straddles my waist. The air in the small cellar changes, and he feels it too.

Mitch looks at me, our faces so close I can smell the crisp apple and spice scent of him, and I want to bathe in it. I decide now is as good a time as any to tease him and see if he really can't stand me or if it's all an act. I wiggle my hips slightly and the movement catches his eye. He gazes down at my body before lifting his eyes back to mine. The grip he has on my wrists tightens and I challenge him by licking my bottom lip.

Immediately he looks at my mouth and I can see the hesitation in his eyes. I hold his gaze as I challenge him, "do it." His eyes flicker back to mine and without anymore hesitation he lowers his mouth to mine. I can feel the tension slowly fade as he eases into the kiss more. I open my mouth for him, inviting him in and he takes the invitation without pause. God, he even tastes like apples and spice.

His mouth has either been scowling at me or making snide comments. Or not speaking at all, so this is quite a different side to him. Waking up this morning I never could have predicted this is how my day would pan out. Mitch keeps his weight off me but releases the hold he has on my wrists. In one swift movement, he reaches down to wrap his hand around the base of my neck giving it a little squeeze.

There's no pain involved, and I sense he's holding something back as he moves his hand into my hair while deepening the kiss. My head is fuzzy and for a moment, I forget we're in a storm cellar with a raging tornado above us.

That fact is quickly brought back to the present when a loud bang sounds from the door.

Mitch jumps up from the couch and rushes over to the door making sure the deadbolts are locked in place, hoping to keep it securely in place. He lets out the breath he must have been holding and slowly turns to face me. I am still as a statue on the couch trying to process everything that just happened in the last five minutes. I went from whacking Mitch in the face with a pillow, to him pinning me down on the couch, to the hottest make out session of my life, to being abruptly reminded that we are in fact hunkered down in a fallout shelter during a storm.

You can't make this shit up.

I sit up feeling a little embarrassed suddenly and watch the last few minutes flash across Mitch's face. We're both brought back to the reality of our situation and sit on separate sides of the room now. "Well, that was something." He breaks the silence first, which is weird.

"I'll say. I haven't seen a storm this bad in years." I'm trying hard not to be awkward, but it feels inevitable. I'm not the best in weird situations and this is about as weird as one can get. Mitch gives me that annoyed look and I can't tell what it is I said that would make him look at me like that right now. After the searing kiss we just shared. He's probably regretting it already, a fact I wait for him to point out with that look on his face. But he doesn't. Instead, he walks over to the shelves and picks up a deck of cards.

"Wanna play Rummy?" He looks at me and waits for a response, so I just nod and join him at the little table. As he shuffles the deck, I study his features. He has these deep dark green eyes, down here they almost look black, which adds to the all-too-serious look he keeps giving me. His skin looks darker down here too, a deep-set tan obviously in place from being outside all day every day.

But I linger on his mouth. The mouth that is constantly scowling at me like I've done something to offend him or smirking at me like I'm his next snack. It's confusing and hard to keep up with. But kissing him, I got to feel those soft lips, taste the crispness of his scent, and experience a completely different side of him.

He clears his throat, and my eyes shoot up to meet his, slightly embarrassed I was caught studying his face. "Ready?" he asks as he starts dolling out seven cards each. I reach for my cards and start arranging them in my hands to keep from looking at him again. When I finally look up, he's looking at my lips now but instead of feeling embarrassed for being caught like I was, he just smirks. Every ten seconds is a trade off for wanting to kiss him or slap him.

Since I've already kissed him, I'm thinking of going for a slap next.

After several rounds of rummy, with me in the lead, something my Dad got a chance to teach me before he died, we hear the wind die down outside. Mitch gets up from the table and unbolts the cellar door. I take a deep breath and prepare myself for what we're about to walk out into. But no number of deep breaths could have prepared me for this.

The once large red barn with beautifully crafted white trim is in shambles. The paint practically ripped off every surface of the barn and scattered around like a wooden massacre. Some of the animals have already emerged from where they waited out the storm and are wandering around.

There are dozens of trees and branches down all around the property, as well as crops completely ripped from the ground. Thankfully the house suffered the least amount of damage and it's clear we didn't get a direct hit. If that were the case, the barn and the house would have been leveled. Dozens of animals would have been lost and who's to say what would have happened to Mitch and I.

As devastating as the damage is, I only have one thing on my mind at this point and that's to make sure my grandparents are safe. The uneasy feeling in the pit of my stomach is growing more and more with each second that passes. "Mitch, I'm so sorry. I know this sucks, but I…"

"You need to check on Joan and Henry, I know. Come on I'll drive us there." He starts for his truck, which also didn't suffer any damage and as much as I want to stop him and tell him I can get there on my own, I take him up on the ride. My nerves are at an all-time high and I don't think I could walk three miles to the bakery right now, let alone ride a bike.

We start driving and it takes twice as long to get down the gravel road due to how much damage there is along the way. When we make it to the main road, reality sets in. Families all along the road waiting for rescues and help, and a huge part of me wants to stop and help in any way I can. But I know I won't be any good to these people until I know my grandparents are okay.

As we pull up in front of the bakery a sob threatens to

escape when I see the damage done to the outside of the shop. It's all fixable, but this is my grandparents' livelihood and to see it wounded like this crushes me. Especially knowing they haven't seen it yet. Before Mitch even puts the truck in part, I jump out of the truck and rush to the door, moving debris away from the front door. Mitch cuts in front of me moving stuff out of the way so I can get to the door and unlock it.

I burst through ready to panic when I see that everything inside is mostly okay. Running around the corner I make it to the door that leads to the cellar and Mitch is right behind me. As much as he irritates me, I'm happy he's here right now.

Opening the door as fast as I can, I rush down the steps to take in the scene. Gran and Pop are with Maureen sitting on whicker chairs *laughing*. They're actually laughing right now, not a care in the world and it almost pisses me off.

Before I say something I'll regret, remembering they haven't been outside to see the damage yet, I take a deep breath and hug them both, then Maureen. "I'm so glad you guys are all okay, I was close to having a panic attack on the way over here." My breathing is ragged, and my chest is heavy from being out of breath. Nothing says fear like thinking you've lost the only family you have left.

"We're just fine dear, don't work yourself up." Gran says as she strokes her fingers through my hair. Something my mom always did to soothe me when I was upset, and something Gran did for her as a little girl, too. Tears prick my eyes, but I brush them away before anyone has a chance to notice. The look on Mitch's face, however, says he either noticed, or he's bored. Hard to say.

"There's so much damage to the town, it's hard not to get worked up thinking something bad happened to you too." I counter. They need to see what this storm did to fully understand that my reactions are entirely valid right now.

"Oh dear." Gran sighs and reaches for my hand. "We were trying our best not to be worried about you at home alone during the storm. We know you're a smart girl and knew how to get to safety, but the thought of you alone..." she sighs again.

"Actually, I was on my way over to the Murphy's when the sirens went off, so I hunkered down with Mitch until it was safe." Gran gives me that look, the one that the cat has after it gets the canary. I can't even imagine what her reaction would be if she knew how we spent our time during the storm. My cheeks flush at the thought.

"Well, isn't that lucky you had a gentleman to keep you safe." She winks at Mitch and pats my leg. What a hopeless romantic. Makes me sick.

Pop gets up and walks over to the stairs ready to inspect the damage. Mitch follows him up, probably to make sure he doesn't trip over anything, then the rest of us join them.

Pop stands outside the bakery with his hands on his hips slightly shaking his head, like he can't believe this all just happened. I walk to his side and wrap my arms around his waist to hug him like I always have. "It's okay, Pop. We'll get everything back to status quo." I assure him, but he just shakes his head.

"That's not what I was thinking about Ollie, I just...I couldn't bear the thought of you alone during this. Knowing there was no way we could get to you or contact you and not know if you were…" he stops and drops his head to look at the ground. Emotion bubbles in my chest and I squeeze him a little tighter.

The last time he couldn't get in touch with someone was when my parents died. I can't imagine the fear they must have felt, not knowing what to do or if they were okay. A tear escapes and slides down my cheek, followed by several more. Pop lifts my chin with his free hand making me look at him. "Knowing you're safe, that's all that matters to your Gran and I. So, please don't fuss over this mess. This place can't hold a candle to what you mean to us."

I stand there with him for a few more minutes, feeling like we both needed this time to appreciate that one another is okay. After ten minutes Gran joins us and wraps her arms around us both. The tension in her body eases as she hold us both and I feel a tear of her own drop onto my shirt. "I'm so happy you're here Sweetie. I had to laugh or else I would just cry."

I want to tell her I know the feeling, that I feel it too, the worry, the fear, the unbearable pain at just the thought of losing them. Instead, I stand here and appreciate that we're all okay. Damaged property can be fixed, and normal life will return. Losing someone, however, that stays with you forever.

A few weeks after the storm hit, things are finally getting back to normal. Mitch came by a few times to help Pop fix up the outside of the bakery, he kept his distance from me, and I was fine with that. Since our little moment during the storm, we've pretty much avoided each other. At first, I wanted to talk about it with him, but when he went back to giving me the cold shoulder, I assumed it was because he regretted the kiss ever happening.

Watching him put the awnings back up outside the shop and seeing the way his muscles flexed had me wanting to kiss him all over again. But one disgruntled look made me realize I was insane for wanting to be anywhere near him. The kiss was amazing, but now that I got it out of my system I can go back to focusing on more important things. Like my art.

I'd sent out a few resumes to art galleries in New York but didn't expect to hear back anytime soon, if at all. The internships there are highly competitive, and I don't know what would make a successful New Yorker choose some random girl from Kansas. Still, I held out a small sliver of hope, just in case.

I didn't even tell my grandparents about the internships because I figured there was no point. Either I tell them, and they get overly excited about something unlikely to happen or worse they're devastated I want to leave. Both options don't sound promising, so until I hear back, I'm keeping it to myself.

Art has always been one of the best ways to express myself in a healthy way. I cringe when I think about it like that because it sounds cheesy. But my high school art teacher, Miss Hayes, had a huge impact on my life during the years after my parents died. She always told me to express whatever I was feeling and just let it out on a canvas. So, that's what I did.

In the beginning my art was dark, and I hardly ever showed anyone except my art teacher. She told me how she went through a dark period in her life and art was the only thing that saved her from herself. She didn't have a mentor around to guide her, she just figured it out on her own. I'm thankful I had her though, not sure where I would have ended up without her guidance. She even wrote me a stunning reference to add to the portfolio I sent out. Every little bit helps is what she told me.

When I was fifteen Gran and Pop set up a space for me upstairs to paint, probably one of my favorite gifts ever. They bought easels and all kinds of paint, acrylic, oil, and my favorite, watercolor. I always enjoyed watching the colors spread and mold together. Like they can't help but move around each other creating something new. Each time I thought I knew what I was painting, the colors would blend and I'd see the piece in a completely different light.

As much as I enjoy painting in my little space, tucked away in the attic overlooking the land, sometimes I just want to paint outside. So, I grab my easel and paints, a stool and some snacks, and head over to the pond. It struck me the other day that as many times as I've painted at the pond, I've never actually painted the scenery around me.

Maneuvering my bike down the gravel path with all my supplies in hand is a much harder task than I anticipated. By the time I make it to the bank I'm tumbling from my bike spilling paintbrushes and canvases to the ground. I lay there on my back for a moment and take a deep breath to keep from getting frustrated. I came here to relax, not get pissed off before I even begin.

A snort from a few feet away has my eyes flashing open and awareness creeping across my skin. Of course, he's here right now, and judging by that incredibly attractive snort I heard stumble from his mouth, I take it he watched me fall on my ass.

I sit up and fix him with the best glare I can imagine. I refuse to let him get under my skin, today I want to be Zen and he's already messing with that. "Can I help you, Mitchell?" I ask using his full name because I know he hates it.

"Just enjoying the view is all." He drawls, clearly unaffected by my use of his full name. That just bugs me even more, I was banking on him hating that. "Didn't realize you came with so much baggage." He adds gesturing towards my paint supplies, but something about it feels personal. Like maybe he isn't referring to my art.

Why does that piss me off? Not five minutes ago I promised myself I wouldn't let him get to me, and now I'm here picturing how many ways I can sever his face from his body. "Yeah, well, what do you even care?"

"Didn't say I did." He shrugs and shakes off the water droplets in his hair. The arrogance of this guy right now. First, he kisses me in the cellar of his storm shelter then acts like it never happened, and now he insinuates he could care less about me or the baggage in my life.

Not that I want him to care, but still.

I must just be a piece of ass to him, hence the impromptu make out session a few weeks ago. I'd love to disappoint him and inform him that I am still a virgin, but I don't want to give him anymore ammo to make fun of me or claim I have too much baggage.

"I came here to relax and paint, so if you don't mind, buzz off." I wave my hands to my side indicating he should leave, but he just smirks at me.

"Last I checked, this is my property." I can feel steam building behind my ears, ready to burst when his phone rings. Probably some other girl he likes to suck face with on a whim. "I'm heading back now. Yup. Five minutes." He hangs up but doesn't acknowledge me as he pulls his shirt back on.

I begin gathering my supplies to set up so I can finally get to painting. As I'm reaching for my easel a strong tan hand reaches out and grabs it before I can. Mitch stands it upright and places a blank canvas on the ledge. Then he grabs my stool, unfolds it, and props it up in front of the easel. I look up at him dumbfounded by this random gesture of kindness to see him scowling down at me. Painting must seem so frivolous to him.

I don't say anything, just watch him grab his work boots and head back up the path towards the farm. Maybe I should have talked to him about the kiss, clear the awkwardness before it gets worse. He apparently wants nothing to do with me romantically or even civilly at this point, then he goes and does something like that. What an ass.

5

MITCH

Apparently four years in college did nothing for my brain, because I'm an idiot. I did the one thing I told myself I shouldn't do. *Anything* to do with Olive Fournier. Instead, I take one look at her perfect lips and turn them into a feast. There is so much wrong with me.

I try to turn my focus back on my work, the damn fence posts that need repairing after the storm a few weeks back. We can't let some of the animals roam as far until the fence is back up.

That kiss was amazing though, and I'd be lying if I said I didn't think about it every goddamn night in bed. She tasted just as good as I thought she would, better even. Now I have to see her every week at our family dinner get togethers, something I'm still unclear of why we started, and at the pond. Clearly my bad attitude hasn't kept her away like I thought it would.

Truthfully, when I saw her at the pond that first time after the kiss I couldn't tell if I was mad she was there or if I would have been more pissed if she hadn't been there. Every time I'm around her, my emotions run around like they're on fire, and she's the bucket of water I need.

I can tell she wants to address the kiss, and part of me wants that too. But I know the second she starts talking about it, my mind will go back to the feel of her soft lips dancing with mine and I'll do it all again. She doesn't deserve this constant whiplash, which is why I've tried to keep my distance.

Guess it didn't help that I set up her easel today by the pond like a gentleman. I go from telling her I could care less about her baggage, which isn't true, I want to know everything about her and why those hazel eyes of hers look lost sometimes. To helping her with her supplies then walking away without a word. If I were her, I would have slapped me by now.

If I had to guess, I'd say she's probably already thought to.

Now I'm distracted by her again and don't realize the wire I'm trying to wrap around the post is sticking out until my palm grazes it to create a perfect slit. "Shit." I mutter, grabbing my shirt from the ground where I dropped it half an hour ago. I wrap the cotton fabric around my hand tightly and tear a piece off to tie it in place. Mom would be pissed if she knew I kept working with an open wound, but I'm so close to being done with this row.

An hour later I finish up and look down to see blood seeping through the fabric of my worn grey T-shirt. Should have wrapped this better. Oh well, too late to change it now. I hop up on Rally and give him a kick to get us back to the farm, pronto. Riding with one hand isn't normally a problem for me, but with my tools hitched over my shoulder, I wish I had both hands for support.

Rally eases up to the stables and waits for his treats as I

guide him back to his stall. I grab a Gatorade from the fridge and head towards the main house to get an earful from mom and proper clean up for my hand.   The screen door creeks open and I step inside to the smell of brownies. My mouth begins watering at the thought of something sweet when I hear more voices.

I turn the corner into the kitchen to see Joan and Olive sitting with my mom on the sunporch off the kitchen. Great, now I have an audience present to witness my idiocy. "Hey sweetie, want a brownie?" Mom asks lifting the plate of freshly made brownies up to me.

Joan turns her head and her eyes snag on my hand first, she clicks her tongue and jerks her head towards my cut so my mom can see too. "Mitchell! What happened?" Mom is on her feet and scrambling towards me to inspect the damage. "The blood is already drying. Tell me you didn't keep working *after* this happened?" She says exasperated.

Rolling my eyes, I shrug her off. "It's fine, just a scratch" I assure her. But I know she's not buying that bullshit lie. She reaches for my hand again and begins unwrapping it. Even I must admit I wasn't expecting it to look as bad as it does. Out of the corner of my eye I see Olive looking at us with her brow furrowed. I don't want her to be concerned about me, because if she's showing even an ounce of concern, that means she cares. I can't have her caring about me.

"Young man, sit down and wait here while I get the first aid kit." When mom uses that tone, I know she means business, so I don't question her, grabbing a brownie as I sit. Joan looks like she wants to say something but refrains and

Olive still looks concerned. As soon as my mom comes back into the room she starts fussing over my cut, whipping out creams and peroxide to clean it. Makes me feel like a little kid again.

After a few minutes of poking and prodding, I hear the inevitable in my mom's voice. "Mitch, honey, it's too deep. You're going to need stitches." Her voice is calmer now, soothing, because deep down even though she's mad I behaved foolishly, to her, I'm still a little boy. Olive gets up from her chair suddenly and we all look over expecting her to leave.

"I can take him." She blurts out and I can't understand why the hell she would want to do me any favors considering how poorly I've treated her. I should say no, insist I can take myself, instead I stay quiet and watch the women exchange glances. Can't wait to hear all the fussing over this gesture later.

"I can take myself." I finally manage to say, and head for the door to grab my keys. I'm almost free when I hear my mom tell me to stop. I don't dare disobey her, so I stop keeping my body facing the door.

"Mitchell Murphy, don't be a dumbass." Well, that was unexpected. "Olive has graciously offered to lend a hand and you will be polite." I turn around to see her hugging Olive and thanking her for taking my so-called dumbass to the emergency room. I drop my keys back in the bowl in the foyer, loud enough for all three women to set their eyes on me again, no doubt. Guess I can't get out of this one without seeming like an ungrateful tool.

Olive leads us out to the car and waits for me to get in the passenger seat, something I hate. If I'm in a car, I'm driving, I don't like handing the reigns over to someone else. I'm perfectly capable of driving with only one hand, hell I rode Rally all the way back to the stables just fine. Almost lost my grip a few times, but no one needs to know that.

She backs out and heads down the driveway towards the main road. I can't help but wonder what's going on in that pretty little head of hers. I've been nothing short of a dick to her and here she is offering to take me to the emergency room. Maybe she's just trying to save face in front of her Gran and my mom and plans on dropping me off at the door. I hope that's the case.

As soon as we pull into the lot it becomes evidently clear she does not in fact plan on leaving me here to deal with this myself. Why can't anything be simple anymore? Trying not to appear annoyed by the chaperone I have by my side, we make our way inside to check in. I don't anticipate this being a quick ordeal, so I take a seat in the waiting room and pray a nap is on the horizon.

Olive takes a seat two spots away from me, which confuses me. If she didn't want to be here, she could just leave. Instead, she decides to stay but doesn't sit with me. Apparently, I'm not the only one who likes to give mixed signals. "I already told you I don't bite." I try to sound humorous, but she can see right through me.

She doesn't respond or even acknowledge me, just keeps her face focused on her phone. I lean over to sneak a peek and see that she's playing solitaire. Here she is ignoring me and not even attempting to look busy. I clear my throat trying to get her to look at me, but she doesn't budge. I want to throttle her, grip my hands around her neck and give it a slight squeeze.

"This is going to take a while, you should go." I don't bother looking at her, expecting that she likely isn't looking at me either, so I just focus on my hands. It's bad enough having to sit here waiting for my hand to get stitched up, I don't need anymore tension added.

"I told your mom I would keep you company." She finally relents. I knew it had to be something like that. I'm a grown man and my mommy sends me to the emergency room with a fucking babysitter rather than taking me herself.

"It's not like your much company right now." I say before my mind can stop my mouth from speaking. Her head snaps in my direction. Well, that got her attention. She's glaring at me, something that is usually my forte, and I just sit here waiting for her to explode. Judging by the look on her face, I'd say she's close.

"Wow. Even when I say nothing at all to you, you still find a way to be an asshole." She stands up and grabs her bag before turning to face me. "Just for the record, people can be nice, it really isn't that difficult. But you, somehow, you've made it taboo. Good luck with that." She says as she points to my hand just before walking out the door, leaving me here feeling like the biggest dick.

Three hours and ten stitches later I finally get to go home. When I exit the hospital it's dark out and in the time I spent getting stitched, I forgot to figure out how I'm getting home. An ambulance sounds from around the other side of the building and I glance over to see a few cars parked in the visitor lot. There, sitting on the hood of her car, is Olive. This girl is killing me. I keep acting like a jerk right to her face, and she keeps being perfect. It makes me like her and hate her.

I stride over to her car, trying to look unfazed, when she glances up at me. Without a word, she sits up and grabs a brown bag stained with grease and tosses it at me. Inside is a hefty number of fries and a double cheeseburger. I smile down at the bag feeling my stomach rumble at the smell of fried food. I didn't realize how hungry I was until I stared into that bag.

Olive hops off the hood and climbs into the driver's seat, starting up the car. Okay, I guess it's time to go. I buckle in and take a handful of fries from the bag shoving them in my mouth like a caveman. The damn vending machine inside the hospital was broken and I was too lazy to look for others. Olive could have brought me liver and onions and I would have eaten it.

"How long did you wait out here?" I ask through a mouthful of fries. There's no way she stayed here the whole time, at the very least she left to get the food.

"Truthfully, I had no intention of coming back. But I made a promise to your mom that I would make sure you made it home. So, after cursing your name a few times, I went and grabbed some food, then came back here."

I picture her gazing up at the stars sitting on the hood of her car like she was when I came out, just like that night

I found her on the roof. She seemed so at ease out there, relaxed. The second she saw me come into view I noticed her body tense. Can't tell if that's a good thing or a bad thing yet.

Probably the latter.

I can't help the smile that spreads across my face, but I hide it quickly before she has a chance to notice. "That's a nice thing to do for someone who seems to hate my guts." I chuckle before taking a large gulp of soda. I notice her hands grip the steering wheel tighter and wonder what it was I said.

"I don't make a habit of hating people, you just make it easy." She bites out. I let out a low whistle and glance over at her as she eases up to the stoplight.

"Damn girl, let me know how you really feel." I stuff another handful of fries in my mouth and catch her glaring at me.

"It's not like you've done anything to change my opinion of you. The way you look at me sometimes…" she lowers her voice and doesn't finish her thought. She really thinks I hate her. My mom would be so disappointed in me for the way I've treated this girl. Hell, I'm disappointed in me.

"I don't dislike you, Olive." I tell her as genuinely as possible. The car slows as she pulls down a small road that leads to an open field with a large tree in the middle. Without a word, she parks the car, turns off the ignition and gets out.

I watch her walk over to the tree, reaching out to run her fingers along the trunk. After one full circle, she finds a spot and sits down leaning against the tree. I watch as she closes her eyes and pulls in a deep breath of night air. Fireflies dance in the distance behind her and the moment feels like something straight out of a romance novel.

Wrapping up what's left of my burger, I place it in the bag with my trash and open the door. As I walk over to her the grass rustles beneath my boots, but she doesn't open her eyes to acknowledge my presence. She knows I'm standing here though.

With a huff she says, "are you gonna sit down or not?" The mouth on her, I love it. I take a seat next to her and process how I want to explain myself and my behavior towards her.

"When I was in high school, I would volunteer at the Raising Hope shelter a lot. There was someone there I wanted to check on, but I didn't want my parents to know." I pause collecting myself before continuing.

"His name is Andrew, or as I always called him, Uncle Drew." Olive's head looks in my direction and I can see the wheels turning.

"He was my Dad's best friend growing up, so not an actual uncle, but close enough. Anyways, he hit a rough patch a few years back and went downhill. Lost his job, couldn't pay his bills, and ended up homeless." I've never really talked about this to anyone, and the fact that I want to tell Olive right now, is weird. Still, I go on.

"My Dad tried to help him, but he refused anyone's help. Said he needed to figure his shit out by himself without taking the people he cared about down with him. When I found out he was staying at Raising Hope, I told my parents it was part of a school requirement and that's why I went every week."

"Truth is, I just wanted to make sure he was okay." I'm quiet for a few minutes and Olive doesn't say anything, just sits next to me waiting patiently for me to collect myself. When I don't continue, she speaks up.

"That day, when we were there together, that's who you were looking for, wasn't it?" She asks and I nod my head.

"A part of me was hoping I would see him while the other part of me was hoping he wasn't there anymore. I couldn't tell which was worse. If he had been there then at least I could have checked on him. But since he wasn't, I'm left wondering where he is."

"Have you asked your Dad if he's heard from him?"

"Honestly, I was afraid to. Talking about Drew has become a sore subject, and I didn't want to upset my Dad by asking about him."

"Maybe now is a good time to come clean about your volunteer work. I'm sure your Dad would feel grateful you cared so much." She reaches a hand over towards me but pulls back quickly as if I might burn her.

"You're right." I concede because she is right. Wondering where Drew is bothers me, so I can't even begin to imagine how my Dad feels.

"Anyways, being back there brought up old feelings, then add in the pressure of working on the farm and the storm we got, it's just been a lot lately." She looks down at her hands, she deserves an apology.

"Olive, I'm sorry. I'm not usually such a prick, but with everything else, I wasn't exactly expecting a distraction too."

She looks at me with a puzzled look on her face, and I want to ease the tension from her eyebrows. "What distraction?" she asks in a whisper.

"You." I say just as quietly. Her face goes blank, and I truly have no idea what she's thinking. For the first time in my life, I wish I had one of those mind reading machines so I could figure out what's going on up there.

"That's why you've been such an asshole?" she asks. "Because I distract you?" She chuckles and I can't tell if it's actually funny or if she's in disbelief.

I laugh too now because I have been an asshole. "That's fair."

"This whole time I just assumed you hated me, for what reason I couldn't figure out, and that you regret kissing me." She touches her lips softly as if remembering the kiss. I know I haven't forgotten, that's for sure.

"I do regret it." I reply honestly. The way her heads whips in my direction should have given her whiplash, and the glare she's fixing me with right now makes me want to do very bad things to her.

"Just not the way you think, clearly." I say gesturing towards her furious expression. She softens a little, but her body is still on guard.

"I have so much on my shoulders right now with helping my parents on the farm. I didn't spend four years getting an agricultural degree to come home and goof off. After the storm hit, my work doubled. So, when I say I regret kissing you, it's not because I didn't like it." I pause before looking at her face again, glowing in the moonlight while fireflies light up behind her. Her hair dances around her face in long waves, she's breathtaking.

"It's because I liked it too much." I finally admit. Olive

nods her head and is quiet while she processes what I just said.

After a few minutes she stands up and hitches a thumb towards her car. "I should take you home, I'm sure you're exhausted."

I am exhausted, but right now I'm more confused that she didn't respond to my confession. Maybe she thought I was kidding or something.

"Olive, I was being serious." I say as I stand to follow her to the car. She gets in the driver's seat and starts it up, so I follow suit and hop back in the passenger seat.

"I know you were." That's all she says as she pulls the car back onto the main road and heads towards the farm. What the fuck? Is this payback for being a dick, making me sweat this out after I just admitted I enjoyed kissing her. Why are girls so complicated?

We drive down the gravel road towards my house and I'm still trying to process how Olive took that information I just plopped in her lap. Her demeanor is neutral so it's hard to say if it pleased her or pissed her off.

As she stops in front of my house, she looks over to me and smiles. "I hope your hand feels better, Mitch." That's it? That's all I get. I stammer out a thank you, feeling like an idiot, as I get out of the car and head towards the porch.

Olive turns the car around and heads back down the road before disappearing completely. I check my watch and the time says 9:30. Time for a drink. I grab two fingers of whiskey and take a seat on the rocking chair replaying the last hour in my mind.

Today has been weird as fuck. All day I act like I can't

stand to be around Olive, then I'm confessing I liked kissing her but that she's a distraction. No wonder she looked at me the way she did, confused while also guarded. If she were smart, she would steer clear of me. A part of me is hoping she's not that smart though

6

Olive

Sundays are my favorite. It's the one day of the week the bakery is closed, and Gran and Pop relax a little. Granted Gran is usually making lists for the shop, but I like seeing them do other things aside from owning a business.

Pop likes to sit on the porch in his rocking chair and read the paper. Gran is usually right next to him drinking her tea and reading some romance novel. None of us have ever been much into watching tv. My parents spent more time reading, something they passed onto me.   As a kid I had so many friends who would talk about their favorite shows, I would just talk about what books I loved. Not something that got me into the popular group.

One glance out my window tells me the sun is a little higher in the sky than I anticipated. I've been waking up earlier these days, so I didn't expect to see the time was nine o'clock. It's quiet downstairs, so I'm guessing Gran and Pop slept in too. I pad barefoot downstairs to start a pot of coffee. Still in my pajamas, hair piled on my head in a messy bun, I'm not exactly in any shape to leave the house just yet.

The coffee machine putters to life and the aroma of coffee beans fills the kitchen. I boil some water in the teapot for Gran to have her morning tea and pull out the scones from yesterday. After another twenty minutes, I'm surprised that no one has come downstairs. The smell of coffee should have reached their room by now, bringing Pop out of his slumber.

A feeling of unease washes over me bringing all my senses to attention. I make my way to my grandparent's bedroom and knock lightly. No answer. I knock again a little louder and call out their names. Still, no answer. I swing open the door, a bit of hysteria coming over me now, and the room is empty.

I feel some relief, but something still doesn't seem right. I grab the landline phone and call Gran to see if they decided to go into the bakery this morning after all. Though it's closed today, they sometimes go in to check inventory or try out new recipes. Everything is probably fine, so I head back to the kitchen and make myself some coffee.

The front porch is cast in a glow of sunlight, highlighting the plants growing wildly around the property. I take a seat in one of the Adirondack chairs and breathe in the fresh air. This time of morning it's still comfortable to be outside. The heavy heat hasn't descended on the day, and I can actually enjoy sitting in the sun without sweating. I close my eyes for a few minutes before my mind starts to wander again.

I hear a car traveling up the driveway at a faster pace than usual and recognize Mrs. Murphy's dark blue SUV. She stops the car and jumps out without turning the engine off. "Olive. It's your grandfather." That's all I hear before a ringing starts in my ears, keeping me frozen for several beats. Elaine says my name again, more urgently and I'm on my feet bounding down the stairs and hopping in the passenger seat.

If she says anything else, I don't hear it. The look on her face says enough though, something is wrong. That feeling I got in the kitchen earlier was right. I can't even think about anything else but getting in the car with her and going to wherever they are. I'm still in pajamas looking like a disheveled mess, surely. But I don't even care enough to grab a change of clothes.

The drive to the hospital is quiet. Once Mrs. Murphy said her sister, who's a nurse at the hospital, called to let her know Pop was there, she came straight here. She knew I wouldn't have known yet. Gran was in such a panic she rushed Pop to the hospital without waking me. Something I should be upset about, but if my partner was sick, my only thought would be about them.

"Alice said they were on the third floor, the cardiac care unit." Mrs. Murphy says as she speeds up a little more to run a light that's yellow. I don't know how many times I've thanked her, but I'd say at least twenty between the moment she pulled up in front of the house and the drive to the hospital.

Instead of pulling up to the doors and just dropping me off, Mrs. Murphy pulls into a spot and turns the car off. "Listen, Olive. These things are never easy, just know you don't have to do it alone. Connor and I are only a phone call away, and I'd be more than happy to bring by some dinners. I'm sure Joan isn't going to want to leave Henry's side right now. So, say the word and we're there."

I could hug this woman and cry in her arms right now if the idea didn't embarrass the shit out of me. I hate being vulnerable, but right now I could use the comfort. As if reading my mind, Mrs. Murphy undoes her seatbelt and leans over the console to wrap me in a hug. I don't even hesitate, just wrap my arms around her and cry.

Through my light sobbing, she brushes the hair from my face, something my mom always did when I was upset. I push the thought away, because I don't need to hyperventilate now too, that would be mortifying. "Do you want me to come in with you? Since my sister works in the cardiac care unit, I'm sure she'd be able to give us some news."

"You're my lifesaver right now, you know that right?" I chuckle through the tears streaming down my face.

"Nonsense, this is what friends do. Actually, I like to consider y'all family at this point. If that's okay with you?" She takes one of my hands in hers, they're soft and warm, and the gesture is comforting and so appreciated.

"More than okay." I smile and wipe away a stray tear making its way down my chin. Mrs. Murphy reaches into her purse and pulls out a package of tissues and hands them to me.

We take the elevator up to the third floor and check in at the nurse's station. Alice is there waiting to show us which room he's in. "Sorry Elaine, it's family only." She says to Mrs. Murphy before leading me down a long hallway.

I glance over my shoulder back at Mrs. Murphy and she offers me a reassuring smile. If only I could tell her how grateful I am she came and got me, brought me here and didn't pepper me with small chit chat in the car. She could sense I needed to process on my own. I'll have to give her a proper thank you once I'm able to speak again.

At the end of a white hallway is his room. Faint noises from various machines are beeping in the background and I can hear Gran speaking softly to someone. The nurse opens the door and gestures for me to enter. I hesitate for a moment, not sure I'm ready to face what's in that room. Taking a deep breath, I slowly enter the room to see a doctor speaking with Gran. She's sitting at the end of Pop's bed and my eyes go from her to him in an instant.

He looks to be asleep, eyes closed, hospital gown on and hooked up to multiple machines. But something about the color of his skin is what has me going headfirst into a panic. His skin is so white it almost appears translucent. I can see the bluish tint of his veins and the shallow breaths causing his chest to rise slightly and quickly. Is he in pain? I can't bear to know he's hurting right now, not after everything he's done for me over the years.

He did his best to find ways to take the pain away from me, help me cope with such a huge loss, both he and Gran. How can I possibly make this better for him? There's nothing I can do and it's making my chest feel tight and heavy.

A realization that hits me like a freight train going one hundred miles per hour. Without a word I turn and run from the room. I'm not sure Gran even saw me enter so I don't feel too bad just walking out. I need air and everything in that room feels suffocating, reminding me of the last time I was in this hospital. The words still ring in my ears, even years later.

"We're so sorry…We did everything we could…"

I just need a minute to collect myself before I go back there. I won't be any help to anyone if I fall apart and start crying. This is not one of those times to be selfish.

I find a couch in one of the waiting areas that's set back in a corner by a small window. No one is sitting over here so I have the small space to myself.

I sit down and bend forward placing my head in my hands as I rest them on my knees. Everything about this place makes me anxious. The smells, all the beeping sounds and people being wheeled in and out.

Just then a stretcher goes by and all I can think about is when they brought my parents in from the ambulance. A nightmare that will forever be carved into my brain.

I lean back in the seat, keeping my eyes closed and focus on something happy, calming.

I'm lying in bed with my eyes closed, a useless attempt to keep the sun out of them as it streams in through the curtains. Never understood the need for blackout curtains until this moment.

I don't need to be at the bakery until this afternoon, so I take my time getting dressed before heading downstairs to make myself some breakfast. My grandparents are usually out of the house hours before I'm up, something I don't mind. I like having the house to myself in the early hours, it's peaceful.

I take my toast and coffee out on the porch and take a seat in the hanging swing. It's not too hot yet, but the humidity is building every minute. Days like these make me feel bad for anyone who works outside, I wouldn't be able to bear it, but that's just me. It makes me think of Mitch, working out in the sun all day, sweating through every inch of clothing he wears while building that insane tan.

I haven't seen him since last week when I took him to the ER to stitch up his hand. Heading there he had been such a prick, then on the way home he admitted he enjoyed our kiss. His mood swings are worse than a group of PMSing girls, something I'd be delighted to inform him of.

We're supposed to all get together for our weekly neighbor's dinner tomorrow, something I've grown to enjoy. I really like his parents, they're down to earth hard workers who know how to cook a damn good meal. I still have dreams about that garlic bread Mrs. Murphy made us. But tomorrow will be the first-time seeing Mitch since his confession.

For all I know he was just saying it to be nice, or maybe the doctors gave him too many pain meds. Either way, I'm not going to let myself fall prey to his charming ways. Because most of the time, he's an ass. Seems like a lot of work to put up with for only a few moments of chivalry.

Before work this afternoon, I decided I wanted to paint. I try to paint as often as I can, but sometimes the inspiration or motivation just isn't there. A few hours in I realized I got lost in my work, again, and frantically tried to get ready for work. Just because my grandparents are the owners doesn't mean I get special privileges. If anything, it's the opposite.

Someone touching my arm pulls me from yesterday's memory and I jump. "Sorry, I was trying not to wake you."

Mitch is standing above me with his eyebrows furrowed and half a scowl. I guess having a sick grandparent in the hospital only calls for partial rudeness.

"I wasn't sleeping. Just thinking about how yesterday everything was fine and today it's a fucking mess." I rub my hands over my face, remembering I'm still in my pajamas and blushing at the realization that Mitch has now seen me in said pajamas. Oh well.

"May I?" he asks while gesturing to the small couch. I give him a curt nod and slide over as far as I can so that I don't accidentally touch him. I keep telling myself there's no attraction there but every time I'm close to him, my body hums in recognition.

Traitor.

Mitch takes a seat and folds his hands together between his legs. I want to ask him why he's here but talking sounds exhausting right now. I could get up but that would mean I need to go in that room again. Also sounds exhausting.

So, for now, I sit here like a coward avoiding all my internal issues. For someone who isn't in college, doesn't have a career and is still a virgin for God's sake, I sure have a lot of issues.

It's not like I planned to be a virgin this long, but the opportunity never came along. Losing your parents at thirteen kind of inadvertently marks you as damaged goods. Not that I was a bombshell in high school, but even if I was, something tells me the guys wouldn't have been lining up to date me.

It's sad, really, my lack of experience. Sometimes I think it would be easier if I just lost my virginity to anyone, get it out of the way. People put so much pressure on their first time, wanting it to be perfect and special, that it becomes the opposite. I'm not waiting for the perfect person or the right moment, and yet it still hasn't happened to me. Might as well prepare to be the next forty-year-old virgin.

Mitch clears his throat lightly, pulling me from my thoughts. He doesn't say anything, just nods his head in the direction of the room my grandfather is in. Without saying a word, I know he's right. Time to put on my big girl pants and go in there.

Time seems to stand still in my mind while things are buzzing around me. Nurses and doctors up and down the hallway in and out of rooms, visitors checking in on loved ones, and then me. Sitting next to a guy who I can't tell whether he likes me or loathes me, while trying to find the courage to walk into that room and see Pop in a hospital bed after suffering a heart attack.

If we sit here, just a little bit longer, then I can put off the news that will inevitably come. The words that will tell us Pop had a heart attack and change everything.   Being here brings out so many emotions that I've tried so hard to bury. It's like I'm reliving the nightmare all over again.

Suddenly, I feel restless, like I can't just sit here and do nothing. I stand up and pace the hallway a few times as Mitch stares at me with concern. We haven't known each other long enough to know how one will react in these situations. He stands up and joins me in the hallway. Looking me in the eyes, he gains my attention and not even saying a word, I know what he's thinking. It's time I find out what's going on and talk to Gran. I nod my head in silent agreement and start walking back to his room.

Standing in front of his closed door, I can hear muffled voices still. Once we walk into that room, things will be different, for everyone. A tear breaks free and rolls down my cheek before I wipe it away. I will hold myself together and be strong, not for myself, but mainly for Gran.

An hour later I'm in the passenger seat of Mitch's truck. I'm quiet as I stare out the window watching the fields pass by in a blur. Mitch doesn't try to make small talk; he just drives in the direction of my house. After spending some time with Gran while Pop slept, Mitch offered to drive me home. If this had happened a week ago, I would have had to deal with this alone.

Gran is staying at the hospital to be by Pop's side and insisted I head home. Maureen, bless her heart, is keeping the bakery open with the goodness of her heart, so we can all heal.

Pop suffered a heart attack, that part was obvious when they sent us to the CCU. But now they want him to stay in the hospital for observations and monitoring in case he develops Arrhythmias or has another heart attack.

Due to his age they're more concerned for his well-being right now, though Pop isn't in the worst shape ever, he's also not in the best. Right now, he's just tired and weak, which is normal, but Gran is too nervous to leave his side. Can't say I blame her.

Before we left the hospital, she asked if I could go up to the attic and look in the filing cabinet for the will and other paperwork she might need. It seems a bit morbid to start going through all these things when he's still here, but I understand her need to be prepared. When her father died, it was so sudden, and her mother had nothing figured out or organized. Gran swore she would never allow that to happen.

"Want some help in there?" Mitch asks, pulling me from my daze. "It can be overwhelming going through all that paperwork, I don't mind helping." Truthfully, being alone is the only thing I want right now.

"I don't mean to sound rude, because I appreciate you waiting at the hospital to give me a ride home. But I think I need to be alone right now."

"I respect that." He starts to turn back to his truck before adding, "Call if you need anything." Then gets in and drives away.

I make my way into the house and up to the attic. When I was little, I used to hate it up here. I was convinced it was haunted, so I rarely stepped foot even near the door. The air is hot and sticky up here and it smells stale. Clearly, no one has been up here in a while to open a window and air things out. Most of the furniture is covered with white sheets, guessing that's why I thought there were ghosts up here as a kid, and everything else is covered in several layers of dust.

In the far-right corner by the window is an old cedar chest, that's where Gran told me the Will should be, along with any other paperwork that she deemed important. I pull it out from the corner and lift the top so I can get to work.

Fifteen minutes later and I still haven't located the folder with the Will. I must have emptied half the chest out with no luck, perhaps it's not even here. I'm about to give up when a folder catches my eye. It doesn't look that old like some of the other folders that have been sitting in here for who knows how long. Something about it stands out and now I'm curious. I pull the folder out and on the front in my mom's handwriting are the words *Letters to Olive*. Why would there be a folder up here with letters addressed to me that I didn't know about?

A part of me wants to rip the folder open and see what's inside, the other part of me is afraid. What if these are letters my mom wrote for me and just never gave me? Opening them would be like opening old wounds again. I've finally started living again, and dragging myself back to the past won't bring my parents back. I'm still staring at the folder waiting for a sign to tell me it's okay to open this.

I rip open the folder to see a dozen letters addressed to me. The address is my parents' house though, so if these *were* from my mom, why would she address them to her own house? I don't recognize the handwriting and there's no return address on any of them. Something feels off and suddenly, my body is covered in goose bumps.

"What the hell are these?" I whisper to myself. So many thoughts and questions are running through my mind right now I can hardly process them all.

Without hesitation, I tear open the first letter to see more of the same handwriting from the front of the envelope. So, these aren't from my parents. I never would have imagined that coming up here and finding these letters would alter my life and everything I've known. But here we are.

Dear Olive,

I don't know when, or if, you'll ever read this letter, but I couldn't go another day without writing to you. I've made some questionable decisions in my life, but the one I can't bring myself to regret is the decision to give you a better life. At sixteen I knew I couldn't raise a baby, even though I loved you so, so much. When I met your parents, instantly I knew they were the right people to raise you and give you everything I couldn't. By the grace of God and their kindness, they allowed me to name you. As soon as you were born, I knew you were meant to be Olive.

I wish my circumstances were different and I could be a part of your life, but I know this is for the best. If your parents ever decide to tell you about the adoption, please just know one thing. I love you more than anything in the world, Olive, and it's because I love you that I gave you up. Not a day goes by that I don't wonder about you and imagine your life. Should you ever want to meet me, I will be here. You are my greatest gift, sweet girl.

Love,

Lucy

My chest is tight with emotion, the pages are soaked with tears that silently fell while I was reading. "What the fuck?" I get up and start pacing the attic, sweat building in my hairline and between my breasts. I don't think I've ever felt so overwhelmed in my entire life. Aside from the day I found out my parents died.

Now, come to find out, they weren't even my biological parents. What am I supposed to do with that information? How did I wake up this morning to find my grandfather had a heart attack and is in the hospital, to now learn I was adopted?

I'm adopted. I can't even fully process that word right now with all the questions running through my mind. How could they keep this from me for so long? My whole life I felt different, and my mom always reassured me I was perfect for them.

Now I'm rethinking so many things she's said to me over the years, searching for clues. Wondering if she tried to tell me and just couldn't find the right words.

How am I supposed to bring this up to Gran with everything else on her plate right now? I may be a lot of things, and in the past, I could have been labeled selfish, but now…Now I need to do what's right for them. Until I figure out what I want to do with this information, I plan to keep it quiet.

I'm trying to breathe through my panic, hoping I don't become hysterical. I need fresh air. I can't be in this attic feeling like the walls are caving in around me when I can hardly breathe. As eager as I am to read the rest of the letters, today has been overwhelming enough. I slip the stack back into the folder and grab all the paperwork Gran requested. A glance out the window I look in the direction of the Murphy's Pond, I head down the stairs taking them two at a time as I try to outrun the reality of my life.

7

MITCH

Harvesting wheat in the middle of the summer is not for the weak. By some miracle, that storm last month didn't destroy all our crops, though right now I'm wishing it had.

I swipe an arm over my forehead and pull it away covered in sweat. Days like these make me realize no amount of water will keep me hydrated, not the way sweat is pouring off me. At this rate, I should just carry around an IV drip to keep me hydrated, much more efficient.

I checked the time and decided to take a lunch break, minus the lunch. I don't like eating big meals when I'm working this much, especially in the heat. It ends up making me tired and sluggish, so I just opt for electrolytes instead. Gatorade in hand, I head to the pond to cool off before continuing my day.

Rounding the corner down the gravel path, I notice that long brown hair I so desperately want to run my fingers through. Olive's back is to me so I can't tell what she's doing, but the way her shoulders move slightly has me wary. I don't want to startle her, so I crack open the bottle in my hand to give her some warning.

She hears me coming and immediately I notice her swipe her hands across her cheeks. Fuck, she's crying. I'm an ass most of the time when people *aren't* crying, not exactly sure how to navigate these waters.

I figure it's best to give her a moment to collect herself before having to interact with me, so I remove my sweat stained shirt and without saying a word, launch myself into the pond. I stay under water for several seconds reveling in the feel of the cool water against my heated skin. No amount of sunscreen can keep the rays from bronzing my body. When I resurface, Olive is no longer sitting on the banks of the pond.

I'm embarrassed to say I frantically look around to see where she went when I hear a splash from behind me. There's an old swing attached to one of the trees on the opposite side of the pond, my brother and I spent every day down here jumping off that thing. Dad hung it for us when we begged and pleaded for two weeks straight one summer. Glad to see it's held up all these years. Mostly.

Olive surfaces and I can see it in her eyes, something is wrong. I'm not about to ask what it is though; I've learned it's best to keep your mouth shut until someone asks you to open it. I don't always have the best bedside manner, and right now she doesn't need sarcasm from an asshole like me.

She leans back to float in the water, closing her eyes and steadying herself before going completely still. She's wearing that simple black bikini that shows off her curves and olive toned skin. From here I can see a few freckles dotting her collarbone and my mouth waters at the thought of kissing each one.

I don't know how long she floats like that while I watch her, but eventually she opens her eyes and looks at me. "Shit day, huh?" she says. I can tell it's rhetorical, but I nod and look up at the sun peeking through the trees. Today, aside from the heat, is one of the most perfect days we've had around here lately. But we both know she's not talking about the weather.

I swim closer to her and watch her movements as I do. She's guarded, but there's something else there. A fire in her eyes that has me melting worse than the sun out in the wheat fields. One look from her and I'm molten, happily melting under her gaze.

Before I have a chance to register how close she's swimming to me, her lips crash into mine in a desperate plea. She winds her hands around my neck, pulling my body closer to hers, slick against each other from the water. My hands find her waist on their own and pull her even closer to me.

In one movement, I'm lifting her legs around my waist and sinking lower into the water to better balance us. Her thighs tighten around my waist and the feeling goes straight to my dick. God, the affects this girl has on me and she doesn't even realize it. Her body tightly pressed against mine is the sweetest sin I've felt in a long time, and I will gladly go to hell if it means I can touch her like this.

Her body is petite, but strong. The curve of her back leading down to her ass has me dizzy with need. I want to press her up against the trunk of the white oak nestled just past the banks of the pond and ravage her. Find every sensitive spot on her body, learn every curve, and taste every part of her. I want all of that just from one kiss.

I want to ask her what the sudden change is all about but can't bring myself to release her lips from mine. She tastes like heaven, just as good as she smells, like coconuts and vanilla, a literal paradise. I could drink her in and never be thirsty again. Slowly, I pull back to look at her, see what storm she's fighting behind those dark hazel eyes, and find out if she'll let me in.

Even if it's just a little.

Just as I'm about to open my mouth, she puts a hand up to stop me. "I don't want to talk." She removes her legs from around my waist and starts to get out of the water. I follow her out and watch her ring out her hair and towel dry her body. She pulls on a pair of light wash denim cutoff shorts and a black tank top. After piling her hair into a messy bun on top of her head, she turns to me. "Want to go for a drive?"

There's still a lot of work I need to get done on the farm, but I can tell she needs a friend right now. Not sure I fall into that category, exactly, but if I'm the kind of friend she wants to keep kissing like that, then I'll be the best friend she's ever had.

I grab my discarded clothes and head in the direction of the house to grab something clean to throw on. Ten minutes later she and I are driving down the gravel driveway in my truck. Olive turns the radio on and some song by Warren Zeiders is playing. I focus on the lyrics while occasionally glancing in her direction to see the wisps of hair around her face blow in the breeze.

The song was practically written for her, the way he sings about some girl being able to paint the sky blue. Olive is that girl, she can light up a room without even trying, something she clearly doesn't see in herself. Somehow, she's gotten me to rethink how I treat people, not become some gruff asshole who scowls all the time.

I don't even know when that all started. It's not like I grew up with two absent parents who didn't pay any attention to me. Growing up on this land, with my older brother, was a dream come true. I guess sometime over the years my exterior hardened, and with it so did my insides. It's something I want to work on, something my mom is constantly reminding me of, too.

I keep driving, heading in the direction of Raising Hope shelter and remembering the first time we drove this way together. Olive is still quiet, lost in thought somewhere in that beautiful mind of hers. It's killing me not knowing what's going on with her but considering how many times I've given her mixed signals; I stay quiet for now. I can't act like I care, even though I do, when majority of the time we've known each other, I've been a dick.

Five minutes from raising Hope I remember a path I found when I was volunteering years ago, it feels like the perfect thing to show Olive. A quiet, beautiful spot that's secluded and away from everyone else. I would go there on lunch breaks to get some fresh air and process my own problems. Volunteering there for so long, just to keep an eye on Drew, had its own stress attached to it. Mainly the fact that my family didn't know that's why I was going so frequently.

Easing the truck to a stop in a dirt lot off the side of the road, I turn the truck off and look at Olive. "Want to go for a walk?" I asked her. She turns to look at me and I catch a small glimpse of a smile. It was gone as soon as it appeared, but still I caught it.

We get out and start walking. I can't guarantee she'll open up to me, but if she wants to, then I'm here. Let's hope I can keep my sarcasm to a minimum. Depending on what's wrong, I might become awkward real quick.

8
Olive

I fall into step with him, and we start walking down the gravel road towards a path that leads into the trees. Much of the land around here is flat and open, but there are clusters of trees here and there that provide secret passages.

When I was little, I used to pretend each patch of trees was a different secret world, with hidden treasures and mythical places. I don't dare admit that to Mitch though, I've been weird enough for one day.

"How did you find this path?" I ask as I pay close attention to the ground, so I don't trip over a root.

"When I would volunteer here weekly, I'd get time to have lunch, so sometimes I'd wander off. Being there was overwhelming sometimes, so coming out here was a nice break."

This is the first time talking to Mitch has felt effortless. Usually, we bicker with each other, or he grimaces at me. He's probably just being nice because he can tell something is wrong, but I'm not ready to talk about it yet. I've barely processed the news myself, never mind the idea of explaining it to someone else, that someone else being Mitch, no less.

But the more he talks the more I feel connected to him in ways that I can't quite explain. Most of my friends in school had other interests than me, I was always reading or listening to music. They often wanted to go shopping and visit the mall a few towns over.

I step on a rock that wobbles a little and for a second, I lose my footing, but before I can trip, Mitch grabs my arm. The gesture is kind and does weird things to my heart. I want him to keep holding my arm, but I know I can't say that.

"You okay?" he asks with a touch of concern, not the kind where he actually thought I might hurt myself, but the kind like he cares about my well-being. There's a pull between us, something I've never felt this quickly, or with anyone for that matter. I'm trying to muster some confidence to ask if he feels it too, but the words keep getting caught in my throat.

Instead of responding, I just smile and nod. I glance down to where his hand is still enclosed lightly around my arm and the gooseflesh where his fingers linger. Realizing he's still touching me; he releases me quickly and instantly I miss his warmth. "Can I ask you something?" He says out of the blue.

My heart starts racing just at the sound of his voice, deep but kind, filling the quiet space around us in the trees. I'm hoping he's not about to ask me what's wrong because as much as I don't want to talk about it, I feel like I would. The sound of his voice does something to me, and if he asked me to, I'd spill all my secrets.

No one is around, if he turned out to be some crazed psychopath, no one would hear me scream. I like to think I have a decent judge of character though, and everything about him screams safe. Which is weird considering a week ago we barely spoke.

"Sure." I whisper.

"Do you have a boyfriend?" he asks, not making eye contact with me. Not what I thought he was going to ask, and the question catches me off guard enough that I start laughing. He snaps his head up to look at me before laughing nervously himself.

"I'm sorry, I don't mean to laugh. It's just, I wasn't expecting you to ask that. I'm not exactly the type to have guys falling all over her." I say gesturing at my worn jean shorts and plain black tank top.

"Why would you think that?" he asks genuinely.

"I don't know. I guess I just never thought of myself as someone guys would be interested in. I'm plain. I have long skinny legs, no chest to write home about, and my parents died. Guys probably see me as too much baggage." I didn't mean to admit that my parents died just then, but he wanted to know why, so I told him.

"Plus, if I had a boyfriend, I wouldn't have attacked your face in the pond." I laugh but there's no humor there.

"Those don't sound like reasons for someone not to like you, Olive. Losing your parents doesn't mean you have baggage. It means you've lived through some tough shit and probably have more appreciation for what you have. It's admirable."

"How do you know I have appreciation for what I have? For all you know, I'm miserable all the time." He can sense I'm reaching with that last statement, but I continue. "Truthfully,

I was that way up until maybe a year ago. They died when I was only thirteen, it changed my whole life overnight. They missed so much, and for a long time I was bitter about it. It's not like one of them got sick, they died in a stupid car accident. Had they not been driving together I would have only lost one, not both."

I realize how morbid that sounds, but it's what I've thought about for years. Losing one of them would have been devastating but losing both nearly killed me too.

"I'm sorry, I know that sounds awful. I didn't mean to bring the conversation to such a depressing place." He tugs on my arm to stop me and turns me around so that I'm facing him.

"Olive, this is part of you, it's part of who you are." He reaches up and gently tucks a strand of hair that fell loose from my ponytail, behind my ear. The feel of his fingers, feather light, across my cheek ignites feelings I've never felt before. "For what it's worth. There's lots of reasons guys should be lining up to date you."

I'm holding my breath and reviling in the feel of his body so close to mine. I've kissed guys before, but only two, and neither one was worth remembering. In this moment, I've never wanted to be kissed as badly as I want Mitch to kiss me, again.

I lift my gaze to meet him and there's a war of emotions in his eyes. I don't know him well enough yet to know what he's thinking. But if I had to make a guess, I'd say he's fighting the same thing I am. I take half a step towards him, testing his reaction and his body meets mine like we're two magnets drawn to each other.

Mitch rests one hand behind my back, pulling me another step closer, and the other finds the lock of hair by my ear again. In one swift movement, he's tucking the hair behind my ear and drawing me closer to him.

Our lips meet in a soft embrace while currents of electricity are igniting every nerve in my body. I lean into him and inhale his scent, crisp apples, and cinnamon. I open my mouth and his tongue invades my senses. This is the kind of kiss you see in movies, gentle but heady, and I want more.

My body arches into him as he holds my back with both his hands. I wind my hands to his face and hold him there as he explores my mouth with his. A soft groan fills the air and at first, I can't tell if it's from him or me. He releases my mouth and gently kisses my neck while one hand plays with the end of my ponytail.

"You smell insanely good, just so you know." He whispers against my neck, and I feel goosebumps arise all over my body. "What is that scent?" He groans while breathing in deeply. I laugh trying to think of what perfume I put on this morning, which was hours ago, and yet he can still smell it. "You smell like coconuts and vanilla." I start to laugh again, and he swallows the sound with his mouth, feeling the laughter rumble between us.

I keep thinking I'm dreaming, anticipating waking up very disappointed this isn't real. But Mitch pulls my front flush against his chest and the sensation has my nipples pebbling beneath my shirt. I don't have much experience with guys, at nineteen I'm probably the only virgin left, and Mitch is more than likely not. That fear brings me back to reality, and he can sense my shift in demeanor.

"I'm sorry, I should have asked if that was okay." He takes a step back and rubs a hand through his hair. I don't want him to think I didn't enjoy myself, so I know I need to come clean about my thoughts, even though it's surely going to be a buzzkill.

"Please, don't apologize. I was the one who attacked you first." I murmur looking at his chest. The muscles there have me itching to rip his shirt off and study each one. He smirks at me and comes closer again, wrapping his arms around my waist.

"I wasn't pulling back because I wasn't enjoying the kiss. Truthfully, it's the best kiss I've ever had." There I go shoving my foot in my mouth again. A blush creeps across my face again and I look down to hide my embarrassment.

"I can say the same." Mitch says as he tilts my chin up to look at him. He kisses me softly, feeling my lips move against his again and all thoughts vanish from my mind. I want to tell him my secret, both secrets, but maybe for now I can just enjoy this moment. I doubt he expects me to strip my clothes off and take him right here and now. Tantalizing as that may be, it's not exactly how I picture my first time. Especially given everything running through my mind still.

Kissing Mitch is unlike any feeling I've had, a welcome distraction. I'm used to being the sad girl who lost her parents. When I woke up this morning, I felt lost, but today with Mitch has been a piece of hope I didn't expect to find. We start walking the trail again for a few minutes before the ranch comes into view. The sun is setting on the horizon just as the horse's gallop laps around their enclosure.

It's picture perfect, and now I want to come back for riding lessons. Quietly, we watch the scene before us, appreciating its natural beauty. But as the sun descends into the earth, it's evident we should get going. Not that I'm afraid of the dark, but I don't particularly want to make an ass out of myself by tripping every three feet. It was bad enough I tripped when there was still daylight. Plus, I need to check in on Gran and Pop, I can only escape reality for so long.

"We should head back." I say quietly when I peek up to see him already looking at me. "I don't want to get you in trouble for not finishing your work today."

"It'll still be there when I get back, I'm not worried about it."

"Why did you do it?" I ask, stopping as I wait for an answer.

"Do what?" He looks at me a little confused.

"You didn't even hesitate earlier when I asked you to go for a drive. I know how hard you work, and how important the farm is to you. I was expecting you to blow me off, so why didn't you?"

"I could tell you needed someone today, and I wanted to be that someone." He replies, and it's so honest it has my knees wobbling.

"But I don't say a word to you, just get in the water and kiss you out of the blue. Then ask you to drop everything you're doing and take me for a drive, while still not letting you in."

"For weeks I thought I disgusted you, then last week you told me you regret kissing me because you liked it too much. If you haven't noticed, Mitch, I'm a bit of a mess. So, please, enlighten me. Why do you want to be that someone for me?"

He marches right up to me, grabs the back of my neck, and pulls me in, kissing me fiercely with a touch of aggression. The hold he has on my neck is biting, but I like it. I want to lose myself in his touch and forget everything else exists. I want him to be the person I can turn to, the person who's there even when they don't know what they're there for. I just need to know why.

"Because I want you."

It's as simple as that. Only four words and yet I don't feel like I need anymore of an explanation. He's here kissing me because he *wants* to. There's no obligation tied to it, it's just that. For years I never felt good enough, like every person looked at me like damaged goods. Unable to see past the flaw of losing my parents. As if it was my fault they died, and no one could stand to be near me afraid I was so delicate I'd break.

For the first time since I was thirteen, I don't feel breakable. I feel strong. Despite finding out I'm adopted and not even knowing where I come from. Learning that Pop had a heart attack and could be at risk for another serious one that likely would end his life.

All this time I just felt lost, never knowing where I was going or what to do with myself. I don't need a guy's approval, that's for sure. But feeling wanted is unlocking something inside me that's long been closed off.

"Don't get me wrong, you still piss me off sometimes." He admits as he runs a hand through his hair.

"Yeah, well you're still a prick most of the time." I counter. We both laugh and then his face goes serious again.

"Last time I told you I meant what I said, you brushed me off. Are you going to do that again? Because I don't think my pride could take it."

I try to look like I'm deep in thought, trying to remember what it was he said when he flicks one of my nipples, clearly visible through my shirt. "Hey!" I yell as I rub the spot he flicked.

"Answer my question, Olive." He looks at me intently, waiting for me to respond, both knowing full well what he's referring to.

My heart is beating wildly in my chest, fully aware of the uncharted territory I'm about to embark on. With everything I have going on, I know I should run. Forget those moments that have happened and focus on the important things.

That voice in my head, though, she keeps telling me *Mitch* is important. Everything I'm feeling is important and happening, whether I want it to happen or not. Walking away now would just leave me with a lifetime of what if's. I've got enough of those floating around my head as it is.

I take a step closer to Mitch, never breaking eye contact and nod my head. Silently answering his question, showing him, I know he's serious, and that I'm serious too.

"Say it, Olive." He grips one side of my neck, tilting my head up to look at him more directly. He's not going to release me until I say the words he wants to hear. Ass.

"I want you, Mitch." That's all he needed to hear before he crushed his lips to mine again in a searing kiss that has electric vibrations reaching my toes. How the hell does he do that?

"That's my girl." He kisses my forehead and pulls me to his side as we walk back to his truck. We didn't exactly label whatever this is that's happening, but whatever we just did feels clear. I'm his, and he's mine. After weeks of bickering and scowling at each other, we admitted there's something here and we somehow ended up here. I just hope I don't fuck it all up.

We drove around for over an hour, listening to music as we talked aimlessly. The windows are down, and the air doesn't feel as humid with the wind blowing throughout the cab of the truck. When we got hungry, we stopped at a diner off the interstate. Mitch called his parents to let them know where we were and to pass along the information in case Gran called. She has enough to worry about without adding the fear of me missing. As upset as I am, I would never intentionally add more stress to her plate.

When I was little, my mom would make breakfast for dinner sometimes. I always thought it was so cool, to have pancakes and bacon for dinner. So, tonight I ordered breakfast at the diner, since they serve it all day, it seemed fitting. My parents may not have been mine biologically, but they raised me and that's not something that can ever be taken away. This woman, Lucy, I know nothing about her or if what she said is even true.

The whole thing feels messy and uncertain, but that voice inside keeps telling me I deserve to know the truth. I'll love my parents forever, but the idea that I have another set of people out there who created me is intriguing. There's so much I want to know.

After eating, we're back on the road again. We drove around aimlessly for so long that we managed to make it two hours from home. I just want to close my eyes and put this entire day behind me. Having to wait another two hours to get home seems unbearable.

"I'm so tired, this day has seemed to go on forever." I rasp. Mitch reaches across the center console to hold my hand.

"Do you want me to stop somewhere? Maybe we can find a cheap place to stay for the night?" He must be tired too; I can't fathom driving right now and he's been doing it all night.

"I'm so sorry, Mitch. You must be sick of driving. I can drive us the rest of the way back." He shakes his head quickly.

"Baby, your day has been eventful enough. I can get us back, I just wanted to offer it as an option." He smiles and directs his attention back to the road.

Hearing him use that term of endearment is doing something to my insides. My heart flutters wildly like a Butterfly taking its first flight. Whatever is going on between us is still fresh, but he can call me that *whenever* he wants.

I focus back on what he's just said. As enticing as it sounds to spend the night in a hotel room alone with Mitch. I don't trust myself enough right now to remain in control. Especially since he just called me *baby*. Virgin or not, I'm quite willing to do anything right now to escape this day and the way I'm feeling. Wouldn't that be quite the story. Lost my virginity to a guy I barely know in some seedy motel after weeks of thinking he hated the sight of me. The idea makes me laugh, attracting Mitch's attention.

"Care to share what's so funny?" He smirks at me as I rest my head against the headrest.

"It's nothing, just tried to picture staying in a hotel room with you and we haven't even known each other six weeks." Mitch raises an eyebrow. I can pretty much tell where his mind immediately went, which makes me laugh again. Louder this time and now I've got his complete attention. He slowly pulls the truck to the side of the road and turns in his seat to look at me.

"I can't exactly focus on the road Olive when you're laughing like that. Your laugh does something to me, honestly it makes me want to kiss you so hard I can taste your laughter."

Now it's my turn to raise an eyebrow at him. How is it he always knows what to say and how to say it? His voice is like honey, smooth and sweet. I know what he means by wanting to kiss the taste right out of my mouth. Without hesitation, I climb across the console to straddle him. His eyes go wide as he accommodates the shift of our bodies. I waste no time and capture his mouth with mine, entwining my hands into his hair. A groan slips free, and I arch my body into his.

We should probably slow down, but all I can think about right now is the taste of him and the intoxicating way he smells. He always smells like spice and apples, probably from working outside on the farm. I can't get enough of it. I nibble the side of his neck, enticing a moan from him, and taste the saltiness of his skin. I can feel his length hardening between my thighs and it's causing my head to spin. I don't want to lead him on in any way, but this is exactly what I need right now.

I pull back and look at him with dazed eyes. "I need to tell you something." I blurt out, feeling like today has had enough bombshells, what's one more?

Mitch grips my waist and nods his head with a breathy "Okay". We're both out of breath and judging by the feel of him and how wet my undies are, both extremely turned on. I look down at my hands clasped in my lap, suddenly nervous to confess this to him.

On a deep breath, without looking up, I find a sliver of courage. "I was going to tell you the other day, but since we don't know each other that well I didn't want to say anything too soon." He looks concerned now but lets me forge on. "When I say kissing you is the best I've ever had, it's true. I've only kissed two other guys and that's…that's it."

I wait, hoping he got what I was implying, but he stays quiet. Shit, this is harder than I thought it would be. "Mitch, I've never…" My confession is cut off by my phone ringing in the cupholder beneath me. I grab it and answer quickly when I see Gran's name.

"Gran? Is everything okay?" My voice comes out on a choke, and I stare at Mitch with wide eyes anticipating bad news. "Okay. Yes, I found the papers. I went for a drive with Mitch to clear my head and honestly, I didn't want to be alone." I listen to her fill me in on how Pop is doing and that she's planning to stay at the hospital with him.

"We're heading back now. I'll have the papers set up for you when you come home. Try to get some rest, Gran. Mhmm…I love you too." I hang up and stare down at my phone. The moment has passed and now feels like incredibly weird timing to confess I'm a virgin.

I climb back to my side of the truck and fasten my seatbelt. "Gran is staying at the hospital tonight, and probably for however long Pop is there. We should head back."

He deserves more of an explanation, but once he looks at me, he gets the sense now isn't the time to push the topic. We drive quietly for a few minutes before Mitch clears his throat.

"Whenever you're ready to tell me whatever it was you were about to, I'm here. No judgement." I offer a small smile before turning my head to look out the window again, just as a tear slips down my cheek.

I must have fallen asleep, because before I know it, we were parked in front of my house. It looks dark and depressing and truthfully, I can't imagine staying there alone tonight. "Mitch? As if you haven't already done enough for me today… would you mind staying here tonight? I just don't want to be alone." Jesus, what's with all the tears lately. It's like I'm thirteen all over again.

"Of course. Let me run home to grab an overnight bag and I'll be back in fifteen. Is that okay?" he replies easily and almost like he was anticipating me asking that.

"I'm so embarrassed." I whisper.

"Don't be. I really don't mind." He assures me. I hop out of the truck and run into the house to turn on lights and get a pot of water boiling for some tea. I have fifteen minutes to collect myself before Mitch is back. If I'm not careful I'll likely fall head over heels in love with this guy.

Twenty minutes, a hot shower, and two cups of tea later, Mitch is back. I hand him a mug and lead him into the den to sit on the couch. This was always one of my favorite rooms here, a sunken in den with big comfy couches and a big television. Since Gran and Pop have always been so busy with the bakery, they hardly have time for tv. This is one of the only ones in the house, so I used to sneak off here to watch. I grab a giant sherpa blanket from the back of the couch and cover myself and Mitch.

This moment makes me want to snuggle into him, inhaling his scent and just relaxing as if I didn't have the most life-altering day. Instead, I put on a random movie and focus on my tea. It's nearly midnight and the events of the day are causing my eyes to droop. I'm not sure how Mitch is even functioning right now, considering he spent most of the day with me and then a few hours driving. I glance over at him to see he's passed out, full cup of tea still in his hand. Carefully I take the mug and set it on the table next to mine. I nestle myself into his side and within seconds, I'm out.

Morning comes too soon, just a sliver of light filtering in through the curtains. I don't even know what time it is, but something tells me it's early. By the time we fell asleep last night it was passed midnight, so the idea of getting up right now sounds worse than high school math.

I rub my eyes and turn my head to see Mitch smiling at me. "Oh God, I must look ridiculous right now." I say groaning into my hands. He just chuckles next to me and pulls me closer to his side.

"Actually, I was thinking how adorable you look first thing in the morning. You always seem so put together, it's cute to see this side of you." If only he knew how far from put together I actually am.

He nudges my chin up with his finger so that I'm looking at him. "You don't ever have to hide from me, Olive." He leans in and places a soft kiss on my lips before sitting up to stretch.

"As much as I want to stay here all day, I really need to head over to the farm and check on things. Will you be okay for a few hours?" That question has me both swooning and wanting to hide in my shell. The fact that he cares enough to ask is sweet, but that also means I was such a mess yesterday he's afraid to leave me alone.

"I promise I'll be fine." I say with a laugh, hoping he'll believe it. "I should check on Pop and Gran at the hospital, anyways." We both get up and I start folding blankets as Mitch grabs his boots.

"I'll come back tonight, if you want." He says as he tucks my hair behind my ear. God, I love when he does that. I give him a kiss and a minute later, I'm alone.

Before my mind can reel from everything going on up there, I head to the kitchen to make some pastries to bring by the hospital.

After visiting Gran and Pop at the hospital, I head to the bakery to check in with Maureen. Pop seemed better today, and by better, I mean at least awake enough to notice my presence and offer a weak smile. Gran was in good spirits in front of him, but as soon as his eyes closed a dark cloud loomed above her. I can't even begin to understand how difficult this situation is for her. Aside from me, all she has is Pop.

After my parents died, she put all her energy towards the bakery and nothing else. Something we have in common it seems; I've done just about everything to distract myself since the news I uncovered about being adopted.

I took my time getting to the bakery, riding my bike leisurely and noticing all the wildflowers that had grown in the fields before town. I know when I get to work Maureen and everyone else is going to bombard me with questions about Pop. They mean well, but I'm not in the mood for all the peppering questions.

Stopping next to a stream that runs under the road, I hop off my bike and climb down to sit on the banks. Everything feels so overwhelming and life-altering that I just want to focus on something simple, like this stream.

My grandfather is in the hospital, and I have no way of knowing if he's going to fully recover. I'm constantly worrying about Gran and keeping the bakery just the way she would. The fact that I was adopted, and my dead parents weren't even my biological ones. Oh, and the secret of being a virgin pushing up against my insides, is like a volcano ready to erupt.

Secrets begging to be freed.

With so much going on there never seems to be a right moment to confess to Mitch just how inexperienced I am. Even though he has been there for me these past few days, I don't know him well enough to expect anything. Mom always used to tell me to trust my gut, so that's all I can do. Wait for the right moment and hope Mitch understands.

I hadn't realized I'd laid back in the grass until the sunshine on my face was blocked by a figure. Are you okay miss?" A tall man with a deep, kind, voice says from the road where my bike is leaning against the guardrail.

I sit up and use one hand to shield the sun from my eyes. "Yes sir, just enjoying the beautiful weather." I smile, sounding pleasant and normal, but the feeling of those words leaving my mouth is like gasoline.

"Saw the bike and figured I'd make sure you were alright. Have a nice day, Miss." He salutes me and carries on with his day.

I lay back down and close my eyes against the summer sun listening to the stream babble along the rocks. Taking a deep breath, I smell honeysuckles and fresh cut grass, the perfect recipe for summer if you ask me. My palms lay flat against the grass, and I move them back and forth, feeling the sensation tickle my hands as I do.

Maybe if I focus on the simple things, I can escape the big ones looming in my mind. So many unanswered questions, so many unknowns, this thing with Mitch, Pop, Lucy, my parents. It's too much.

I feel a tear slip down my cheek and I quickly wipe it away. I need to get to the bakery to distract myself and focus on work. Laying here on any other day would be peaceful, but today it's just giving me too much space to dwell on the shit storm that currently is my life.

9

Olive

It's been a week since Pop had his heart attack. The doctors kept him for five days and now he's home. The transition has been smooth overall, Gran and I set up a bed for him in the den, so he doesn't have to go up and down the stairs so much. Plus, there's a bathroom between the den and kitchen, so he has everything he needs close by.

A nurse is supposed to come by once a day to administer meds and check vitals, something Gran made very clear to the doctors she wouldn't do. "I am not going to be responsible for giving this man his medication and risk fucking it up!" Is what she said loud enough everyone at the nurse's station and surrounding hallways could hear. It made me laugh, something Gran did not find amusing in the least.

I'm sitting at the kitchen table when Gran ambles in, looking more tired than I've ever seen her. For someone her age, she's always kept up with work and life in general. Nothing, except the death of my parents, has ever aged her until this week.

Despite the awful initial feeling of Pop's heart attack, and everything this week piled on top of that news, seeing the love between my grandparents, so honest and pure, has given me some kind of peace.

I stir some honey into my tea while I watch Gran shuffle around the kitchen, grabbing a mug for herself and joining me at the table. Her gray hair is pinned back in a French twist, like she always has it, and little fly away's frame her face. She's always worn delicate framed glasses, with no trim, that rest low on her nose.

If you were to look up the definition of Gran in a dictionary, Joan Fournier is likely the picture next to the description. She lets out a soft sigh as she settles into her seat, tea in hand. Without saying a word, I lean over and hold one of her soft wrinkled hands, hands that know hard work, and offer her a gentle squeeze.

Gran smiles down at her mug of tea, unable to look at me for fear of tears cresting her eyes. Can't say I blame her. Every time I go to talk about anything with her, I feel tears build behind my lids. There are so many things I want to ask her, things I need to know. Given any other day, I would march right up and ask. But her heart is heavy enough as it is right now, I can't dig up the past and dump that on her as well.

I may want answers, and I know I am entitled to them, but I'm not a selfish little teenager anymore. The well-being of my grandparents is far more important currently. The truth of my lineage can wait until the dust settles a little.

After a few quiet moments, Gran rises from her chair and wipes her face as if she felt phantom tears there out of habit. This week she has probably cried more than I've ever seen in my life, aside from the loss of my parents.

"Gran, I was thinking we could host the Murphy's for dinner this week. I'll handle the shopping list and preparations, but this way Pop can join us but still be at home." I watch her back as she mulls it over, hoping she'll take me up on the offer.

"That sounds fine, dear."

"Is there anything you think Pop would prefer now that he doesn't have to eat hospital food anymore?" I ask as I pull out a notepad and pen to make a shopping list.

"He loves Elaine's garlic bread, center the meal around that and have her bring a loaf or two." She grabs her purse off the hook by the back door and pulls out some money to hand to me.

I hold up my hand to stop her, "Gran, I got this, you just rest, okay?" She smiles at me weakly but stuffs the money back in her bag and walks outside to sit on the porch.

List in hand, I head out to the grocery store to get everything I need to make meat lasagna. Gran has this recipe that my mom always made, one of her specialties, she would say. I know I won't be able to make it exactly the way she did, but I can try.

Halfway through my shopping, I bump into Mitch's mom. "Mrs. Murphy, how are you?"

"Olive! I'm well, sweetie, how are you? How's Joan and Henry holding up?"

"They're okay, all things considered." I say with a shrug. "I'm glad I ran into you. I was thinking we could host dinner tonight, that way Pop doesn't need to leave the house."

"We can skip this week, dear. With everything you've all been through, dinner can wait." Elaine says as she kindly places a hand on my arm.

"If it's okay with y'all, I think it would help a lot to have you over. Gran is in a funk, understandably so, and Pop has been eating hospital food for a week." I make a face at that, and we both laugh lightly.

"Well, in that case, of course we'll be there! Can I do anything?" she asks with a bright smile.

"Pop really loves your garlic bread…" I say while letting the end of the sentence hang in the air. Elaine picks up on it easily and smiles.

"In that case, I'll make two loafs."

"Thank you so much, Mrs. Murphy."

"Olive, I told you, call me Elaine. We don't need to keep up this formal charade, we're practically family." She goes in to hug me and I can smell her perfume, lavender and bergamot. It reminds me of my mom, and I have to choke back the emotion building in my throat.

I smile sweetly and thank her again before heading back to my shopping. As I round the corner, I hear Elaine call my name. "Olive! I forgot to mention, Collin is coming to visit, is it alright if he joins us for dinner?"

"Collin? Your eldest son, right?" I ask, vaguely remembering Mitch mentioning him. He works for a big law firm in New York City and hasn't been home for months.

"The one and only." She giggles to herself like only she is in on the little secret.

I smile and nod my head, "Of course, the more the merrier." I'm sure Gran won't mind one more person for dinner. Plus, I've been wanting to meet this older brother I've heard practically nothing about. All Mitch told me was that he lives in NYC, a place I very much want to visit.

A few of the resume's I sent out for internships were to NYC, I wonder if Collin will answer some questions for me.

I pay for the groceries and head home to start prepping for tonight. I've never made the lasagna my mom perfected over the years, and now the idea that I'll be cooking for guests has me a little nervous. Baking I can handle, with my grandparent's guidance over the years, I've gotten good. But cooking in the kitchen with my mom wasn't something I had the opportunity to do.

All the groceries are laid out on the counter staring at me as if mocking me, like they know I'm nervous about cooking for everyone. I've cooked dinner countless times and never had a problem. But knowing I am now cooking dinner for Mitch and his family suddenly makes me want to vomit.

Filling a glass with water, I chug it, shake my head and shake the nerves from my hands. This is silly and I'm making a big deal out of nothing. At the very least, Elaine is making garlic bread, so we won't starve.

When I'm almost done with the lasagna, I check the clock to see how much time I have before everyone arrives. I throw together a quick salad with olive oil and lemon zest dressing and set it on the table. I decided to use our nice dinnerware and set the table with cloth napkins and candles in the center. I'm probably overdoing it, but I want this to be nice for Pop.

Ten minutes later, the doorbell rings and I race towards the front door to answer it. Thankfully, I set aside a few minutes to clean myself up before the Murphy's got here. Brushed my hair and pulled it back into a sleek ponytail, threw on a clean shirt and quickly applied some mascara. I'd like to say I didn't try too hard to look good, but adding the mascara told me I was lying to myself.

Taking a deep breath, I open the door with a smile to greet everyone. My eyes find Mitch immediately, then snag on the taller man behind him, Collin. He looks just like Mitch, but taller and cleaner cut. Where Mitch has stubble and tan skin from being outside every day, Collin is refined and tailored. He's handsome in every way, but my eyes shift back to Mitch, and that fluttery feeling is back.

I welcome them inside and call for Gran and Pop to join us. It takes them a few minutes since Gran has to wheel Pop out in a wheelchair, something he isn't too keen on.

"I can walk just fine, dammit. This chair is pointless." He says with a huff.

"Henry, shush, we have guests and I'm sure they don't want to hear you gripe about the damn chair." She looks up with a mischievous smile and welcomes everyone in. "Don't mind my husband's poor manners. The sooner we get some of that garlic bread in him, the better off we'll all be." She chuckles and makes her way into the dining room with all of us following.

Despite how difficult this week has been for Gran; she knows how to plaster on a smile and put her best foot forward. I admire that about her. I can only hope she takes the conversation about my adoption with as much poise. I try to imagine how it will go and I can't. No scenario prepares me for how she'll take me knowing the truth.

There's a small part of me that's hoping she didn't even know.

Every time I want to ask, I clam up and busy myself with household tasks. I can't tell if she's noticed how distant I've become or if she just assumes it's because of everything with Pop. I'd say it's a little of both at this point.

We all take our seats and I bring in the lasagna and place it on the table next to the salad bowl and *two* loafs of garlic bread Elaine brought. The aroma of good Italian food swirls around us giving me a warm and content feeling. Whoever said good food can bring people together, was right.

No one appears to be gagging over the lasagna, so at least I know it's edible. I take a bite and my eyes widen. It's actually good. Not something I expected, I just assumed it would be mediocre at best. Gran winks at me and nods towards her plate, her way of saying she's proud of me in a subtle way. I'm not the best at receiving compliments, something Gran is aware of, she's always been good at subtly complimenting me, so I don't get too flustered.

Wish that memo was passed onto Elaine, who boasts about how good a cook I am. I blush and practically melt into my chair from embarrassment when all eyes land on me. "Don't look embarrassed dear, this is wonderful, let us compliment you!" She says with a smile.

"Olive here isn't great at accepting compliments", Gran says, "not sure where she got that from considering her mama loved to be praised as a girl."

I know she means well, and a week ago I would have smiled and shrugged it off. But now I question what mannerisms came from my parents and what came from my birth parents. *So many questions.*

Gaining control over my flushed cheeks I turn my attention to Collin, trying to focus all eyes on him instead of me and my cooking skills. "Collin, how do you like living in New York City?" I ask, hoping he'll take the bait and give me all the details of living in the city I've dreamed of seeing since I was a little girl.

"A stark difference from here, that's for sure." He says with a chuckle. "I love it, truthfully, but it is nice to visit home every now and then." He goes to take another bite of Elaine's garlic bread, eliciting a soft groan of appreciation. "This right here is why." He lifts the bread up before taking another heaping bite. The table laughs and we all nod our heads in agreement.

I steal a glance at Pop and for the first time in over a week, he's smiling. It's small and disappears quickly, but it was there, fleeting, but there. Something in my chest warms and I feel a smile of my own crest my face. Before I realize it, I'm suddenly hyper aware of a set of eyes on me. I peek through my lashes to find Mitch watching me.

His eyes on me, even in such a PG way, has my skin bursting into flames. His green eyes pierce into mine and it feels like we're the only ones in the room. I brush off the reaction and focus on my food because the last thing I need right now is for one of the adults to notice our quiet moment and make it a thing.

Considering Mitch and I never labeled what we are, I don't want to make it bigger than it is to anyone, including myself. I have next to zero experience with guys and for all I know I'm just a summer fling to Mitch. He spent four years at a university and the chances of him being pure are slim to none.

The conversation we never got to finish the other night looms over me multiple times a day. I haven't found the best way to bring it up and it's not something that is likely to come up naturally. I'm embarrassed to admit I spend more time than normal thinking of all the ways he could take the information of my virginity. And way too much time thinking of all the ways he could *take* my virginity.

How am I supposed to admit that not only have I not had sex before, but how badly I want him to change that fact, repeatedly. For someone who has never had sex, I'm very aware of how badly I want to. I don't think it even has anything to do with sex directly, but more to do with Mitch. That thought scares me. That's the kind of thinking that comes with attachment, and I don't think that's good for either of us right now.

The sounds of plates clinking pulls me out of my thoughts and I look around to see Gran and Elaine clearing dishes and bringing them to the kitchen. Mitch is looking at me with a quirk in his brows like he knows exactly what I was just thinking about.

"Stop looking at me like that, you weirdo." I say as I stand to bring my plate to the sink where Gran and Elaine are in a private conversation. I don't want to intrude but the sight of Gran wiping away a tear from her cheek causes me to pause in the doorway.

"It'll just take time for things to get back to normal, Joan. Try not to worry too much, even though I know that's easier said than done." She wraps an arm around Gran's shoulder and pulls her into a full hug. I can feel a tear of my own threatening to spill but I shake it off quickly before making my way to the sink.

"Gran why don't you and Elaine go sit on the front porch with a glass of wine. I can handle the cleanup in here."

"Sweetie, you cooked for us, you shouldn't have to clean up too." Gran says but Elaine is shaking her head.

"Olive is right, Joan. The boys can help her here." She reaches for the dish in Gran's hand and places it on the counter before leading her to the dining room. "You get Henry settled and I'll finish clearing off the table with Olive, we'll meet outside in ten. Sound good?"

There's something in Elaine's voice that no one dares to argue with. I see Gran hesitate for a moment before her shoulders relax, she needs this. We all know it and it's clear she knows it too. She walks back to the dining room to help Pop get settled into bed while Elaine and I finish clearing off the table.

Ten minutes later she and Gran are on the back porch, wine glasses in hand, talking under the stars and fireflies. Mitch and Collin meet me in the kitchen rolling up their sleeves to help dig into the mountain of dishes in the sink.

"Alright boss, tell us where you want us." Mitch says with his hands on his hips waiting for further instruction. I roll my eyes at him as I throw him a dish towel.

"I'll wash, Collin can rinse, and you can dry. Deal?" I say

with a smirk, knowing he's not going to object to anything I say right now since it's all to help my grandparents.

"How about you guys handle the dishes and I take out the trash and wipe down the table." Collin pipes up and something about his statement makes me believe he suspects something going on between Mitch and I. Immediately my face gets hot, and I think back to how obvious our exchange must have been to everyone at the table.

I want to find a way to crack a joke and accuse Collin of just not wanting to hang out with us, but I can't form words past the lump in my throat. Mitch on the other hand seems unfazed. Just waits for me to get my ass in gear washing dishes so he can get to rinsing and drying them.

I'm sure this isn't exactly how he saw his evening going. Having dinner with my family and his, then having to clean up the mess with me. I know I'm not the most secure person in the world, and even though Mitch has made his intentions regarding me somewhat clear, I still have doubts. Maybe I need to go back to a therapist.

Mitch nudges me and tilts his head towards the sink indicating he wants to get this over with. Can't say I blame him. "Sorry about this." I say as I join him at the sink. He looks at me with a puzzled look, waiting for me to let him in on some secret. "I'm sure this isn't how you wanted to spend your night."

"I'm with you, aren't I?" He smiles at me coyly. A smile of my own creeps across my face and I look down to start rinsing the dishes. It's weird how easy things are with Mitch now, when in the beginning it was like he could barely stand to be near me. On top of everything looming in my mind about my parents, I have questions I want to ask Mitch too.

A few weeks ago, my world was so mundane and predictable. Things have changed so much in such a short amount of time, it's hard to keep up with everything. For what seems like the millionth time this evening, I'm lost in my thoughts and don't even see the suds flying at me until they're plastered on my face.

I let out a gasp as the bubbles roll down my chin and drip onto my shirt. I glance up to see Mitch smirking at me with a handful of more bubbles ready to go.

"Choose your next move very carefully, Olive."   Oh, he's dead. With a calm shake of my head, I smile sweetly as I wipe the bubbles from my face. In seconds I'm grabbing the wet dishcloth hanging over the side of the sink. "Seems to me, you're the one who should tread carefully, Mr. Murphy."

I chuckle just as I swing the wet dishrag across his chest, it connects with a thwap sound and water saturates his shirt. The idea seemed good for a total of two seconds before reality sets in that he's going to get me back ten-fold for that. I shriek as I head for the front door, knowing he's hot on my heels.

Launching myself out the screen door, I take off down the steps and into the field in front of my house. The grass rustles beneath my feet and I can hear Mitch charging after me. The chase feels good, fueling me to move my legs faster, running harder than I have in probably years. I laugh nervously as he gets closer. I can practically feel his breath on my neck just as an arm reaches out and grabs me.

I shriek with laughter and allow Mitch to tackle me to the

ground. We land in a soft patch of tall grass, both laughing and panting from the chase. I roll onto my back as Mitch looms over me with a devilish look in his eye. Gently, he brushes the hair off my face and tucks it behind my ear, my breathing is still labored but not from the run.

He slowly leans down parting his lips while staring at mine with a hunger I've only read about in books. Just as I think he's about to kiss me, I feel a gush of water trickle over my face and chest. Gasping, I spit water out of my mouth and rub my eyes clear to see Mitch laughing with the dishrag in his hand. "Told you to choose your next move carefully, baby."

"I can't tell if you did that in retaliation or because I'm wearing a thin white t-shirt." I say breathing heavily and looking down at my now transparent shirt. Mitch follows my gaze, and his eyes go glassy as he takes in the lace bra under my shirt, now on full display. He swallows audibly and I watch his Adams apple bob in his neck.

My whole life all these major things have been out of my control, and it drives me crazy, keeping me up at night. Right now, I can decide something that's mine, something I can take control of. Before I lose my nerve, I sit up and pull my t-shirt up and over my head tossing it in the grass next to us. Mitch turns to stare at my discarded shirt before looking back at me.

I love watching him fight for control, but sometimes I want him to just take charge and show me how he feels rather than be so gentle with me. I'm not breakable, and I'm done feeling that way. I lay back down in the grass and stare up at Mitch, hands propped on his knees looking down at me.

With one hand, I reach up and fist a handful of his shirt in my hand and pull him towards me.

His resolve is melting away, being replaced by the guy with the hungry eyes and God do I want to get lost in them. He hovers over me, careful not to put any weight on me as he leans down keeping his face mere inches from mine. I breathe in his crisp scent and lick my lips, hoping he can see the clear invitation. Slowly, he lowers his lips to mine, and I moan into his mouth as our lips meet. If I could, I would bottle his taste to keep it with me knowing I'll never get enough.

He deepens the kiss and slips his tongue in my mouth to get a better taste. I arch into him pulling him closer to me, needing to feel his weight over me. Mitch uses one hand to keep himself propped over me while the other caresses my neck slowly moving lower as he cups a breast through my bra. Squeezing me gently I hear him groan against me, needing more. I need more too, and I want to say that without sounding so desperate.

With both hands, I push him back slightly so I can sit up and reach around to the clasp on my bra. Without giving it much thought, I flick the clasp and let the lace material slide down my chest and rest in my lap. This is the first time I've ever been this exposed to someone, and somewhere in my mind I know I should feel embarrassed or scared, but the feeling is invigorating. I feel brave and craved as his eyes roam over my bare chest.

"Touch me." The words sound foreign coming out of my mouth, but I've never wanted to be touched more than I do right now. Mitch looks at me with those hungry green eyes that never leave my face as he lowers himself to take one nipple in his mouth. His breath is hot on my skin and suddenly my entire body is in flames. He sucks and nibbles my breast while kneading the other with his hand, twisting my nipple between his fingers. I can feel the desire pooling between my legs, and I don't know if I'm going to be able to stop him if he tries to take this farther.

I still haven't told him I'm a virgin, and a part of me doesn't want to at this point. I don't want him overthinking what we're doing right now and assume I'm not ready. I want this. I want him.

"I've thought about what you taste like for weeks now, Olive. Now that I know, I'm never going to get enough." He switches breasts and starts sucking on the other nipple a little harder than the first. I arch into him needing more friction somewhere else.

Mitch reaches down to unbutton my jean shorts and my breath hitches in my throat at the proximity. I want him to touch me, but no one ever has, myself included. He senses my reaction and looks back up at me. "Have you ever touched yourself, baby?" he asks while staring at me intently. I think about his words, feeling them explode in my chest like moths fluttering wildly.

It's not something I've ever even thought to do and now I'm feeling extremely inexperienced. Mitch looks at me while he plays with the hem of my shorts. The feel of his fingers brushing the sensitive skin just below the seam has my skin blazing. I may not have ever touched myself, but I'm suddenly desperate for him to.

I shake my head slowly, never taking my eyes off his to gage his reaction, hoping he's not about to pull back. "No one has ever tasted you?" He asks me as he slowly unzips the zipper of my shorts. I shake my head again, breathing heavily now as he begins to slide my shorts off. I help him pull them past my knees and kick them off to the side with my shirt.

For the first time in my life, I am practically naked in front of someone. I want his eyes all over me and I want his tongue all over me, tasting every inch of my skin. Mitch lowers himself over me again, capturing my lips with his and kisses me eagerly. His fingers toy with the lace of my underwear and I can feel how slick I am without him even touching me.

"Is this okay?" he asks before sliding a finger under the hem. I nod and wait for the sweet pressure of his fingers against me. Slowly he circles my clit being gentle even though I know he's trying to restrain himself from being rough with me. He slides a finger across my slit and gently presses it between my folds and inside me. The feel of his finger has me delirious with need and I grind into his hand wanting more. He adds a second finger and starts moving them in and out faster.

My head falls back into the grass, breaking our kiss and a sigh leaves my mouth when he curls his finger up in a C motion. Even if I had ever done this to myself, it sure as hell wouldn't have been like this. Mitch finds my lips again and eases his tongue in my mouth just like his fingers inside me.

"Fuck, Olive. You're so wet." He moans between kisses, moving his fingers in and out of me faster now. I can feel how slick I am on his fingers, and it turns me on even more somehow. "Let me taste you."

I'm terrified to let him, but more terrified not to. It never felt right to do this with anyone else, but I trust Mitch. Reaching down, I pull my underwear all the way off and add them to the pile of my clothes. Mitch moves to his knees again and looks down to take in all of me. "You're perfect."

He moves his hands up my legs and rubs my thighs. I squirm beneath him, missing the feeling of his fingers inside me, but very aware of what's about to be inside me. Without breaking eye contact, he nestles himself between my legs and slowly licks my slit from top to bottom. My eyes roll back at the feel of his tongue tasting me. He's gentle at first, tasting me slowly before burying his face in me.

The pressure of his tongue and now two fingers working me is almost too much and not enough at the same time. He looks up at me with such intensity I feel like I could come just from that look alone. "You taste so fucking sweet, baby. What an honor to be the first to taste this pussy." My cheeks heat at those words and before I know it, he's back between my legs feasting on me.

I've read plenty of romance novels describing this feeling, but never expected to experience it like this. Mitch sucks my clit into his mouth with the perfect amount of pressure and I can feel an orgasm blooming. I've never had one, so I really don't know what to expect, all I know is I don't want him to stop.

"Oh my god, Mitch, don't stop. Please don't stop." I chant while he continues licking and sucking me. I can hear how wet I am each time he slides his fingers in and out of me, and

I feel like I should be embarrassed but I'm not. Not even a little.

Mitch curls both fingers up to that spot again as he sucks me into his mouth harder and I'm about to come undone. "Right there!" I yell just as I feel the flood gates open, and my release comes crashing over me. I scream out his name as he keeps working me through my tremors. It quickly becomes too much as I come down from the high and I chuckle as I slap him away. "Holy shit." I say breathing heavily.

"Holy shit is right." He laughs as he licks his lips. I blush again when I see the result of my orgasm glisten on his lips in the moonlight. "I think I found my new favorite dessert."

"No more oatmeal chocolate chip cookies?" I tease as I sit up to face him.

"After tasting you, those cookies couldn't hold a candle to how sweet you are."

Mitch grabs my clothes and hands them to me so I can get dressed. I didn't realize how scratchy the grass was until right now, too absorbed in all the other sensations my body was experiencing. I pull my shorts and shirt on and lay back on the grass next to Mitch. We're quiet for a few minutes as I allow my breathing to return to normal. I watch the fireflies dance around us in the night as the moon shines on us from above.

I hope Gran and Elaine aren't looking for us. Thankfully I ran far enough into the field that it's unlikely anyone heard my screams of pleasure. That would be an awkward thing to explain.

My Dad and I used to come out here at night sometimes

to look at the stars, it was our special thing. The memory suddenly has my throat thick with emotion. In some ways Mitch reminds me of him, the rough exterior but warm heart. When I first met Mitch, I thought he was just a self-absorbed guy, but over the last few weeks I've gotten to see another side of him.

Mitch nudges my arm and I look over at him to see he's already studying the look on my face. I hope he doesn't think I'm quiet because I didn't enjoy myself a few minutes ago. If anything, I'd think my screams were proof enough. "What's going on in that head of yours?" he asks.

"I was just thinking about how well you and my Dad would have gotten along." I rasp.

"Tell me about him." Mitch reaches over to hold my hand, a comforting gesture. Meeting him only a few weeks ago feels surreal. He already feels like someone I've known for years. Someone I can actually confide in. I was close to my parents, but there were a lot of times where I felt different in a way I couldn't explain. My skin tone was different, my hair was darker and some of my personality traits were nothing like them. I told my mom once I felt like an outcast. She hugged me tight and told me I fit in perfectly for them. That's all I really needed to know at the age of eight, so I didn't let it get to me too much.

Sitting here with Mitch, telling him about how my Dad loved fishing, going on walks through the field behind my grandparent's house at night with mom, and his appreciation for a good beer. I feel like I can tell him anything, it's exhilarating and terrifying all at once. I've always been too afraid to give too much of myself to someone, afraid of getting close just to be let down. Guess it makes sense I never had a steady boyfriend. I didn't allow myself the opportunity to get close to them and inevitably hurt in the end.

"Dad told me when I was younger that he loved walking the field with my mom because when they started dating, she would sneak out to meet him. He would throw rocks at her window and wait for her to come outside." The memory hits me as if my Dad is telling me for the first time again. "They would lay in the field watching the fireflies. It's where he first told her he loved her." I can feel tears building so I shake it off quickly, hoping Mitch doesn't notice.

"Sounds like they really loved each other. A rarity these days." We're quiet for a few minutes, just sitting together listening to the sounds around us. A dog barking faintly in the distance, leaves rustling above us from the soft breeze and the crickets singing their tune.

"Can I ask you something?" I ask while running my hands through the grass around us.

"Shoot." He says.

"Do you think there really is one person out there for everyone?" I realize it's a weird and random question, but I want to see his take on it. Watching my parents be so in love made me truly believe in the power of it. Ever since losing them, I feel like I've lost a little of that hope.

"I do." He says without hesitation. "Are you thinking about your parents...or you?" I thought about that for a minute, I asked mainly because of my parents, but I guess a part of me wonders if there is someone out there meant for me. The idea exhilarates me and frightens me.

"A little of both, I suppose. Growing up, my parents were always so in love. I could see it. When they died, it felt like I lost some of that magic along with them. I haven't found it again, so it made me wonder if it really exists." Mitch turns his body towards mine and places a hand on my cheek.

"Olive." I look at him, giving him my full attention. "I think it comes down to the right place right time, nothing is guaranteed of course, but sometimes the perfect person comes into your life when you don't even know you need them. I don't think there's anything more powerful than that."

Those words hang in the air, thick with meaning. I nod my head in agreement and look back at the moon.

"How old are you?" I ask, out of the blue. Mitch speaks like someone who's lived a lot of life already, so sure of himself and what his future holds. It's endearing, and extremely sexy. He laughs, probably at my second random question but just smiles and says, "I'm twenty-two, remember?"

I forgot that I asked him that back when we first met. Three years doesn't seem like a big age gap, and it's not, but knowing he's already gone to and completed college makes me feel like we're eons away from each other. Experience wise, and life. I sort of want to know how experienced he actually is, but then again, the idea makes me sick.

Judging by the skills he just used with me, I'd say very experienced. I'm not typically a jealous person, but Mitch brings out a feeling in me that's so unfamiliar and new, the idea of him being with another girl makes me physically ill. I would never admit that to him, probably make myself seem like a clingy lunatic. My experience with guys is just kissing. The first guy who ever kissed me accidentally touched my boob one time and nearly fainted. Safe to say, we didn't continue.

Kissing Mitch was probably the farthest and most intimate experience I've ever had, up until thirty minutes ago. Knowing that I haven't done much should make me self-conscious and nervous, but it really just makes me want to do it more.

Mitch notices my quiet spell again and softly nudges my knee with his. "Did I say something weird?" he asks nervously.

"Just the opposite, actually. I was thinking about how much more experienced you probably are, and kind of went down a rabbit hole." I laugh nervously, hoping to play it off like I'm not some jealous girlfriend. "It's none of my business, of course. But knowing you've been to college, and I've just been here…makes me wonder." I'm rambling again, he can tell because he just smiles at me.

"Can I tell you something?" he asks with one eyebrow cocked. I swallow and nod my head slightly, wondering what he's about to say.

"I'm probably about to put my foot in my mouth and scare you off. But kissing you, tasting you is the most connected I've felt to someone, ever. I'm mad at myself for trying to keep my distance for so long. Yeah, I've been with other girls, I won't lie about that. But with you, it's just different."

I don't respond right away, soaking in what he just said and internally doing cartwheels. Mitch makes me nervous and comfortable and confident in ways I'm not used to. So, before I lose my nerve, I move to straddle him, lacing both my hands into his hair and pull him to me.

I kissed him softly at first, my way of showing him how much that statement meant. Then I deepen the kiss and lean into him, pressing my breasts against his chest. They pebble at the contact and when Mitch dips his tongue into my mouth, a gasp escapes. I could do this all night, but I know everyone will start to wonder where we are. For a few minutes though, I want to just be present here.

He grips my waist and pulls me against him, resulting in a soft moan slipping from my mouth. I can feel the length of him beneath me and suddenly my skin feels like it's on fire. I press into him firmly, enjoying the feeling of him and wanting more. He pulls back to catch his breath and smiles his full dimple smile at me.

"I take it you like weird." He laughs and I kiss him once more before sitting back beside him.

"I'm good with weird." I insist. "But that wasn't weird, that was perfect. Thank you." Mitch lifts my hand and kisses my knuckles.

10

MITCH

Last night I admitted things to Olive I've never said to another girl. It felt right in the moment, but it also scares the shit out of me. I never bothered getting close to a girl because I always figured there was no point. In high school everyone ends up going off to different places. In college I knew I was eventually coming back here, so again there didn't seem to be a point to put down roots with anyone.

Now though, something feels different. I don't know if it's because I'm older or what, but I want to be around Olive all the time and I'm not even embarrassed to admit it. I can sense my feelings for her growing, but I know it's too early to tell her that.

I keep thinking about being in that field with her last night, feeling her warm body against mine and tasting her. The memory has me hard within seconds, and I'd be lying if I said it wasn't what I jerked off to in the shower later when I got home. When she told me no one has ever touched or tasted her, I nearly came just from those words. What an honor to be the first one to do that for her.

I've never worried about my skill level because I have had my fair share of experience, but I've never been more concerned with pleasing someone than last night. Sure, I'm stoked to get to be the first, but that comes with a lot of responsibility too. If it was bad, then she would always remember that. I just remind myself of the way her body reacted to mine and how she screamed my name as she came.

Core memory unlocked.

It's still morning and the thought of finishing out this day before getting to see Olive again has me groaning with annoyance. When did I become someone eager to finish work and go see a girl? I've always enjoyed working on the farm, but today we're harvesting lettuce and that's a bitch.

Hunched over for hours chopping lettuce heads isn't exactly how I want to spend the day, especially since it's hot as hades out here. Sweat pours off me in heaping amounts as I chug my fourth water bottle in two hours. Dad always told us boys that if you're gonna work the farm it can work you just as hard. You have to stay hydrated, or you're done for.

Collin hasn't left for the city yet, so he's out here helping me with the harvest and I'm a little surprised. He's so clean cut now with his big city law firm job and crisp suits, I never thought I'd see him willingly in the fields again.

"Missing the city yet?" I tease as he chops a head of lettuce and throws it over his head into the barrel. He stands up straight to stretch out his back and swipe an arm across his head to wipe the sweat away.

"At this moment, yeah a little bit." He laughs in response, chugs a bottle of water and bends down to get back to work. "I do miss being here though, as much as you might not believe that."

A part of me doesn't believe it. Because as soon as he graduated, he made it clear this was the last place he wanted to be. Whereas I went to school to come back here and help run the farm, Collin left and never came back. He visits occasionally, but never more than a week. The city is his life now, and I guess I have to respect his decisions. Even though I don't like it.

"I know Col, we all just miss having you home, especially Ma." Collin and I aren't ones to have a heart to heart, we grew up slugging each other and fighting like brothers do, but as we've aged, we've changed. I can talk to him in a way we were never able to as teenagers. We've always been so different, it seemed pointless getting his opinion on anything.

"I miss you guys too, I really do. But for now, the city is home, I know that sucks to hear, but it's the truth." He confesses. I focus on chopping lettuce again and for a while we work in silence alongside each other. When I stop to take a break Collin does too, joining me on the edge of the truck bed we guzzle more water. Hopefully only another hour or two before we can call it day with the damn lettuce.

"So, Olive seems really sweet." Collin says between sips of water. He says it sincerely, not because he's interested in her. "What's going on there?" he asks.

How do I answer that? There's a lot going on there but also not much. I have feelings for her, real ones but I'm not even ready to say that to her, let alone my brother who I only see a couple times a year. We're still in this in between phase of getting to know each other, so I can't say we're dating, but she's also more than a friend at this point.

"It's hard to explain." I finally relent. "We aren't dating or anything, but we're also more than friends if you know what I mean." Collin laughs and nods his head.

"Yeah, I think I do. You like her, I can tell. I'm sure neither of you were trying to be obvious last night, but at dinner the tension between you two was palpable." I look up at him with an 'oh shit' look because I can't have my mom noticing things like that, she'll be up my ass constantly.

"Don't worry, I'm the only one who noticed, I think. Ma was too worried about Joan and Henry to focus on anything else. But I could definitely see something, especially the way she looked at you all night. The air was sizzling between you."

That makes me smile, like I just won a prize or something. Knowing she was looking at me the way I look at her, it's undeniable. Guess I should have known my brother would pick up on it, he's always been intuitive. When we were younger, Collin always knew what girl I had a crush on, said he could tell just by the way I'd look at her. Grace Meadows was probably my first real crush when I was twelve. Every time she was around, I turned to mush, and Collin always noticed. He used to tease me about it, but he was also four years older and already hooking up with girls.

Fast forward to now, he still has that niche. "She's amazing and doesn't even know it. It kills me." I laugh even though I'm dead serious. "When I compliment her, it's as if she thinks I'm just saying it to be polite, not because I mean it. Even Joan said she's not good at accepting compliments."

"Sounds like you need to change that." Collin says. At first, I didn't know what he meant, and I can tell he sees that in my eyes because he elaborates. "When you give someone a compliment, you have to make them feel it not just hear it. When you say something a certain way it can truly be felt by the other person based on how much you feel it. If it's true, then show her that."

He says that like it's so easy, and the more I think about it the more I realize it is that easy. I always tell Olive how amazing she is or how beautiful she is, which is true, but those are just words. I need to find a way to make her feel beautiful and special.

"I don't even know how to do that." I say rubbing my face with the hem of my shirt. Even in the shade I'm sweating profusely. This goes back to what I was thinking about earlier. I've never connected with a girl before, they were always around in school, but I never wanted anything from them. With Olive, she's different, and I want to show her why she's important to me. Without looking like a lovesick moron.

"Find something she's passionate about and show her it's important to you because it's important to her. What are some things she's into?" Collin asks as he bites into an apple from a cooler we have at the back of the truck.

I think about some of the things she's told me over the last few weeks. The other night she told me about spending time in the field at night watching the fireflies. She bakes, but that's her job so I can't imagine she wants to do that in her spare time as well. Then it clicks.

"She's into art, says she wants to intern at a studio in New York City. That's her dream." I tell Collin. He lets out a whistle and smirks at me.

"Brother, you're talking to the right guy." He nudges my arm and gestures to the crops indicating it's time we get back to work. I want to know what he's thinking, and I won't budge until he gives me a clue. A few paces ahead of me he turns around and cocks his head to the side. "Look, I know some people in the city who could take a look at her resume. But in the meantime, do something that shows her you're interested in her art."

Show her I'm interested. How the fuck do I do that? I know nothing about art. I can't ask Joan because she'll hound me with a million questions just like my mom. I need someone's advice, preferably a female, who could steer me in the right direction. Within seconds, just the right person comes to mind. Someone Olive looks up to, has spent a lot of time with and would probably have some good straightforward advice. I smile to myself already planning on when to make my escape and take a drive.

Four hours later, one hot shower and an extreme amount of back pain from harvesting lettuce, I'm in my truck driving to the shelter. Olive has known Gwen since she started volunteering at Raising Hope and it's obvious they've grown close over the years.

I park the truck and head inside to see Gwen hunched over her desk in the back office with a very focused face. She's frowning at a stack of papers and muttering something under her breath. I tap lightly on her door to gain her attention without startling her. "Am I interrupting?" I ask in the doorway.

"Mitchell! Not at all, please come in." She gestures to the chair in front of her desk and pushes aside the stack of papers she was just scowling at. "Right now, I could use a distraction." She smiles softly and I can see the stress lining her features.

"Everything okay, Gwen?" I ask because I'm not about to ask a favor without first checking on her. She looks the most stressed I've probably ever seen her. When she's out with the residents staying here, she's always her happy cheerful self. But back here in the confinement of her office, she can let her guard down a little.

"Oh, you know, just stress, but it's nothing for you to worry that handsome little head of yours about. What can I do for you?" Typical Gwen, always trying to defuse a problem like it's no big deal.

"Gwen, you know I'm not blind right? I can see the stress written all over your face, something is up. Spill it." It takes a few seconds, but I see her shoulders relax a little and she leans her head on the arm propped on her desk.

"We just don't have as many sponsors helping out like we once did, so cash flow is a little grim right now."

"How bad?" I ask, almost afraid to hear the answer.

"At the rate of people coming in, I can't keep up the cost it demands to keep everyone fed and bathed. It's too much." She places her face in both hands now and her shoulders tremble a little. Shit I hope she's not about to start crying, I am not the best at dealing with that.

"Hey, hey don't worry. We can figure something out." I

lean in and take one of her hands in mine, wrinkling with age and likely stress now that I know what's been going on. "I'll talk to my parents about a way to raise some money. Maybe we can have an event on the farm or something."

She laughs softly and pats my hand, "You're a good kid, Mitchell. Your folks raised you right."

"Does that mean you'll let us help?" I ask with a sudden excitement in my voice. "I know it's tough accepting help, but don't be stubborn Gwen. There's a lot of people willing to help, I promise."

"Fine. But I don't want your folks throwing in money on my account. If you're going to have some kind of vendor event, it must be volunteer based. Got it?" She looks me sternly in the eyes and I know she's serious.

"Scout's honor." I pledge. As I stand to leave, I remember why I came here in the first place. Seeing Gwen stressed and upset made me forget all about asking for her advice. "I forgot to ask you something." I say sitting back down.

"Oh, yes, I'm sorry. I'm sure you didn't come here to listen to me gripe. What's up?" She asks.

"Please don't pepper me with a bunch of questions or say anything to my parents because my mom will for sure do just that, but I need some advice about Olive." I look down at my hands in my lap, suddenly afraid to face her even though I'm a grown man.

"What kind of advice?" She asks with no hint of humor in her voice.

"She's an aspiring artist. How can I show her that what she's passionate about is important to me?" I sound like a lovesick puppy, exactly what I didn't want. But I'm here so I might as well see this through.

"I see." Gwen nods her head as she thinks. "It's simple but will make her feel appreciated. There's an art supply store ten minutes from here. Go there and ask Rick for help, he owes me." She chuckles at that but continues. "Get her an eight by ten canvas, maybe two, some watercolor paints, and a few different size brushes. Set it up somewhere and ask her to paint for you, tell her you want to see what it is she loves about it. She'll be shy at first and probably brush you off, don't let her."

That's genius, and I know exactly where to set it up. "Gwen, thank you. Seriously, if I asked my mom or Joan, they would have just squealed with excitement instead of actually being helpful." I laugh and see that Gwen is too. I hope we can help her out with funding for this place. If it went down, a part of me would be devastated. Knowing what this place was for someone close to me for so long, I couldn't bear to know others wouldn't get that same second chance here.

Per Gwen's instructions, I headed over to the art supply store in search of supplies. How I went from being a grumpy farm boy to picking up art supplies to show a girl how much I care about her, I'll never know. The bell above the door dings as I walk through and immediately, I'm overwhelmed by this place. Rows and rows of paintbrushes, different kinds of paint and canvases line the aisles. I try to stay focused on what I came here for instead of being sidetracked by everything else.

An older man with salt and pepper hair walks over from behind the front desk. "You must be Mitch." He says as he extends a hand for me to shake. My brows pull together in confusion just as he says, "Gwen called."

"Good old Gwen", I chuckle. "Nice to meet you, Rick." I take his hand in mine and am a bit taken back by how soft his hands are yet strong. It's not a combination I'm used to, seeing as my hands are always rough and calloused.

Over the next fifteen minutes, Rick takes me around the store grabbing what I need before bringing it back to the cash out desk. "She must be a special girl." Rick smiles without looking at me and begins scanning the items. Jesus, how much did Gwen divulge to this guy?

"Did Gwen tell you her name too?" I laugh.

"No names. Didn't even mention who you were buying this for. But I can tell it's not for you, no offense." He shrugs a shoulder, and I'm not the least bit offended. "Judging by your deep tan, I'd say you spend a lot of time outside. That handshake of yours was strong and tight, which tells me you were raised right and work hard."

He continues scanning the supplies, but I'm no longer watching the price on the screen. I'm looking at this guy, someone who clearly has good intuition, I can see why Gwen recommended I come here.

"I take it you don't paint since you were unsure of what paintbrushes to use but you knew exactly what paints you needed, so all roads lead to this is a gift." He finishes scanning and places everything in a brown paper bag then looks up at me grinning. "I've been around a long time." He chuckles.

I can't help but smile in return, this guy is good. I wonder if he would be of any help in the fundraiser I want to set up to benefit the shelter. I drop my gaze down to my wallet and pull out my credit card. "Her name is Olive, and she's an amazing artist. Just wanted to do something nice for her."

"Well, she's going to love it." Rick swipes my card and hands it and the receipt back to me. "Thanks for coming in, I reckon I'll be seeing you again."

"I hope so. Actually, I was wondering if I could talk to you about something. It's about Gwen." Rick looks up to me and furrows his brows like he's concerned. Makes me wonder if there's more than just a friendship between the two of them.

"The shelter is low on funding, and I was hoping to put together some kind of fundraiser at my family's farm to help raise money for the expenses. She's stressed, I'm hoping the town can pull together and help."

Rick nods his head and already I can see wheels turning in his mind and ways he can help. "Anything y'all need, I'm in." He shakes my hand again and I smile as we exchange numbers. I'm grateful he's willing to help for Gwen's sake, but I'm betting Olive will be happy to talk to him as well.

"Thanks Rick, talk to you soon." I say as I exit the store and head back to my truck. Now to plan the surprise. I might need to call in reinforcements for this one. I pull out my phone and dial Collin's number. He answers after two rings.

"I need your help this afternoon. Can you pull down the Christmas lights from the attic?" I ask as I pull out onto the road hitting the gas.

I hear him laugh into the receiver. "Sounds like you

figured out what's important." Yeah, as well as a few other things today that are still running through my mind. Before I can respond, he speaks again. "Tell me where to be, and I'm there brother."

11

Olive

It's slow at the bakery today, some days there's a constant flow of people in and out, and then there's days like today. Not a single soul entered the shop in forty-five minutes. Gran is at home with Pop, still not ready to leave him alone just yet. Something that bugs the hell out of him. *"I'm not an invalid."* He would say.

Judging by the lack of customers I tell Maureen she can head out early and I'll close myself. We close at six tonight, so there's no sense in keeping her here for another hour. When six rolls around, I count the register and put the deposit bag in the safe back in Pop's office. I turn off all the lights and type in the security code at the door before locking it.

Walking over to my bike, I see Mitch's truck sitting in the lot with him leaning against the front fender looking sexy as hell. My mouth goes dry instantly. As I stride over to him, I can see my bike is already in the bed of his truck.

"I love how you just assume I'll go with you now." I say gesturing towards my bike.

"Would you prefer to ride your bike home?" He asks with a hint of humor in his voice.

"Not a chance." I say as I walk up to him and stand only a foot away waiting to see who makes a move first. I'm stubborn so a part of me wants him to lean in and kiss me first, but I'm also hungry for those lips on mine and don't know if I have any patience to wait.

Just as I'm about to reach up on my tip toes, Mitch leans down and pulls me close. The hand on my neck is gentle while his other on my waist guides my body forward to meet his.

"These lips." He says and leans in to sample them. I can't help the sigh that leaves my lips as I part them, welcoming him in. I savor the flavor of him and deepen the kiss by sliding my tongue against his. The hand holding my neck tightens in my hair as Mitch fists a handful.

"How do you always smell so good?" he asks as he nuzzles my neck leaving soft kisses along the base of my throat.

"I probably smell like flour and baked goods right now." I laugh into his chest, and he continues sampling my neck. He lightly licks up my neck from the base to just below my ear.

"All I can taste is you, and you're sweeter than any baked good." A shiver rocks my body as I remember what we did just a few nights ago. After tasting me for the first time he claimed I was his new favorite dessert. Those words cause a deep blush to cover my face and chest as the memory washes over me as if he just said it.

"Did you come over here just to kiss me? Because I'm totally fine with that." I laugh and give him a quick peck. Mitch wraps an arm around my shoulders and leads me to the passenger seat, lifting me into the truck like he always does. At first it bugged me, I didn't like him thinking I was too fragile to get into a truck by myself or ride my bike home alone. Things I have always been more than capable of doing.

Now I look at these gestures differently. It's his little way of showing he cares, and now I find it endearing. My mom always used to say people have different love languages and that it's important to learn the other person's so you can show them how you love them appropriately. Mitch is an acts of service guy, with a side of physical touch, I've learned. It makes me think about what my love language might be.

I've never given it any thought because I've never been close to intimate with someone. But the closer I get to Mitch, the more I think about what matters to me. I can easily admit that I enjoy it when he touches me, so much so that I crave it. When he's close I just want to feel him, smell his crisp apple scent invade my senses. So many times, I've had to resist the urge to run my fingers through his hair. Honestly, I never found longer hair that appealing, it always gave a surfer vibe in my opinion. But Mitch's hair isn't surfer boy long, its shaggy and unruly and downright sexy.

Working outside all day has given his dark blonde hair lots of natural highlights from the sun, and I can tell he's constantly wiping it out of his face when it falls in his eyes. I wonder why he doesn't just cut it, keep it short to avoid the hassle of pushing it away all day.

"You're doing it again." Mitch says beside me in the driver's seat as we make our way to my house.

"Doing what?" I ask although I'm pretty sure he's referring to me zoning out like I often do.

"That thing where you get quiet and too in your thoughts."

"Not in a bad way this time." I laugh. "I was just thinking about your hair, actually."

"What about my hair?" He asks while subconsciously running a hand through it while the other keeps hold of the steering wheel.

"Absolutely nothing. I just wonder why you keep it long instead of getting it cut shorter. It must be a pain when you're in the fields sweating all day." He's thinking about what I just said, brows furrowed, and head tilted to the side slightly.

"When you put it that way, I don't know why I haven't cut it. I never gave it much thought, and truthfully, I usually have a hat on when I'm working, so it doesn't get in the way." Now I'm picturing Mitch with a worn faded baseball cap on keeping his head protected from the sun rays. Oh God, I wonder if he ever wears it backwards, shirtless…My mouth goes dry thinking about that, and I think I have a new mental image to pull out when I need it.

"I don't think I've ever seen you work. I've seen the aftermath," I chuckle, and he glares at me from his seat. "I don't mean that as an insult! I can tell by the look on your face you think I'm bagging on you for sweating. Truthfully, it's the other way around."

"And what does the other way around mean, exactly?" Mitch arches a brow at me, amused by this conversation now.

"You're a hard worker, that's all I meant." I can feel my skin blushing and I'm thankful we're in the dark cab of his truck so he can't see how much he affects me. As we round the corner where the road splits taking you to either my house or the farm. Mitch turns right, heading towards his property and I look at him confused. Did he invite me over without me hearing it?

"Wh-where are we going?" I ask, looking out my window as we pass his house. If he isn't bringing me home, or even to his house, then where is he taking me? Is this the moment in the horror movie where everyone is screaming at me for not seeing the signs of the psychopath about to chop me into a million pieces and feed me to his dogs. Yeah, I really do need that therapist.

"I have a little surprise for you, that's all." He smirks at me and directs the truck down a gravel road heading towards the pond on the edge of their property. The same pond where we first met, and I've enjoyed spending time at the last few weeks. Now it's likely my final destination.

I'm dead.

"Listen, if you wanted to murder me, you could have done it long ago. You didn't have to make me like you first, ya know?" I laugh a little and he just smirks at me again. We haven't known each other that long so I don't know if that smirk is supposed to mean something. Before I can let myself panic about what we're actually doing and the reality that he likely isn't planning to murder me subsides, I see a few twinkling lights along the path to the pond.

Mitch pulls the truck to the side of the road and cuts the engine. He unbuckles his seatbelt and turns to face me. "You ready?" He asks before hopping out of the cab. He walks around to my door and opens it for me, waiting for me to follow him. I've never been to the pond at night, I've always wanted to but it's incredibly dark here at night. Feels a little too much like Camp Crystal Lake. But I can see lights lining the trees and now I'm curious what this surprise is.

I take Mitch's hand and let him guide me towards the pond. The truck disappears from view behind us, and we're surrounded by the trees. The closer we walk to the water, the more lights I can see. Within a few seconds I gasp, taking in the scene before me. Lights are loosely hung like canopies in the trees along the bank of the pond and a few feet away is an easel.

Lanterns with white candles rest on a tree stump with a tall wooden easel set up next to it. A plain white canvas is already in place, with a few others down below. There's a small vintage table next to the easel with a handful of new paintbrushes and paints. I walk closer and see a palette of watercolors resting on the table. My throat feels tight, and my mind is reeling. I feel slightly guilty for even thinking for one second, he was going to hurt me.

Despite our start, Mitch has never been anything but kind and gentle with me. This is the most thoughtful thing anyone has ever done for me. Tears sting my eyes and I close them before any can stain my cheeks. I reach out and touch the brushes with feather light fingers and smooth the tips feeling the softness of an unused brush.

I can sense Mitch standing close behind me, waiting for my reaction, but I know if I turn around now, I'll cry. A hand reaches up and brushes the hair off my shoulder, then his hand is grazing my cheek feeling a single tear. His chest connects with my back, and I lean into him, taking a much-needed deep breath. "You did all this?"

"Art is important to you." He says quietly while still standing behind me. "I wanted to show you it's important to me now, too."

So many things run through my mind at warp speed. I'm unable to process exactly how I feel right now. He did all this to show me that what's important to me is important to him, and yet somehow, we haven't talked about what we're actually doing. Does he think of me as his girlfriend or am I just a summer fling to pass the time?

I wish I could say I know for sure, but the truth is I don't. This gesture right now has me more confused than I've ever been. No one goes to these lengths for someone if they don't have genuine feelings, right? I look up at the lights hanging from the branches around us, the lit candles illuminating the canvas propped up on the easel. How did he even know what supplies to get? I can't remember if I told him watercolors were my favorite to work with, and yet here they are.

I'm in my head, again, and I need to shake it off, because this is the ultimate romantic gesture. Breathing in the summer night air, I turn around and look up into Mitch's eyes. "How did you know what to get?" I have a lot more questions, but I'll stick with the easier ones for now. Mitch comes to stand closer to me, pulling me in by my hips and giving them a gentle squeeze.

"I have my ways." That's all he says as he winks at me. Once again, I can't tell if he's being serious or if those are nervous ticks. I'm hoping it's the latter because that I could understand. But if he's doing all this so I'll sleep with him, he's going to be sadly mistaken.

I look down to where his hands are planted on my hips and feel my heartbeat kick up a notch or two before speaking. "Mitch. People don't do stuff like this for just a friend. I mean, maybe they do, but this feels incredibly personal and I'm just trying to figure it all out."

Soft, strong fingers grip my chin and lift my gaze up so that I'm looking right into those piercing eyes of his. He is staring at me so intently, everything inside me melts. My body is molten from that look, the feeling of his hands gripping the flesh of my hips, the words he told me circling my brain on repeat. *Art is important to you.*

"Well, allow me to be clear. Clearer than the dozens of candles lit around us displaying a rare moment where I show someone I care about them." His words sound impatient, but he says them quietly, softly. "I like you, Olive. I like spending time with you, and I want to learn everything about you. This isn't casual for me; it hasn't been for weeks now. I tried to push it away, this attraction between us, and just focus on my work. But it's evident now, that's not going to work." Mitch tucks a strand of hair behind my ear, grazing his fingertips along the curve of my lobe and my body erupts in gooseflesh.

"You've given me pieces of yourself, whether willingly or not, and now that I've gotten a taste of you, literally and figuratively, I can't go back to not having as many parts of you as you're willing to give." Shit, he wasn't kidding. That message is loud and clear and I'm not sure how to respond appropriately.

Instead of using my words, I let my body do the talking for me. Something I never would have imagined myself doing, but Mitch has changed things in me that didn't seem possible a few weeks ago. I'm learning new things about myself by being with him. I don't feel like the damaged, fragile little girl anymore who lost her parents. I feel worthy, sexy, and strong in front of him.

I rise on my tiptoes, thread my fingers through the hair at the base of Mitch's neck and pull his face to mine. Slowly, I sample his lips, feeling the warmth of them spread throughout my body like a wildfire engulfing trees and everything in its wake. I allow the inferno to overtake my whole being and give in to this moment with him.

Mitch wraps his hands around my waist, pulling me even closer to him until my front is flush with his. He lowers his hands to cup my backside and squeezes, eliciting a groan from my lips as I deepen the kiss. I may not always know what to say and when to say it, but I'm hoping Mitch can hear my words through my body without me having to speak them. Words aren't always enough, sometimes you must *show* someone how you feel. Another life lesson my mom was able to instill in me before she died.

Without breaking the kiss, Mitch lowers us to the grass along the bank of the pond, careful not to tip the easel. He sits first and guides my body over him so that I'm straddling his lap. I nestle in, my thighs tightly pressed against his and hold him to me for dear life. I keep kissing him, needing more than what he's already giving. I feel desperate and needy for his touch, his taste, his smell. Memories of the other night flood my mind and I feel my skin blush at the thought of him touching me again.

I know I'm still not ready to tell him about being a virgin, even though at this point I don't think he would care. Hell, he probably already knows. Mitch has already shown me how much he cares for me in so many ways. But I want to be able to give back to him the way he's already given so much to me.

I lift myself off him and scoot down his legs until I'm hovering over his feet. He places both hands behind his back and leans on his elbows for support as he looks at me with a question. Before I can lose my nerve and psych myself out, I reach for his belt buckle and begin undoing it. I don't make it far before Mitch's hands grab mine and pull them away.

"Olive, you don't have to do anything. Tonight was supposed to be about you." He's holding my gaze so sternly, but I know he's fighting with himself. He wants this as much as I want to give it to him. He just needs to let me.

"I know I don't. But I want to." I look at him with heated desire, hoping he'll relent and allow himself to be vulnerable with me. I've never done anything like this and I'm nervous I won't know what to do. Doubt is creeping in, at a rapid pace and I need to shut it out before it consumes me, and I ruin this before I even start.

"Can you help me? Tell me what you like." I say as I reach for his belt buckle again. This time he allows me to undo it and pull it from the loops on his jeans. Slowly I lower the zipper and I feel his gaze hot on my face. He's barely controlling himself; I can feel his desire radiating off him in waves. It fuels me, giving me the courage I need to keep going.

"You've never done this before, have you?" he asks as he gently pulls my hair away from my face. I should probably pull it back, so it doesn't keep getting in my way. As I pull the elastic band from my wrist and wrap it around my thick hair, I shake my head slowly. I don't even need to tell him I'm a virgin, something tells me he's already figured it out.

"I was the first to taste you, and now I'm the first you'll ever taste." Those words fall from his lips like thick honey, dripping with sweetness but thick with emotion too. I want to taste his desire so badly it has my mouth watering. I lick my lips and focus back on getting his pants down.

Once they're off, he just sits there in briefs, looking at me with something I can't decipher. I run my hands up his muscular thighs, reminding me of thick tree trunks. He's all muscle, strong and healthy and he really knows how to take care of his body. Reaching for the hem of his black t-shirt, I begin to lift it up his torso and over his head. I rise on my knees to reach where his shirt comes over his head and our eyes meet.

"Olive." He whispers against my face, and I can practically taste the spice from his breath. With both hands, Mitch cups my face and meets my lips with his own. He holds me in place, and I plant my hands on his bare chest, enjoying the way his muscles feel under my fingers. They're trembling slightly, from the nerves, and Mitch notices. He looks down and takes them in his as he pulls each hand to his lips, kissing them softly.

"If you want to stop at any time, please do. I don't want you doing anything you aren't comfortable with, okay?" He's frowning and it feels like maybe he's a little nervous too. Weirdly, that makes me feel more at ease. I lower myself down his body again and nestle between his legs. I can see his bulge lining his underwear and it just now hits me how big he probably is.

I can see the outline perfectly through his black briefs and now I'm wondering how he'll possibly fit in my mouth. Pushing away my fear, I reach into the opening of his briefs and grip him firmly between my hand. He hisses, already growing larger at the contact. Despite my fears, I slowly pull him all the way out and take him in for the first time.

He's bigger than even my hand realized not five seconds ago. Thick and long, and hard as a rock as I stare down at him. Our eyes meet briefly before I look down at his cock again. Yeah, he's definitely going to have to coach me through this. Where the fuck is all of that supposed to go?! "You should have warned me." I say as I slowly stroke his length, chuckling nervously. It feels like we both need a little warm up before I jump into this.

"You wanted me to warn you about the size of my dick?" He laughs and I feel the movement throughout his body as I grip his shaft in my hands.

"Yes. I didn't realize how much you were working with here, Mitch. I don't have much experience to go on, but this is porn star worthy." Mitch lets out a barking laugh and I can't help but pout a little that he's finding this funny.

"Baby, I can assure you I'm not a porn star, and I already told you we don't have to do this." He grabs my chin again. "Look at me, Olive." His eyes soften and he kisses me gently.

"I want to. I really do. Just talk me through it, okay?" He releases me and allows me to settle myself between his thighs again and I lean down to take my first taste.

My breath is hot on his skin as I breathe heavily against him. I fit my mouth around the head of him and slowly start sucking. Mitch drops his head back between his shoulder blades and curses quietly to the night sky. Feeling him react this way only motivates me to keep going. Circling the tip a few times I take more of him into my mouth and begin moving in an up and down rhythm. I may not know what I'm doing but he seems to be enjoying himself, he hasn't given me any tips on what to do so I go on instinct.

I bob my head up and down a few times and Mitch takes a fistful of hair into his hands and begins massaging my scalp gently as I work him. As if it were even possible, I can feel his length grow impossibly bigger in my mouth and I groan into him. His body is taut beneath me taking everything I give. I use my free hand to grip the base of his shaft and squeeze slightly.

"*Fuck*, Olive." Mitch grunts beneath me. "I'm close, baby." I suck him harder and squeeze the base again just as he pulls back, my mouth makes an audible pop sound and I look up to see Mitch let loose onto his stomach as he curses. Taking a few deep breaths, he looks at me and cocks his head to the side. "You said you've never done that before."

"I haven't." I shrug and wipe the saliva from the corner of my mouth. Maybe being inexperienced isn't the worst thing ever.

"Fuck. That was amazing. I can't believe that was your first time doing that." He pulls his underwear and jeans back on but leaves his shirt off. "Usually I last a lot longer than that, but it felt amazing." I sit up and Mitch reaches his arms out to me, pulling my back against his chest as we sit in silence for a few minutes. The warm breeze filters around us causing the loose hairs on my face to blow. The leaves in the canopy above us rustle and with them the lights hanging there.

It's quiet and peaceful sitting here with Mitch, feeling his chest rise and fall beneath me. His heart rate is slowing down post orgasm and something about it makes me chuckle. Mitch tickles my ribs at the sound of my laughter, and I squirm against him. "What's so funny?"

"Honestly, nothing. I was just feeling you breathe behind me and the sound of your racing heart made me chuckle." I laugh again and turn to look at him. "I really don't have more of a reason." I confess. Mitch tilts my chin up and brushes his nose with mine before capturing my laugh with his mouth.

"I love your laugh. I can practically taste it every time I hear it." I feel his nose trace my jawline, inhaling my scent as he goes. My back is still against him, but my face is turned towards his as he continues breathing me in. He grips a hand around the base of my neck and gently squeezes before tickling my ribs again.

The hold he has on my throat keeps me in place as he swallows my laughter, tasting me and dancing our tongues together. After another minute he releases me and jerks his head towards the easel still sitting next to us, untouched. "I didn't bring all this out here just for it to watch us make out." He jokes.

Mitch gets up and reaches down to help me to my feet. I walk over to the easel and pick up a paintbrush, playing with the bristles. I can feel Mitch's eyes on my back as I stand awkwardly in front of the blank canvas. I don't even know what to paint right now, especially with an audience. I've always painted in solitude, so this is new for me.

I'm aware that by sending out my portfolio, people would be seeing my work. But I don't have to see their faces when they do. It's easier to accept rejection when I'm not face to face with the person delivering it. What if Mitch sees my art and doesn't think it's any good. That would be embarrassing.

His arms come to wrap around me from behind and I relax into his hold. "You don't need to be nervous. Stop overthinking it, Olive." He whispers in my ear, and I can feel the hair on my neck come to a stand.

"Well, apparently tonight is a night for firsts. I've never painted for anyone before…" I let the end of the sentence hang in the air as I dip the brush into the first color. Closing my eyes, I inhale a sharp breath and brush the first stroke across the canvas. For the next twenty minutes, I paint in silence hyper aware of Mitch behind me, watching. He doesn't say anything, but I also can tell he's not bored.

I was worried for a few minutes that he would lose interest in the process and pull out his phone or something. But each time I glance back at him, he's there watching me intently with a serious expression. I can't figure out what he's thinking, and I'm constantly resisting the urge to ask him.

I hear his feet move in the grass as he walks to where I'm perched on a stool in front of the easel. My elastic has loosened and has my hair hanging sloppily over my shoulder. Mitch carefully lifts my long tresses back up into a ponytail, securing it with the tie. It's intimate in such a basic way and I lower my hand holding the paintbrush.

"Breathtaking." Mitch breathes against my ear, and I smile feeling proud he likes what I've painted. The landscape before us is the pond, dark water lining the banks with the white oak tree in the background. I used a small brush to paint delicate white and yellow dots to recreate the lights he hung for tonight. Just below the trees stands an easel with a blank canvas and unused brushes in a cup beside it. Laying in the grass below is Mitch and me.

"I'm glad you like it." I blush leaning into his embrace.

"Yeah, the painting is beautiful too. You're an amazing artist, Olive." I turn around to face him and he holds my face in his hands. "But the breathtaking comment was meant for you." He leans in and kisses the tip of my nose. Mitch checks his watch and heads over to the bag he brought down here with him. Pulling two wrapped packages and some soda from the bag, he sits down in the grass again and gestures for me to join him.

"It's not super romantic, but I brought us some sandwiches. Wasn't sure how long we'd be here." He admits with a wink.

I take the sandwich and thank him just before taking a huge bite. I guess I was hungry. Oftentimes I get lost in my work and forget what time it is or when the last time was that I ate. I'm glad Mitch had the foresight to bring food with him.

Out of the corner of my eyes, I can just make out the time on his watch. Not as late as I was expecting, but still later than I usually stay out. Guess one of the perks to Gran being so consumed with nursing Pop back to health is that I can go under the radar without being questioned all the time. I've always had space to go and do as I please, but there are still rules.

After finishing our sandwiches, we talk about random things for a while. How I got into painting and how Mitch decided to go to school for agriculture to help back home. "I don't regret my decision, but sometimes I wonder what I would have majored in had I gone to school for me rather than the benefit of my family." I can relate, working at the bakery is great and I love being near family and Maureen, but I can't say it's what I want to do for the rest of my life.

That's why I sent out my portfolio to several galleries around the country. If I never try to put myself out there and strive for more, then this is all I'll ever be. I don't want to live my life that way. "I know the feeling. I love being around my grandparents, but this place hasn't felt the same since my parents died. Not sure I even belong here sometimes."

"Why do you think you don't belong here?" Mitch asks and I don't even know how to answer that.

Can't say I planned to have this conversation tonight, but right now feels like the right time. "Growing up I always felt misplaced in a way. I would express that to my mom, and she always assured me I was perfect for them." I'm twisting the bracelet on my wrist, feeling the nerves kick in. Mitch is the first person I'm about to talk to about the adoption, something I've lived with by myself for a few weeks now.

"I tried to brush off the feeling of not belonging and then they died. That abandonment feeling grew and I felt more and more lost. The first few years after they died were dark. I was hell on wheels and my grandparents did their best to help me through such a tragic loss. I owe them everything, honestly, because I don't know how I would have made it through my teens without them." I feel tears pierce my eyes and swallow hard trying to push the feelings back.

Rubbing my hands together to warm them even though they aren't cold is a good distraction. I want to cry, break down and let the dam that's been built behind my walls flood my senses and take over. But if I allow all the feelings to be set free, the good and the bad, they'll consume me. I let out a heavy sigh just as a single tear escapes past my lids.

"The day Pop had his heart attack, Gran asked me to gather all the important documents we might need, like his Will, in case something happened. It's morbid to think like that, but when Gran was little her father died suddenly and her mom wasn't prepared. She vowed never to allow that to happen to her."

"I respected her wishes and went home, up to the attic where we keep our safety box inside a cedar chest and searched for the Will." Shit, this is already hard. My palms are sweating, and I can't tell if it's because I'm nervous or because I've been rubbing them together. Probably a little of both.

"I found the Will after a thorough search, but something else in the chest caught my eye. There was this thick manilla folder and on the front in my mother's handwriting were the words *'Letters to Olive'*." I can feel Mitch's gaze on me, and I want to look at him, feel the reassurance in his eyes that I can do this, I can talk about this without completely breaking down. I'm afraid if I look at him, though, I'll see the look. The look everyone gave me for years, that pity look that I fucking hate.

Taking my chances, I take a deep breath and look up to see Mitch gazing at me with such an intensity it should be illegal. His eyes are piercing, and they make my insides hot. Only Mitch could manage to turn me on when talking about something serious, without even trying. "You know if you keep looking at me like that, I'm not going to be able to finish this." I laugh but the sound falls flat.

"I've got nowhere better to be right now." He smiles and I take that as encouragement to continue.

"The letters were from my mom." I let the confession hang in the air, feeling like it sounds anticlimactic because it's not a weird thing to find letters from your mom. "My birth mom…" saying it out loud feels surreal, like maybe it wasn't real before but now it is. It's not just me who has this knowledge anymore, I can release some of it now when I couldn't before.

"Your…birth mom? As in…your parents weren't your real parents?" Mitch asks, sitting up a little straighter now. I can't even speak anymore; I just look at him with glassy eyes and nod my head once.

"Shit, that's heavy stuff Olive. I wish I knew sooner; I could have been there for you." He reaches over and takes one of my hands in his. A few more tears slip down my cheeks and I smile despite the crying that's now inevitable.

"That's the thing, Mitch. You have been." My voice is shaky, and I gather my thoughts before telling him exactly what these last few weeks have been for me. "You're the first person I've talked about this with. I knew I couldn't ask Gran, not with everything she already has on her plate. I'm not sure if she even knows, which if she doesn't, now is not the time to inform her. I was selfish for so many years, and while I had good reason to be, it didn't make it okay. The way I treated them, challenged them on a regular basis for no reason at all. For once in my life, I was given an opportunity to show I'm not that selfish thirteen-year-old."

"Despite knowing all that and feeling like I made the right decision to keep this to myself for now, it's been hard living with it alone. Being able to talk about it with you doesn't make it easier in any way, but it makes it feel lighter, if that makes sense." I'm suddenly so tired, like the events of my life recently have caught up with me and drained me from the inside out. It's nearly midnight and we're still seated in the same position we have been since I stopped painting.

I feel guilty bringing up all this heavy stuff when Mitch went to great lengths to make me feel seen and important tonight. I just hope I didn't scare him off with the added baggage I now carry in addition to all the shit I've been carrying for over six years.

"Sorry I just dumped all that on you, I didn't mean to bring down the night." I admit feeling embarrassed.

"I want to know everything about you. So, don't apologize." He tells me.

"Thank you for this. I don't even think I officially thanked you yet. This was – this was unbelievable, one of the best nights of my life." I tell him as I turn around to kiss him softly. It's late and I'm not sure what time Mitch has to be up tomorrow, so I stand and start packing the art supplies up. I hope he doesn't take the lights down just yet; I like them being here illuminating the pond. If they stay, I feel like I could come here at night now and not be worried about falling on my ass in the dark.

Glancing up at the lights again, Mitch practically reads my mind. "I'll leave them up for now." He smiles at me then his face darkens with some kind of desire I can't place. He touches my face and slides his hand down the edge of my jaw before gripping my chin and tilting my face up to his. "I have a feeling we'll be back, soon." He kisses me deeply once more before grabbing the easel for me as we head towards his truck.

Just as he opens the door for me to get in, he pauses and looks me right in the eyes. "So, what comes next?" He asks me and every nerve in my body knows whole-heartedly what he means by that question. I don't know what to do about my birth parents yet, but I know when I decide, Mitch will be there

This girl. Where she came from and how I managed to make her mine I'll never fucking understand. Last night was easily one of the best nights of my life. Sharing something with her that makes her who she is, feeling her lose herself in me and vice versa, and then hearing a deeper part of her story. It all makes me more connected to her than I was already feeling.

I grew up a farm boy, looked at life as black and white, right and wrong for as long as I can remember. Olive blows into my life carrying massive amounts of color with her, colors I didn't know existed until I got to know her. It's as if she's not just a painter bringing images to life with a stroke of her paintbrush. The colors become more vivid and alive simply because she touched them. It's entrancing to watch her work.

She joked that she wanted to see me at work, and at first, I thought she was kidding. But here she is, striding over to me in tight blue jeans cuffed at the bottom just above her cowgirl boots. Wearing a loose-fitting white T-shirt and a baseball cap. She looks adorable and I don't have the heart to tell her that by the time she's done here, that shirt won't be white anymore.

Cutting the tractor's engine, I hop off the seat and meet her by the fence where all the pigs are gathered waiting for their feed. It's a little past eleven in the morning, and sweat is pouring off me. I grab a shovel leaning against the fence and start shoveling the pig's food into their troughs.

"Well don't you look sexy at work, glistening with sweat and all." She jokes as she comes to a stop next to me. I give her a quick wink before focusing back on the pigs. I don't miss the subtle way she licks her lips though. Maybe a working guy covered in sweat from the day *is* appealing to her. Willing to bet she wouldn't like me wrapping her in a hug though.

"You got a thing for blue collar workers, Butterfly?" I ask, swiping a hand at the sweat trickling down my face. Her face looks confused as she absorbs the nickname I just gave her. The more I think about it, the more fitting it seems.

"Butterflies are beautiful, gentle creatures. Most of them are full of color and their main purpose in life is to pollinate and feed on nectar. They collect it and then bring it to other plants to keep populating more seeds. It's incredible when you think about it." I scoop another shovel of food and toss it in the trough on the far left where the biggest pig, Bertha waits. I named her when I was ten.

"I remind you of butterflies?" she asks as she chews on her fingernail, processing. A smile spreads across her face and she nods. "I like it. Thank you." She blushes then takes in the area where all the pigs are now eating at a rapid pace.

"What do they eat?" Olive asks as she watches me shovel more food in.

"It's mostly a combination of wheat and corn. We grind

it up so it's easier and makes it amount to more. They eat *a lot* if you can't tell." I chuckle just as Bertha grunts and snorts as she inhales her food. Olive watches them all with wide eyes, and I watch her. She grew up on farmland but clearly has never spent much time on an actual farm. I'll change that.

"Want to help me harvest wheat today?" My voice comes out gritty, and I reach for my bottle of water chugging half in ten seconds flat.

"How do you harvest wheat?" Her voice is soft. It thrills me to show her, considering the wheat her family uses at the bakery comes directly from our farm. I think this will be good for her to see.

"We use a combine, which is a big machine that harvests the wheat efficiently. Using the combine makes it easier, and faster, to harvest more grain." I grab my gloves and start walking to the back field where the combine is. It's one of our biggest pieces of equipment on the farm and cost a pretty penny. A few years back Dad and I learned how to make repairs to it when something went wrong, knowing we could easily do it ourselves rather than pay someone else to do it.

Collin likes to call it the Green Monster, a nod to Boston even though he lives in New York City. I open the door, climb up into the seat and reach for Olive's hand to have her join me. She climbs into my lap, and I have to focus my thoughts on the combine rather than how her ass in those tight jeans feels against my thighs.

"As you can see, this is a massive piece of machinery and has to be handled right. One wrong move and you could fall out...I don't have to tell you how bad that would be." Olive turns around to see the cutter bar behind us. The blades are incredibly sharp and the thought of her riding out here with me doesn't fill me with excitement, but rather anxiety. She's not allowed near this thing when it's in use.

"Are you ever nervous driving it? Or just used to its colossal size?" She tips her head up to ask. As she does, the sun hits her face and I notice clusters of small freckles dotting her nose. They're hardly noticeable, but in the bright sun I can see them. Makes me wonder what else I may have missed about her.

A smile pulls at my lips, "are you concerned about me, Butterfly?" She looks down as she shuffles her feet in the dirt surrounding the pig pen, both hands hooked in the loops of her jeans.

"Concerned is a strong word, more like curious." She continues. "If I had to drive that thing, knowing the dangers surrounding it, I don't know that I could do it with a level head. All the what if's would give me too much anxiety." I ponder that for a moment never having thought about it quite that way. I've always just done my work and am used to the dangers that come along with farm work.

When I don't respond for several beats, a look comes over Olive's face like she realizes she may have put her foot in her mouth. I want to laugh, but now I kind of want to see her sweat. "I didn't mean to imply you shouldn't have a level head when operating that thing." She's nervous now and it's adorable.

"I never really thought about it like that before." I say as I tip her hat a little so she can look me in the eye. "But I promise you, I've been around combines my whole life and I don't get nervous operating them."

She turns to watch the pigs again and even though I feel I've convinced her I can handle the combine, my mind wanders to that scene from *The Man in the Moon* where Court died from falling off his tractor. It gave me nightmares for weeks, but I was too embarrassed to admit it. Knowing if I did, Collin would make fun of me.

I'm hoping Olive has never seen that movie, no need to freak her out. It's just a reminder that no matter how well you know what you're doing, accidents can still happen.

Grabbing Olive's hand, I pull her away from the pig pen and start walking towards the horse enclosure. Rally is doing laps and seeing him gallop like his heart depends on it always makes me smile. I glance over to see Olive with a wide smile on her face as she watches the horse's pure beauty.

For years I took it for granted, just how beautiful it is here. When I went to college I was in a completely different kind of place, and it made me miss home. This is where I want to put down roots.

"You asked me the other night how I knew what kind of paint supplies to buy." I say to Olive as we come to rest on the fence posts, watching Rally do laps. "I had a little help from Gwen, I went to see her."

Olive looks up at me, squinting against the sun. "Why didn't you just ask Gran? She knows what I like too." Before I have a chance to respond, realization dawns on her face and she giggles. The sound goes right to my core. I could listen to her laugh on repeat like a favorite song and never tire of it.

"Scratch that. Had you asked her you would have been answering a slew of other questions for over an hour." She laughs again. "Gwen was a smart choice."

I tap her nose with my pointer, so she knows she hit the nail on the head with that statement. "Well, when I was there, she seemed stressed. She wouldn't disclose why at first, but I pulled it out of her. Seems she's having some funding issues at the shelter."

I lean my back against the fence post before continuing. "Thought maybe we could have a fundraiser here at the farm with vendors and food to raise money on their behalf." Olive whips her head in my direction so fast I'm surprised it doesn't snap off. This look comes over her face and I can see it in her features, the wheels turning and ideas coming into place.

I love how caring she is, always ready to step up and help others. I know how much she loves Gwen and the people at Raising Hope. She's smiling now, she hasn't said anything yet, but I watch her thinking as the sun sets a warm glow across her face. Her eyes are warm pools of green and brown flecks, and with those light freckles from the sun underneath, I'm a goner.

Just then, Olive claps her hands together with a loud smack and straightens her back ramrod straight. That determined look is back on her face, and I notice a gleam in her eyes now, something fiercer than the soft glow they just had. "What needs to be done first?"

With that, we get started. We rushed back to the house to talk with my parents about having the event on our property and discuss possible vendors. Within three hours, we have a date, several committed vendors, and a list of others still to call.

I don't want to involve Gwen just yet, Olive and I decided this was best to be a surprise. Gwen is a proud person, and never asks for help. So, keeping her in the dark is best for now.

We ate pizza on the porch that night, talking about the fundraiser and telling stories about volunteering at the shelter. I remember the first time we went there together several weeks ago, Olive knew I was looking for someone but at the time I wouldn't tell her who.

"That day we went to the shelter, when Joan asked me to go with you." I say seeing Olive nod her head in my peripherals. I was a jerk to her then so I'm sure that's what she's remembering. "I told you I volunteered a lot in high school…" I let my words hang in the air for a few minutes before continuing.

"My Dad's best friend used to stay there. He went through a rough patch and basically hit rock bottom. Lost his job, turned to some bad habits and ended up losing his house." The memory lodges in my throat and I think back to how upset my father was during that time. We had lost contact with Drew for months, and it wasn't until I found him at the shelter that we at least knew he was alive.

"When we got there that day, memories flooded my mind reminding me of what it was like to see him there. I always wanted to know what had gotten him to that point, but figured if he wanted me to know he would have told me." To this day I still don't know why he went off the rails.

"It's been a few weeks, and I can't stop thinking about

where he might be." The porch swing Olive and I are sitting on creaks under our weight as we slowly rock back and forth. I feel her hand wrap around mine and just watch her soft fingers play across the back of my hand. It's a comforting gesture.

"Maybe Gwen knows where he is. It's worth asking, at least." She speaks softly and reassuringly. A small part of me feels better with the unknown. What if we ask Gwen and get a lead on him only to find out he's worse, not yet back on his feet. A heavy feeling descends on me when I think what's even worse than worse, is that he never got better. I was away at school for four years, and in that time my parents never heard from Drew.

As morbid as it sounds, Drew could be dead, and we never got any closure. My heart hurts for my father, for his best friend.

The next morning, Olive and I headed to Raising Hope to talk to Gwen about the fundraiser. We wanted to keep it a secret, but Gwen is a fountain of information when it comes to fundraising and honestly, we need her help. It gives me a good excuse to ask about Drew, too.

The gravel crunches beneath the tires as we pull into the lot outside the shelter. Gwen is already outside, working in the garden with a few residents. She wears a floppy sun hat and a wide smile, something I hardly ever see her without. For a woman who has been through as much as she has in life, she's never without a smile. All the more confirmation we're making the right decision in helping her.

Turning her head, she spots Olive and me getting out of the truck. Dropping her shovel, she stands and makes her way over to the two of us, wrapping us in a hug. "This one here can be quite romantic, eh?" She smiles at Olive while nudging my ribs.

Olive blushes, remembering the night I set up the paint and easel for her, and judging by the scarlet shade of her cheeks, she's remembering more than the paint. That makes two of us. "That he is." She smiles shyly.

"So, what brings you two back this way?" Gwen asks as she heads back to the garden.

"Olive and I would like to talk to you about something, if that's okay." Gwen squints her eyes at us, detecting we're up to something.

"Should I sit down for this?" There's humor in her voice, but also skepticism. Nothing in life comes free, something she's learned over the years. Convincing her we want to help raise money for the shelter with no strings attached might be a challenge.

Walking away from the garden and towards the small gazebo by the basketball courts, Olive dips her head and waves an arm at us. Gwen and I follow her over and take a seat under the shade of the gazebo.

"The other day you told me you were having trouble finding funds to keep the shelter going, especially at the rate you have people coming in. We'd like to help with that." Before the last word is out of my mouth, Gwen is rising to her feet shaking her head with both hands held up in surrender.

"No. I am not taking anyone's money, Mitchell. We

talked about this." She shakes her head again, more defiantly and before I can ask her to sit back down, Olive's voice cuts in.

"Gwen, sit." Her voice is stern and unwavering, it's kind of hot if I'm being honest. Gwen turns to look at her as Olive continues. "I was a bitch to everyone for years, don't make me pull that side out of me again, we both know it's not pretty." She is clearly kidding, but I get the feeling she's kind of serious.

Fifteen minutes later, we sit across from Gwen as she takes in everything we've said, realizing our plan is a good idea, I hope. Giving her a few minutes to process, I take Olive's hand in mine giving it a reassuring squeeze.

"We're doing this whether you want us to or not, Gwen. It would be helpful if you got on board and helped us find suitable vendors. You have far more connections than we do, and we want to do this right. Raising Hope deserves this, but more than anything Gwen, *you* deserve this. You do so much for everyone else, let us do something for you." Olive's words hang in the air, and I don't miss the tears that well in Gwen's eyes before she swipes them away.

"You know she's right. Say yes."

With a shake of her head and one last wipe of her eyes, Gwen stands. "I'm in. These people deserve this, too. I will always strive to make this place better, a place where people can come to feel safe and get back on their feet." Olive and I rush her, hugging her tightly as we smile at each other. This feeling, warmth spreading through my chest igniting something in me that I haven't felt for a long time. The satisfaction that comes with helping someone selflessly. It gives me a glimpse into how Gwen hopefully feels daily, knowing she's making a difference in these people's lives.

"I've got calls to make!" Gwen yells as she grabs her sun hat and heads back to the shelter. "I'll send you a text with some people to contact, food vendors and such." She bustles away, a new pep in her step that wasn't there twenty minutes ago.

I grab Olive's hand and pull her with me back to the truck. Just as we were about to hop in and head back, I remembered I didn't ask Gwen about Drew. "Gwen!" I yell just as she gets to the front door. "Do you remember Andrew Harper? He stayed here a few years back." I'm nervous, not sure what to expect and not even sure what I'm hoping to hear at this point. Anything is better than nothing, I guess.

Gwen tips her hat back, a soft smile painted on her face. "He's well. Called here two weeks ago to catch up." Something in my chest loosens, a tightness that I didn't realize was there before. He's okay. I can at least give my Dad that much if nothing else. "I'll get you his number, dear." And with that, she disappears inside.

Opening the door to my truck, I slide in the driver's seat and stare at the wheel for several moments. He's okay. All this time I feared he was dead, dreading the fact that my Dad might have lost his best friend. His little brother, as he always used to say. Hope is coursing through me, for Gwen and the shelter, for my Dad and for Drew.

Hope can be a heavy thing. But right now I'll take it.

13
OLIVE

*I*t wasn't hard to get the town on board with the fundraiser to help Gwen with Raising Hope. The last two weeks have been nonstop planning and prepping for tonight. The fundraiser kicks off in a few hours, so it's all hands-on deck.

Vendors have set up all around the field behind the Murphy's house, creating a large circle for people to walk easily. We ended up with six food trucks and a dozen local vendors happy to donate fifty percent of their earnings to the shelter. My heart is bursting with appreciation for these people willing to help.

It's midafternoon and the sun is high in the sky shining down with such intensity I feel like the top layer of my skin is melting off. Elaine and I are hanging lights on the fence posts around the barn for extra lighting and I see Mitch and Collin out of the corner of my eye. They're laughing as they race to see who can push the hay bales faster. We decided to use the smaller hay bales as seating rather than renting a ton of chairs.

In the center of the circle is a dance floor set up in front of where a live band will play. We're hoping people will want to eat, dance and shop more than they care to sit. But still, we needed some options.

The skin on Mitch's chest glistens with sweat and the smile on his face reminds me of what he probably looked like as a boy. Innocent and care-free. It's a nice change from the rugged tough guy I met a few months ago. So much has changed in that time, some of it makes my heart warm. But seeing Pop not back to his old self has other feelings swirling around.

He's been recovering well, but at his last check up it was clear he can't continue the way he has. His workload is too much for his age, and if he doesn't care about what it does to him, he cares about what it's doing to Gran. She's the love of his life and he wouldn't do anything to cause her more stress. As hard as it's been for him, he's pulled back at the bakery and allowed people to help.

Right now, he wants to assist us with the setup, instead he sits in a chair under some trees in the shade scowling at us. Pop likes to appear tough, but all that face is doing is making me laugh. I reach down to take the string of lights from Elaine and hang them on the clip to secure them in place.

"What has you chuckling up there?" Elaine asks as she dabs a hanky across her glistening forehead.

"Pop is trying to look unfazed over there," I point to him under the tree and Elaine follows my hand. "But really, he just looks like a toddler who isn't getting his way." I can't help the laughter bursting from me now and soon Elaine joins in.

"Bless his heart, he tries." She replies easily.

Once we finish hanging the lights I go check in with

Gran before heading home to shower and get ready. It's hot as Hades out here today, but instead of riding my bike back to the house, I walk. The last few days have been hectic, to say the least, and I haven't exactly had much time to myself. I'm either with Mitch or working on the fundraiser.

The feelings it's brought me though, are thrilling. Doing something productive and helpful fills my heart with a feeling I haven't had in a long time. I enjoy the hustle of being around people, working towards a goal and feeling useful. The bakery is a family business, and while I love it, it doesn't give me that sense of purpose. Sometimes I wonder if that's why I want to move to a big city or if it really is to further my future in art. The last few weeks have been so busy I haven't had time, or the thought, to check my email on any of the internships I applied for. I don't feel ready to look rejection in the face just yet, especially not today.

I make my way up the worn front steps, hearing them creak under my weight and remove my dirty sneakers by the door. Since Gran and Pop are both still at the farm, I know I have the house to myself. I take off my sweat stained T-shirt and toss it in the hamper by the stairs. I need to do a load of laundry anyways, so I strip the rest of my clothes off and toss them in as well.

Steam billows throughout the bathroom and I'm about to hop in when I remember the new body wash I bought is still in my room. Wrapping myself in a towel, I quickly go grab it. As I round the corner, I hear the screen door shut and feel grateful I had half the mind to throw a towel around me. If Gran or Pop walked in to see me naked, I'd have to leave town and never come back.

"Gran?" I yell down the hall, but my next question dies on my tongue when I see Mitch, sweaty yet still looking edible, round the corner. His eyes are dark as he takes in my current state. My body freezes and my skin prickles at the awareness of his eyes on my bare body. He knows I'm naked under this thin towel and it has blood rushing to my cheeks.

"I thought you were still at the farm." I manage to choke out.

"I was. I came looking for you, and boy am I glad I did." He stalks towards me slowly, fixing me with a smirk that starts at the top of my head and reaches down to my toes.

I fidget with my towel, suddenly unsure of what to do. The sound of water pelting the shower curtain grabs my attention and I turn to look back towards the bathroom. In two seconds, Mitch is down the hallway burying his face in my neck. He grips my waist and starts backing me up towards the door to the bathroom. My back meets the wall and I heave a breath as I push my palms into Mitch's sweaty chest.

"You're soaked." I laugh as my hands slide down his sweaty shirt, itching to feel his glistening skin underneath. Usually, I'm not particularly aroused by guys covered in dirt and sweat, but Mitch wears it well. The sheen of sweat adds to the bad boy farm image and I'm certain this moment will star in several new fantasies.

"Something tells me, so are you." He breathes out a growl as his hands tighten on my waist. The dampness between my thighs confirms his suspicion, but I don't let him know that. I rub them together to abate the ache that's growing in my core,

Mitch notices immediately.

"Are you wet for me, Butterfly?" God that nickname, something that seems so sweet goes right through me like a hot branding iron and I melt for it. My back slips past the threshold and I'm able to put a little distance between myself and Mitch. That doesn't stop him from invading the small space of the bathroom. My head is fuzzy with need and all I can think about is having his body crowd mine in that tiny shower.

I place the bottle of body wash on the edge of the tub and turn away from Mitch. He stays where he is, and I can feel his hot gaze on my back as I slowly release the hold on my towel, letting it pool at my feet. Without sparing him a glance, I open the curtain and step under the water. Anticipation pools in my stomach, waiting to see if he politely leaves, or joins me. I'm scared of both options.

Having only been naked in front of Mitch once, while it was dark out, my nerves are in overdrive. My breathing is ragged, something he can probably hear, even over the sound of water rushing down the drain. I close my eyes and stand under the spray to get my hair wet and wash off some of the sweat from the day. I hear Mitch's belt buckle clink and thud as it hits the floor.   *Shit.*

The curtain pulls back slightly, and Mitch peers in, just his bare chest visible. He watches me as I run my fingers through my hair, wetting the ends before reaching for the shampoo. I don't dare open my eyes to look at him, because I know the second I do, he's coming in. I can feel him waiting impatiently for me to look at him, waiting for permission to join me, instead I make him sweat. "Olive." His tone is piercing, causing goosebumps to erupt across my skin.

"Every second you make me wait out here is one second more I will torment you with my tongue." My eyes flash open in surprise and settle on his gaze. His dark green eyes, almost appear black with lust, pierce through the steam in the shower and slowly cascade down my wet body. "I'll bring you to the edge over and over again, until you're begging me to let you come." With our eyes locked, he pulls the curtain back and steps one leg into the tub, never leaving my face. Waiting for a reaction, I suppose. When I don't protest, he fully steps in and closes the curtain behind him. His body takes up more than half the space in here and suddenly I'm having a hard time getting air into my lungs.

The air is stifling in here from the steam, add Mitch's tall, muscled body and I might as well be in an inferno. Taking the shampoo bottle from my hands, Mitch squeezes some into his palm and moves his finger in a circular motion telling me to turn around. I do as I'm told and feel his hands come to my long tresses. Massaging the shampoo into my scalp as suds bleed down my body. He removes the shower head from the wall and begins rinsing the suds from my hair. Then repeats the process with the conditioner.

Once my hair is free of soap, he turns me around to face him, grabbing my new body wash as he does. He squeezes a generous amount in his hand and begins lathering it through his fingers. The sweet lavender aroma fills the air around us, I swallow audibly as Mitch lowers to a knee to begin washing me from my feet and up my legs. Gripping my thighs, he massages the soap in circular motions, and I can't help the groan that escapes my lips.

From beneath me, I see him look up grinning, pleased with how my body is reacting to his touch. Careful not to touch the one spot I desperately need him to; he washes my back and stomach before finishing with my arms. Like he did with my hair, Mitch removes the shower head again and washes all the bubbles from my body. Feeling delirious with need and suddenly brave, I say, "you missed a spot." He crowds me, gazing down into my eyes as he reaches for the body wash once again.

Squeezing a small amount into the palm of his hand, he looks at me and raises a brow. "Show me." He knows exactly what spot he didn't touch; he just wants to hear me beg for him. At this point, I gladly will if it means he'll touch me where I need him to.

Slowly, I trail a finger down between my breasts, chest heaving, I stop just below my belly button and look at him. His eyes are zeroed in on where my finger stops, and his jaw twitches. Self-restraint is wearing thin; the beast is looming just beneath the surface, and I want to see that side of him take over. Lose control and stop being so gentle with me. I want him to see that I'm not breakable, I'm not some fragile little girl.

The water washed the soap from his hands, but before he could grab the bottle again, I take his hand in mine and place it just below my bellybutton. I lace my fingers over his and slowly dip them lower until the tips of his fingers brush that sensitive spot. My body is vibrating with want and need as he slides a wet finger through my folds. My eyes flutter shut and my breath hitches in my throat as he adds a second finger increasing the pressure.

I push my body into his touch, needing more than what he's giving, and he chuckles, deep and sexy. "Needy girl." Sliding one finger into my heat, my head falls back against the tile of the shower, and I move my body in tandem with his finger. He increases the pressure and adds a second finger, pushing deep and curling up to hit that sweet spot.

I grip Mitch's shoulders, needing his support as he adds a third finger, causing my vision to go splotchy. I've never been stretched this far. My forehead rests against his chest and I cling to him, desperate to hold him to me as his fingers continue their assault inside me. "Fuck, you're so tight." He grunts into my neck. Feeling my orgasm building, I can't help the scream threatening to spill from my lungs. It feels so good, but fear pricks the back of my brain that anyone could be coming by the house any second.

Mitch works his fingers inside me faster and harder and I'm about to lose all control. I'm grinding into his hand, not even concerned about how desperate I am for his touch. I gasp, "I'm close…Mitch, I'm so…" I bite the base of his throat just as a scream threatens to break free. I'm coming so hard, and he doesn't let up until I'm practically falling to my knees with euphoria. "Fuck." I say between pants.

Mitch smirks at me and holds me up under my arms because my knees are still wobbling. He's hard as a rock, and right now it would be so easy to let him have me. The thought crosses his mind too, I can see it the way he's looking at me and I'm about to tell him to do it when I hear the screen door slam shut.

"Shit!" I whisper, though it comes out more like a shriek. "Did anyone know you were coming here?" I ask frantically. Mitch shrugs his shoulders as if being caught in the shower together is no big deal. "Mitch!"

He laughs and pecks a kiss to my forehead. "You're adorable when you're nervous, Butterfly." He reaches out to grab a towel and steps out of the shower, locking the door. Guess I should have thought to lock the door, at least one of us is thinking clearly. Not my fault he just rocked my body with an intense orgasm, so I can't exactly be blamed for my lack of responsibility.

A knock sounds on the door, and I freeze, too terrified to speak. Surely Gran will be able to tell if something is wrong, so I need to pull it together. "Olive?"

"Y-yes Gran? I'm just finishing up here. Did you need the shower?" Not that she'd want to shower in here since the water has practically run cold. I'll never tell her the other reason she wouldn't want to shower in here anymore.

"No dear, just letting you know I'm grabbing my bag for tonight and hanging out with Elaine until the festival begins." Before I respond I hear her footsteps disappear down the hall. I let out the breath I didn't realize I was holding and turn off the water. I pull the curtain back to see Mitch grinning at me like a kid who just won a damn goldfish at the county fair. He hands me a dry towel and I swat him with it.

"Don't look at me like that!" I whisper yell as I wrap myself up. We could have been caught if he hadn't thought to lock the door. Gran gives me privacy, certainly, but if she needed something in here, she would have just come in. I can't begin to imagine the horror on her face had she opened that door to see a naked Mitch.

He just laughs again as he zips up his jeans. He just showered and now has to put on his dirty clothes he's been sweating in all day. I'm looking at him like I want to eat his face when he smirks at me. "See something you like?" He drawls.

"I see everything I like." I hum as I reach up on my tiptoes to drop a kiss on his cheek. "Sorry you have to put on those dirty clothes after getting clean, though."

"Baby, what we just did in there is anything but clean." He winks at me and pulls me flush against his chest. "What would have happened if Joan hadn't come home?" He asks and the blood drains from my face. What would have happened? I don't think I would have stopped him if he tried to go farther. We've done everything but sex now, and I know I won't be able to hold off much longer. Can only imagine how he's feeling.

"Guess we'll never know." I wink, but he sees through me, I know he does. I get the sense he knows I'm a virgin, which is why he never asks about sex, but he's gentleman-enough to wait until I'm ready to confess that part of me. There is no scenario in my mind that doesn't want Mitch to be my first, I know it and I'm pretty sure he knows it too. But, rushing in a shower when anyone could come in is not the place. I don't need it to be special, but I need it to feel right. Today wasn't the right time.

A few hours later, the fundraiser is in full swing. I'm amazed at how many people came to show support for Raising Hope, and more importantly, Gwen. She'll never admit she needed this, but judging by the look on her face, she's more than grateful.

The tents are arranged in a semi-circle around the back of the barn with all the food vendors in the middle. The smell of meat sizzling and fresh baked goods wafts in the air as a live band plays in front of the barn on a raised stage. The strung lights Elaine and I hung are twinkling and we added lanterns at the last minute to illuminate the tables set up on each side of the stage. For pulling most of this together in just over a week, the place looks beautiful. I'm amazed at what hard work and dedication from people all around town can do.

We set up a table with raffles from each vendor here tonight, in addition to them volunteering their time, they all agreed to donate gift baskets to help raise even more money. I'm currently in line for a dough boy because the last time I had one was at the county fair when I was maybe ten.

I take my sugary treat, covered in powdered sugar, to one of the tables and take in the scene all around me. People are dancing on the dance floor in front of the band, while others sit at tables, laughing and eating. My heart could burst from the sense of community and support here tonight. If more people cared about others, the world would surely be a better place.

Just as I take a bite from the dough boy, a hand snakes

around my waist pulling me in. I don't even have to look to know who it is, the cinnamon apple scent wafts around me and I silently bathe in it. His scent causes delirium in my mind, almost like I'm in a trance. I would gladly follow him to a tower and allow myself to prick my finger on a spindle. As long as he is the one kissing me awake in the end.

"Want a bite?" I ask as sugar falls onto my lap. Mitch hands me a napkin and wipes the powdered sugar from my lips with his thumb. He sucks it into his mouth and I've never been so jealous of a thumb before.

"No thanks, I've already had my treat for the day." His gaze darkens as he looks at me through hooded eyes. Memories of our shower this afternoon filter in and I'm reminded of how he licked his fingers clean after touching me. A deep crimson is likely painting my cheeks right now as I relive those moments.

"Butterfly, we're in public right now. You can't be fantasizing about me without someone noticing." He murmurs against my ear and the feel of his hot breath sends a shiver down my spine. I just want to be alone with him again. I need to remind myself that tonight is about Gwen, any other feelings can wait until tomorrow. Or tonight when I'm alone in bed dreaming about Mitch and his skilled fingers.

"I was doing no such thing." I brush off his comment with a wave of my sugary hand, but he can smell the bullshit a mile away.

Dropping my napkin on the empty plate, I relax in my seat and sigh as I take in the scene around us. Everything is perfect. "What's on your mind, baby?"

"It's just…I can't believe we actually pulled this off. Tonight is exactly what Gwen needed. I don't know the numbers yet, but I'm sure we were able to raise more than enough to keep things going at Raising Hope. There's no better feeling in the world than helping the people you care about." I feel tears brimming my lids, I can't explain why, but I allow them to fall. For the first time in a long time, I cry not because of sadness, but because of pure joy.

For so long I cried about the loss of my parents, them missing out on so many milestones in my life. I cried when Pop had a heart attack, I cried when I learned about my adoption. I've cried in frustration of what my life has become instead of being grateful for everything it already is. Tonight, I'm allowing myself to cry for a reason unrelated to grief, and in a weird way, it's freeing. I feel Mitch place a hand on my thigh, reassuring me without any words, that he's here with me.

"I think I'm ready." I say on an exhale. Mitch keeps his hand on my thigh and gazes over at me. My eyes are trained on the people laughing and dancing under the stars, but out of the corner of my eye, I can see Mitch. He's gazing at me thoughtfully, but with a touch of confusion. He's in for a ride with me. I chuckle at the thought and turn to him with a smile. "I'm ready to find my birth mom, Lucy."

Mitch nods his head once, and I turn my head back to the dance floor. Before he has a chance to respond I'm grabbing his hand and pulling him to the dance floor with me. We make our way through the crowd of people to the center just as a slow song begins to play over the speakers. The band is taking a break, so Luke Combs voice fills the air around us as 'Love You Anyway' plays.

I wrap my arms around Mitch, and he rests his hands low on my hips as we sway to the music. "I love Luke Combs," I say quietly against the sensitive spot next to Mitch's ear. "I've always wanted to go to one of his concerts."

"We should go the next time he comes around." He insists, and it causes my heart to do summersaults at the idea of planning something that far in advance. I don't even know where Luke Combs is on his tour right now, we may have already missed our chance. But Mitch whispering in my ear that he wants to make those plans has me crushing on him harder than a girl in middle school.

As the song ends, Gwen makes her way over to us. "I can't believe y'all did all this for the shelter. I can't ever thank…" Her voice hitches as she tries to tamp down the rising emotions. "I'll never be able to thank you enough for what you've done here tonight. This is incredible and Raising Hope will forever be grateful. *I* will forever be grateful." She sniffles and swipes a hand under her eyes to dry the tears that are threatening to spill over.

"Gwen, this wasn't just for the shelter." I say as I take her hands in mine. I can feel Mitch right behind me, like an anchor of strength, ready to stand by me through anything. "This was for *you*, Gwen. *You* deserve this, and so much more." Now the tears are painting both our cheeks as she pulls me in for a tight hug. Mitch stands back and watches the exchange before Gwen sticks an arm out and drags him into the hug. A moment later, I hear Elaine and Gran's voices come around us and they huddle into the hug.

There's so much love here tonight, friends and neighbors all together in support of someone important to our community. By the end of the night, it's clear we'd raised enough money for Gwen to keep things running smoothly for several months. That gives her plenty of time to apply for more grants and state assistance.

Mitch walks me home after we help clean up around the barn, the rest we'll do tomorrow. His fingers are intertwined with mine and it's quiet as we walk the dirt road to my house. I'm focusing on the crunch of our feet as I watch fireflies dance in the field in front of us. There's an elegance to the way they light up the sky, reminding us that in even the darkest of times, you can always find that glimmer of hope. As the fireflies take turns glowing in front of us, I think about Lucy, and what I want to do moving forward. My words from earlier ring in my head, *'I'm ready'* and the way Mitch looked at me. I brought him to the dance floor before he had a chance to say anything.

"Earlier tonight, I said I was ready to find Lucy. I didn't give you a chance to respond before I pulled you on the dance floor." Mitch squeezes my hand in his and locks eyes with mine, glowing in the moonlight.

"I'm here for you, whatever you need Olive." His voice is a whisper, and its softness is reassuring. We were almost at my house when he stopped me at the end of our gravel driveway, pulling me against his chest. He kisses me softly and tucks a strand of hair loose from my ponytail behind my ear. Cradling my head between his hands, he holds my gaze and whispers, "so, what comes next?" Lord help me, I'm a goner for this man.

14

Olive

Today Gran is taking Pop to see the cardiologist who did his surgery. It's been a month since the heart attack and Pop has shown so much progress. The first few days at home were rough for him, and Gran. Getting him to stick to a new diet was like trying to shove shaving cream back inside the can. So many times, I could practically see steam come from Gran's ears, but she always kept it together for him.

They started taking walks around the property in the evenings, a way to increase Pop's physical activity. He was reluctant at first, but that time spent together seems to have helped in more ways than one. I like to watch them from my window sometimes, seeing how dedicated they are to each other is something I long for.

Once they leave for his appointment, I head to the attic to pull out the letters from Lucy. I only read the first letter that day after Pop's heart attack, too stunned to read any others. Last week when Mitch asked me what came next, I didn't even know. How am I supposed to move forward and process everything this means? I don't know the first thing about finding someone, and what if I find her and she no longer wants contact? Or worse…I can't allow myself to believe for one second that could possibly be the case. I've already lost one set of parents, I'm not sure I could handle losing more. Even someone I've never met.

My feet climb the stairs slowly, like concrete has dried to the bottom of my shoes. Ever since I found the letters I've felt the weight of the attic above me, taunting me. Having the fundraiser to pour all my energy into was helpful, but now reality has set in again. I can't avoid this forever, and dealing with it alone hasn't helped either. Mitch offered to come over and read through the letters with me, hoping to find an address or any information that might lead us to Lucy. As much as I want him here, I need to do this by myself. I can't explain why.

The cedar chest sits in the same spot it always has. Under a stained-glass window looking out over the field. Sunlight pours in and rests on the chest, as if lighting the way. Taking a seat on the floor, I wipe a layer of dust off the top before opening the chest. On the off-chance Gran came up here for anything else, I hid the envelope on the side of the chest under a bunch of old newspaper articles.

Lifting the envelope, I tip it upside down as a dozen letters fall to the floor. Suddenly feeling overwhelmed I don't even know where to start when I notice a number on the back of one envelope. Apparently, Lucy had enough foresight to number them, not sure if she expected my parents not to give them to me or what. But in any case, I'm grateful. Taking a deep breath, I open letter number 2 and prepare for what I'm about to read.

My dearest Olive,
After my first letter, I wasn't sure I should write again. You're too young to read and I can't imagine your parents pulling these out at bedtime to read to you. In any case, here I am writing to you again. I still don't expect anything, but in a way, these letters are a form of dealing with the loss of you. If there ever comes a day when you read these, I felt it might be helpful to tell you a little bit about myself.

I grew up on a beautiful farm with my parents, who were truly great people. They would have loved you. While my upbringing was good, I was different in a lot of ways. I was always doodling, and painting the fences around our property. Thankfully my parents encouraged me rather than smother my dreams. It often makes me wonder if you're just as creative.

I've always been slightly introverted, listening to music and reading more than anything else. And I was always outside. Your parents seemed like the right people to provide you with the kind of life I would have given you. I felt it in my gut, giving you to them was the right choice.

When I was sixteen, I met a boy, someone kind and so handsome I felt butterflies every time he looked at me. I'm sure it's easy to guess what happened next; nine months later came you. I didn't expect to do it alone, but I found myself in exactly that position. While I fell head over heels for this boy, it was clear he did not feel the same. He was a few years older and away at school so I hadn't gotten the chance to tell him about you before he had moved on. We were so young; can't say I blame him for wanting to act his age.

To this day, I'm still not sure he knows I had his daughter. I never told him, and that's something I'll need to live with for the rest of my life. My main purpose in writing these letters is to assure you I did not want to give you up. You are still the love of my life, Olive. I will never not think of you and wonder where you are. Should you ever find these and feel inclined to reach out, I've included my address.

I hope your life is everything I couldn't give you, sweetheart. You deserve the world, and I hope that one day I can be a part of it, in whatever way you wish. I love you with all my heart, Olive.

Lucy

My heart is thudding wildly in my chest as I read these words written so many years ago by the woman who birthed me. I didn't even notice a few tears had started falling until they landed on the envelope, smudging the ink. I'm so much like her, and now my thoughts are spiraling at what else I may have inherited from her and my birth father.

There's a part of me that wants to rip through every envelope and read the words she's written, but there's an even bigger part of me that can't. One letter at a time is kind of my limit it seems.

On the back of the page at the bottom is an address. I stare at the words for several beats before realizing the town listed is only a few over. Literally a short drive away could be my birth mom and she's likely been there all this time. My mind is reeling from the information and the only thing I can think to do is run. Run from these letters invading my blood stream and taking root in every part of me. Run to Mitch and wrap my arms around his strong body and allow him to hold me until the shock wears off. Run to my grandparents and let the flood gates open, ask them if they knew and why I was never told. Running is all I can think of doing so I grab my sneakers, run down the steps of the attic slamming the door behind me and out onto the porch before launching myself into a sprint.

Sweat pours off me but I don't let up. I keep pushing myself forward, running harder than I ever have until I reach the path to the pond. Two miles isn't a long distance, but I ran here in a full sprint, and my chest is heaving as I lean forward resting my hands on my knees. A few minutes later once my breathing has calmed, I take my shirt and shoes off before diving into the water.

The water surrounds me as I dip beneath the surface, allowing the temperature to cool my face. As I resurface, I float on my back and think of the day I was here with Mitch. We could hardly stand each other then and the idea of how things have progressed since makes me laugh. In so many ways it feels like I've known him for longer than a couple months, but then I'm reminded it's only been a short amount of time since we started getting along with each other. I have to fight the urge to ask him what it was he didn't like about me.

My insecurities start to take over when I rid them from my mind. Now is not the time to spiral down that road again. Reading Lucy's letter made me feel like I was suffocating in that attic, all the realizations of her not wanting to give me up came flooding in and it was too much. This woman who I didn't even know existed, let alone birthed me, *loves* me, and thinks of me. It's a hard thing to grasp when I've spent so much time feeling like I didn't fit in. Especially now when I know I'm a lot like her. I've always felt loved, but this is a new kind of feeling, one I can't put into words.

Every time I go to talk to Gran about the letters, I feel my throat closing in. Physically incapable of voicing the truth in fears of how she'll react. The words Mitch has said keep floating around my mind, trying to figure out what comes next isn't as easy as hearing them roll off his lips. It would be so easy to drive a few towns over to the address Lucy gave me and introduce myself. But to me that feels underwhelming, I feel like it should be grander.

How is this woman going to react to the daughter she put up for adoption nineteen years ago showing up on her doorstep? I can't even imagine it because the idea seems unfathomable. I make my way out of the water and lay down in the grass under the white oak tree imagining different scenarios of meeting Lucy. Maybe it's like ripping off a band aid and I need to just go without overthinking it. Sitting up suddenly I grab my shoes and shirt and rush back home.

15

MITCH

The sun is blazing today, hotter than it has all summer and every inch of my tired body can feel it. It's the middle of summer, so not only is the heat nearly unbearable, but it's prime sweet corn season. All summer we harvest sweet corn to sell to locals and our neighboring towns. You haven't had sweet corn until you've had it fresh picked from our farm with warm butter and salt. My mouth waters at the thought as I toss another ear over my shoulder into the barrel.

Without realizing it, I've worked through lunch, again, and my stomach assaults me with loud grumbles urging me to take a break. Seeing as I'm almost through this row, I tell myself to finish strong and head to the house for something to eat. Ma likes to make a heaping tray of cold cut sandwiches, leaving them in the fridge for Dad and I to grab easily. With Collin home the tray has been empty more often than full. Ma doesn't seem to mind, having both her boys home has seemed to bring her a sense of purpose. I wish she could understand just how much she means to us all already, but none of us men are much for mushy talk.

Thirty minutes later I heave the last of the barrels of corn onto the truck and head for the house. Any kind of food right now has my mouth watering and stomach grumbling but I certainly don't expect to walk in and find Ma pulling fresh bread from the oven with a tray of cold cuts laid out on the counter. She used to do this a lot when we were kids and eating everything in sight.

Ma would make a few fresh loafs of bread and lay out a spread of meats and cheeses for us to make our own subs. We haven't had lunch like this in years, partly because I was away at college and partly because Collin was never here. Having us both under the same roof for the first time in who knows how long, must have triggered the memory for her.

Nothing beats the smell of bread baking, a smell I didn't realize how much I missed until it smacked me in the face with the teasing aroma of carbs. My mouth waters like the sweat pouring off me so I take a swig of water before rounding the island to wash my hands.

"It smells amazing in here, Ma." I say as I scrub the dirt and sweat off my hands and forearms. Once they're rinsed I turn to see a megawatt smile grace my mothers face and it warms my heart in ways the sun will never be able to.

"Well thank you my sweet Mitchell. I just decided that with Collin bein' here and all, we should have a proper lunch like when you were boys." She brushes the flour from her hands across her apron and reaches for the plates to hand to me. I take them from her and give her cheek a peck, a small gesture I hope she takes as gratitude. "Collin is up in his room workin' I think, will you holler for him to join us while I get your father?"

I nod my head as I head to the stairs with a slice of salami in hand, not discreet enough to pass Ma though, she swats me with her dishrag and shakes her head in mock annoyance. Not much beats getting a rise out of her these days, or any day for that matter.

"Coll! As if you can't already smell the delightful aroma of fresh bread rising to your room, Ma made lunch and if you don't get your ass down here now I'm gonna eat all the meat!" My voice carries up the stairs while also out the side window and to Ma walking out to the barn.

"Language, Mitchell!" She yells from across the lawn. I chuckle just thinking about all the times she's caught us cursing as kids. We got more than a swat from her dishrag, that's for sure.

Thirty minutes later, the four of us are gathered around the kitchen counter, stomachs distended from the amount of bread we've consumed, and more full than I care to admit. Dad pats his stomach before leaning over to place a soft peck on Ma's cheek. "As always, dear, that was wonderful. Thank you." He stands to head back out to the barn leaving just us boys and Ma. A core memory races to the forefront and it takes an absurd amount of energy to push it back where it belongs. After an amazing lunch, now is not the time to bring up the past.

Life isn't meant to be perfect, and lord knows I have made some questionable decisions in my life. But sitting here with Collin and my mom has memories of one of the worst nights of my life racing through me. A simple mistake nearly cost my Dad his life and it took me a real long time to let go of my guilt and move forward. Sitting around this island is like being thrown back to that night all those years ago where we weren't even sure he was going to make it.

Suddenly the heavy amount of bread in my stomach isn't sitting well with me so I stand to hopefully walk some of it off. I quickly thank Ma for lunch and pat Collin on the back as I head out the side door and down the steps towards the barn.

Dad and I never really talked about the incident, and I know he doesn't hold it against me, but a part of me still wonders if he still thinks about it the way I occasionally do.

I'm about to head into the barn when I see a car pulling down the dirt driveway towards the house. I recognize the car immediately and head over to greet Gwen as she exits the drivers side. "Gwen, to what do we owe the pleasure?" I ask striding over.

"Oh, you sweet talker, it's no wonder Olive fancies you something fierce." If I wasn't already flushed from the sun I would probably blush at that comment and then never admit it happened. Little does Gwen know, I feel the same if not something more intense towards Olive. Something I haven't even fully admitted to myself, let alone anyone else.

Brushing off her comment, I fall into step with her as she heads towards the shaded area of trees to get out of the blazing sun. She's fidgeting with the hem of her button down, giving off an anxious vibe that has the hair on my arms coming to a stand. Whatever she came here for was important enough that a phone call didn't feel appropriate.

"I was hoping to catch you, and not your Dad." She says

as she glances around, probably making sure he hasn't spotted her here. My steps falter as I wait for her to spit it out. I'm not always the most patient person, and Gwen is not someone I want to be on the receiving end of that.

"Gwen, is everything alright?" I ask with a slight edge to my voice.

"Yes, nothing you need to worry about dear, it's just that… well, Drew came into the shelter last night." Her admission leaves her mouth and goes right through one ear and out the other without fully taking root in my mind. Surely I heard her wrong. With a shake of my head I look up at her and ask her to repeat herself, there's no way she just said that.

"Drew stopped in last night to talk with me. I guess he had more to say after our phone call a few weeks ago." Probably noticing the look of unease on my face, she gently places a hand on my arm, giving it a gentle squeeze before continuing. "I assure you he's alright Mitch, very well from the looks of it."

That admission does little to ease the tension in my shoulders right now, because I still have so many questions. The words just aren't forming on my tongue at the moment, so I stay silent, waiting for any other information Gwen plans to share.

"You must have a million questions." She says as if reading my mind. "Listen, all I can tell you is that he's well and healing. Which to me, is always the most important thing." Walking ahead of me, she takes a seat on one of the large rocks rested under the trees. I join her moments later, still absorbing the information she's just dropped on me.

A weird feeling courses through me when I realize I'm not rushing to tell my father. Don't get me wrong, I want him to know his former best friend is alive and well, having not heard from him in years. But, a stronger emotion is taking root at the moment, one I'm unfamiliar with. More than anything, I want Olive here beside me. Her presence is calming, always grounding me to where I am, keeping me present.

"He gave me his contact information, I thought you might want it." Gwen extends her hand to me with a folded white piece of paper between her pointer and middle fingers. A tiny piece of paper holds the information I need to reach out and find out what really happened with Drew. We all knew he went through something hard, but when he cut off my parents specifically, we weren't sure what else we could do. How do you help someone who doesn't want help? If they want to get better, it needs to come from them first. This is the first sign of reaching out, and it's coming from him. That strikes me right in the chest.

"Thank you, Gwen." I whisper while turning the folded sheet over and over in my hand, never looking away from it. Afraid that if I do this will all just be a dream and the idea of being able to see him again after so many years will vanish. I decide right there that I'm not going to tell my father about this until I know for sure Drew is okay. I'm the one who unknowingly kept tabs on him, keeping it a secret from my family all those years ago. What's one more secret now?

Gwen rises to her feet and pats her hands on her sides before stepping over to place a hand on my shoulder. "I'll let you decide what to do with this information. I remember back when you would volunteer, your parents were unaware of Drew being at Raising Hope. I trust you'll do what's best now, just like you did then." How she keeps reading my mind is beyond me, but I just offer a weak smile and another thank you before she heads back to her car and drives off.

A while goes by where I just sit beneath the tree, holding the piece of paper. My fathers voice penetrates my thoughts as I hear him walking closer to my spot in the shade. Quickly shoving the paper in my pocket I stand and walk in the direction of my father.

My thoughts from earlier, wanting to talk about the night of his accident rings in my mind, a warning bell telling me either now is the time to bring it up, or warning me to shut my mouth. I choose the latter and instead help him moving hay bales in the barn. In the days following the fundraiser, we've had to rearrange and put a lot of things back in order, the hay bales being the most tedious.

Feeling like a coward, I swallow my thoughts and keep focused on our task, rather than spewing word vomit all over my father. We keep our conversation light, like how fucking hot it is outside Weather is always a safe topic. Both of us have sweat pouring from our bodies like fountains, and I use that as the excuse to pause our work. "Hey Dad?" I say tentatively, not sure what I even plan on saying when he looks at me with a raised brow. The words I want to say die on my tongue and I shake my head hoping a new idea will arise.

"I-I was thinking maybe we could visit Collin to see a Yankees game sometime. Think you'd be up for that?" He drops the hay bale he's holding and reaches for a bottle of water, chugging it until it's nearly empty. Before he can answer, I'm rambling again. "I know it's hard to leave the farm, but I'm sure it would be okay just for one weekend. Plus, I know Coll would love us staying in his fancy New York apartment." I laugh knowing how much Collin would *hate* to have us stay with him. He thinks we're a bunch of barn animals.

My Dad laughs at my joke and perches both hands on his hips as he thinks. He didn't immediately say no, so that's a good sign. I may not have planned to ask that, I chickened out about both topics I *really* want to discuss. But now the idea of a weekend New York trip is enticing. He looks down at his boots just before he lifts his head and looks right at me. "You'll have to run it by your mother." He finally says and a smile tugs at the corner of my mouth.

Dad isn't a man of many words, but when he speaks he's right to the point. His instructions were clear, don't get my hopes up until Ma is on board. With that, I grab my empty water bottle and head in the house to wash off the dirt and sweat my body has accumulated and expelled today. As I walk up the porch steps, I'm hyper aware of the folded piece of paper in my pocket. Feeling as if the information on it weighs a hundred pounds keeping my attention locked in place.

I don't know what I want to do yet, but I do know one thing. I want to wrap my arms around the beautiful brunette who smells like coconuts and sunshine. I strip off my clothes in the bathroom ready to wash the stench of the day down the drain. As the water rushes over my body I'm brought back to that moment in the shower with Olive last week. My cock twitches and I groan into my hands at the memory of her coming on my fingers. Right now I want to breathe in her beauty as if it will give me the strength I need to confront my past. Then I want to make her come over and over again until I can think of nothing else but my name on her lips.

16

Olive

"Where's the fire?" I jump at the husky voice just a few feet from me and catch Mitch leaning up against the railing on the porch. My chest is already tight from running back here in a sprint, my breasts heaving from exertion and it catches Mitch's attention immediately. His eyes land on my chest, holding still for several beats before returning his eyes to mine. They're smoldering, and I can sense more than desire in them. No, there's something else lurking beneath the lids.

We're quiet, except for my labored breathing, now completely due to his perusal of my chest, not physical exertion. Sometimes I wonder how it's even possible to so easily loose my train of thought, but when I'm around Mitch everything else seems to fade to the background. All I can smell is his scent, crisp with a hint of spice, and it makes my mouth water. My body always reacts the same when he's within reach, goosebumps taking over every inch of exposed skin in anticipation of his touch. Due to the heat of the day, my body is already flushed and yet I can feel a deeper blush start at my ears and course down my neck.

"I-I ran from the um… the pond," I lift a hand to my head

scratching a spot that isn't itchy because I can't even form a normal sentence without sounding like I need an oxygen tank for support. Mitch just nods his head, I can feel his thoughts racing through his mind, likely the way mine are. I need to get some distance, and a cold shower. "I probably look like a ripe tomato and desperately need a shower."

"I love tomatoes." Is all he responds with, his eyes still searching mine. I want to tell him about my revelation, how I found Lucy's address and was running home in such a hurry to head over there. But I can't force the words to the surface. They're marinating in a sea of worry, self-doubt and undeniable fear. So much is riding on this and if I just say it nonchalantly it feels like I'm not giving it the weight it deserves.

This isn't something I'm doing on a whim. I mean, maybe a little, but finding Lucy has been on my mind since the moment I found her letters. I was able to distract myself with the fundraiser, working at the bakery and helping around here. But every night when I get into bed, she's there. I wonder what she looks like, how her voice sounds and if I look like her. Sometimes the what if's become so potent I end up climbing out my window just to breathe in the clean night air. Everything that comes with meeting Lucy is so massive, it feels wrong to play it down as anything but.

My body tingles, pulling me from my thoughts when I realize Mitch has taken a few steps closer and is gently pushing a lock of hair behind my ear. I don't know why, but I fucking love when he does that. It feels intimate in ways not related to sex. "Did you know tomatoes are actually botanically defined as a fruit, Olive?" His question seems random, and not really like a question at all as he leans in to inhale just behind my ear. My body turns to mush as he lightly licks the spot just behind my earlobe and I shiver despite the heat.

"So sweet." He murmurs against the sensitive skin. I take a shaky breath and count to ten before speaking knowing if I don't, my voice is going to come out as a squeak.

"Tomatoes, um…they're not really sweet though." I say as I lean into him, needing more. More of what, I don't know. I just know that anytime I'm near Mitch, I always want more. *Need* more.

"Not technically. But you are. You're sweeter than any fruit out there. It's a shame no one will ever be able to taste it." He clicks his tongue and my hands find his muscled chest on their own volition. I press my body into his and feel him take a deep lungful of air in. "Now that I've gotten a taste of you, it'll never be enough. I'll always want more of you."

Mitch plays with the hem of my shorts, running his finger along the lining that rests just below my most sensitive spot the one aching to be touched by him. It seems we're in agreement, because no amount of Mitch is enough. Even when he's touching me I want more.

Slowly, Mitch lowers his lips to mine, capturing them in a sweet and gentle embrace. I lean into the kiss and feel his tongue tease the seam of my lips, waiting for me to open for him. He deepens the kiss, grabbing the back of my neck pulling me further into him, as if it were even possible to get any closer. After several beats, he pulls back slightly and pierces me with those dark green eyes. "But Olive…" I look up at him with hooded eyes, desire pooling deep within them. "I don't like to share."

His admission has my heart racing and my underwear soaking through, no doubt. Is this his way of saying we're official? I'm afraid to ask on the off chance I'm wrong and he thinks I'm crazy. But why else would he stake claim like that if he didn't want us to be official? I feel his hand tilt my chin back up so we're face to face again. "You're mine, Olive."

"In case I haven't made that clear until this point, I wanted you to know where I'm at with you. With us. I don't want anyone else, you're the one who invades my every thought from the moment I wake up until the second my eyes close at night. And even then, you're in every dream."

This is the point in a movie where everyone would be screaming at the screen for me to kiss Mitch and accept what he's just said for what it is. We're together. In every sense of the word and that feels right. I rise up on my tiptoes and place a soft kiss on his lips before lowering myself back down. I keep his eyes locked with mine and offer a playful smile. "I don't like to share, either."

I took my shower, alone, after I was able to convince Mitch to sit downstairs and wait for me. Once I was dressed I headed into the kitchen to find him waiting at the island for me. Hearing me enter the room, he turns to face me with a mouthful of cookie and a guilty expression. I chuckle as I take in his boyish charm sneaking cookies, versus the rugged farm look he usually wears. The one that makes my heart race and insides turn to lava.

Swallowing audibly, he holds up his hands in surrender. "They were just sitting here, practically begging to be eaten."

"I get the sense Gran likes having you around. She's been making these cookies more often lately." I grab one as I round the counter and head to the fridge to pull out the glass bottle.

We get our milk delivered weekly by the local diary, and I swear its the best milk there is. I never had to suffer through that store bought shit some kids get. I gag at the thought.

Pouring two glasses of milk, I join Mitch and take a seat. We're quiet for a few minutes, sensing each other has something to say. I'm hoping he breaks the silence first because I still haven't figured out the best way to bring up my recent revelation.

When he doesn't say anything, still enjoying the fresh baked cookies Gran left on the counter, I break the silence. "I read another one of Lucy's letters today. I went to the pond after, needing something to cool me off." Mitch wipes the crumbs at the corner of his mouth on his napkin before turning in his seat to face me. "That's where I was running back from when I saw you on the porch."

"Are you okay?" He asks softly. Such an interesting question to be asked. It's simple enough, yet the answer weighs me down like a massive boulder. Am I okay? In the moments that followed reading the second letter, I just got up and ran to the pond. Needing to get my mind off the heat coursing through my body, lighting me up from the inside out. When I finally came to the conclusion I was going to find her, I ran home and got distracted by everything Mitch said.

Feeling the contradiction, I allow it to slip past my lips to Mitch's waiting ears. "Oddly, I am, but I'm also not. Does that make sense?" I ask with a light laugh. If anyone understands the feelings of being torn, it's Mitch. When he admitted he was attracted to me, he finally explained it in a way that made sense. He kept his distance from me because I was a distraction he didn't plan for. Wanting to give in, while trying to maintain control isn't easy.

Finding Lucy is a lot like that feeling. I so desperately want to meet her, get to know her and understand the decisions she was forced to make at such a young age. But on the other hand, I'm terrified. These letters are nearly two decades old, her feelings could have changed. I'm not a mother yet, so I can't begin to understand that pull one has to their child. I'd like to think feelings like that don't dissipate over time, but again, how the hell would I know?

Mitch nudges my chin up lightly with his finger. I resist his touch for a millisecond before meeting his gaze. "Whatever you decide to do is up to you, baby? No one can force you to make a decision you aren't ready for." His words are soft and sweet, genuine care flowing so easily off his tongue I'm ready and waiting to drink them in. "If you want to get in the truck right now and drive to where she is, I'm game. But if today isn't that day, that's okay too."

I lean forward until my head reaches his shoulder. I can feel tears brimming my eyes, and I wipe at them before they have a chance to spill over. Maybe this is where the expression *cry on my shoulder* came from. Mitch rubs a hand up and down my back in soothing motions. His other hand holds mine steady in his lap between us. Giving it a gentle squeeze, a reassurance or a term of endearment, I don't know. Nonetheless, it causes the butterflies in my stomach to take flight.

I look up to see Mitch inspecting me, "what comes next?" I wish I could give him an answer, not just for him but for me too. I know he would do anything to help me with this, and I want that so bad it's nearly suffocating. But I'm in no place to make a decision as big as this right now. Instead, I lace my fingers around his neck drawing him closer to me. I breathe in his scent and exhale feeling lighter and like no matter what comes next from this moment forward, I have him in my corner. What a fucking feeling that is.

Without answering his question, I jump up from the stool and head towards the backdoor. I look over my shoulder right at Mitch and hitch my head in the opposite direction. He takes the hint and rises to his feet, pushing the chair in like the gentleman he is, and takes my hand in his. I walk through the squeaky side door and go to take a seat on one of the Adirondack chairs nestled in the far corner of the porch. Before my butt fully hits the seat, Mitch lifts me up under the arms and cradles me against his chest as he lowers himself in the seat. A blush warms my cheeks at the simple gesture.

"What would I even say?" I ask after a few quiet moments together. Sitting here with him is like being in our own personal bubble, nothing can penetrate it. But I'm not that naive. Life is still out there pushing to get in and take control, as much as I want to stay inside this peaceful place, I have to face my life sooner or later.

"To Lucy?" He asks as he nestles his head into the crook of my neck. I nod, unsure of how else to respond. My voice feels weak, not able to articulate things in a normal decibel while it feels like my heart is literally ready to beat out of my chest cavity.

"I think its just one of those things you'll have to feel out once you see her. I doubt it's an easy thing to map out ahead of time." He's right, undoubtably. The reality is, there's no rulebook or manual to this kind of thing. I should just be happy I'm one of the people who was lucky enough to find letters from their birth parent. Some people have to go off of nothing and face rejection without any real preparation. Lucy at least confessed how much she loved me and didn't want to give me up, but ultimately did what she felt would be best for me in the long run.

I don't think I would have the guts to do the same. The idea of creating a life and having to hand them over to a stranger, trusting that person to raise the one thing you love most in the world. It gives me chills just thinking about it. Heaven forbid Mitch and I ever got ourselves in a similar situation, I don't think I would have it in me to give up my child. Seeing a baby that's half of me and half Mitch, my heart would shatter into a million pieces of love just looking at them.

Slowly but surely as they grow, those small fragments get pieced back together, because your child is the one thing that makes a heart whole. I can't imagine there ever being a love stronger than that of a child and parent. Having to give up that part of you is like accepting you'll never be whole again without them in your life. I wonder if that's how Lucy has felt all these years. Walking around knowing a part of her, a part she so desperately wanted to keep, is out there.

A single tear streaks down my face, painting my cheeks with the pain of this revelation. It's no longer a question. I have to meet Lucy, now. If not just for myself, but for her as well.

With my back against Mitch's chest, I turn to look at him. I know I don't even have to ask him to come with me, and a part of me wishes I could do this on my own. But I know I need his support and I know he'll be there for me in any way I ask. "I'm ready."

The windows are open, blowing in a sweet breeze off the fields on our right. The smell of summer is in the air, thick with the heat and harvest swirling around us like a soft blanket. It's comforting as we drive an hour to the address Lucy left me. I try to focus on the fields rolling by, the feel of Mitch's hand resting on my thigh, keeping my mind occupied with anything but where we're going. If I let myself realize the severity of what I'm doing, I'll fall apart.

I want to make a good impression, and if I show up crying hysterically that will just make things even more awkward, for everyone. I keep convincing myself none of that matters. It's not like I had a phone number to contact her and give her the heads up that I'm coming. What would I have said anyways? *Hey, this is Olive. Your long lost daughter you gave up for adoption nearly twenty years ago. Want to get some coffee?'* I cringe at the thought.

Showing up out of the blue feels like an ambush in some ways, but I truly think this was the only way to do it. Rip off the bandaid. Planning sets up expectations and I don't want to expect anything. I *can't.* By expecting anything to come from this meeting is just ensuring failure. So here I sit in the passenger seat of Mitch's truck, twenty minutes away from potentially meeting the woman who birthed me. I'm not freaking out. I'm internally combusting into a pile of ash that could easily be swept away with a gust of wind.

The car ride is quiet, except for the soft music Mitch has playing in the background. I try to focus on that so I don't spiral completely out of control. It reminds me of that first car ride we took together on our way to Raising Hope. A song came on that for whatever reason struck a nerve. I hadn't thought I'd ever heard it before, but my reaction to it was so strong.

I remember the look on Mitch's face, probably thought I was insane for acting like the song bothered me, then demanded he leave it on so I could hear it. Something about this drive feels like that one. Other than the feeling that Mitch hated me back then. It makes me laugh silently at how far we've come since then.

"Do you remember the song that was playing the first time we went to Raising Hope?" I ask.

I lift my head to look at him, his eyes never wavering from the road. "I do. Silver Springs by Fleetwood Mac. What made you think of that?" He replies easily. I'm a little surprised he remembered so quickly. Makes me feel like being around me wasn't as much of a bother as I originally thought.

"I don't know, it just came to mind. I was so worried you were going to think I was crazy for how I reacted to it. I don't know why but it did something to me." I laugh again at the memory.

"Well, to be fair, I did think you were a little crazy." He looks over and smirks at me. Jerk. "I'm kidding. I told you, sometimes we just hear something that resonates with us. Doesn't always have to be some deep kind of meaning to it." He shrugs and focuses back on the road. Not that it really needs his undivided attention. It's basically all flat out here, straight roads and open fields on either side. It would be dull as shit if I didn't find it oddly soothing.

I sift through what he said a few times before conceding that it must have just been a fluke thing. Maybe the song reminded me of something I've heard before and that's why I reacted. I take Mitch's phone in my hand and lift it up to him asking permission to change the music. He nods and I search through hundreds of artists from Cody Johnson to Florence + the Machine to Green Day. His taste in music is wider than these fields.

The name Fleetwood Mac catches my attention and I scroll down until I see Silver Springs. I want to hear it again and test my body's reaction. As soon as the song begins with instruments playing in perfect harmony, the goosebumps arise. Why does this song affect me so much? I look at Mitch and see him already glancing at me, trying to figure out my facial expressions and blanket of gooseflesh. I shrug lightly and shift my focus back out the window.

The next twenty minutes fly by until we're pulling down a dirt road that leads to a farm tucked behind a sea of trees. It's breathtaking here. The property is lined with tall white oak trees on either side, completely blanketing it from the road. It's like a peace of heaven tucked away in secret. Though I love where I grew up, I can't help but wonder if this is the farm Lucy grew up on and has always lived here. This might be where I would have grown up had she not placed me for adoption.

My heart is beating rapidly in my chest, drawing a look of concern from Mitch. He eases the truck into park and cuts the engine before turning to look at me. Taking one of my hands in his, he squeezes it reassuringly. "If you need to do this alone, I'll understand Olive."

I mull over his words and look at him with tears brimming my eyes. I smile weakly and nod my head. "I think I just needed your help getting here. But...I need to this on my own. I'm sorry." My words tumble from my mouth on a whisper and Mitch is already shaking his head.

"Baby, no. You don't need to apologize for a thing. I'm

happy you trusted me enough to share this with you. I'll be right here, okay?" He pulls me against him, hugging me to his chest before placing a soft kiss on my forehead.

With shaking hands, I reach for the door handle, pausing before opening it. My breathing feels erratic and my hands are shaking so bad you'd think I was epileptic. Mitch places a hand softly on my back. "You can do this, Butterfly." I use his words to fuel my need for answers, my need to meet this woman. I can't let the fear keep me from discovering where I came from. I can do this.

Mitch stays in the truck parked along the dirt road we drove in on. A short cobble path weaves to the left leading up to a beautifully crafted farmhouse with a tall brick chimney. The white shiplap is the perfect contrast against the black frame windows lined with dark greenery. It's like a Home Living magazine come to life.

The wrap around porch is completely wood, stained a dark walnut with intricate detailing around each banister. This property is well maintained, taken care of with precision to detail and a shit ton of hard work. The window boxes are a copper metal overflowing with flowers adding pops of color and greenery to the space. A wave of unease washes over me as I climb the steps to the porch slowly and one at a time. At home I skip every other landing as I bound up the steps, but here, I take each one deliberately.

The door to the farmhouse is open, only a screen stands between where I stand and potentially meeting Lucy. My finger dances just over the doorbell and I watch as my hand trembles, unable to press the little white button. Inside I can hear shuffling around and the smell of something heavenly. It reminds me of Gran and Pop, cooking at home with them or at the bakery. I feel a strong sense of guilt wash over me knowing that I have yet to tell them I know about the adoption. I can only imagine what my parents would say if they knew I was here. Hell, they probably already know.

With a quick shake of my head, in hopes to rid my body of the tremors, I wipe my hands on my shirt and firmly press the doorbell. My heart stops as reality sets in and I start to panic. Ready to back away and run to the truck where I'm in the safety of Mitch and the sense of peace I feel when he's near. Maybe I should have had him come with me after all.

Mid freak out, I hear a woman's voice coming from just inside the door. I turn abruptly and am met with the face of the woman I *know* is my mother. I can't explain how I know, call it intuition if you want, but nonetheless, it's there.

Our eyes meet and her shoulders slump forward ever so slightly. She assesses me for a brief moment before locking eyes with me once again. I can see the emotion behind her lids, the need to do something, evident on her face. I want to hug her, cry with her, ask her a million questions and learn everything I can. But I can't get to any of that before I even greet her.

Raising one hand awkwardly, my face blushes and I whisper softly, "Hi, I'm…". I try to smile but I know it's strained. This is the most surreal moment of my life and I can barely speak.

She opens her mouth to finish my greeting, and abruptly closes it, second guessing whatever she was about to say. Composing herself, she closes her eyes and takes a deep breath. When she reopens them, she offers me a gentle smile as she opens the screen door and steps onto the porch. Only a few feet away and no longer having the barrier of a door between us, I can smell the lavender and honeysuckle on her. It's comforting and inviting and I desperately want to lean into it but I also don't want to make this more weird than it already is.

We stand there for what feels like hours before she slowly reaches a hand out and takes one of mine in hers. With tears threatening to spill down her cheeks, she squeezes my hand and whispers, "Olive."

That's all it takes. Tears are streaming down both our faces as she pulls me into the hug I never realized I needed. All those times in my childhood when I didn't feel like I belonged, have disappeared. It all makes sense now, standing here hugging the woman who birthed me, who undoubtably loves me. I can feel the emotion coursing through us as we continue to embrace for several minutes. I guess I was right about this feeling, hoping she would know who I was and that I would know her as well. The second she rounded the corner and I saw her face, I knew her. Immediately.

We take a step back from one another and I laugh before I have a chance to cry more. "Hi." I say again because I'm still having a hard time formulating words at the moment. She looks exactly how I imagined she would. Long auburn hair, like mine, and the same skin tone. Her eyes are a dark chestnut color, whereas mine are hazel green. It makes me wonder if that's something I got from my birth father.

"Everyday I wake up wondering if it's going to be the day I get to see you again." She squeezes both hands in hers and smiles, but there's a touch of pain behind it. This must be so difficult for her, knowing I've been out there all these years and not be able to have some part in my life. I only just found out about her, and that alone still has it's challenges. But I can't even fathom spending the amount of years she has, in pain and longing to meet your first born.

"I take it you got my letters." She states matter of factly. I nod my head, unable to talk just yet. I know if I try, my voice will crack and come out as a squeak.

"We have so much to talk about, would you like to come in? Have some tea?" She gestures to the house and I look back over my shoulder to where Mitch is waiting in his truck. I hadn't thought this far ahead, clearly. I was so worried about getting here that I didn't think through what happens next. I can't leave Mitch waiting in a hot truck for who knows how long while I talk to Lucy. But he can't exactly leave either. We're an hour from home and I would never ask him to come back and get me. Sensing my hesitation Lucy speaks up, "Unless now isn't a good time."

"No, I'm sorry. I-I just have someone waiting for me in the car, and I didn't think this far ahead and where he might go while we...talk." I'm nervous, and it shows. My hands are clammy and I keep scanning the area around us hoping Mitch didn't listen when I said stay in the truck.

"He's welcome to join us if that makes you feel more at ease. I'm afraid there isn't a manual in dealing with these types of situations." The joke rolls off her tongue and instantly I laugh, because I had that same thought just a few hours ago. I wonder how many other mannerisms I have that are like her.

Needing a minute to breathe, I tell Lucy I'm going to get Mitch and we'll come back. As long as we aren't putting her out. She tsks at that remark and assures me our presence is more than welcome. "I'll start a pot of water for tea, take your time."

I jog down the path in the direction of Mitch and find him jumping from the cab of his truck to meet me. Before I reach him his eyes are laser focused on me, causing my breath to hitch. Shit, he really is nice to look at. "Are you okay?" He asks with a shaky voice. I'm sure waiting in the truck had his own mind reeling.

"I'm…Shit." I start to cry, but tamp down the raw emotion so I don't scare Mitch into thinking something is wrong. "I'm okay. She's…She's exactly what I pictured." I murmur against his chest because halfway through that sentence he was pulling me into a gripping hug. His familiar scent grounds me and I breathe in deeply, focusing on how he calms me.

"She asked if I wanted to come inside, but I didn't want to leave you out here sitting in the heat. Would you come in with me?" My voice sounds shy, probably due to all the emotions coursing through me right now.

"I'd be honored." Normally I would think he was being sarcastic, but Mitch knows how big a moment this is for me. So when he says he'd be honored, I know he means it.

We stayed at Lucy's for hours, not even realizing how much time had gone by. I could have talked to her well into the night, but knowing we have a drive ahead of us, we decided to call it a night. There's still so much I want to know about her, who she is now and who she was back then. How can one possibly get to know someone in such a short time? I feel like we've barely scratched the surface.

Today was perfect though, just the right amount of information without being overwhelming. Mitch was like an anchor the entire time, holding steady next to me keeping me grounded and safe. I'll have to properly thank him later.

Halfway through our drive home, I call Gran to check in and let her know I'm with Mitch. I don't like lying to her about where I am, but discussing this over the phone is not at all how I want to go about everything. We stop at a little diner for a quick dinner before getting back on the road. Thankfully Lucy only lives a little over an hour away, but that commute will get old quick I'm sure. Especially when there's nothing to look at but endless fields.

A yawn escapes my mouth and Mitch laughs from the drivers seat. "I don't know how you're so tired, Olive. It's not like today was a monumental day or anything." I swat his arm and settle into the seat a little more. I'm exhausted but also invigorated. I haven't felt this good in a long time, like I have something to look forward to again.

Organizing the fundraiser gave me a sense of purpose, something meaningful to work towards. I want that feeling back, and as tired as I am, I'm ready to dive head first into a new project. Meeting Lucy has awakened something, that has quite literally lit a spark in me.

An idea comes to mind and I bounce it around for several minutes before voicing it to Mitch. "I was thinking about something…" I let the words hang in the air, gauging Mitch's reaction.

"Uh oh. That can't be good." I frown at him. "I'm kidding Butterfly. What were you thinking?"

"The fundraiser we did for Gwen. Something about putting my energy into a good cause gave me a feeling of belonging, a feeling of purpose. I want to have that again." I let my admission swirl around before continuing. "With everything that's happened with Pop, I think we should do something nice for him and Gran."

Years ago Gran teased Pop about renewing their vows. He brushed it off playfully, saying they already have so much on their plates. But I could tell it was something Gran really wanted.

Mitch sits up straighter in his seat, a smile stretching wide across his face. "What were you thinking? I mean truthfully it doesn't even matter, I'm on board either way."

Gazing at him, I feel another wave of warm emotion course through my veins taking root very close to my heart. I've never been in love, not with anyone, and I'm not sure if what I feel towards Mitch is even that. But I can tell with absolute certainty, what I feel for him is stronger than anything else I've felt. That knowledge surges through me with equal fervor and fear

17

MITCH

Another excruciatingly hot day comes to an end as I grab my shirt, soaked with sweat, and head back to the house. It's been a week since I took Olive to meet her birth mom. Since then she's been in full swing planning a vow renewal for her grandparents. Collin is planning to head back to New York in a few days so Olive and my mom are frantically trying to pull it all together before he leaves.

Since the fundraiser was only two weeks ago, we decided to reuse a lot of the lights and hay bales we used for that. A simple setup with lots of lights and flowers. Olive decided to keep it a secret for now, so with the help of my mom they've already managed to get a lot of the details locked down.

Most of the vendors we had for the fundraiser are more than happy to come back and help, one of the many reasons it's evident how loved Joan and Henry are around here. This community pulls together at the drop of a hat, something you don't see everywhere. I'm amazed at how easily people are willing to lend a hand, and now I can see why Olive enjoys this so much.

I can hear her voice before I'm even inside the house. The sound carries through the air like the sweetest ballad.

going straight to my chest. I rub the spot where I can feel the familiar ache, something I've grown accustom to since being around Olive. I've dated a lot of different women since high school and throughout college, but none of them ever made me *feel* anything.

Rounding the corner to the kitchen, I spot Olive and my mom huddled together looking at something on the counter. Neither of them has seen me yet so I take this moment to stare unashamedly at Olive. The way the loose strands from her hair fall around her face, framing it perfectly. The way her smile seems to light up the room with a natural glow that can't be replicated. The sound of her laugh as she squeezes her eyes shut and throws her head back at something Ma said. I could watch this all day.

When it comes to Olive, I'm so fucked. She already has such a hold on me and I doubt she even knows it. I'm constantly thinking of ways to make her happy, prove to her how much she already means to me. I shift my weight as I lean against the doorframe and the floorboards beneath my feet squeak, drawing the attention of my mom and Olive.

"Mitchell! You startled me." Ma places a hand on her heart like the dramatic soap opera actress she is and I don't miss the way Olive giggles into her hand. I can't help but smile in return, unashamed of being caught staring and uncaring that my mom is grabbing her dishrag likely planning to throw it at me. "Don't just lurk in the doorway like that, you'll scare off our sweet Olive here." Ma wraps an arm around Olive's shoulder and pulls her in for a side hug.

"Ma, I've been around Olive long enough now that I think

if anything were going to scare her off it would be you." I duck out of the way just as her dishrag comes flying at my face. I chuckle and stick out my tongue at her since she missed. Raising two rambunctious boys trained Ma for these kind of interactions, this is nothing new.

"Olive, dear. I apologize for my sons lack of manners this afternoon. Surely he must be spendin' too much time out in the sun, it's fryin' his brain cells." Ma fixes me with a stern look, only making me laugh even more.

"Well, despite his comment just now, he's been a perfect gentleman. You and Mr. Murphy have raised him well." I don't miss the way her face blushes slightly. My sweet Olive is thinking about less than holy things as she sits right beside my mother. I plan to give her shit about that later.

I wink at her and make my way around the kitchen island to grab an apple in the bowl by the sink. There's never a lack of fresh fruit around here, or vegetables. One of the perks to living on a farm I suppose.

Biting into the apple, I lean over to see what it is Ma and Olive are working on so intently. There's papers and magazines spread out all over the countertop, all jumbled together in a heaping pile. My brows pull together in confusion just as Olive turns to face me.

"We're sifting through ideas for the renewal this weekend. It seemed like such a great idea to have it so soon until the actual planning came into play. We may have bitten off more than we can chew." Olive worries her bottom lip, drawing it into her mouth and nibbling it gently. I want to be the one to nibble that lip and other things…

I should really go shower before my mom catches me with a hard on right in front of her. That would earn me more than a swat from her dishrag.

"Nonsense." My mom says to Olive, patting her hand sweetly. "We have lots of help already, and everyone from the fundraiser is happy to pitch in again. I think they genuinely enjoyed that night." I exchange a smile with Olive, remembering everything that transpired that day. The shower leading up to the fundraiser as well as the event itself. Seeing how happy Gwen was, that made everything worth it.

"If I can get your father on board, I was thinkin' we could have regular events on the farm going forward. Maybe like food truck Fridays or somethin' akin to that. What do you think?" Ma asks.

Olive's eyes light up at the mere idea of that, and if I had to guess she's more than delighted. "Sounds like a great idea, Ma. Between the two of you and the town behind you, I'm sure it would be a hit."

Finishing my apple, I toss the core into the compost bucket by the back door and face the women still huddled over the counter discussing seating arrangements. I say we just use the hay bales again, but I don't dare cut into their planning.

"I'm gonna head upstairs to shower." I say as I lean in to give Olive a quick peck. I'm not sure how she feels about public displays of affection, especially in front of my mom, so I keep it chaste.

As I skip every other step on my way up the stairs I realize Olive and I haven't been alone since we went to meet her birth mom last week. I've been so busy on the farm while she and my mom dove right into planning for this weekend. I never got a chance to talk to her about Gwen coming by to tell me she saw Drew.

The piece of paper with his information on it has been burning a hole in my desk drawer, I never even unfolded it to see the contents. Too afraid that by seeing them would make the reality that much more real. All Gwen told me was that he seemed well, but that could mean a number of things. One persons definition of *'well'* isn't always another.

I strip off my dirty clothes, tossing them in the hamper as I head to the bathroom. If my mom weren't here, I would have invited Olive to join me for round two in the shower. I don't know when my mind started acting like a teenager going through puberty again, but touching Olive in any way I can is *all* I seem to think about these days. My fingers twitch with the need to touch her soft skin, feel her writhe against me as I explore her most sensitive spots.

As soon as I'm done with this *cold* shower, I'm taking her out. With everything we've both had going on, I'd say it's well earned. Selfishly, I want her all to myself. As of late, I've had to share her between both our work schedules, her spending time with Ma, and meeting her own mother. I may have to share her during the day, but tonight, she's *mine*.

At seven o'clock on the dot, I walk up the steps to Olive's house. The door is open and I can hear the tv on in the adjacent room where Henry sits next to Joan. They always seems so content to just be with one another, I hope one day I find that same happy stillness with someone.

I knock lightly on the screen door, attracting Joan's attention. She waves me in with a smile and I make my way over to greet them both. "Good evening you two, watching anything good?"

"Just some old re-runs." Henry declares. He looks well, despite what he's been through the last several weeks, he seems to be recovering. This weekend might be just what they need.

After a few minutes chatting with Olive's grandparents, I hear the squeak of the stairs just before Olive rounds the corner. Her hair is down in loose wavy curls, she has a smattering of makeup, highlighting her natural beauty and making her eyes pop against the black mascara.

My eyes travel down to the simple white cotton dress she's wearing, thin straps hanging delicately on her shoulders. It's the same dress she was wearing the day we met. Her cheeks flush as my eyes shamelessly roam her beautiful figure. My fingers twitch by my sides, desperately wanting to reach out and touch her, knowing I can't considering the company we're in.

She stops short, eyes scanning the room and I realize not only am I enamored with her entrance, but her grandparents are also eyeing her. Her cheeks blush a deep scarlet and I can't help the smile that spreads across my face.

The way Joan is looking at Olive is far different from the way Henry is looking back and forth between the two of us. Brows furrowed with a scowl on his face, if I wasn't worried about what he was thinking, I would find it funny. Olive is his only grandchild, and a beautiful girl at that. I imagine he's looking at me like the guy who's about to whisk her off and get her pregnant.

Joan would probably be thrilled by that, along with my mom. Jesus I can't stand here thinking about impregnating Olive when we haven't even had sex yet. The thought crosses my mind to inform them of that fact. But that would imply pure intentions, and when it comes to Olive, my intentions are anything but pure.

The attention is making Olive nervous, it's easy to detect as she fiddles with the strap of her purse hanging by her side. That and the fact that her cheeks are still a rosy red. She clears her throat and focuses on me, "Should we get going?"

"After you." I smile and lift my arm gesturing to the front door. Joan rises to her feet and points a finger at me then directs it at Olive. I freeze under her gaze, reading for whatever warning she's about to throw our way.

"Don't bring her home too late." She fixes me with a stare I'm sure she's trying to make menacing, but honestly she looks adorable with her glasses resting on the bridge of her nose and her housecoat tied firmly around her waist. "I'm sure you're aware of a reasonable hour Mitchell."

She then turns her attention to Olive, still pointing one finger. "And you…Better bring me home dessert from wherever he's taking you." I have to stifle a laugh. I know for a fact she is as serious as a heart attack. Fuck, Henry literally just had a heart attack just a few weeks ago and I have the gall to make a joke about it. Albeit in my mind, but still.

"Of course, Gran. I know what you like." Olive leans in to give her a soft hug, looking over her shoulder to roll her eyes at me. This time I can't help the laugh that escapes, and Joan turns to looks at me. Olive distracts her by saying goodnight and then ushers me towards the door.

Joan is one of the kindest people I've ever known, but she can still pack a punch. She's protective over the things that matter to her, probably why her and my mom hit it off right away. Kindness matters to them, but above everything else, family comes first.

"That was close." I laugh as we walk down the front steps towards my truck.

"I'm surprised she let that slip, you laughed pretty loud and Gran doesn't like to be left out of an inside joke. Though, I wouldn't call me rolling my eyes at her an inside joke." She says on an exhale.

I round the side of the truck to open her door for her, rewarding me with one of her megawatt smiles. The one that reaches my toes. I feel like a lovesick puppy when I'm around her, and I'm kicking myself for not taking her out on a proper date sooner.

She is absolutely stunning, and I'm almost certain she would brush off that compliment if I tried telling her such. I hate when people have a hard time seeing themselves the way others do. To me, Olive could hang the moon, the stars and everything else in the universe, and I would still find her even more captivating than the day before.

After helping her into her seat, I climb in the drivers side and start the truck, heading down the gravel road to town.

"May I ask where you're taking me this evening, Mitchell?"

I glance in her direction, "Olive, only my mom calls me that. First warning." I try to sound playful, but I also want to temp her into doing it again.

"Ooh, I'm scared." She holds up both hands in mock horror. Oh yeah, I'm going to enjoy giving her a punishment to my liking. Something tells me she'll enjoy it too...

"You're playing with fire Ms. Fournier. I would like nothing more than to bend you over my knee and smack that tight little ass of yours." She releases a gasp, and I like that I've stunned her to silence. I chance a look at her and all the color has drained from her previously pink cheeks. Now all I want to do is find all the ways to paint it back.

She doesn't say anything for several minutes, and I enjoy the state of shock I've put her in. If she's quiet for a reason other than surprise, I'd say she's fantasizing about me holding true to my word. In due time.

"It just so happens, I got us a table at Della's." I wouldn't say it's fine dining, but it is the nicest restaurant around. I could have taken her a few towns over but I didn't want to waste time driving. I have other plans for her after dinner. Not that I plan on telling her that.

"Mitch. You didn't have to do that. Della's is a *really* nice restaurant." She looks down at her dress and tugs at it self-consciously. God, this woman really doesn't know how breathtaking she is. I plan on finding every way possible to show her just how beautiful she is.

Inside and out.

"You look perfect, Olive. Stop worrying." I reply easily.

"How do you know I'm worrying?" She counters.

"Baby, you're biting your bottom lip, something you do when you're anxious I've come to learn. And if you keep doing it, I'm going to have to take over and bite it myself." My eyes are dark, I'm sure she can't tell in the darkness of the cab, but I'm willing to bet she can feel the hunger emanating from me.

Before she has a chance to respond, I ease the truck into a spot outside the restaurant. I'm glad I had the foresight to make a reservation, it would have been embarrassing to usher her in there just to be turned away.

Olive starts to open her door, but I'm around the truck and taking her hand before even one of her feet hit the pavement. Chivalry isn't dead, Ma would say if she were here. My Dad always did little things like this for her, opening doors and pulling out her chair. It's not like she isn't capable of doing it herself, but it's a small act I always viewed as respect.

Taking Olive's hand I lead her to the restaurant. There's a slight gleam in her eyes, no doubt wondering where this gentleman act came from. We didn't get off to the best start in the beginning, something Ma smacked me for, so I'm trying to make up for it now.

"When I was a teenager, both my parents, on separate occasions, told me how to treat a girl." I wink as I open the door to the restaurant for her. "I guess a few things stuck." She meets me with a smile before heading inside.

Dinner was perfect. One of the best steaks I've had in a long time, cooked just the way I like it too. Olive searched the menu several times, trying to find the least expensive dish I'm sure, until I assured her she can order whatever she wants. Her experience with guys is minimal, something she disclosed to me when we first started getting to know each other. I'm guessing what little experience she does have was spent with guys who didn't deserve an ounce of her attention.

I plan on changing her outlook.

"How's your ice cream?" I ask just as she darts her tongue out to sample it. Something as simple as licking an ice cream cone has my body drunk with need. I clear my throat and focus back on my own ice cream cone as she hums in delight.

Guess that's my answer.

18

Olive

The day of my grandparents vow renewal is here, and I'm freaking out. A few days ago I snuck into their closet and pulled out a suit for Pop and a dress with Gran's measurements. I wanted to do something special for her and have a dress made. The idea was great at first, but now I'm anxiously pacing the store of the seamstress praying it'll all work out.

Gran never has an excuse to dress up, so I didn't want to make it too fancy that she's uncomfortable. However, I did want to make it a little dressy considering the occasion.

I'm trying not to appear impatient, but we only have a few hours until the renewal and my grandparents don't even know about it yet. I'm starting to worry keeping this a secret was a big mistake. I know Gran wants this, even if she'll never admit it. But what if it's too much for Pop? Before I can freak myself out any more than I already am, Bridget comes out with the dress.

She smiles widely at me holding up the garment bag containing a custom dress just for Gran. I have some money saved up but you can never tell how much these things will cost. I'm nervous to ask but right now I just want to focus on the dress itself and deal with the price after.

"I'm really excited about this one." Bridget says as she hangs the garment bag on a hook to unzip it. "Miss Joan has been a wonderful role model in my life throughout the years, nothing makes me happier than to do this for her."

"I can't thank you enough, Bridget. I know this was a lot to ask on such short notice." She simply waves me off and begins unzipping the bag to reveal a long cream colored dress with delicate lace overlays. The sleeves are elbow length and the see through lace matches the overlay throughout the dress. It's perfect. Simple enough that Gran won't feel overwhelmed, but dressy enough to hopefully make her feel special.

"Bridget…It's perfect! Thank you!" I can't help myself, I pull her in for a hug feeling my throat thick with emotion. My grandparents are wonderful people, and they truly deserve a special day like this to remind them why they're right for one another. I release her, wiping away tears before they can slip down my face. I already had my makeup done, and I don't want to risk ruining it before the ceremony even begins.

She zips the dress back up and hands it over to me, beaming with pride and love. "How much do I owe you?" I ask, hoping what I have with me is enough.

With a smile and both hands held up she simply states that it's on the house. I nearly choke on my tongue because there's no way in hell I'm going to allow this sweet woman to work this hard, on such short notice, without being paid for her time. "Bridget, absolutely not." I begin to protest.

"Olive, stop. I was honored you came to me and asked

that I do this for Joan. It wouldn't sit right with me to accept your money." She takes my hands in hers since I practically dropped the garment bag when she told me the dress was free. "I only ask one favor." She states.

"Yes. Anything!" I reply eagerly.

"If anyone asks where she got the dress, you direct them here." She says playfully.

"Are you kidding? I'm about to steal a bunch of your business cards and hand them out as parting gifts." I chuckle but Bridget doesn't miss the not so subtle way I glance around her in search of said business cards.

"I appreciate the enthusiasm dear, I'll see you in a few hours." She hugs me again and five minutes later I'm rushing home to break the news of tonights festivities to my grandparents. Thank heavens for Elaine. She's meeting me at the house to tell them and help them get ready. I'm suddenly really nervous as I round the corner and head up the drive to the house.

I park the car and get out with Gran's dress just as Mr. And Mrs. Murphy pull in. They both get out and a wave of ease washes over me. I'm not in this alone, every step of the way the Murphy family has been there helping me pull this off. Who knew this idea that came to me out of the blue would turn into such a big event with dozens of people pitching in?

I hoped it would feel similar to the way I felt leading up to the fundraiser, and after. And it does, but there's also another emotion wrapped in it as well. Gwen means so much to the town and to so may people, myself included. But these are my grandparents. The two people who helped raise me and get me through the most difficult time of my life. I owe them everything. I owe them for the person I am today and for every gap they filled in my heart over the years. I am who I am because of *them*.

I want tonight to prove to them how grateful I am. I want them to feel special and most importantly, I want them to feel seen.

Elaine smiles at me so big, and her confidence helps my nerves, but only slightly. I can feel my anxiety building with each step I make towards the house. "Jesus, I'm so nervous." I confess as I ascend the front steps. "What if they aren't up for this? Maybe I shouldn't have kept it a secret." Mr. Murphy is the one who stops me, and I glance back at him confused. Not sure what to expect from him, this is not a man of many words.

"Olive, dear. Years of living with this wonderful woman by my side, I've learned a few things." He winks at Elaine then returns his attention back to me with both hands lightly holding me in place. I look up and focus on the man with eyes like Mitch and a heart of gold like Elaine.

"What you've done here, what this will mean to Joan and Henry…It's not something that can be fabricated. You've put your heart and soul into planning a beautiful night for the two people who mean the most to you. You have *nothing* to be nervous about. I promise you."

Elaine wipes away a tear behind us and I let out the deep breath I'd been holding. I couldn't have done this without them, something I hope they know. "Okay." I breathe out again, "Let's do this."

With Mr. And Mrs. Murphy behind me, I make my way into the house and find my grandparents sitting on the back porch reading together. They're always so content around each other, existing in a comfortable stillness. It makes my heart expand with so much love and adoration.

"Hi Gran, Pop. Beautiful afternoon, isn't it?" My voice sounds choppy and nervous, and I feel Elaine wrap a reassuring arm around my shoulder, keeping me grounded. "We have a little surprise for the two of you." I whisper, and both their heads snap up to look at me.

"What kind of surprise dear?" Gran asks as she sets her book down. Now I feel like my nerves are seeping over to her and getting her anxious. I remind myself of my life motto these days, and decide to rip it off like a band aid.

"With the help of the Murphy family, as well as the rest of the town…We have put together a vow renewal ceremony for you and Pop…tonight." I let the news sink in for several seconds before my heart rate kicks into overdrive. My body is vibrating with nervous energy and Elaine has to practically hold me still to keep from bouncing off the porch.

They're quiet for far too long, longer than I expected. At the very least I figured Pop would have grunted with some kid of disapproval by now. Instead, they exchange a glance. The kind of glance only a married couple who has spent more than half their lives together could understand. The kind of unspoken language meant only for them.

Pop nods his head ever so slightly at Gran before she turns her eyes, brimming with tears, back to me. Without a word, she rises from her chair and comes to stand in front of me. She takes my hands in her own and smiles at me. "Thank you." She murmurs, quiet enough that I'm sure I'm the only one who heard it. I'm momentarily puzzled, having not expected such a calm reaction from either of them. But when she pulls me into a rib crushing hug, I know this was the right thing.

Elaine claps her hands behind us, wiping tears from her eyes. "Okay! Let's get a move on. We have a bride and groom to get ready!"

Mr. Murphy takes Pop into the house to help him with his suit, while Elaine and I begin doing Gran's hair and makeup. We keep the makeup light and simple, just the way she likes it and her signature French twist with a beautiful barrette. I haven't told her about the dress yet when she gets up to scan the items in her closet.

"I'm not sure I have anything suitable for a vow renewal." She worries her bottom lip, the way I always do, and the similarity bring me an odd sense of joy. Even though we aren't blood related, we're family. That's not something that can ever be changed.

"Well, I took the liberty of having something made for you, Gran." I say as I ease up beside her holding the zipped garment bag. Her eyes find mine in a sweet and pleading gesture. "Bridget made you a one of a kind custom piece, and it's beautiful. I hope you like it." I hang the bag up and begin unzipping it to reveal the elegant dress masked inside. When Gran gets her first full look at the dress, she cries more than before.

"Oh my." Her fingers reach out to stroke the material with

feather light touches. "This reminds me of the gown I wore when I married Henry forty-five years ago." She sniffles as Elaine hands her a handkerchief. "Did you give her a picture of my wedding dress, dear?" Gran asks and honestly I never even thought to do that. I shake my head in disbelief that Bridget was able to capture something so memorable without having seen Gran's first dress.

After we get Gran into the gown, which fits like a glove. I have her follow me out to the field in front of our house. Mr. Murphy is planning to bring Pop out there as a surprise first look before we head over to the renewal. As she steps out onto the porch, I see the moment she notices Pop standing with his back to us in the field. It's as if everything else around her fades away, and all she can see is the love of her life waiting for her.

Wren, a local student is working on building her photography portfolio, so I recruited her for the day. She offered to work for free in exchange for use of all the photos she captures today. She's standing a few feet behind Pop waiting for Gran to walk down so she can capture the moment. It almost feels like a real wedding, and I'm thankful I get to witness their love this way.

I help Gran through the tall grass until she's a few feet away from Pop. Giving her a hug and a smile of encouragement, I step back and allow them their moment. The entire time Wren is clicking away, grabbing as many candid moments as her camera will allow.

With tears brimming her eyes, Gran steps forward and gently places her left hand on Pop's back. On a deep inhale, he turns around to face Gran, after a few seconds he releases his breath, tears of his own threatening to spill over. Myself and Elaine have given up hope of keeping it together, as we stand arm in arm crying like a bunch of babies. Mr. Murphy stands strong behind Elaine, holding her left hand in his and I don't miss the gentle way he whispers in her ear.

I'm witness to two great love stories, right before me. The growing and glowing evolution of marriage and creating a strong partnership with one person you've given the most sacred part of yourself to. The tears continue to flow as I watch Pop take Gran in his arms and hold her close to him, silently ensuring he'll never let her go. This moment makes me wish my parents were here. They shared a love a lot like my grandparents and the Murphy's, I can only hope to have a love as great as all theirs one day. Seeing this display of true love makes me never want to lower my own standards for happiness.

After a few minutes in the field taking pictures, we head over to the Murphy's to begin the ceremony. It's twilight, and the lighting was breathtaking as Wren had Gran and Pop pose candidly for photos. Once she develops them, I plan to have a few black and white prints made to hang next to their original wedding photos.

It took some convincing, but I managed to blindfold my grandparents so that everything is a surprise as they walk down the aisle arm in arm. We worked so hard on bringing together a simple yet elegant look, I just hope they both love it the way I think they will.

Everyone is gathered outside the barn, seated on hay bales

covered with soft blankets to keep from being pricked by hay. The lights we used for the fundraiser a couple of weeks ago, are strung up like canopies above us giving off a soft glow. Gwen was gracious enough to officiate the vow renewal, and she smiles at me as she waits by the doors to the barn. I quickly take my seat next to Mitch in the front row, along with Mr. And Mrs. Murphy.

"You look stunning, Butterfly." Mitch whispers in my ear as the soft instrumental version of *'Turning Page'* begins to play. Call me girly, but once I heard that song during Edward and Bella's wedding in Twilight: Breaking Dawn, I knew it would be perfect.

"You clean up nice too, Mitchell." He pinches my hip and I cover my mouth to stifle the laugh threatening to ruin this moment. I guess it's my own fault for using his full name at a time like this. I should have known he would do something as payback. Before I can say anything else, Gwen raises her arms indicting us to please rise.

Turning around, I see Pop guiding Gran down the aisle lined with babies breath, both glowing with megawatt smiles and acknowledging the guests in attendance. They make their way to the front where Gwen is waiting to begin the vow renewal. Mitch takes my hand in his and squeezes gently. I rest my head on his shoulder as I watch my grandparents once again vow to love one another not only in this life but in the next.

What I wouldn't do for a love as powerful as theirs.

After fixing my makeup, again, I walk into the barn where we're hosting the reception. After the ceremony, we opened the big barn doors to reveal the inside. Modern light bulbs hang from every rafter above us casting the barn in a warm glow. I loved the contrast of modern and vintage when Elaine and I spent hours upon hours looking through wedding magazines for inspiration. The dark beams in the barn up against modern lights with tons of greenery and babies breath. Simple and elegant.

The live band that came out for the fundraiser generously joined us again to celebrate tonight. Something we were thrilled about considering how much the crowd loved them a few weeks ago. People are already dancing, enjoying themselves as trays of hors d'oeuvre get passed around. With the help of people in town, we managed to set up a huge buffet for everyone to eat and sample as much as they want, rather than a traditional sit down meal.

Maureen and the staff at Fournier's took care of all the desserts, and judging by the looks of it, I'd say the dessert table is just as big as the food table. Plus, we have a s'mores station set up around the fire pits for anyone who wants to roast marshmallows. I will most definitely be making a few.

My grandparents sit at a small sweetheart table centered in the room as guests make their way over to congratulate them. I haven't had a moment alone with them since we told them about tonight, but right now I just want them to enjoy themselves. They truly deserve a night like this after everything they've been through.

Before heading to my seat, I stand at the entrance to the

barn, taking in the event before me. People laughing and dancing, enjoying good home cooked food in the company of this town. My heart is full of love and pride, and there's no one I'd want to share this with other than Mitch. I catch him out of the corner of my eye striding towards me with his farm boy swag and my heart skips a beat.

He sidles up next to me and folds me into his chest, kissing me softly on the head. "Do you always smell this good?" He asks as he breathes me in. I'll never get used to the ways I seem to affect him, or the way my body hums in recognition. At first it was weird, the way I reacted to him when he was close, now it's like second nature. My body knows his like it knows my own. It's like we're two perfectly cut pieces that just fit together seamlessly.

"I don't know." I tip my head back to look at him. "Do you always taste this good?" I ask as I lift up on my tiptoes to kiss him deeply. I snake my arms around his neck, pulling him in closer as I explore his mouth with my own. I open for him just as he slips his tongue past my lips. The taste of him is almost intoxicating, setting my skin on fire. After dinner I was planning to make s'mores, but now I'm thinking of indulging in a different kind of dessert.

Mitch pulls away and looks at me with hooded eyes. If I could extricate us without being seen, I would in a heartbeat. But the evening is just beginning, I can't take my leave just yet. As if reading my mind, Mitch snakes a hand around my neck and nibbles the sensitive flesh just below my ear. "If I could sneak you out of here unseen, you'd have no chance of escaping me."

Blood rushes to my core, engulfing me in an internal inferno, and if I don't get a little distance from his tight grasp, I will literally combust. I place my hands on his firm chest and give a slight push. "I need some air or you're going to make me miss the rest of this celebration, Mitchell." I smirk at the use of his full name again, and if I didn't know better, I'd say he's starting to like it.

He pulls me in, groaning into my neck again before biting my earlobe. "Butterfly, you're going to pay for it every time you use my full name. That's twice tonight." He releases me and steps back before offering me his hand and leading me to our table. I'm flustered froths words, but hide it quickly as we approach his parents and Collin at the table.

Collin decided to extend his stay a few days so he was here for the celebration. He leaves the day after tomorrow and I have yet to bend his ear on New York City. I have so much I want to ask, and I'm hoping he might have some connections to the galleries I sent resumes to. I thought about asking Mitch if he knew, but with everything we've been doing the last two weeks, it kept slipping my mind.

Can't even figure out how I form coherent sentences when I'm around him.

It's nearly ten o'clock, and I can tell Gran and Pop are exhausted. Just a few hours ago they didn't even know any of this was taking place. Add in all the emotions of the day, and I can see how beat they are. Elaine and Mr. Murphy offer to take them home after saying goodbye to all the guests. Quite a few people are still happily dancing and drinking while the rest have either gone home or are gathered around the fire.

I make my way over to my grandparents just as they're about to head out. Gran pulls me in to one of her bone crushing hugs and I can feel a few of her tears dot my shoulder. "Olive, how you ever managed to pull this off I'll never know. But your grandfather and I are so touched." She pulls away to look at me, my own tears matching hers. I don't know when the hell I became so emotional, but these waterworks lately are fucking with me.

"The detail, the amount of work y'all did to make this come about, it's…I'm so proud of you, honey." She sniffles again and Pop comes to join us, wrapping an arm around us both.

"My sweet Ollie, thank you for this. Your grandmother has always joked about having a vow renewal, and you made that dream come to life for her." His soft hand touches my cheek in a loving gesture and I let a few more tears fall. "My only dream is to see her happy, and you made that happen tonight." He pulls me in for a full hug and I cry into his shoulder allowing my love for them both to consume me.

After another round of hugs and a fit of laughter at our show of waterworks, they're in the car and heading home. Mitch wraps his arms around me from behind and nuzzles into my neck. My thoughts from earlier tonight come rushing back. I'm tired, but exhilarated. This night went exactly as I'd hoped and while crashing in bed and sleeping until noon sounds great, I have something else in mind that sounds even better.

I turn around in Mitch's arms and wrap my own around his neck. Kissing him softly, I memorize the softness of his lips on mine. As I pull back I see a wave of emotions run through his deep green eyes. I could get lost in them and never find the need to be found.

He gently pulls me onto the dance floor as *'Love You Anyway'* by Luke Combs comes on. I'm brought back to when we first slow danced to this song at the Raising Hope fundraiser. That feels like eons ago when it was only a few weeks. We sway to the music as Mitch pulls me against his chest and I settle against him allowing him to lead. Thinking about everything that's transpired between us this summer, it makes me wonder what changed for him. How he went from smug and detached to caring and attentive.

I pull back and look up at him to find him already looking at me. "In the beginning," I start, trying to find the right way to ask. "You acted like you hated me when we first met. What changed?"

He's thoughtful for a moment, thinking of how he wants to answer another one of my random thoughts. With a soft expression he replies easily. "I didn't hate you, Olive. I only did that to convince myself to stay away from you." He tucks a loose curl behind my ear and my knees tremble a little at the gesture. "But it didn't work. I never should have wasted so much time keeping my distance, when all along you were the thing I needed." Without caring about the dozens of curious eyes around us, Mitch leans in and kisses me sweetly.

I never expected to have a moment of clarity where I felt the time was right. But I can say with full honesty, now feels right. Being with Mitch, and connecting with him in every way possible feels more right than anything else I've experienced. Releasing my arms from around his neck, I take one of his hands in mine and tug gently. Looking a little puzzled, just pull him behind me until we're alone outside.

"Did you leave the lights up at the pond?" I ask as I turn to face him.

"Of course." His eyes are laser focused on me and my breath hitches in my throat.

"Good. Let's go for a walk." I lace my fingers through his and start walking towards the path that leads to the pond. No one can see us from here so slipping away unnoticed isn't a problem. I should feel nervous knowing what I want to happen when we get there. But if anything, I feel confident. I know what I want.

I want Mitch.

19

MITCH

Olive takes my hand in hers and leads me in the direction of the pond. I can already feel where this is going, and I'm more than ready. But I want to make sure she is too. We never had a full conversation about how inexperienced she is. Knowing I was the first to ever touch her though, I'm more than positive she's a virgin. It's not something I felt I should bring up, if she wanted to tell me then she would have. But if I had to guess, I'd say she's self conscious about it. Something I wish I could tell her she has no reason to be.

Olive being a virgin just makes her all the more special. If she allows me the privilege of getting that part of her…Fuck, that's not something I take lightly.

We walk hand in hand down the tree lined path that leads to the pond. The lights are solar powered, so they're already twinkling above us like our own personal patch of stars. The warm lights illuminate Olive's face, making her look ethereal, especially in her dress from the vow renewal.

She's wearing a lavender colored floor length dress that hugs her body in all the right places. The fabric is silky with delicate lace cap sleeves. It's simple and elegant, everything she is and as much as I love her in this dress, I am more than ready to get her out of it.

After the night I brought her here to surprise her with the paint supplies, I brought a bin down with blankets and pillows. Not just for when we're here together, but if she ever needed a comfortable place to relax there would be something for her to rest on. At the time I hadn't given it too much thought, but tonight I'm feeling extra thankful I had the foresight to bring them here.

Olive releases my hand as she walks to the edge of the pond and dips one of her bare feet in, testing the temperature. I hook my hands in my pockets and lean against a tree, just watching her. She's captivating, I just wish she could see herself the way I see her. If I could paint as well as she can, I would paint her exactly the way I want her to view herself. Breathtaking and confident.

"How's the water?" I ask. My voice coming out gravely with desire.

"It's perfect, actually." She replies easily as her eyes find mine. There's a nervous energy around her, but there's something else there too. It's like fear and desire melding together leaving her body unsure of what to do. It would be so easy to go to her, slowly undress her and show her how much she means to me. But everything we may or may not do, I want to be her choice. She's completely in control.

I'm still watching her, trying to control my own need to touch her when she reaches behind her and starts unzipping her dress. My breath hitches in my throat and I cough a little before regaining my composure. My body is rigid against the tree as I watch the fabric pool at her feet, leaving her standing there almost bare. From here she looks naked, but as my gaze focuses more closely, I can see she's wearing a matching nude bra and panties set. It's completely see through and made entirely of lace. My fingers itch with the need to caress the fabric over her nipples, waiting for them to pebble at my touch.

Just when I think she's about to wade into the water, she unclasps her bra dropping it to the ground with her dress and panties. Shit. Now she actually is completely naked and on full display for my hungry eyes. I take her in as she slowly walks in the water, submerging herself to her neck. The water hugs her every curve as it dances around her soft skin glowing under the lights in the trees.

I'm frozen in place, still standing next to the tree. Although now I need it for *actual* support. She turns in the water and locks eyes with me once again, a hunger of her own emanating from them. Olive lifts her hand out of the water and hooks a finger gesturing me to join her. In an instant, my dress pants and shirt are hitting the ground next to her clothes, and I'm meeting her in the water.

I'm careful not to touch her just yet, if I do I'm afraid I won't be able to restrain myself and take my time with her the way I want to. The way she deserves. "This feels amazing." She murmurs softly and for whatever reason, it makes my dick hard with need. A need so fierce I can't not touch her.

I swim closer to her and wrap my hands gently around her waist, pulling her flush to my chest. Her breathing is more ragged than a few moments ago, and my own nerves are starting to kick in. "*You* feel amazing." I whisper in her ear just as her thighs clench tighter around my waist. I'm sure she can feel my hard length pressing up against her, dying to get a feel of her. I've had Olive in every other way except one. I want to slow things down and take her gently, but the beast inside is begging to be let free. I have to keep reminding myself she's a virgin, even though she never fully admitted that, and be gentle with her.

This is new territory for me, I've been with other women before Olive, but it's never even for a second felt like this. I would burn the world to the ground if it meant keeping Olive safe. A strong sense to tell her how I feel crashes over me and the words are tumbling out before I have a chance to think them over. "My heart has never beat for anyone else the way it does for you, Butterfly."

Olive's green eyes sear into mine, every emotion possible swirling inside them. Without any hesitation, she lowers her lips to mine in a branding kiss that has every part of my body vibrating for her. This moment is tattooed on every inch of my body, inside and out, and I would gladly wear them for everyone to see.

Olive is mine forever, undoubtedly.

When she pulls back, her eyes search mine. I'm not sure what reassurance she's trying to find, but I'll give her anything she needs right now. She unhooks her legs from around my waist and starts to walk to the edge of the pond. Her long legs step out and her skin glistens as water trails down every curve. When she turns around she doesn't say anything, just waits for me to join her under the white oak tree where the box of blankets is.

I unfold one and lay it down in the soft grass just beneath the tree, grabbing a second one to lay over us in case she's feeling demure. She lays down first and I start to pull the blanket over us as I join her. Her hand snakes out to stop me, and I look at her slightly puzzled. "We don't need it." She whispers.

"I want you to be comfortable baby, so please, keep talking to me. Okay?" This is her first time, I can't even fathom fucking it up for her. I think I'm more nervous for her first time than I was my own.

"I'm okay. Just come here, Mitch." She pulls me close to her and I lay on my side so that we're facing each other. Her curls cascade down her back in waves and a few loose strands frame her face beautifully. Her chest is rising and falling and I can almost hear how fast her heart is beating.

Olive moves first, wrapping her hands gently around my neck and guiding my face to hers for a slow and sweet kiss. As my mouth dances with hers, I shift my body so that I'm over her as she lays back. I'm careful not to put any weight on her, keeping myself propped up with one elbow. Slowly, I trace my hand down the middle of her chest playing with her nipples as I go. Olive arches into me and I can feel the warmth of her pebbling against me.

The way her body reacts to my touch is like a man dying of thirst in the dessert. She's so hungry for it and it gives me all the reassurance I need to continue. I open her legs with one of mine and settle between her thighs, still careful not to crush her under my full weight. A soft gasp elicits from her lips as my fingers graze her slit. She's already wet, and not from being in the water moments ago. I tease her softly, playing with her folds until she's squirming beneath me, desperate for more.

"Feeling impatient, are we?" I tease as I slide one finger into her wet heat. I"m rewarded with a moan as my fingers works her painfully slowly.

"Please, Mitch." She breathes.

"Please what? Butterfly."

"I need *more*."

With that, I add a second finger, curling them both to hit that sweet spot that has her arching into me with delicious force. I'll never get enough of how her body reacts to mine. *Never.* Fisting the hair at the base of my neck, she tugs firmly. The sensation is erotic in a way, feeling her grip me tightly as I bring her closer and closer to release. Little does she know, I don't plan on giving in to her that easily. I want this to last, for both of us. I want to replay this in my mind like a movie on the big screen, and rewind it back to my favorite parts. But *everything* about Olive is my favorite.

I withdraw both fingers and a pout immediately paints her face. It's adorable. I can sense her about to protest, but stop her when I place a finger coated with her arousal on her lips. Her body goes still as she watches me, waiting for my next move. "Can you taste yourself, Butterfly?" I ask as I gently run my finger along the seam of her lips. Her eyes are hooded with desire as she nods slightly. "Nothing has ever tasted as sweet as you."

I bring my finger that was just on her lips to my own and suck it into my mouth. My eyes shut as I take in the taste of her and a frenzy begins to take over. I'm rock hard against her stomach and I feel Olive's soft hands wrap around me tugging gently. I can't help my groan of approval as my body revels in the contact. She strokes me from base to tip over and over again, making me even more hard. With such confidence, Olive lines me up at her opening, swiping me along her wetness a few times. My own desire mixing with hers.

Her eyes flutter to meet mine and she searches for something. There are words on the tip of her tongue and I reach down to taste them. She doesn't say anything, but she doesn't have to. We're so connected in this moment, words wouldn't make that fact any more evident. "Mitch." She breathes against my lips

"Yes, Butterfly. Tell me what you need."

"I just need you. I'm…I'm ready."

Fuck. I feel like I'm thirteen all over again, about to come before I've even felt her tight pussy wrap around me and bring me to places I've never even heard of. I hold her gaze in mine and focus on my breathing, I need to stay in control no matter what. As much as I want to unleash the beast and ravage her repeatedly, I want to make this perfect for her.

"Please tell me if it's too much, okay?" She nods her head softly and smiles. I reach for my pants and pull a condom from my wallet. I've carried it around for weeks now never knowing if the time was going to be right. I'm glad it never was before tonight. I slip on the condom and line myself up at her entrance again, adjusting her legs around my waist. She tightens them around me instinctively and I have the strange urge to praise her for how well she's doing. Olive's arms are gripped tightly on my shoulders, her nails digging in slightly adding another layer of desire to my growing need for her.

"Look at me, Olive." Her eyes find mine instantly and I slowly ease my way inside her. She's wet, but so, *so* tight. I have to actively keep reminding myself to be gentle. The grip she has on me tightens even more as she squirms beneath me, trying to accommodate my size. I wouldn't say I'm porn star worthy, something she said to me the first time she saw my dick, but I know I'm on the bigger side. I've always been confident with what I'm working with, but right now I almost feel guilty because of how uncomfortable Olive looks.

I make sure my movements are slow as I inch in little by little. The first time usually hurts for most girls. Luckily I've had my fair share, and while I know it'll hurt at first, I know what I'm about to do will help her body adjust. I withdraw from her achingly slow, reveling in the feel of how tight she is around me. Warning her will just make her tense more, so I wait a beat before sheathing myself completely inside her. Her body arches into me and a cry escapes her lips as I bury myself to the hilt. "I'm sorry, baby. I would have warned you but that would have made it worse for you. Are you okay?"

Her breathing is ragged and her face is scrunched slightly, but her eyes meet mine with pools of desire. "Yes. Keep going." She moans and I almost come undone. Slowly I start working myself in and out of her, waiting to feel her muscles relax around me. As soon as they do I'm pumping into her with more force, while still remaining somewhat controlled.

"More, Mitch. *Please.*" She begs and if I didn't know any better I'd say my sweet Butterfly wants it rough. Not something I expected, especially for her first time, but I'm not one to disappoint. I hook her legs around my waist and hold her hips tightly with both hands as I begin pumping into her harder and harder. Her breasts bounce in my face and I lower myself to take one taut nipple in my mouth. Her body reacts and I can feel her getting even more wet as I continue my assault on her breast.

She clenches around me and her breathing is coming out in heavy pants now. She's close, I can feel it. I reach down and rub her clit while I sheath myself inside her, moving at a pace that's about to make me come along with her. I close my eyes and feel her lips meet mine with hunger and desire. She's unable to control her moans as I rub her clit, pinching it lightly between my fingers. Just when I think I can't hold on any longer Olive erupts around me, screaming my name in ecstasy. It's by far the hottest thing I've ever witnessed in my life.

"*Shit*. Oh my God, Mitch. I can't...That was..." she laughs, not able to form a sentence and when her eyes open to meet mine, searing into me with a desire I can't describe, I spill inside her with such force I wouldn't be surprised if I overflow the condom.

"I know." I pant against her chest. I gave up on trying to keep my weight off her, and now my head rests against her breasts. They're heaving beneath me and I kiss each one before circling my tongue around both peaks.

When I lift myself off of her and roll to my side, I search her face for any sign of discomfort. I promised myself I wouldn't lose control like that, but when she practically begged me to go harder I lost all voice of reason. "Tell me you're okay, baby."

Olive looks at me as the sweetest smile lights up her face. She looks even more breathtaking now than she did all done up in her dress and makeup. Her hair is framing her face in an unruly manor and her lips are plump and red from the assault of my kisses. Her eyes hold a new kind of sparkle and if I could photograph this moment to keep forever, I would. "I'm more than okay."

"I always planned on telling you before, but never found the right time to say it." She lets her words hang in the air for a moment, and I wish I could tell her I already know. Assure her that it didn't matter either way if she had been a virgin or not. I'm just thankful she was willing to share this part of herself with me.

"That was my…I'm a…virgin. Well, I was." She chuckles at her own joke and the sound of her laughter goes right to my chest. "I was worried if I said something to you, you'd try to wait or be too gentle with me. I didn't want anything holding us back, I just wanted you."

"Baby, I already knew." I kiss her knuckles softly and she looks at me confused. "You may not have ever said it outright, but you alluded to it a few times. I never brought it up because I figured if you wanted to tell me, you'd find the moment that felt right to you."

"I'm the only man who has ever touched you, tasted you and felt you come around my cock and that is an honor I will hold in the highest regards." She swats my hand away and covers her eyes from the compliment like she's embarrassed.

I pull them down and turn her face so she's looking at me again. "Olive, you are perfect. And everything about what we just did was so perfect, I doubt I'll ever be able to find something to top it. I love that I'm the only one who gets you like this." The words I feel in my chest are right there on the tip of my tongue, but I'm afraid if I speak them too soon it'll ruin this moment.

I'm almost certain I love Olive Fournier. But if tonight was proof of anything, it's that great things can't be rushed. When I tell her I love her I don't want to just say it.

I want her to *feel* it.

20

Olive

"Y ou know what one of my favorite things is?" I ask Mitch as I trace circles over his bare chest. We're still lying in the grass, blanketed by the stars and string lights hanging in the trees above. We came here straight from the renewal, not even telling anyone where we were going. Gran and Pop already went home and something tells me everyone else knew what we were doing anyways.

"Laughter. It's like this funny feeling that comes from within, radiating all around until it bubbles to the surface." My head is resting in the crook of Mitch's arm and I can feel his heart beating beneath my ear. Steady and strong, and all *mine*. I haven't told him I love him, neither has he, but I feel it. Just like laughter flowing all throughout my body, just waiting to surface.

"You know what *I* love?" Mitch asks. "How random you can be." He laughs and my head lifts with his chest. "I love how your mind works."

"Is that some kind of back handed compliment?" I reply dryly.

"Not at all. If I could burrow into your head and listen to

the way your brain works, I could be occupied forever."

"Burrow into my brain? That's weird, Mitch. And I'm the random one." I mumble against his chest and he laughs contentedly. I just want to stay in this place forever. I don't even know what time it is, but it's probably well past midnight. My grandparents headed home around ten but Mitch and I didn't walk right over here as soon as they left.

Sitting up, I look around us to see all the lights casting a warm glow on the water. It was already serene here before Mitch added the lights. I've loved coming to this pond to paint and relax, and now every time I come back I'm going to think of this night. I always told myself my first time didn't have to be this over the top perfect experience. But being here with Mitch, it's more than I could ever have hoped for.

I didn't get home until sometime around two in the morning. By the time we managed to untangle ourselves from one another, it was already so late we didn't feel the need to rush. Mitch insisted on walking me home though, and then had to walk all the way back to his house. I felt bad because if he were anywhere near as tired as I was, that four miles would feel more like forty.

This morning we're supposed to start the cleanup, but I'm dragging my feet. I think I managed to get five hours of sleep and the bags under my eyes are proof of that. When I got home, I quietly made my way upstairs to shower quickly and get ready for bed. As soon as my head hit the pillow, I was out. I must have slept hard too, because when I woke up my body was in exactly the same position as when I fell asleep.

The stairs creak beneath me as I make my way into the kitchen. Gran is sitting on the porch with a cup of coffee, so I grab one myself and join her. She greets me with a warm smile and eyes tired like my own.

"Good morning, dear." Gran says softly.

"Good morning. How did you sleep last night?" I ask as I take the seat opposite her.

"I think I slept better than I have in years. That celebration wore us out!" She chuckles into her coffee mug and then sets her gaze on me. "Olive, I still can't believe everything you did last night. It was one of the best nights of my life." She reaches across the chair to take my hand in hers.

"Nothing made me happier than seeing the two of you renew the vows you made to each other years ago, in front of the whole town. It's something I was honored to be a part of." I give her hand a gentle squeeze.

We're quiet for a few restful moments, and the words I've been wanting to speak are on my tongue practically vibrating with the need to be vocalized. I think this is my chance to come clean about finding the letters. For all I know, Gran never even knew about them. But something tells me she had to have known.

"Gran, can I ask you something?" My voice is a whisper, but she still hears me. I'm not even sure how to begin, I've thought about this moment so many times, but never gave thought to how I would bring it up. It's not an easy thing to talk about, especially since she doesn't even know I'm aware of the adoption. They'll always be my grandparents, nothing could ever change that, but this information has been weighing me down and I need to be able to talk to her about it.

"Ask me whatever you like, sweetie." She takes another sip of coffee, and I take another deep breath. Rip off the band aid.

"Did you know?" I ask hesitantly.

"Know what?" She turns to look at me, a confused expression furrowing her brows. I don't say anything for a minute and I swear she knows what I'm about to ask. The color drains from her face, and her eyes almost completely bug out of their sockets.

"I-I found the letters, Gran. I know."

A tear slips down her cheek and she doesn't bother to wipe it away. She just breathes in the morning air as she gazes out across the field. "When your mother was a little girl, she would always talk about becoming a mom. She knew what her purpose in life was, and it was to raise a family."

"When she met Thomas, I knew instantly he was the one she was going to marry. They fit together, like two pieces of a puzzle connecting seamlessly. And we all knew without a doubt, he would make an amazing father."

Emotion is thick in my throat and I desperately want to cough, loosen some of the strain there, but I can't chance pulling Gran from this memory. She's finally opening up, and I'm desperate for her words.

"They were devastated when they found out she couldn't conceive on her own, and back then IVF wasn't as common, and certainly not cheap. They were given a beautiful opportunity to adopt, and they jumped at the chance." She contemplates her next words carefully, adjusting her glasses before continuing.

"About an hour away, a young girl reached out through an agency about putting her unborn daughter up for adoption. Without hesitation they drove the hour to meet her. She was very young, and scared beyond belief. I don't know what it was, but they bonded immediately and by the end of their meeting, Lucy agreed to let your parents adopt you."

"I never got the chance to meet her, but from what your mother told me, she was lovely. I can't even imagine how difficult it must have been to give you up, dear. We've had the privilege and honor of loving you your whole life, and while I'm sure she has as well, she didn't get to be a part of it. That used to keep your mother up at night. The guilt would chip away at her, and she felt like she was keeping the two of you apart."

I'm trying to absorb as much as I can, but my emotions are clogging my airways, making it harder to breathe. Still, I keep listening, needing to hear everything she's willing to share.

"I asked her once why they decided to have a closed adoption. The look of true grief altered her features and I was almost sorry I asked. She told me she couldn't bear the thought of losing you once they got you. She knew how much your birth mother loved you, and she was terrified she would try to take you back. Josie used to call me in the middle of the night terror stricken, crying uncontrollably. There was nothing I could do to help her through it, I just had to be there and listen."

"Around your first birthday, they received the first letter from Lucy. It took your mother a week before she finally opened it. She kept thinking of the worst possible scenarios, but finally relented. When she read it, she felt terrible for thinking the worst, Lucy just wanted you to know she loved you unconditionally."

Gran stops to take a few deep breaths. It's like this information has been waiting to spill out of her for so long she can't talk as fast as her brain is running. I can only imagine what it's been like having to keep this secret even after my parents died. If I were in her shoes, I wouldn't feel like it was my place to say anything. How do you make that decision, and when is the right time? Finding the letters on my own seems like the only scenario that worked for everyone.

I was shocked and incredibly upset, yes, but I was able to process the information on my own. I didn't have to sit down awkwardly with my parents or my grandparents and hear about where I came from. That conversation would have felt more like an ambush.

"Why didn't they tell me? I mean, I was thirteen when they died. They could have told me way before then."

"Oh honey, they wanted to. But it never felt like the right moment. The idea that they were keeping this monumental secret form you, was killing them both. They didn't know how to tell you they weren't your biological parents, and I think a part of them worried you would feel some kind of abandonment or lack of belonging."

"Yeah well, Mom knew I felt like I didn't belong. I used

to tell her that all the time. When I think back on it, it breaks my heart to think of what those words must have done to her. I always felt like an outcast, that I looked different and liked different things. Now I know why." I whisper as a tear slips past my lids. I'm already so tired, and this conversation is sucking what little energy I thought I had left out of me.

I was supposed to meet Mitch and the rest of the family at the farm to clean up from last night, but I don't have it in me to put this conversation on hold. I pull out my phone and shoot off a quick text to Mitch, letting him know I'll be by soon.

"Gran, did Mom read all of the letters or just the first one?" Because when I opened the second letter, it was sealed. I didn't think much of it at the time, but now I'm eager to go and check to see if the rest of them were sealed as well.

"She only read the first one. Josie felt it wasn't her right to read them when they were addressed to you. I think she was hoping you could read them together, once the shock of the news wore off a little. How many have you read?" She asks softly.

"Only two. I can only take so much in one sitting. The day I found the letters was the day you asked me to get the Will after Pop's heart attack. It took me weeks before I could open another." Gran looks at me with a pained expression and I wish I could soothe her worries.

"Oh lord, Olive I am so sorry. I never even thought about those letters being in there for you to find." Gran sits up in her chair, nervous energy flowing from her in waves. "With everything that was going on with Henry, it slipped my mind." She reaches over to take my hands in hers once more. "I can't apologize enough, dear."

"Gran, please. You have nothing to be sorry about. No one does, really. I'm not upset with Mom and Dad for not telling me either. I've tried putting myself in their shoes, trying to understand what I would have done and I can't fathom it. I just wish I had known when they were still alive, I think our relationship would have been stronger in a way."

I hate to think that the bond I shared with my parents wasn't strong, because in fact it was. But knowing now that I felt different my whole life has helped me cope with things as a child. My mom always tried to reassure me that I was just right for them, and that probably hurt her to say knowing she was keeping the truth from me for so long.

"They loved you so much, Olive. If there's only one thing you take away from all of this, let it be that."

I smile and wipe away the tears that have made their way down my face and are pooling on my chin. I stand and pull Gran in for a much needed hug. Her frail body is warm and comforting, and there has never been a moment where I felt more connected to her than right now. Finding out about my lineage changes nothing when it comes to them. I love them just as much now as I always have, and I always will.

The warm breeze coming off the field whips around us, Mother Nature's way of giving us a subtle hug I suppose. I stare out at the field and think about my parents meeting a young Lucy, pregnant with me and scared about what her future holds. My heart aches for all three of them. Lucy having to give up her first and only child, and my parents being unable to have their own naturally. Life can be so unfair sometimes, and if I could hug them all and tell them how much I love them, I would in a heartbeat.

Gran has sat back in her seat while I lean against the railing, studying the field and remembering all the times Dad said he would come out here with Mom at night. It's why I've always loved fireflies so much, they remind me of my parents.

I turn to face Gran and find her already looking at me with a warm gaze. "I can't walk away from this conversation without letting you know…I met her. I met Lucy." My hands are clammy and I feel my body shake with silent tremors as I watch Gran absorb that last piece of information.

"It didn't feel good to go behind your back and find her, but I needed to do it on my own. I wasn't sure how much you and Pop knew, and with everything that happened with his heart attack…It felt selfish to make something about me, *again*."

"I would have done the same thing, honey. Sometimes we need to do the big things alone. If we always have someone there to catch us then we'll never know if we had the strength to do it on our own." She rises to her feet and pulls her housecoat firmly around her waist, tying it in place. Slowly she makes her way over to me with tears threatening to spill.

"I'm so proud of the woman you are, Olive Fournier." With that, I'm resting my head on her shoulder, allowing the silent tears to soak her sleeve as we both cry about what is and what never was. Life is funny, just like laughter. When I said that to Mitch last night I meant it. Laughter bubbles out of you and it would be a shame to try and keep that inside.

Now that I know about Lucy, I don't want to keep it inside. Telling Gran, hearing her side of things from my moms perspective, has me feeling lighter than I have in weeks. It's time I stop keeping this to myself, I don't want to let it bubble beneath the surface anymore. I want to let it free and enjoy everything that can come from it.

It's been a week since my grandparents vow renewal. A week since I lost my virginity to Mitch, and officially one week until my birthday. I didn't tell Mitch when my birthday was and he's never asked, so I plan to keep it to myself. I don't want him thinking he has to make a big deal about it, turning twenty is hardly anything to celebrate.

Growing up my parents always did a big thing for my birthday, which was fine, but I was never one to enjoy the attention. I never told my parents, but sometimes the night before my birthday I'd break out in hives and have panic attacks. I hated the idea of being the center of attention, something I knew my mom wouldn't understand. She grew up doing pageants and relished in the spotlight. It would crush her to know I didn't feel the same.

I thought about bringing it up to my Dad once right before I turned thirteen. As soon as I mentioned my birthday he started gushing about how excited my mom was. If I had known then that would be my last birthday I got to celebrate with them, I probably would have felt differently. Sometimes I wish I could go back, I would be more open with them about who I was, and not be afraid to disappoint them in some way. Talking to Gran has made me realize my parents always wanted what was best for me, if I expressed my feelings more clearly, they would have understood.

Ever since they died I couldn't bring myself to care about birthdays anymore. I only enjoyed them because of how much they did, even if I hated the attention it brought. Every year I get older is just a reminder that they'll never be here to celebrate with me again. It fucking sucks. Gran and Pop tried to make my birthdays special after that but I think they could tell I just wasn't into it. It's hard to fake happiness when everything inside you feels cold.

Even though I'm in a much better place, and have come to terms with the things my parents have missed, I still can't bring myself to say anything to Mitch about it. Knowing him, he'll try and pull off some grand gesture and I wouldn't know how to break it to him that I secretly hate my birthday. If I'm honest with myself, the only thing I want for my birthday this year is to spend it with Lucy. The last time she saw me was the day I was born, and we've never had the opportunity to celebrate together.

Mitch is working and I'm off today, I asked Gran if Maureen could handle the bakery so I could spend the day with Lucy. I didn't tell her the last part though. Even though everything is out in the open and there's no more secrets, I can't help but keep this little one. I don't want my grandparents feeling weird about how much time I do or don't spend with her, so for now, I'll keep it to myself.

Checking the time I grab my bag and keys off the counter, heading out the front door to my car. This is the first time I've gone to see Lucy by myself, and I feel almost more nervous this time than when I first met her. I knew I had Mitch with me, and he was like a suit of armor, protecting me in ways I can't protect myself. Climbing into the front seat, I start it up and back down the driveway. It's beautiful out today, hot but not sweltering the way it has been for weeks.

There's a soft breeze, filtering in through the windows with a sweet nature smell. I inhale deeply and head in the direction of Lucy's house, passing the expansive fields across massive flatlands, remembering what it felt like the first time I took this drive. Such a pivotal moment in my life and we were surrounded by subdued fields, a contrast to the uncertainty of my future in that moment. I had no idea what to expect, could hardly anticipate meeting her and yet he I was surrounded by fields cloaked in predictable terrain.

Thoughts buzz throughout my mind, stuff Gran told me about my parents meeting Lucy that first time. Taking this very same drive out there, not knowing what to expect. Similarly to how I felt the first time. Anticipation swirls in my gut as I inch closer and closer to her farm, but it mixes with that feeling of uncertainty again. There's so much we don't know about each other, things I desperately want to know. But these are uncharted territories, for both of us, and now I'm almost wishing I hadn't made the decision to come alone.

With someone else, there's a buffer, a helpful distraction when the conversation lags. How am I going to fill the void or stay calm when I can barely breathe as it is? I'm not even there yet and my nerves are bouncing around inside me like a damn tennis ball against a brick wall. On the verge of a panic attack, I ease the car to the side of the road and reach for my bag. I threw a few snacks in there as well as a bottle of water, grabbing it, I untwist the cap and guzzle the cold water. Feeling it work its way down my throat, cooling my racing heart and insides that are burning up.

I used to get panic attacks more often, but as I've gotten older I've been able to recognize the signs and stop it before it takes over. On few occasions, I've needed actual assistance to calm down, the times where I can't do it myself. My chest gets tight the way a corset sucks a woman in, crushing her ribcage and my mouth goes so dry a cotton ball is hardly comparable. Whenever it would happen, Gran or Pop, occasionally Maureen, would have to coach me threw the panic attack until I was able to breathe easily again. I haven't had one in over a year, and I sure as shit don't need one now.

The air in the car is stifling, turning on the air conditioner, I blast it and position the vents to point directly to my face. After a few moments, the tingling of my skin subsides and my breathing slows to a normal rate. I'm embarrassed I let myself get to this point, I don't want Mitch knowing about my panic attacks, and thankfully he hasn't seen one. I don't even know how I'd explain it to him without sounding like a drama queen. Anxiety is something a lot of people don't understand, if they haven't experienced it themselves, they think it's an overreaction. If only that were true.

Feeling a little more stable, I pull back onto the road and make it the rest of the way without too much anxiety. This time Lucy knows I'm coming, so that element of surprise is gone. I hated feeling like I was ambushing her, no warning at all, just showing up out of the blue after two decades. Even though she didn't know I was coming that day, in a way it's like she expected me. She said she woke up every day hoping it would be the one she would see me again. That night in bed I cried at the pain I felt for her, the sense of loss she must have endured for years and years. All because she did the right thing by me at such a young age herself. How many sixteen year olds can make that kind of decision when they're practically still a kid themselves?

I grieved for her, I cried so hard you would have thought someone died. It was in those moments, lying in the dark that I realized something. To her someone did die, not literally but metaphorically. A part of her, a part she never even got the chance to learn, died the day she birthed me and had to give me away. The part of her who wanted to be a mother died, the part of her that wanted to keep me and raise me the way she would have if she were older, died. All the dreams and fears of parenthood vanished before she even had a sliver of it, barely able to hold on before the possibilities were taken. I laid there wondering if there was a moment where she changed her mind. If she took one look at me and decided she couldn't go through with it.

The what if's kept me up well into the night and it hurt to know that those feelings have likely been within her for nearly twenty years. Adoption is a crazy thing. Good people who know they can't provide the kind of life they'd want for their child, have to make the decision to give them more. They have to hand over the most precious thing that will ever exist to them, to strangers, and hope it was the right choice.

What if Lucy had the support of my birth father with her? What if he wanted to raise me with her, even though they were so young? She never even told him about me, and I can't say I blame her. What if she had and he only stayed out of obligation? That's not how I would want to raise a child. All these questions circulate in my mind as I drive down the long dirt road to Lucy's home. Feeling a little like I'm about to ambush her, I swallow down my questions and fears. The last thing I want to do is barge in there with a list of the heaviest questions I can think of.

I need to start off slow and ease into what happened twenty years ago.

"Nice to see you again, stranger." Lucy addresses me with a smile as I make my way up the stairs, stepping inside the house. I know she means it in a way that says she hasn't seen me since before the vow renewal, but it stings a little too. We *are* strangers, and I want to fix that, starting today. "How did the renewal for your grandparents go?" She asks over her shoulder, leading me into the kitchen. On the counter is a pitcher of lemonade with little sprigs of lavender and lemon slices. Beside it rests a plate of scones that if I had to guess what heaven smelled like, I'd say it was those blueberry scones.

"It was beautiful, truly. I wish you could have been there." The words are out of my mouth before I have a chance to stop them, I cover my lips with my hand, a blush covering my cheeks. Way to go, *dumbass*.

"I'm sorry, I didn't even think before I just blurted that

out…" I need to get a handle on my nerves, or I'm going to word vomit all over the place.

Lucy turns and faces me, a slight smirk painting her features. "Olive, one thing you can learn about me right now, so you don't stress you're going to upset me all the time, I don't get offended easily. I know you didn't mean anything cruel with that statement." She takes a seat at the counter after pulling a chair out for me.

"If the situation weren't so unknown yet, I would have loved to be there. Get a chance to see where you grew up, meet the people who helped raise you. I bet it was beautiful." She's so at ease when she speaks, unlike me who choked on the first statement I made coming in here. I remind myself, I haven't had as much time to wrap my head around our situation.

Lucy pulls me from my thoughts again, before I spiral down the rabbit hole. "I know how much your grandparents mean to you, how much they meant to your mom and Dad." Hearing her call my parents that feels odd and I wonder if it does for her too. Calling someone else mom would feel like acid on my tongue. I offer her a weak smile, still trying to get my nerves tamped down, as I reach for a glass of lemonade.

"When the time is right, I'd love to meet them. Assuming the feeling is mutual." She breathes out a sigh as she lifts the glass to her lips, taking a long pull of lemonade. Maybe she's more nervous than she lets on.

"Actually, I had a talk with Gran the other day. About… "I gesture between the two of us, "Well, everything." I laugh and fidget with the hem of my shirt nervously.

"Oh. How did that go?" She asks, setting her glass down.

"Better than I thought, if I'm being honest. I went into the conversation not knowing if they were aware of the letters. In a way, I'm glad she knew because if she hadn't it would have felt like double the information I was throwing at her. It was hard enough admitting I knew." My voice comes out ragged, sometimes when I speak too fast from nerves it sounds like I'm a chain smoker.

"I'm sure it's been difficult keeping this to yourself, but it's good you have at least one person in your corner." Lucy gives me a knowing look and I know she's referring to Mitch. The day we met her I clung to Mitch like a life preserver, hoping that if I started to go under, he'd keep me up. It's weird to think so much has changed with Mitch since I met Lucy. Things I want to open up about, have that motherly advice in a way since I can't have that with my other mom. *Other* mom. I don't even know what to call either of them at this point. Everything is still incredibly confusing.

And overwhelming.

A scarlet blanket covers my face and neck at the mere mention of Mitch. Even if I didn't want to talk about him and what's going on between us, my face gave it away before I could even open my mouth. The smirk on Lucy's face grows wider and now I know I'm gonna need to spill the beans. "I don't even know where to start." I drop my head into my hands and laugh nervously before returning my gaze to Lucy. Her features have softened and she's leaning casually against the counter.

"How about you start at the beginning and tell me as much as you're comfortable with?" Her voice is so soft, so genuine and I'm practically in a trance. Wanting to confide in her and hear what advice she has for me. I think I'm falling in love with Mitch, and I sure as shit have no idea how to tell him. Or if I even want to. The thought he doesn't feel the same terrifies me and I'd much rather have him the way I do now than not at all. My life has been a series of unfortunate events, one after the other. I can't risk fucking it up with Mitch when he's the first real thing that has made me happy in six years.

With a deep breath, I dive into the story that is Mitch and I. I don't know when or how it happened, but I felt comfortable enough to tell Lucy *everything*. An invisible weight lifts off my shoulders by the time I'm done and a calming feeling washes over me. It's a relief I was able to talk about my personal life, but the one I really want to hear about, is Lucy's.

I can only hope she's as willing to be vulnerable the way I just was.

21
MITCH

Sweat trickles down my forehead as I pace my room back and forth, threatening to wear a hole in the rug. It's hot as fuck up here, even with the windows open and the fan circulating above me. I can't go downstairs though cause Ma is in the kitchen with her Vulcan hearing. I swear I couldn't get away with anything as a kid, she could hear me curse before the words even left my mouth. It's like she had a superpower for detecting bullshit.

Still does.

With my phone in one hand and the piece of paper Gwen gave me in the other, I'm ready to combust with anticipation. Drew's contact info has been sitting in my desk drawer for far too long now, it's time I do something about it. I can't keep letting the fear cloud my need for answers. For my father more than anything else. If I'm able to give him the good news that Drew is okay, then it will soften the blow of how I lied to them in high school and knew where Drew was. I was put in a shitty situation, because they had already had a falling out because of Drew's spiral. But he also asked me not to say anything to my parents. He was embarrassed, that much I could tell. But it was more than that.

It's like he knew if my parents offered to help, he would take it. But he needed to know he could get out of that rut on his own, without our help. I've always respected him for that. What I didn't respect was that he up and left Raising Hope without any intention on telling someone where he was going. I spent years thinking he left to off himself. Not something I wanted to carry around for years, in private no less.

Turning my neck to the left and then the right, hearing a satisfying crack, to relieve some of the tension, I take a deep breath and begin dialing. The number listed isn't one I recognize, another thing that used to piss me off. It was bad enough he left without a word, but he changed his number too. All I ever did was try to help him and be supportive, and he repaid me by ghosting me. I felt like a high school chick who got stood up.

Fucking ridiculous.

The dial tone rings in my ear and I almost drop my phone from how sweaty my palms are. Fucking hell, it's hot up here. As the dial tone continues, I stick my head out the window and breathe in some fresh, but not much cooler, air. On the fourth ring, I hear it. The voice that has plagued me for years, trying to memorize it so that if one day I did discover he was gone, I could at least remember how he sounded.

"Hello?" He says easily, and my response gets lodged in my throat. A weird croaking sounds slips past my lips and I cough to regain control. I wish a part of him knew it was me, so he could save me this awkward silence.

"Drew? It's…" My voice dissipates into a whisper and I'm unable to say my name all of a sudden. It would be so easy to pretend I'm a sales person trying to sell him a subscription, but then I would just be chicken shit.

"Mitch? Is-is that you? Holy shit." His breathing is rough through the receiver, seems I'm not the only one struggling with this. That brings me some relief in an odd way.

"Yeah, hey man. Ho-how's it going?" For christ sake, I sound like an illiterate moron. I really should have done this somewhere rather than my sweltering bedroom. I might have been able to function more clearly.

"Jesus. I was hoping I would hear from you. I gave Gwen my number to pass along but I didn't expect anything, especially considering how I left things." He pauses, collecting himself before continuing. "I'm sorry, Mitch. You didn't deserve the way I left back then, and if I could change how I went about things, I would. I was in a dark place, which is no excuse, but I didn't want to drag you down with me." I know I should make him sweat a little, make him feel bad for how he left me hanging, left my parents hanging, but I just can't. All I ever wanted was to know he was okay.

"I had already made the decision to keep your Dad in the dark, not wanting to strain our relationship by feeling like he was obligated to help me. Then you showed up at the shelter, and I…Fuck, I didn't know what to do."

I have to cut him off before he works himself into a panic over what happened all those years ago. He can't keep thinking he was a burden on me or our family. "Drew, stop. This is all unnecessary, man. I can't begin to understand what you went through, and quite frankly I have no idea. You never told any of us, but that's not what matters. It didn't matter then and it sure as shit doesn't matter now. All that matters is you're okay." I pause, listening to his end to make sure he's still listening and didn't hang up to disappear again.

"Are you? Okay, I mean?" I ask quietly now that my breathing has returned to normal.

There's a long silent pause, and now I really think he's hung up. I check my screen and see that the call is still connected, and I sigh with relief. "I am. I'm okay. Took a while, but I got to where I needed to be. I just had to do it in my own time, and I had to do it alone. I'm sorry I couldn't voice it that way. Like I said, if I could change how I went about everything…I would do *so* many things different."

Talking to Drew right now is like maneuvering around a sleeping baby. I'm treading lightly, afraid if I poke to hard I'll spook him. But even through a phone call, he sounds good. "At the risk of sounding too forward, can I ask you something?" I say.

"Ask away."

"It's been years since you've seen him, and he deserves answers, Drew." We both know who I'm talking about, and I take my shot knowing it could backfire. "What are the chances I could get you to come out here? Just talk to him. I'm not sure what you've thought over the years, but he's still there for you, even if you never let him in."

The silence on his end is deafening at this point, but at least I know I extended the Olive branch, I just hope he takes it. My mind momentarily drifts to the beautiful brunette who invades my mind every waking minute, before I hear Drew's response. Surely I heard him wrong and it takes me a minute before I ask him to repeat himself.

"I said, I was hoping you'd say that. When I didn't hear from you right away, like I admittedly thought I would, never assume things, you know what they say." He chuckles lightly at the joke. "Because I'm in town, and if he's home, I'd like to come by…today."

Well, that escalated quickly.

As if pacing my bedroom wasn't bad enough, now I'm pacing the dirt driveway. Kicking up dusty rocks just before turning around and walking right through it, choking on little particles of dirt. I never expected Drew to say he wanted to come by *today*. I haven't had any time to prepare my parents, or talk to them about knowing where Drew was and that I saw him weekly at the shelter. I feel like a little kid again, about to be punished for bad behavior. Maybe I can spin it in my favor somehow…Fuck!

Slapping both hands across my face, I drag them down wiping the dirt and sweat with them. He's going to be here any minute, and I have no time to do this the right way. The way I always told myself I would if I ever found Drew. Gulping in fresh air, free from the dirt I've been kicking around, I remind myself of my new motto these days, and rip off the bandaid. The goddamn bandaid that I've ripped off too many times to count as of late.

My parents are in the kitchen eating lunch, and if I wasn't so nervous I'd eat the shit out of the sandwiches Ma just made. When I don't immediately start scarfing down food,

Ma looks at me with a confused expression. She knows better than anyone how much I love her fresh bread and cold cut sandwiches. You'd think I was about to tell them I knocked up a girl, between my fidgeting and now both their wary eyes on me.

"Mitchell, whatever it is, just spit it out. You're giving me more grays than I care to have at this age." Years have hardened my mom I see, I guess raising two boys will do that to a person.

"I told myself I was just going to rip off the bandaid, so that's what I'm going to do." I don't have a chance to say anything else before my mom is screeching at me, waving the dishrag in her hand.

"Oh god! Is Olive pregnant?! Jesus, Mitch, we had the talk with you, how could you let this happen?!" Pacing must run in the family because Ma is frantically doing just that as she mutters something under her breath.

"Ma, no! Fuck, calm down." I mutter. Dad gives me a stern look, the one that tells me I need to watch my tone, and my language. "Sorry, I just - no! That's not what I'm getting at here." I pull in a lungful of air and blurt out the words as fast as I can before anyone has a chance to cut in again. "I found Drew, he's okay and he's on his way over here right now." I check my watch and look back up at my parents gaping faces. "Like five minutes."

Dad just stares at me, no doubt trying to process my words and before I can look at my mom, she's tossing the dishrag in my face. "Really?! You got me all scared it was something bad, you little shit." Woah, not the reaction I expected. It makes me want to laugh, but judging by the still stoic look on my fathers face, laughing is not the best thing to do right now.

"Listen. I always told myself I would do this the right way, have a conversation about everything that happened with Drew, but we don't have time." Now or never, I chant to myself. "When I was volunteering at Raising Hope in high school, it wasn't mandatory. I went every week because Drew was staying there. I was put in a shit situation." I hold my hands up in apology. "He didn't want you guys to know he had fallen that far, and I promised I wouldn't say anything."

Mind racing, and palms sweating, I chance a look at my Dad and watch him as he absorbs this new information about his former best friend. "I didn't want to ambush you like this, but Gwen recently gave me his contact info and I wanted to make sure he was alright before I got your hopes up about any kind of reconciliation. I think he's ready to tell his side of things and make amends."

My father gets up and make his way around the counter to stand in front of me. I feel like he's about to yell when he does the opposite and pulls me in for a rib crushing hug. "I'm sorry, Dad. I really wanted to tell you sooner..." My throat feels tight and the emotion that's been clogged there for years threatens to break free. My body's way of ridding me of this weight I've been carrying, this guilt.

Pulling back, he looks me in the eye, emotion of his own mirroring mine. Dad isn't one to express his feelings, especially to his sons. I've never even seen him cry. But right now the raw emotion painting his features is as close to him crying I'll probably ever see. "Thank you, son." He pats my back and walks to the side door and onto the porch. Through the kitchen window I can see him take a seat on the bench swing facing the driveway. If I didn't know any better, I'd say this is like Christmas morning for him and he's waiting on the present he's always wanted. His best friend.

Ma finally looks at me, with tears silently falling down her rosy red cheeks. I know she wants to say something, but the wife part of her is tamping down for my Dads sake. I'll get an earful later I'm sure.

She goes to join my Dad on the porch just as a dark grey sedan makes it's way down the driveway, kicking up dust as it goes. My heart is in my throat and my palms are drenched in nervous sweat. I join my parents on the porch, leaning up against the railing as Drew puts the car in park and slowly gets out.

His hair is shorter than I remember and is peppered with grey. He's no longer clean shaven, rocking the salt and pepper beard look. The last time I saw him his hair was long and unruly, always looking disheveled and unkept. He was a lot thinner then too, unlike the tall healthy man striding up the steps to greet us. I can't tell if I want to punch him or hug him now that he's *finally* here. Guessing that I'm likely the first to make any kind of move here, I go with the latter and pull him in for a hug.

Drew wraps his arms around me tightly as he whispers *'I'm sorry'* in my ear, low enough for only me to hear. Nodding my head I release him, offering a small smile before stepping aside as my Dad approaches. I never thought we'd get this moment, something we've all waited years for.

They stand awkwardly in front of each other for a moment, silently talking in a way only best friends can understand, before they hug. Years of questions, years of uncertainty is washed away. There's still so much we need to know, like what happened all those years ago, and why he left without a word. We'll get to that, right now all that matters is he's here and he's okay. Sleepless nights wondering if my uncle Drew was missing, or worse…are gone.

After a long exchange of greeting, Ma is responsible for that with all her crying and hugging. We make our way onto the sun porch with iced tea Ma made, the best around, in my biased opinion.

I sit next to Ma so my Dad and Drew are closer in proximity, this meeting is really more about them than anything else. Since Dad isn't the best with words and expressing himself, I plan on asking all the questions I've had since I saw him that first day at Raising Hope. I tried asking back then, but he was so far gone from the man I knew growing up, I couldn't get him to budge.

"Man, it's so good to see you all. This is long overdue, and all my fault, I know." Drew speaks easily but his voice has a slight tremor to it, he's nervous, and judging by the looks on my parents faces, they are too. "You all deserve an explanation, and more importantly, an apology. So, I'm just going to dive right in, if that's okay with y'all?" Ma nods her head aggressively fast as if she can't wait another second without this information Drew is *finally* willing to give us. I laugh quietly to myself, she doesn't have a poker face, at all.

"A few years back, when everything happened, I had gotten some news that rocked me. Long story short, I didn't know how to process it in a healthy adult way, so I went off the rails. Lost my job because I kept showing up drunk and then stopped showing up altogether. When I lost my job, I couldn't pay rent anymore and everything just spiraled from there."

"Realizing that I was now homeless, I heard about a shelter outside of town, Raising Hope, and when I got there, I met Gwen. She saved my life, I don't know where I'd be right now if it weren't for her help and guidance." His confession guts me, the idea that he allowed a stranger at the time to help him, more than us, his family. The adult version of me wishes I could go back and encourage the seventeen year old to make Drew see we would have been there for him. No judgement. As he continues, though, I realize that's not what he needed at the time.

"I just want y'all to know…I know you would have been there, you would have helped me in any way possible. For that I want to say thank you. But, I couldn't allow my mistakes to drag down the ones I love, especially you, Connor." He looks at my Dad with heavy eyes, trying to abate the tears. "You were my best friend and as much as it killed me to shut you out, I had to know I could do it myself. You didn't deserve my silence, but more than that, you didn't deserve my burdens."

I knew it was like this for him, that was the only thing I managed to get out of him back then, that he refused to lean on my parents and take their help. He wanted to get himself out of the hole he dug. "Can you tell us what happened, back then?" I ask, unable to hold in the question any longer, it's practically bursting out of me.

Drew nods his head slightly, and lowers his head. Keeping his eyes on his hands in his lap, he takes a few deep breaths. It's evident this is still a hard thing for him to talk about, even years later. Ma is holding her breath next to me, preparing for whatever bomb it is he's about to drop. My Dad looks stoic, as always, and I'm about to jump out of my seat with anticipation. For years it's been on my mind, wondering what could be so big he allowed it to alter his life in such a massive way.

"I found out I have a daughter." The room goes silent, and thoughts are racing through my mind a million miles per second, so I cover my mouth to keep from blurting anything out before Drew has a chance to continue. "I've never met her, she was placed for adoption at birth and her mother never told me. Can't say I blame her, I wasn't exactly boyfriend material back then, so she must have assumed I wouldn't be father material either." Heaving a pained laugh, he pauses, and I'm ramrod still in my seat. All the breath has left my lungs and a pit has formed in my stomach.

"Oh, Drew." Ma says as she reaches across the table to offer him her hand. Squeezing it gently, he smiles at her then looks to my Dad.

"I was embarrassed that I had been so careless back then. I wish I could say I would have been there for her, but I don't know if I can. If I'm honest with myself, I probably wouldn't have been around and that's part of what gutted me. Knowing that I had a daughter out there somewhere, someone who is half of me that I've never met…It killed me. As you know, it didn't take long for the pain and guilt to consume every facet of my life."

It's on the tip of my tongue, threatening to spill out of me. But I know once I let it out, there's no taking it back. I bite the inside of my cheek, trying to refrain from asking the *only* question I now want an answer to. This is uncharted territory for me, I never imagined in a million years he would come here and admit he fathered a daughter that was then given up for adoption before he ever even knew of her conception.

This is some Jerry Springer shit.

"Drew?" That's all I manage to say before I shut my mouth, trying to figure out if I really want to know. Both of my parents and him look at me expectantly, waiting for me to continue. Fuck. I can't look at him, I close my eyes and let the question slip past my lips, practically a whisper. "What was…? The mother…Wh-what was her name?"

My body tenses, it's like I already know the answer without having to look at Drew. My heart races and with the amount of perspiration seeping from my pores at an alarming rate, I know I'm going to need another fucking shower. I look up just as he says her name, allowing it to fall from his lips effortlessly. "Lucy."

Fucking shit. This is more information than I bargained for.

22

Olive

"You have so much music." I state as I peruse the rows of CD's and albums, all stacked neatly and alphabetically. After unloading everything going on with Mitch, I needed a conversation break. Lucy is making us lunch so she told me to make myself at home and look around. The wall of CD's caught my eye first, floor to ceiling in height, it also spans the entire width of one wall. Her home library is right on the other side of the kitchen wall, with two large glass French doors separating the spaces. I couldn't help but notice it as we sat at the kitchen island to talk.

Ever since I was little I've been interested in the arts, specifically painting, but music has always been a close second. My parents had great taste in music, a wide variety of genres, whereas my grandparents listened to the classics and oldies. I've grown to appreciate the way a song can make you feel, kind of like that song did in the car with Mitch that first day. Thinking back on the way gooseflesh erupted all over my body, I can't help but wonder if Lucy has anything by Fleetwood Mac in her collection. Lightly tracing my fingers until my eyes snag on several cases with Fleetwood Mac.

Humming in the kitchen, I watch Lucy as she flits about setting up a lunch tray complete with Sammies, fresh fruit from her garden, and pasta salad. Everything smells delicious, and I'm momentarily sidetracked by my growling stomach. Pulling a few cases off the shelf, I turn them over until I see the song I'm looking for. I find it on a live edition album called *'The Dance'*. Studying the case and all the songs listed, I try to remember if I've ever seen this album around my house growing up. I come up short, and am convinced I've never heard any of it until that day in the car with Mitch. Lucy calls me in for lunch, and I grab the CD, bringing it to the table with me.

"Whatcha got there?" She asks as she passes me a plate and gestures me to dig in. The tray is set up almost like art, I feel bad touching anything. Taking a seat across from her, I set the CD on the table before plating my dish with food.

"This album, is it one of your favorites?" I ask before biting into one of the Sammies. A solemn look comes over her, and she stares at it as if remembering something.

"I haven't heard this in years, if I'm being honest. But, I used to listen to it *all* the time when I was younger." Younger as in when? I ask myself. The album was released in 1997, so she had to have been a teenager when it came out.

"There was a song on there I must have listened to a hundred times, I loved it. When I was a teenager I looked up the lyrics and some of them really struck a cord I suppose." She admits. Something in my chest is tightening and my stomach is doing weird little flips. My gut says I know which song she's referring to, and her confession of listening to it as a teenager just gives me more reason to believe I *have* in fact heard this song before. Just not the way I originally thought.

"Was it Silver Springs by any chance?" I ask calmly, never taking my eyes off her face.

She looks up at me with a confused expression, slowly morphing into understanding. Tears prick her eyes, and she wipes her napkin across her mouth. The air in the kitchen is stifling all of a sudden, and this new connection forming between us is palpable. "Yes." She whispers. "I used to play it when I was pregnant with you…" The tears that threatened to fall have spilled over and stream down her face in gentle rivers. I knew I felt something when that song came on, I just couldn't explain it.

Until now.

Up until that day with Mitch, I had never heard that song before. Or if I had, I certainly don't remember it. Now I know it wasn't just a fluke thing, my body somehow remembered that song and reacted to it even though I had no understanding. I can feel tears of my own brimming my eyes, and if this moment wasn't so profound, I'd be irritated with the fact that I'm crying, *again*.

Guess I can add crying to my list of characteristics, since I'm so good at it these days.

"How did you know it was that song?" She finally asks. I sift through ways to explain it without sounding weird, but it doesn't matter, everything about this situation is weird in a wonderful way. Hearing that song and feeling a connection to it without knowing why is about as weirdly wonderful as one can get.

"The first time I was alone with Mitch, we were on our way to a shelter to drop off baked goods when Silver Springs came on. My whole body responded to it, chills and goosebumps all over. Mitch looked at me like I was insane." I laugh at the memory and Lucy smiles as she listens.

"I knew I had never heard the song before, or seen the album around the house growing up, but when I played it a second time I knew there something about it when I reacted the same way." We sit quietly, and I can hear the sounds of both our labored breathing. Our lunch is all but forgotten, which sucks because I *was* starving before we started this conversation. Only have myself to blame for that.

"What was it about that song that made you listen to it so much when you were pregnant?" I ask, genuinely curious.

Sighing, Lucy places her napkin in her lap and pushes her plate away from her slightly. "Some of the lyrics just rang true to how I felt about my situation with your birth father. As much as it pained me to hear it in a song, it was also the only thing I wanted to listen to. Counterintuitive I guess."

Since I heard the song the second time, I added it to a playlist and listen to it all the time. I've dissected the lyrics a few times, trying to find something in them that would make sense. Something that would be a hint or reason to be so affected by it. Now that I know the meaning behind the song, I think I know which lyrics stuck out to Lucy. My heart hurts for the sixteen year old girl, alone and scared to bring life into this world without the boy who is half of me. The boy she probably could have loved had he not left without a backward glance.

"I know I could have loved you, but you would not let me." I reach across the table and hold one of Lucy's soft hands in mine. When her eyes meet mine, there's so much compassion and understanding in them. She knows this has been hard for me like I know how hard it's been for her. I want to help her through it like I know she wants to do the same for me, but the fact is, we can't erase the years of hurt. We can't go back in time and change the outcome. We just have to be thankful that we're here now and make the most of what we're being given.

A relationship, of any kind, takes hard work and compromise. Now that I've found Lucy, found the truth about where I come from, I can't just treat it as an everyday thing. This is a gift, being able to connect with the woman who birthed me, who loves me, *after* already being loved by two amazing parents. It's overwhelming, and at times too much to take in, but now that I know…Nothing can take that feeling away.

We spent a few more hours talking and learning as much as we could about the other. We also reheated our food and finally ate. I think I had three Sammies by the time we were done. My cheeks hurt from smiling so much, and tomorrow I'm going to check for a six pack after all the laughing we did. Lucy feels more like the best friend I never had, rather than another mom. We're a lot alike and have many of the same interests, another thing I didn't have with friends growing up. I always felt like an outcast with how much I enjoyed art and reading. Up until I met my high school art teacher, Ms. Hayes, I didn't have anyone to connect with on the same level.

By the time I'm heading out, it's dusk. I'm not a huge fan of driving in the dark, especially since it's an hour away. But we decided the next time we get together, Lucy is going to come to me. I think I'm ready to have her meet Gran and Pop, now that I told them I know everything. I would never dream of ambushing them by bringing Lucy over unannounced. Gran may not have said it directly, but she wants to meet Lucy, that much I can tell.

The sky is black by the time I'm pulling down the road to my house, but Mitch's truck catches my eye immediately. My heart beats in my chest, just the anticipation of feeling his arms wrap around me, pulling me in for a searing kiss. The kind that has butterflies flapping wildly against my rib cage. Gran told me she and Pop were going to the Murphy's for dinner tonight and that she would save me a piece of garlic bread since I wasn't going to make it.

As I cut the engine and climb out of the car, I notice there aren't any lights on in the house. My grandparents aren't home yet and awareness pricks at my skin that Mitch and I have the house to ourselves. Probably the first time since we took our secret shower the day of the fundraiser for Raising Hope. I don't know how long we have before someone comes home, but I plan on taking advantage of what time we do have.

The porch swing creaks as Mitch rocks lightly back and forth. In the moonlight I can just make out the smirk he's fixing me with and the finger that pulls me closer and closer to him without any thought. I stop in front of him, my knees brushing against his, and feel both of his hands snake out to wrap around my legs. His touch, even through my clothes is scorching and I'm desperate to feel more of him, without any barriers.

We haven't done anything since the night of the vow renewal, and I want to change that, *now*. Without any greeting or explanation, I place one leg on the side of his thigh and swing the other over so I'm straddling him. Hooking my hands into the hair at the base of his neck, I pull him into me and kiss him deeply. The warmth of his lips spreads down my chest and straight to my core. I don't even need any prep tonight, I'm ready and willing. After all the emotions of this past week, I only want to lose myself in Mitch right now.

Using both hands, Mitch grips my thighs and slides them up and around until he's holding my ass. He drags my body down and against him until I feel his hard length pressing into me. A soft gasp escapes me as I release his lips for a lungful of air. He captures the sound with his mouth and pushes his tongue through the seems of my lips, tasting and savoring me. "This is the best hello of my life." His voice caresses me.

We're out in the open, but there's no lights on in the house casting a glow on us as we sit on the porch. The moon is slightly shielded by passing clouds, so before I lose my nerve, I pull back and yank my shirt off. I place it on the swing next to us, because at least I have some foresight someone could come home at any moment. I could have left my shirt on, but the feel of Mitch's lip pulling my breast into his mouth is not something I'm willing to pass up.

Sliding his hands up my body, Mitch finds the clasp of my bra and releases it with ease. The lace material falls to the porch floor and I'm too lost in this sensation to even care. Mitch latches on to one nipple, sucking it into his mouth on a groan. I push farther into him, enjoying the feeling of his mouth on my peak and his hard length against my pulsing center. I need him now, hard and fast. No more being gentle like he was our first time. I get why he did it, he wanted to make sure I was okay, but I want all of him, guard down.

"Mitch?" I say in a breathy whisper, my body involuntarily grinding into him. "Did you…do you have another condom on you?" He doesn't respond, just moves to my other breast and sucks my pebbled nipple into his mouth. He looks up at me with a piercing stare and he practically feeds on me with fervor. It's heady and my body practically melts at the way he's looking at me. Like he's a starving man and I'm his last meal.

I'm ready to be devoured.

The pressure building between my thighs is becoming unbearable. I never knew I could be so desperate for Mitch to touch me, but now that I've had a taste of it, I don't think I'll ever get enough. I don't know how much time we have or if I'm even able to pry myself away from him long enough to move into the house. The hand holding my hips against him grips me harder and I bite his lip, eliciting a satisfying moan from him.

"In my pocket, baby. Can you get it?" Mitch mumbles against my breast, the feel of his hot breath giving me tingles all the way down to my toes. I fist his wallet out of his jeans and pry it open searching for the condom. A triumphant smile overtakes my face as I rip it open not able to wait until minute to have Mitch sinking into me.

He releases my breast and leans back as I begin unbuckling his belt, then yank his jeans down just enough that he's able to slide the condom on. Lining himself up to my entrance, he looks at me and grips my chin in his hand. "If it's too much, tell me. Do you understand?" This is the side of Mitch I love to see. The side of him that loses control, unable to restrain himself from how badly he wants me. It's empowering, invigorating and I relish it in.

I lift up onto my knees, positioning myself over him and slowly sink down onto him. Gloriously impaling myself on his dick, feeling him grow even bigger as he stretches me. I'm so wet already, it doesn't take long for our bodies to move in tandem, slick against each other. Setting the pace, I move up and down on Mitch, moaning each time I'm seated completely on him, grinding my pelvis into him harder and harder with each pass. He holds my hips in his tight grip, guiding me down each time, working together as we set the pace for release.

I would make this last all night if I wasn't afraid of getting caught. Something about that arouses me more though, the fear of being seen only adds to the moment. It's provocative and so goddamn empowering, I can't get enough. The reserved girl who was always sad as a teenager, losing herself in art and books is gone. Replaced by the woman confidently riding the man beneath her, taking what she wants unapologetically.

I've never felt so strong, like I'm the one in control, and

that's exactly what I am…in control. I set the pace and I shift my hips into Mitch with delectation, enjoying the way he watches me. His eyes roam over my body in slow perusal, causing gooseflesh to erupt across my arms and legs. When he looks at me, I don't just feel like Olive, I feel desired, I feel transcendent. Euphoric feelings pulse throughout my body and I know if I allowed myself to, I would come right now. As easy as it would be, I slow my movements down so I can delay my orgasm and enjoy this feeling for just a few more minutes.

I roll my hips against Mitch, leaning in to kiss the smirk right off his lips, tasting his pleasure with my tongue. It feels fevered and I'm high on it. When I move into Mitch, he takes it all and gives it back ten fold. Our movements are languid, and I simply enjoy the feeling of him pressed so tightly to my chest I can feel his heart thrumming beneath his shirt. His restraint is waning, and I can feel his need to thrust into me hard and fast building underneath me. I'm ready for him to lose control, fuck me the way he's dying to, the thought plainly written all over his face.

I nip his bottom lip, pulling it into my mouth and sucking hard as I arch my body further into him, as if that were possible, picking up the pace as I do. That's all it takes, he's wrapping a fist around my ponytail and yanking my head to the side so he can sink his teeth into my neck. I cry out, in pain and ecstasy as he drives into me harder. Gripping his shoulders I grind myself against him, getting impossibly deeper, and feel my orgasm building.

I have no idea if we're being loud or not, and truthfully a car could pull down the drive as we speak and I don't think

I would let up. My thighs clench against Mitch, riding him until I feel my release about to detonate me from the inside out. I'm close, my movements become erratic, and I'm moaning uncontrollably. I can tell he's right there with me, his shoulders tensing beneath my grip, attempting to hold off his own release until he knows I've had mine. We lock eyes and on an exhale I mumble, "come with me, Mitch." As soon as the words leave my mouth, I feel myself lose control. Catapulting over a cliff of blinding euphoria, unable to stop.

Mitch comes a second later, growling into my neck, licking at the salty skin there as his fingers dig half moons into my thighs. We stay like that for several seconds, allowing our racing hearts to slow and return to normal. I lay my forehead against his heaving chest and breathe in his crisp scent, hoping I can memorize it. I've never felt so craved by someone, so connected, and it makes me want to cry. Not tears of sadness for once, but the good kind.

Lifting my chin so that I'm looking at him, Mitch kisses my lips tenderly. His voice is low and sexy as he whispers against my cheek. "Believe me when I tell you…A tornado could tear apart this farm and all the land around it. A tsunami could sweep me away and out to sea…and I could be ripped to shreds by sharks. All that and nothing, I mean *nothing*, could break me the way you could. The power you hold over me is terrifying, Olive." He says as he tucks a loose strand of hair behind my ear. His confession hangs in the air between us, and I wish I could respond and tell him how much I love him. How I'm *in* love with him. His words play over and over in my mind, like a symphony of what I mean to him. The feelings are mutual, I can feel it between us, but something prevents me from saying what's desperately trying to work its way out of my chest and out in the open.

Instead of saying anything, I twine my fingers in his hair, sweaty from exertion, and kiss him softly. My body gives him the words I'm unable to voice and I can only hope he feels them the way I need him to. Whatever this is between us, it's the realest thing I've ever felt. My heart swells with the love I've come to experience in the last few weeks. If I told myself a year ago this is where I'd be, I'd laugh without any humor.

I just wish it was enough to quiet that voice in the back of my mind telling me this is all too good to be true.

That voice can fuck off.

The fact that Mitch and I managed to get dressed and sit casually on the swing just before my grandparents got home, has me laughing as I walk up the stairs to bed. Since neither of us lives alone, it means we don't have a ton of privacy or the luxury of spending the night together. One day, maybe.

Freshly showered and ready for bed, I climb under the thin sheet just after midnight. It's humid tonight so I opted for my silk two piece silk pajama set. They leave little to the imagination, a point made abundantly clear as my pebbled nipples cut through the thin fabric. The sky is clear through my window, and I decide to climb out onto the roof to watch the stars for a while. I haven't come out here in weeks, always exhausted after the day.

Whenever I come out here I feel more at ease, even on

hot nights like tonight where the air feels thick. My legs brush against the rough roof tiles, prickling my sensitive skin. I brush my hands under my thighs wishing I brought my blanket out with me. Lying back, I gaze up to see a blanket of stars crowding every inch of black. Out here the stars are like tiny diamonds, unobstructed by bright city lights.

It's quiet too, serene, with just the sounds of crickets in the field and a few northern mockingbirds serenading the night. Mother Nature's symphony at work. I'm about to head in when I hear the sound of gravel crunching. Straining my eyes, I see a figure walking towards the part of the house I'm perched on. It's past midnight and people don't typically lurk around here at night.

At least, I didn't *think* they did.

"Olive!" I hear someone whisper shout, my body tingles with awareness and I try to decide if it's best to ignore the voice and climb back in my room slamming the window shut and locking it. Or, see who it is. Two conflicting sides of myself battling for dominance. Ten seconds later, I hear it again, only louder and more clear. "Olive, it's Mitch." Relief courses through me and I laugh at how paranoid I just was.

"What are you doing, creeper?" I tease. He disappears to the side of the porch and I hear him heft himself up the trellis until I see his face peak over the edge of the roof. "Mitch! What the fuck are you doing?" I shriek. This dumbass is scaling the side of my house like a damn koala in a tree, and he just laughs at my distress.

With ease, he uses his upper body strength to pull himself up until he butt plops down on the roof next to me.

He's smirking at me, probably assuming he impressed me when really I want to whack him upside the head for being so careless. I kind of got used to him being in one beautiful piece, I'd hate to see him fuck himself up over something stupid. "Are you trying to impress me? Cause I gotta be honest, that's not the best way to do it."

"I'll always try to impress you, Olive. But I'd much prefer to do it in other ways…" Mitch was just inside me a mere three hours ago and already he's ready to go again. That makes two of us, I can never get enough of him, and I want to hold on to that feeling for as long as possible. Mitch toys with the strap of my pajama top, fingers grazing just above my breast. It doesn't matter how simple a touch can be, he elicits a gasp or a moan out of me every single time. We could make this a fun little game, I have to try and control my reactions and sounds every time he touches me in an intimate way.

I'd lose during the first round.

"I couldn't sleep and hoped you might be out here." He says, tracing his fingers down between my breast now. I'm finding it hard to focus on his words, but I want to ask why he thought I might be out here. I can't remember ever telling him it's something I do, but that's the part I'm struggling to focus on. He makes my brain turn to mush every time his hands are on me.

"H-how did you know I'd be…I'd be out here.?" I stutter as he sucks one of my ear lobes into his mouth, biting down with little force.

"I saw you watching the stars one night when I went for a walk, back when we first met." He switches to the other ear now as one of his hands gently massages my inner thigh. "It took a lot of restraint not to climb up here and sit with you that night. I was already failing miserably at trying to stay away from you. Then I find you sitting up on the roof like a fucking moon goddess." This is news to me. I wonder how many other times he's watched me up here.

"That's pretty creepy, Mitch." I murmur against his shoulder just as a single finger grazes my clit. Without a word, Mitch lowers me until I'm on my back and he's hovering between my legs. He grips my knees and widens them as he stares at me licking his lips. Well, this escalated quickly.

"Do you know what I thought about doing to you when I saw you up here?" He asks as he lowers himself until his face his hovering over me. I can feel his hot breath against my pussy and I try clenching my thighs together to abate the need for him to touch me. I hope he doesn't expect a real answer, cause I think I may have lost my voice and I'm far too preoccupied with his head between my legs to go looking for it. "I dreamed of taking off your sweet pajamas, laying you bare beneath the stars and then sucking your clit into my mouth until I make you see a different kind of stars." Oh, *fuck*.

Using one hand, the other keeping my knees form closing around his head, lifts my tank top until my breasts are on full display. I doubt he can even see them clearly, the only light coming from the partially obstructed moon. Then he begins lowering my shorts, moving out of the way to remove one leg from it's side and then sliding them completely off. It's still really humid but suddenly my body is shaking with chills, goosebumps popping up everywhere as I wait to see what Mitch does.

"Are you already wet for me, Butterfly?" He asks, lips brushing my sensitive folds. Lightly, he sticks his tongue out and leisurely slides it from the bottom of my slit until he reaches the top of my pelvis. I quiver beneath him, enjoying the feel of him but needing more. I'm ready to grip his head in my hands and bury his face in my pussy until I'm coming so hard I'll wake the whole town. If anyone could accomplish that, it's Mitch.

I don't respond with anything but a garbled moan and Mitch pulls back to look at me. "I'm dying to taste your sweetness, Butterfly. So you better tell me now, are you wet for me?" He pinches my clit between two fingers and I cry out, quickly covering my mouth to keep from waking my grandparents. No way in hell could I explain myself out of this situation.

"Y-yes! Yes, I'm wet for you, only for you, Mitch." He groans in satisfaction but still doesn't do what I desperately need. I'm not above begging, and if he doesn't do something soon, I'll take matters into my own hands. *Literally.* "Why don't you taste me and find out?" I wiggle beneath him and arch so that my center is pushing towards his face. He chuckles against my flesh and plunges two fingers in without warning.

I position my arm over my face, bending at the elbow, attempting to keep my pleasure that's fighting to be let free, from filling the quiet night. He works his fingers inside me with such precision, I could come apart just like this. When he lowers himself to sample me, my eyes roll back and I can't help but arch further into his touch. I'm moments away from grinding my pussy into his face when he grips my hips harshly to keep me still. Pulling back for only a second, he levels me with an intense glare. "If you suffocate me, I won't be able to finish baby." That would make two of us.

Controlling the urge to smother him, I settle my hips against the roof and focus on the intense pleasure Mitch is giving me with just his tongue. How the fuck is he so good at this? I've heard some girls don't like oral sex, and now I'm assuming it's cause the guy doing it was shit at it. If every girl got to experience it the way Mitch is doing it right now, they'd never want to stop.

Thinking of Mitch will other girls has me curling my hands into fists at my sides. I don't want to be thinking about that while he's going down on me, but even now my insecurities get the best of me. I try to push the thought to the back of my mind when he hooks finger back in, curling it up into a C shape. I open my eyes to stare at the stars, focusing only on them and Mitch's mouth covering me. I might have to come out here more often if this is how my night will end up.

Working his tongue and fingers together, I feel my orgasm building and I want to chase it, feel it crash over me in heavy waves taking me higher and higher. My body reacts to each flick of his tongue and I'm shuddering beneath him, my arousal leaking onto my thighs. Just when I think the pressure is too much, I'm coming, hard and fast. I grip my thighs around Mitch's head, keeping him planted in place as he sucks my clit into his mouth. My body goes limp, and I loosen my hold on Mitch, legs flopping to the side.

Chest heaving, I watch the stars as I get my breathing under control. I don't even know where Mitch is, for all I know he's still lying between my legs. He lifts up onto his elbows, staring at me with a look of contentment. "You're amazing." He says smiling with proof of my orgasm glistening on his lips. I feel the blush creep over my face and chest and am thankful it's too dark for Mitch to see.

Instead of sitting up next to Mitch, he lies down next to me, interlocking my fingers with his. I never want to leave this place. This place of belonging, where I feel wanted for once. The thought of something happening between Mitch and I, of everything falling apart is too much to even process. More than anything I wish I could just tell him how I really feel about him. This connection between us has morphed into more than a summer fling or simple crush. I wake up thinking about him, my heart recognizes him as it's own and beats for only him.

I try to quiet my thoughts for a moment, listening only to the crickets and Mitch's breathing beside me. If one day he were to decide I wasn't right for him, I would accept it, understand that maybe we just aren't right for each other. It would still hurt like hell, but at least he'd be honest about his feelings. I couldn't stomach being lied to, especially in a relationship that feels as strong as ours.

I roll onto my side, even has the rough surface of the roof bites at my sensitive skin. I should probably put my clothes back on, but the soft breeze feels nice against my flushed body. Mitch is looking up at the stars, and for a minute I just stare at him. The way the stubble lightly covers his face, his strong cheekbones and the way those green eyes of his pierce mine with such intensity it gives me chills. His hair is shaggy and frames his face in rivulets of dark blonde and brown. I'm suddenly wishing I had my paints out here, or my phone at the very least. I'd like to capture this moment of him looking happy and at ease.

He turns his head slightly to face me, and furrows his brow. "What's on your mind, Butterfly?"

"Promise never to lie to me. Please, Mitch." I sit up so I can look at his face more clearly as I get this out. "I've had enough lies in my life already, I couldn't bear one from you too."

Mitch lifts up into a seated position next to me and takes one of my hands. "I won't promise something unrealistic, Olive. People lie, sometimes for good reason. I can't assure you I'll never lie to protect you, because I would, without question." Not exactly what I was hoping he'd say, and he can tell. My face falls slightly, wishing he could have just lied and reassured me he'd never lie to me, but then there's the problem. That's already a lie.

"When it comes to the important things, I wouldn't lie to spare your feelings. I'm only saying it would be hard not to lie if it's to protect you from something that could cause more damage than good."

"I get that, thank you. I just don't know how I'd be able to get past something like that, after everything that's been kept from me my whole life." I turn to face his, holding his gaze. "But, I trust you, Mitch. It may not be an easy thing for me to admit, but I really do trust you. I know you wouldn't keep something from me that would hurt me." I rest my head on his shoulder, and tell myself he only stiffens for a second because he didn't see it coming. If I let myself begin to doubt his words, then we'll be downhill faster than a kid on ice.

I said I trust him, so that's what I plan on doing. Even if it scares the shit out of me.

23

MITCH

I don't deserve Olive. That's the first thought I have when I open my eyes the next morning. She pleaded with me never to lie to her, and I just sat there with the biggest secret. I should have just told her I know who her father is, but I couldn't get the words out. I don't even know why. Maybe because it's not my place to tell her, I feel like it should come from Lucy or Drew. On the other hand, now that I know it's like I'm purposely keeping it from her. *Fuck.*

I'll just talk to Drew, see what he knows about Lucy and maybe they can set up a time to meet and tell Olive together. What the fuck is wrong with me? I'm over here planning family meetings like I'm the host of Maury trying to find out who the father is. Only problem is, I *know* who the father is, I just don't have the balls to tell the one person who deserves to know. I'm not super religious, but I definitely feel like God is looking down on my very disappointed.

Another scorching hot summer work week in the books. This one felt particularly tough, between the heat and knowing who Olive's father is, it's like my sweat is sweating. Every time I see Olive, I want to tell her, she deserves to know, but something always stops me. It's like I've reverted back to my old self when we first met, staying quiet and avoiding eye contact. I'm hoping she won't notice, so instead of being completely closed off, I just keep giving her orgasms. She doesn't seem to mind.

The way her face flushes each time, it's like a drug I can't get enough of. I'm addicted to the way her body responds to me. Like she needs me just as much as I need her. If I didn't love it so much, I'd say it's unhealthy.

She's coming over tonight with Lucy, and I know she's nervous about it. They talked about it and decided our weekly dinner was as good a time as any, Lucy will have an opportunity to meet my parents as well as Joan and Henry. No pressure.

With all the changes thrown at Olive the last few months, she's handled it with such grace, it's transcendent to watch. If it were me, I'd probably sulk about it and distance myself from everyone. Or drink too much. If I'm being honest, it'd probably be the latter. When I was in college, I was known to throw back the drinks fairly easy, not something I'm entirely proud of. Sure, it got me laid more times than I can count, but that life got old real quick. The high can only last so long until it eventually fizzles out and all your left with is shame.

When I got home, I promised myself I would buckle down and grow up. That's why I kept my distance from Olive in the beginning, or at least tried to. It's not like I'm an asshole by nature, I just put up walls and try to keep everyone out no matter how much it hurts.   Myself included.

Every night I'd lay in bed and think about her, and that's what pissed me off even more. The fact that this one girl was controlling so much of my headspace, I wanted her to hate me so I wouldn't risk getting close to her and ruin everything. She was always so sweet, it killed me to be such a dick, but every now and then she'd let that fire out. Once I saw that side of her, I knew I was fucked. I wanted nothing more than to be on the receiving end of both her soft and fiery side.

She's given me that, and then some.

After washing up, I head to the kitchen to check if Ma needs any help. She brushes me off at first, but then abruptly turns around and shoves a stack of dishes in my arms. "Set the table while I finish up in here." Before I can get a word out, she's bustling back to the stove to pull the garlic bread out of the oven. The smell of garlic fills the room and my mouth waters in anticipation. If I ever got stuck on a deserted island and could only have one thing the rest of my life, it would be Ma's garlic bread.

The doorbell rings just as I set the last spot at the table, and a smile tugs at my lips. My body can practically sense when Olive is near, and right now it's tingling with anticipation.

Olive and her grandparents stand just outside the door smiling as I open it and welcome them inside. Joan says a quick hello before hustling to the kitchen. Henry shakes my hand and then he too is off in the direction of the kitchen to talk to my Dad I'm sure. The way they all get along is almost too sweet. Instead of neighbors, we're like family.

Olive stands in the doorway looking at me like a piece of meat, and I have to actively try not to get a hard on in front of the family. "You know when you look at me like that it makes me want to do very bad things to you. Which would be kind of awkward considering the company we're in." She leans into me, inhaling my scent and looking up at me with hooded lids.

"Yeah, well, when you walk over looking like *that*," she gestures to my whole body and I can't help but chuckle, "then it's kinda hard to keep my desires at bay. Plus, you smell *so* good all the time. How the hell do you do that?"

"You're adorable, you know that?" I say just before capturing her lips in mine, tasting the laughter that escapes her.

"I don't know if you'll think I'm so adorable when you see me inhaling Elaine's garlic bread." She laughs. "I'm *starving*. I only ate breakfast because we were slammed at the bakery and I didn't have time to eat lunch."

I hate when she tells me she doesn't have time to eat, she's already so petite, the thought of her skipping meals makes me want to drive to her work everyday and force her to sit and have lunch with me. I'd be a hypocrite though, because I often forgo lunch, too. Especially on the really hot days.

"Well, then I'm making sure you get as much garlic bread as you want, you can even have mine." If there were any other way to say I love you right now without using those three words, that would be it. I *never* give up my garlic bread. But I'd steal it off everyone's plates if it meant she was full and happy. That wouldn't go over too well, but I would at least try.

Just before we all sit down to eat, the doorbell chimes

again, Olive jumps up and races to the door. It's cute to see her excited about this. Sure, I get to see it when she paints, and my favorite, when I make her come and she screams my name so loud my ears ring. But this is different, I get to witness her growing connection to her birth mother, something I never would have gotten to see with her parents since they passed. This is a significant moment for them, as well as her grandparents. As much as I want to enjoy it completely, that sinking feeling lingers in the back of my mind, knowing I have information she deserves to know, but can't find the right way to tell her.

Olive reappears with Lucy close behind, she's smiling but I can sense the nerves. This isn't a normal situation to be in, but the fact that we're all here willingly says a lot. Each one of these people *wants* to be here for Olive, I just hope she understands how monumental this truly is.

"Gran, Pop, this is Lucy…my birth mom." Olive's hands are clasped tightly in from of her, and I wish I could walk over and hold them. Reassure her I'm here if she needs to lean on me at any point. But she's much stronger than she gives herself credit for, she doesn't need anyone to hold her up. I would in a heartbeat, but Olive can do anything, she just needs to believe it.

Joan walks over ahead of Henry, and her eyes are already brimming with tears. After only a moments hesitation, she pulls Lucy in for a hug, and now they're both crying. I'd be lying if I said I wasn't feeling emotion thick in my throat, but I just cough quietly to dislodge it. Henry walks over next, shaking her hand firmly before also giving in to the inevitable hug. This isn't the time for formality.

Lucy is the first to speak once they've all exchanged hugs, my mom included. She can't help herself, she's a hugger by nature. "I can't tell you what it means to me, to have you welcome me into your home. I know the circumstances are a little out of the norm, but I'm grateful you're allowing me to spend this time with you, and Olive." She turns her attention to Olive, love and adoration painting her features. It's abundantly clear how much she loves her, how she's *always* loved her. I can't imagine spending the last nineteen years not knowing if you'll ever see your child again. The thought is like a puncture wound right to the chest.

And I don't even have kids yet.

"I've wanted to meet you for a very long time, dear. I have so many stories to tell you and so many questions to ask. But before we get to all that, I say we sit down together and enjoy a lovely meal Elaine has prepared for us." Joan gestures to the table and Ma leads the way, passing food around the table as we take our seats and then leading prayer.

Dinner goes off without a hitch, and by the time we're done, my stomach has distended so much I can hardly move. Ma went above and beyond tonight, making enough food to feed a small army. She did however have the foresight to bring out to go boxes so that Lucy and anyone else can take home leftovers.

"Shall we sit on the porch for some drinks?" Ma says, leaving the dishes in the sink for later. I plan on recruiting Olive to help me, reminding me of that first time we did dishes together at her house. I got to taste her for the first time that night, and now I'm itching to get my hands on her. A few more hours and I'll hopefully have my way with her.

"You guys head out there, Olive and I can start the cleanup." I wink at her and she rewards me with a soft blush. Guess I'm not the only one who remembers the first time we washed dishes together.

"Thank you, Mitchell." Ma pats my face and grabs some glasses before disappearing outside with a bottle of wine. I think Henry and my Dad headed out there too, which is a nice change considering they usually excuse themselves to the barn.

"Shall we?" I ask, turning my attention to Olive. She's sitting on the counter, with a gleam in her eye and I'm thinking the dishes are going to have to wait. I make my way over to stand in between her legs, resting my hands on the counter caging her in. "Something on your mind, Butterfly?"

"I was just thinking..." She lifts her head to place a soft kiss on my lips. "About the last time we washed dishes together." Another kiss. "We had quite a bit of *wet* fun, didn't we?" Jesus, she's going to kill me right here in my kitchen. Just as I go to brush the loose hair out of her face, I feel a wet cloth slap against the side of my head, followed quickly by a shriek of laughter and Olive pushing past me to run out the front door. Oh, so we're back to this game? She can run, but I'll always catch her.

24

Olive

s soon as the dishrag connects with Mitch's face, I'm off the counter and sprinting towards the front door. He'll catch me, he always does, but the chase makes me push my legs faster than they've ever gone. Adrenaline pumping through my veins, as I stifle my laughter, slightly laced with fear.

Everyone went out back to sit on the deck, so I knew running for the front door was safest. As soon as I leap off the front steps, I can hear Mitch bounding heavily behind me, which only fuels me to go faster. Tall grass tickles my legs as I run through the field, and I catch sight of the fireflies doing their nightly dance. I make it to the fence on the edge of the front yard, right where the road meets their driveway. I'm a little impressed with myself for making it this far without him catching me, but I know it's only because he's allowed me to get this far. If he really wanted me, he would have grabbed me before my feet hit the grass.

Just as I make it to the gate, a strong arm wraps around my waist and yanks me to the ground. I fall on top of him, laughter bubbling out of me as I wiggle against his chest.

We're both gasping for air, but I'm afraid to turn around, knowing he has a wet dishrag in his hand ready to soak me.

Mitch flips me over so that I'm on my back and he's hovering over me. Straddling both legs on either side of me, keeping me right where he wants me. His muscles ripple beneath his shirt, and I have this strange urge to lick them. He grips my chin in his hand, using light force to make me look up at him. I defy him, but only for a moment before I relent. As soon as our eyes meet, he lowers his mouth to mine and feasts on my lips hungrily. All throughout dinner, I had to push away thoughts of him touching me, but out here…no one can see us. It's thrilling.

He breathes heavily against my cheek. "You know, when you said we had wet fun that night, I thought you were referring to something else." He pinches one of my nipples that are already pebbled under my shirt, and I arch into him. I hope he brought that rag out here to soak me, it gives me an excuse to shrug off my clothes faster.

With a wicked smirk, he lifts the cloth rag from behind his back, dripping with soapy water. So not only did he manage to catch me, but he took a few extra seconds to put soap on the rag *before* chasing me. I'm impressed.

I wiggle beneath him in a futile attempt to escape his hold. Just as he lifts the rag dripping water over my chest, car lights flash across us. Mitch sits up, looking to see who's driving down the driveway towards the house. I don't think much of it until I see the horror stricken look on his face. His breathing halts momentarily, before picking up pace until his chest is heaving. Now I'm nervous.

"Mitch? What's wrong?" I ask, slightly worried at how quickly his body tightens with tension above me. "Who is it?" He doesn't respond, just pulls me up with him, all playfulness gone. Replaced with a worry that I can't place. Who would come here that would have Mitch distressed like this?

The second we're off the ground, he's running towards the house. If that car didn't interrupt us and stop in front of the house, I'd think I did something wrong. I run after him, yelling out to him to see if he'll stop and explain what's going on. But he doesn't, he just keeps running like he's trying to win a race, until he stops in front of the car that just pulled up.

I'm several paces behind, when I see a man emerge from the car. From here, he seems relaxed, and they clearly know each other. But Mitch is speaking fast, waving his arms in the direction of the house. Whoever this man is, I get the feeling he wasn't supposed to be here. My skin prickles with unease, and I walk slowly towards them, trying to decide if they need space.

The front door opens and the screen slams shut behind my grandparents, Lucy and Mitch's parents. Something feels off, but I don't know why. As I near the back of the mans car, I notice Lucy stop short on the front porch. Her eyes bug out and she looks from me to the man several times. If I didn't know any better, I'd say they know each other. Mr. Murphy pipes up from the porch, drawing my attention to him momentarily. "Drew, what brings you here?" Okay, so he seems calm. Maybe the tension is in my head, except for the way Lucy is still staring at him.

As soon as that thought crosses my mind, I'm right back

to feeling the air thicken and the sense that something is very *off.* "Lucy?" The man, who I can only assume is Drew, says in a disbelieving tone. She doesn't speak, just stares at him like she's seen a ghost. They know each other, and judging by he pale white face and wide eyes staring, I'd say they haven't seen one another in a long time. Maybe not since they were kids... Oh, *fuck.*

I'm seconds away from panicking when I feel Mitch rush to my side, trying to pull my attention to him. He looks frazzled, and more than anything, he looks *scared.* I can hear him talking quickly, trying to pull me back towards the field, but I can barely hear him. Just like when I met Lucy for the first time, I knew it was her before she even spoke. So as soon as the man, still standing next to his car, turns to face me, all the blood drains from my face.

It's my father.

"Olive, baby, *please*, let's go somewhere. Let's talk." Mitch is still tugging my arm, and suddenly I understand why he's in a panic, desperately trying to pull me away from this situation. He knew. He fucking knew for God knows how long, and he didn't tell me.

Feeling my limbs get weaker by the second, I turn to look at him, disbelief and betrayal washing over me. I look him in the eyes, tears threatening to spill over, and whisper the words I'm afraid to voice. Knowing that once I do, everything changes. "You knew." It's not a question, and he knows it. He can't even focus on me, can't even look me in the eyes and confess that he knew.

I rip my arm out of his grasp, and his face falls, shame

written all over it. Fury fills my veins, begging to burst out of me in a fiery explosion. "You fucking *knew*! Didn't you?" He doesn't say anything, and out of the corner of my eye, I can see my grandparents come to stand beside me. I'm not sure how much anyone else knows, and suddenly I'm feeling like the walls are caving in around me, despite being outside.

"Olive, please, let me explain…" I hold up a hand to silence him. Not wanting to deal with any more explanations or lies right now.

"Don't. Don't you fucking *dare*." I scream. Mitch stays quiet, and I glance around to see everyone focused on me, all except Lucy and this man who is likely my father. They're in stunned silence, unable to process the bomb that is currently exploding in my face right now. Heartbreak cracks my chest open, and I know as soon as I let it all the way in, hurt will begin seeping through my pores. With a deep breath, I swipe the tears from my eyes and look up at Mitch. The man who I was in love with a mere ten minutes ago. The man who now looks like a stranger through my eyes, cloaked in betrayal.

"One thing. I only asked you for *one thing*, Mitch. Don't lie to me." The tears I wiped away are back and spilling down my cheeks as I turn and break out in a sprint, running back home. I need to get out of here. Not knowing who was in on this secret is threatening to break me more than I already am right now. I try breathing in and out but each time I do the breath gets caught in my throat. The emotion clogged there keeping me from getting air to my lungs, even though my body is desperate for it.

I can hear Gran yell my name, and then again before I'm

far enough away the only thing I can hear is the sound of the crickets and my feet beating against the ground. Mitch doesn't follow me, a feeling that greets me with equal parts relief and disappointment. What do you do when the one person who makes everything feel better, is the one who made it all hurt? As soon as I make it to my front steps, I collapse against the railing, chest heaving and tears flowing down my cheeks in rivers. The emotion is too much right now, I can't run it off, as much as I wish I could. I just need a distraction.

A thought pops into my head, and I'm racing up the steps to my bedroom, throwing the door open. My eyes scan the room until I see my laptop. I push the fear aside, and bring up my email, something I've been too chicken shit to do for weeks now. I never checked to see if my application to the gallery in New York accepted my internship. I'm already at my lowest, so what better time to check than now?

I scroll through junk mail before my eyes snag on the letter M. The Museum of Modern Art is a well known art gallery in Manhattan, and my dream is to intern there. I put off checking my email in case I was rejected, afraid of seeing that I wasn't accepted. Without thinking, I click on the email and scan it until I see the words I never expected I would. *We are pleased to inform you…*

Holy *fuck*. I got it. I got the fucking internship! My only regret right now is opening this email during one of the worst moments of my life, aside form losing my parents. Mitch's betrayal burns deep in my gut, but I shove it aside, focusing on this news instead. Without thought, I yank my suitcase out of the closet and start packing my bags. I never told my grandparents about applying to galleries, especially a few hundreds of miles away. But given what happened tonight, I think they'll understand why I want to leave.

Once my bags are packed and waiting by the door, I pace my room several times. I keep waiting to hear my grandparents come through the door, but they aren't home yet. I lay down on my bed, and look at the stars outside my window. I'll miss this, and I'll miss my grandparents, but I need to do this. I can't stay here where I feel like all I'm surrounded with is grief and lies. I need to go, and do this for myself. There's only two things left to do now. One will be easy, and the other is going to gut me.

Mitch always tells me I'm stronger than I think. I plan on proving just how strong I *really* am.

I don't hear from Mitch, not because he hasn't tried to get in touch with me, but because I've blocked his number. After what happened a few nights ago, I told my grandparents everything. I told them about the man who's my birth father, and how Mitch knew but lied about it. *Kept* it from me. I'll never understand why, but I don't care anymore, I'm leaving in the morning.

It was really hard, but I told them about the internship I applied for months ago, and about my acceptance. Gran cried for what felt like hours, and though Pop had a solemn look on his face, I knew deep down he was proud. Last night we celebrated, just the three of us, at home with all my favorites.

It didn't take any convincing to have Collin let me stay

with him in the city, he said it would be nice to have a friendly face around. I felt a little weird asking at first, especially given everything that happened with Mitch. But Collin already agreed not to say anything to him about me staying there. I wouldn't be able to get through Mitch just showing up out of the blue one day. The less he knows, the better.

I can't sleep, and laying here in bed on my last night before I leave, I can't help but wonder if I'm overreacting a little. I could go to Mitch, and ask him why he did what he did, listen to his reasoning. But I don't feel like I owe him that at this point. The one thing I begged him not to do, he did. That's not something I can just move on from, trust is everything to me.

When we first started something, I felt like he was too good to be true, and he proved that theory right. I won't say he's a bad person, because I've gotten to experience first hand how amazing he is. But at this stage of my life, I'm not willing to settle for someone who won't put me first. Whatever his reasons were for not telling me, he should have pushed aside. The second he found out, he should have told me. I repeat that in my mind over and over again as I fall into a restless sleep.

Around three in the morning, I wake up, feeling overheated and claustrophobic in this room. Opening my window, I climb out onto the roof. Another thing I'll miss, laying on the rough tiles watching the sky for a long time. Trying my best to memorize the stars, knowing I won't see them like this in the city.

Before I head in, taking a moment to inhale the night air, smells of wildflowers and fresh cut grass invading my senses.

A lone figure catches my eye, out past the field, against the fence that runs along the road. I rub my eyes, assuming I'm seeing things in my tired state. But he's still there, and I know it's him. Mitch doesn't know I'm leaving early in the morning, I never told him, and I pleaded with Elaine not to say anything either. She doesn't want to lie to him, so she said if he asks she'll tell him I took an internship in the city, but nothing else.

The guilt I feel for that stings at the back of my eyes, but I know this is what I need. A clean break.

I wake up as the early morning sun streams in through the curtains. Laying in bed, I try to soak everything in, knowing this is my last morning in this room for who knows how long. A tear slides down the side of my cheek, followed by a river of others. A look at the clock tells me I only have a few minutes to pull myself together before we leave. My flight is at nine this morning, so Gran and Pop are driving me to the airport.

At first I just wanted to go alone, unsure if I could handle them watching me leave at the airport. I thought it would be easier on us all if I said goodbye here at the house. But Gran insisted. She wanted to make sure I got there safe and that I could find my gate without getting lost. She's not ready for me to leave, and if I'm being honest with myself, a part of me doesn't feel ready either.

I've dreamed of working in the city most of my life, and when my parents died it felt like the perfect thing to put my energy into. Living here has been hard the last few years, and up until a few months ago, I was ready to leave without reservations. I always knew I would miss my grandparents and the comfort of home, but now there's a whole other thought occupying my mind.

Fisting the sheet in my hands, I angrily wipe away the tears I've allowed to fall. This isn't about upsetting my grandparents, or leaving Mitch behind without any explanations. This is what I want. This is what I *need*. For the first time in my life, I'm following the path I've made for myself. I refuse to stay here and fall into a comfortable life without taking any risks. I'm scared shitless, but I'll never know if I can truly make it on my own unless I try.

My alarm sounds next to me, and I finally sit up, ready to face my new life. After getting dressed and grabbing my bags, I head down the stairs to have one last breakfast with my grandparents. We're all more quiet than usual, and I know if Gran tries to say anything, she'll cry, and then so will I .

The drive to the airport is equally as quiet, and I have to hide the silent tears threatening to spill down my cheeks. I watch the fields buzz by us in a blur, and wonder how Mitch will react when he finally hears the news. I can't allow myself to feel guilt over our situation. I only asked Mitch for one thing, to never lie to me because I didn't think I could take any more betrayal. Whatever his reasoning was for keeping the truth from me, doesn't matter at this point. Selfishly, I'm leaving it all behind and focusing on myself. Never thought I'd revisit the selfish thirteen year old girl I once was, but here we are.

As soon as I say goodbye to my grandparents and board

the plane, it all sinks in. The reality of what I'm doing crashes over me in tidal waves, and I spend the majority of the plane ride to New York silently crying into the neck pillow Elaine gifted me before I left.

Maybe one day I'll be able to let go of all the hurt, and return home with the hopes of a clean slate. As the plane begins its descent, I see the skyline of the city come into view and my breath catches in my throat. Fear of the unknown settling in my belly. Until the day I decide I can go home again, this will be my new life.

Whether I'm ready or not.

<h1 style="text-align:center">25</h1>

<h1 style="text-align:center">MITCH</h1>

TWO YEARS LATER

I'll never get over the feel of Olive's soft skin beneath mine. The way her hair fans out across my chest as she listens to my thudding heart. The one that wholly beats for her. No one has ever come close to making me feel the way she does. *Did.*

It's been two years since I've seen her, and yet I can still smell the coconut paradise of her skin. Every now and then I'll catch her scent somewhere in the air, causing me to stop dead in my tracks in the hopes that she's nearby. She never is, of course, just my brain playing tricks on me, but I'll never give up hope.

The days after she left were torture, and truthfully I almost got on a plane to find her. When Ma informed me that Olive asked to keep her location private, I almost lit everything in my wake on fire. The embers would be representative of the painful inferno demolishing my heart. I felt betrayed, my own family not willing to give me the *only* thing I was asking. Until it hit me, the only thing Olive asked of me was to never betray her, never lie to her, and I promised I never would.

Until the day I did.

It still keeps me up at night, and on the particularly bad nights, I take a walk to her grandparents house. I watch the roof where she used to sit, gazing at the stars. My mind tricks me sometimes, making me think I can actually see her up there, the way I did for months. I almost climbed up there one night but was afraid of waking up Joan and Henry. Olive leaving was hard on them too, I didn't want to be the cause of any more stress for them.

Our weekly dinners fizzled out after a while, and I feel responsible for that as well. Ma and Joan became so close that summer, and then it was like every time we saw each other, the pain was too much. They missed her just as much as I did, and seeing each other without her sunny presence just made it harder. So eventually, we just stopped getting together.

I'm supposed to make a delivery to the bakery this morning, something I've come to almost dread, another thing that makes me feel like shit. I used to love catching up with Joan, eating her fresh cookies and talking shop with Henry, but it just doesn't feel right anymore. Nothing has been right in two years.

As I ease my truck up in front of the bakery, I notice the shades are drawn and none of the lights are on inside. That's weird, I had just spoken to Joan about a delivery, so I know she was expecting me. Thinking I got the day messed up, I check my calendar and see that I am in fact right. Besides, they're only closed on Sundays and it's Tuesday. Something feels off.

Reaching across the cab of my truck, I grab my phone and

call Ma. If something happened, she would likely have heard about it by now. After three long rings, her solemn voice hits my ear and fills my inside with dread. "Mitchell." That's it, that's all she says before I hear her sniffles through the line.

"Ma, what is it? What's wrong?" My body is buzzing with adrenaline, is it my Dad or Collin? I can't even bring myself to think something happened to Olive. But that would make sense why the bakery is closed. Maybe…Fuck…*No*…She stays quiet for barely five seconds before I'm raising my voice, demanding she tell me what's happening. I can't live with the what if's, I'm already losing my mind without Olive.

"It's…Henry. He died last night." She lets out a sob, and my heart aches for my mom, for Joan. I can practically feel Ma's body shaking through the phone with despair. Without another thought, I'm throwing my truck in drive and barreling down the road towards home.

I can't remember if I said goodbye to my mom before I threw my phone to the passenger side of the truck. "Goddammit!" I yell, punching the steering wheel, feeling unshed tears welling in my eyes. I just spoke to him two days ago, and now he's just…*gone*. Joan must be a wreck, I can't imagine losing the other half of my soul. And yet in some ways, I have. Olive leaving gutted me in ways I didn't even think were possible. But at least I knew she was alive and okay.

As I make my way down the driveway, I see my parents on the front porch with Joan. Jesus, I don't know if I'm ready to face them. I'm not the best in situations where people are crying, I don't know how to comfort someone the way they need. Taking a few deep breaths, I slowly get out of the truck and walk up the steps to where they're all sitting.

Joan's eyes are red and puffy from crying, matching Ma's perfectly. Even my Dad looks emotional, even though he never cries, he still feels deeply. He's just not one to show it. Joan doesn't look at me as I approach, something she stopped doing a long time ago. It's not like there's any bad feelings there, but looking at each other is a reminder of the one person we wish would come home.

I kneel down in front of her, taking both her small delicate hands in mine. I stare at them for a few moments, lightly squeezing them so she feels my grief without having to speak. When she finally meets my eyes, the pain in them almost knocks me clear off the porch. I've never seen such sadness, and knowing that not only has she lost her daughter, and her granddaughter moved miles away, but the one person she chose to spend her life with is gone now too.

"Joan…I can't even begin to understand what this feels like, but one day I hope to." Everyone looks at me with a confused expression and I swear if this moment weren't so raw, Ma would whack me upside the head. "I can only hope to be as fortunate, as rich in love as you and Henry were, and be able to feel love this deeply. Grief is a bitch, but it's proof of how hard we loved someone. That we gave them everything we had knowing one day we will eventually lose them." I keep her hands in mine and she nods up at me slowly, a tiny smirk gracing her features.

"You'll get to feel it one day. Just pull your head out of your ass, and go get our girl. Yeah?" She fixes me with a stern look, and I can't even blink. I want to laugh, but now is an entirely inappropriate time to do such a thing. Instead, I meet her with a smirk of my own, giving her hands one last squeeze before nodding and simply saying, "yeah."

Message received. It's time I win back *my* girl.

26

Olive

Living in the city is more than I ever thought it would be, in good ways and bad. The gallery is amazing, and I've met so many people who have connections to other galleries around the country. Staying with Collin has worked out too, something I was nervous about at first. I didn't know if it would be awkward living with Mitch's brother, especially since we didn't get to know each other that well when he was visiting.

But Collin works seventy hours a week, so I hardly see him. It's like I get to live in a beautiful apartment rent free, by myself. At first it was a luxury, but as the months went on, I became home sick. City life is great for a few weeks, but I miss my quiet home town, I never thought I'd say this, but I miss people recognizing me. I can go days without having any kind of conversation. People at work are too focused on their own tasks, and it's not the most friendly environment. Collin is never home when I am, so I don't even get interactions with him much.

The person I probably talk to the most these days is the coffee barista at the shop I go to every morning. She's pretty cool, but I don't plan on asking her to hang out anytime soon. I'm sure she has her own friends and I don't need anyone pitying me.

It's been two years since I've been home, a fact that crosses my mind often. I miss my grandparents, *a lot*. We talk all the time, but it's not the same. I miss having breakfast with them every morning, our weekly dinners with the Murphy's, and I even miss working at the bakery. I just miss the comfort of home, and I miss Mitch. It took a long time for me to admit that to myself, but it's the truth. I never gave him a chance to explain, and for that I feel the guilt woven into my veins. A tattoo that's branded itself from the inside out.

The apartment is dark when I get home, like always. I drop my keys in the bowl by the door, and set my bag down on the floor, too exhausted to put things where they actually belong. This week felt longer than usual, like a weight has been constantly sitting heavily on my shoulders, causing me to slump around in a sour mood. I can't explain why, but I just feel off lately.

Maybe it's a touch of being homesick, or maybe it's because I haven't felt the surge of excitement at work in a long time. It's as if the shock has worn off and reality has set in, reminding me that this life isn't as glamorous as I always dreamed. I don't regret my decision to move here though. I needed to know I could do it, live on my own, almost, and work at my dream gallery.

Now that I've done it, I feel like it's time to move on

and find a new dream. I plop down in one of the decorative armchairs by the big window that looks over the city skyline, and heave a sigh. I should feel more grateful for the opportunities I've been given, but that little voice in my head is telling me it's time to go.

Collin has been a great roommate, and I've enjoyed getting to know him better, in the times we're actually here at the same time. Sometimes I lay in bed at night and wonder if Mitch ever found out where I went and who I'm living with. I half expected him to come here in a rage, knocking the door down. After months went by, and then a year, I realized he probably moved on and never really cared about me the same way I cared for him. The sting still hurts, and even after two years, I feel his absence like a lost limb.

It's almost midnight, I'm hungry and I need a shower, but I'm exhausted. Shuffling into my room, I lay down face first on the bed, still dressed in my work clothes. I'm ready to zone out and let sleep take me, when I hear my phone ping from the front hall. Groaning into my pillow, I contemplate letting it go. The thought of crawling back out there to get my phone makes me want to shut it off and ignore it for the rest of the night. The only people who would contact me from that phone is Gran, Pop or the Murphy's. I'd be lying to myself if I said I didn't on occasion get excited at the prospect of Mitch reaching out.

It'll never happen, I remind myself. If he cared enough to reach out, he would have by now. Deciding it's probably nothing important, I pull back the covers ready to settle in and shut out the world. As soon as my eyes flutter shut, I hear the ping again. My earlier thought pops back to the forefront, reminding me that no one calls that phone but my grandparents or Elaine. It's midnight, and they should all be asleep by now. Unless…

My eyes flash open and I fling myself from bed, racing around the corner into the foyer to get my phone. In my frantic search, I miss it several times before dumping all the contents out on the floor. When I finally have it, my hands are shaking and I'm faced with the screen lighting up with several missed calls from Gran. Alongside that are half a dozen text messages from Elaine. Something is wrong.

Not caring about the time, I dial Gran's number in a blind panic, pacing the hallway as the dial tone rings in my ear. She doesn't answer and I'm about to book a flight home when her picture appears on my screen. "Gran! I'm so sorry I missed your calls, is everything okay?" I almost don't ask, because I know it's bad. She wouldn't have called that many times to tell me something little. Whatever it is, she felt inclined to call me until I knew the news. My stomach sinks in anticipation, and I feel like I'm about to throw up.

I hold my breath as I hear her heavy sigh on the other side, she opens her mouth to speak, choking on the words before taking a deep breath and trying again. I'm about to pass out from holding my breath when she finally speaks the words I knew in my gut before they hit my ears. "Oh Ollie, I wish I didn't have to do this over the phone…"

"Don't say…Gran, *please*…" I choke on my words, a sob threatening to burst up my chest and out of my mouth. I can't even ask, I can't even process the thought of it being Pop. The man who half raised me. But I know that's what she's about to say, I can feel it in every part of my body and soul.

"He loved you so much, sweetie." That's all she says. That's all she has to say, because we both know I already knew what this was about before she answered my call. The breath I was holding leaves my body in a gush, nearly knocking the wind out of me. I collapse to the floor as silent sobs rack my very being. This hurts just as bad as losing my parents, because this time I'm losing one of the only two family members I have left.

Neither of us says anything for several minutes as Gran lets the news sink in. She just stays on the other line listening to me cry uncontrollably, slowly losing any sense of normalcy I had left. Everything about being here lately has felt wrong, and now I know why. He needed me to come home, and I couldn't do it. Once again for my own selfish reasons. Goddammit, I thought I was past this shit. But here I am again, sobbing on the floor, thousands of miles away from the two most important people in my life. I should have been there for his last few days. Fuck, I should have been there these last two *years*.

What's worse, is I should be there for Gran right now. Instead I'm crying into the phone as she listens to my heart break, *again*. I try my best to calm my breathing so I can try talking, right now my throat feels raw and swollen. I can barely get words out, let alone air.

After a few shaky breaths, I tell Gran I'm sorry and ask if she's okay. I need to be there for her, and I need to book a flight, right fucking now. "I've had some time to accept it, we all knew his time here was limited. After the heart attack, I took every day after that as a gift. Knowing that he could go into cardiac arrest anytime and that would be it."

"I'm so sorry Gran, I should have been there for him, I should have been there for you…I should…" I can't help it, the tears come again, just as hard as they did five minutes ago. I wish I could be one of those strong people, the ones who don't wear every emotion on their sleeve, and are able to compartmentalize. But that's just not how I'm wired. My grandparents have always known this about me, which is why Gran isn't surprised by my lack of control right now. I just wish for her sake I could have handled the news better.

She's always been so strong, the rock of our family. Hell, she's the rock, the glue, and all the craft supplies. We wouldn't have functioned had it not been for her all these years. She held us up when my parents died, when her own daughter died, she was the one keeping us from crumbling from the pain. Who's going to be there for her after the loss of her one true love? *Me.*

Keeping the phone crooked in my neck, I open my laptop and look up flights, I'd fly home right now if there was a flight available. But since there isn't, I'm able to snag a last minute flight out tomorrow night. I'll be home in just under twenty four hours, and the thought fills me with hope and dread.

"Olive, listen. I know coming home will be difficult, for a number of reasons, just…" She pauses, and I know she's trying really hard not to mention Mitch. After my first few months here, she stopped mentioning him altogether. She could tell it was painful for me to hear his name, and I was thankful when she stopped talking about him. Even Elaine caught on fairly quickly.

"I just want you to do what's best for you when you get here…okay?" That's her not so subtle way of saying whatever feels right regarding Mitch, go with you gut.

"I will, Gran. I love you so much. I'm sorry I wasn't there for you, for him…I wish…" I can't even get the words out. I want to tell her how sorry I am, how I wish I could have been there. But nothing can change that now. I knew something was off in my gut, and that should have been the first and only sign I needed to go home. Instead I stayed here like the coward I am. A little girl always running from her problems.

"Olive Josephine, you listen to me. You listening?" She asks in her *I'm not fucking around* voice.

"Yes, Gran, I'm listening." I manage to choke out before she goes off on her tangent.

"What you did, moving out there to pursue your dream, well, it's fucking incredible. I wish I had the gall to do such a thing at your age. While I don't have any regrets in life, I do wish I had been more like you. You were scared to go, but you did it anyways. I am in awe of you sweetheart, and your parents are looking down at you proud as can be."

"Coming home wouldn't have changed the inevitable, all it would have done was cause you pain having to watch your grandfather, the man I know you've looked up to since you were a little girl, wither away. That's not what he would have wanted for you. So don't you go thinking you're a selfish person for staying where you are. We are more than proud of you, Olive. And if you don't listen to another goddamn thing

I say the rest of your life, let *that* be the last thing you take away. You hear me?" She's breathing heavily, winded from her stern speech.

I'm having a hard time breathing as well, as I take in everything she just said. I always knew they loved me and were proud of me, but hearing it in this way is a punch to the chest. I make them proud. I never realized how little I needed in life, aside from their approval. I didn't get to say goodbye to Pop, and that will kill me for the rest of my life, but knowing how much he loved me and that he was *proud* of me for living my life. That's more than I could have ever hoped for.

"It's late, and there are an awful lot of emotions being thrown around. Get some sleep, if you're able, and I'll see you tomorrow night. I love you Ollie." Gran using Pop's nickname for me, makes me want to crawl under my covers and never come out. I'm going to miss that so fucking much.

"I love you Gran. See you tomorrow." We hang up, and I do crawl back into bed, if only to cry until I fall asleep. Just before sleep comes, I whip out my phone and search through my voicemails, praying to God I find at least *one*. My eyes snag on his name, and I click on the voicemail, bringing the phone to my ear just as Pop's voice flows from the speaker. Silent tears roll down my cheeks as I listen to Pop's voicemail, asking me to check the deposit slip from the night before at the bakery. He was always double checking things like that, and it makes me laugh a little.

But the thing I was waiting for comes right before the message ends, "Love you, Ollie." He says and then his voice is gone. I sob into my pillow, listening to the voicemail over and over again until my throat is raw from crying, and my tears have run dry. I fall asleep clutching my phone, with *'I love you, Ollie'*, playing on repeat in my dreams.

"Are you sure you don't want me to switch my flight so we can arrive together?" Collin asks from the counter where he's brewing us coffee. As soon as I heard him get up this morning, I came out of hiding and told him the news. I have to give him credit, he held me while I cried, *again*, and if I wasn't so heartbroken, I'd be mortified by my actions.

"It's okay, I promise. You're flight comes in tomorrow afternoon, so there's no need to switch now and pay hundreds more." Collin looks at me with an eye roll, as if he cares about the money right now.

"Olive, come on. You know that shit doesn't matter to me. I'm about to switch my flight anyways, so you don't feel bad for asking." He laughs as he pours me a cup then one for himself. He joins me on the couch, and takes a seat on the opposite end. When I first moved here, I was worried it would be awkward being around Collin so much, considering everything that happened back home. But he's like the big brother I never had, I feel safe around him. In ways I clearly didn't around Mitch.

"You know, I don't think I ever properly thanked you for letting me live here the last two years. I don't think I would have been able to make it on my own, as much as I wish I could say I could have." I stare into my mug, as steam billows out above my coffee. In addition to being terrible at accepting compliments, I'm equally as awkward at expressing my gratitude.

"No thanks needed, truly. It's been nice having a friend to come home to, even if said friend is usually passed out by the time I get here." We both laugh, because truth is, I have been sleeping more than usual it seems. I'm still not sure if it's because of my job and living in the city, a place that's exhausting as it is. Or, if it's because I'm just tired in general. "For real though, I can tell a part of you has one foot out the door, but if you decide to come back after the funeral, you still have a place to stay. Just do what feels right in your gut, Olive."

I mull over Collin's words, all morning as I pack my bag to head home for the first time in two years. When I'm sure I have everything I need, I sit down on my bed and glance around the room. Other than a few personal items, there's nothing sentimental left in this room. Once I walk out that door, I could go home and never return, knowing I didn't leave anything important behind.

I try convincing myself that's true, but there is one thing I could leave here, or I could take with me. The weight of it's contents won't lessen whether they're here or with me back in Kansas. Rising from the bed, I make my way over to my dresser, opening the hidden drawer I never would have even seen if Collin didn't show me. It's a great place to hide spare cash, considering it's barely noticeable if you don't know to look for it.

I ease the drawer open, holding my breath as I do, until I see the stack of letters resting inside. I got the first one about a month after I arrived in New York. I didn't expect Elaine to keep my secret forever, and truthfully, a month is longer than I thought she'd hold out on Mitch. Just like when I found the letters from Lucy, I wasn't able to open them at first. Each month, a new letter would come, and each time I would add it to all the unopened letters Mitch had sent. I couldn't bring myself to open them, knowing I wasn't strong enough to stay here if I read his words. If I was able to understand his reasoning and read his apologies, then I'd run back to him. I had to see this through.

After the first letter arrived, I convinced myself he was just giving me a blanket apology, trying to clear his conscience in a way. But once the letters kept coming every month, I knew it was more than just guilt causing him to write them. As much as I wish I could let him go, I never could. Which is likely why I'm pulling the letters from the hidden drawer and stuffing them in my carry on bag. I only ever read the first one, maybe it's time I read them all.

No amount of deep breathing exercises in the mirror could have prepared me for this. I haven't been back home in two years, and now I'm standing in the airport waiting to board my flight. My flight home to attend my grandfathers funeral. It still doesn't feel real. I always thought when I was ready to come home, I'd be flying home to see them *both*. It hurts knowing I'm not going to be able to hug him the way I always did, or hear him call me Ollie. I'll never get to smell the tobacco and sugar scent of him, sweet and herbaceous.

I'm not ready for any of this, and I desperately want to run away. But I need to grow up and stop running from my problems. If I could have been stronger two years ago, I would have been able to hear Mitch out. Maybe now is the time to face all the reasons I left, if he even still cares. The woman on the speaker calls out my section, and I walk towards the doors of the plane. Ready or not, I'm doing this.

27

MITCH

enry's funeral is tomorrow, and I know Olive is already home. It's taking everything in me to leave her be, for now. She has enough on her plate with the grief of losing her grandfather, I can't barge in on her and clobber her with apologies. She's already in a vulnerable state, it would be wrong to beg for her forgiveness.

Ma isn't home, she's been helping Joan with funeral preparations and a part of me is happy to see them come together again. It's been hard knowing our families grew apart because of me. I tried talking to Ma about it once, but she brushed me off and said not to worry, everything will work out.

My Dad walks in from the barn, washes his hands and grabs something from the fridge before sitting next to me at the kitchen island. The man of not so many words is the first to break the silence, a rare occurrence.

"How you doing, son?" Simple enough, but still a hard question to answer.

"Honestly? I don't know. Olive is home, that much I'm sure, but I don't even know how to approach her. Or what to say if I even find the courage to."

"Mmm." He says thoughtfully, then sips his water. I wish he would say more, but I also appreciate the silence. He's giving me room to open up if I choose to. I want to, but I don't know if I can talk about her just yet. I've kept everything inside for so long, I'm not sure how to open up. I never even told anyone about the tattoo I got the first year after she left. I had put a lot of thought into it, but decided to go and get it done one day, spur the moment.

A few inches above my wrist, there's a tiny Butterfly with delicate black lines. I put it there as a reminder of how much she meant to me, how much she still does. I wanted it in a place where I'd always see it, at work, at home and use it as proof that she was real, proof that she was once mine. All I have left is this tattoo. A tiny symbol of how much I love her, how much I wish I had told her when I had the chance.

"Dad…" I say after a few minutes in my head. "I'm sorry about that night." I let my apology hang in the air, positive he knows which night I'm referring to.

"We never talked about what happened, not really. I just want you to know how fucking sorry I am, a day hasn't gone by where I don't think about it. Such a stupid decision I made, one that almost cost you your life…I…"

"Mitchell." Dad says abruptly, and I'm thankful he stopped me before I rambled on, embarrassing myself. "I know, son. It was a stupid decision, yes, but I don't hold it against you. You need to know that."

Shit. I don't want to cry in front of him, but I'm suddenly feeling like it's inevitable. I grip the counter top, squeezing it in the hopes that I can channel my emotions there instead of the impending tears about to fall down my cheeks.

"I appreciate that, Dad, I do. But I was reckless, I shouldn't have been drinking that night and I sure as shit shouldn't have agreed to come pick you up knowing that I wasn't sober. I promised myself I would do well in college so that I could come back here and make you proud. I can't change what happened, but I'll try to prove to you now that I can handle things." I want to say more, but the emotion in my throat is becoming too thick, so I shut up before I start blubbering like a toddler.

Dad turns in his chair so that he's facing me. It takes me a moment to turn so I can face him too, then I feel his hand gently rest on my shoulder. I close my eyes against the emotion, and just nod my head slightly, letting him know I'm listening. I didn't think this was going to be so fucking difficult to talk about.

"You have always made me proud, Mitch." He doesn't say anything else, just pats my back one more time, before giving my shoulder a squeeze and heading back outside. Maybe to some, that would seem insensitive, but to me it was everything. That small gesture was his way of reassuring me he's past it. The words I'm sorry always sound so simple, not strong enough to express one's regret. All these years they've been festering in my chest, waiting to be voiced, but I was always too afraid it wouldn't be enough. No amount of apologies could have expressed how I felt about that night.

This is the first time since the night I sat in this very kitchen, next to my mom and brother, that I've felt lighter. Collin rushed home from college as soon as he heard, and the three of us sat here waiting for word on Dad. Waiting at the table, hoping and fearing the phone would ring. Knowing that one way or another, Dad would be okay or he wouldn't. Those moments haunted me for years. I should have said what's been on my mind a long time ago, and it occurs to me I should have done the same with Olive.

If it wasn't too late to say I'm sorry to my Dad, then maybe it's not too late to say it to Olive.

When I see Gran's face as I make my way off the plane and over to baggage claim, I nearly fall into her arms, weak in the knees. She captures me in a gripping hug and neither of us makes any move to let the other go. I told myself I would be strong, and not cry the second I saw her. But as soon as her arms wrapped around me, I realized how much I'd missed her.

People watch us, taking in what clearly appears to be a reunion, as we hug and cry uncaring of all the spectators. There are so many things I want to say, things I practiced in my head on the plane ride, but now that I'm here, I can barely form the words. "Gran, I…"

"Shh, now don't you worry that pretty head of yours. You hear me?" She says against my ear as she calmly strokes my hair. It's how she and my mom always comforted me, and it makes me miss her too. I've stayed in contact with Lucy over the last two years, and learned more about my birth father. Something I couldn't do from Mitch. Besides, it felt right hearing it from her, it wouldn't have been as authentic to hear it from someone who didn't experience it the way she did.

I thought about reaching out to him when Lucy gave me his contact information, but I chicken out every time. One day I'll be ready to meet him officially and get to know him, but for right now it's still too weird. Every time I think about talking to him I'm reminded of the night I saw him for the first time, the night I realized Mitch kept it from me. I don't want to always associate him with that evening, so until I'm ready, he remains a bit of a mystery.

I grab my suitcase, and walk with Gran out to her car. We don't say much at first, neither of us willing to cut through the tension. But eventually I pipe up, asking if there's anything I can do to help with the funeral arrangements. "No dear, everything is all set. I'm just happy to have you home. Elaine has been an angel taking care of practically everything."

"How is she? I miss her, and her garlic bread." I admit, laughing lightly when Gran chuckles at my admission. Another thing I regret, in my emotional irrational state, I left without saying goodbye to anyone. I was desperate to get away from my problems and Mitch, but there were people here I never got the chance to explain myself to. Explain why I was leaving so quickly. About a month after I left, I got a call from Gwen, and as much as I tried not to, I broke down crying. It's like the weight of my life caught up to me in that moment and I let it all out, clobbering Gwen. It was humiliating, but she kept reassuring me she'd seen worse.

Elaine was like another family member to me, like the aunt I never had, and leaving without saying goodbye must have hurt. She's the first person I plan to go see once I'm settled. "She's doing fine as always, I swear that woman never tires. Must be from raising two rambunctious boys." Gran laughs at her own joke before turning to look at me. She didn't even say his name, and my body is tensing up at just the thought of seeing him.

"I'm sorry sweetie, I'm sure you're nervous about seeing him again."

"No, it's okay. Really." Can't tell if I'm trying to convince her, or myself. But judging by the way she side eyes me, I'd say its the latter. Maybe it's like ripping off a band aid, I just have to do it and hope for the best. Even though my skin is rough and has yet to heal.

It's just past lunch time, and now feels like the perfect time to visit Elaine. Mitch has either had lunch already, or skipped it like he usually does. Or *did*, I wouldn't fucking know. The house looks the same as it did, still big and beautiful with the wrap around porch and swing that holds memories too painful to revisit.

I take the steps slowly, listening for any voices in the house I may want to avoid, if I know he's in there I can run without being seen and avoid an awkward reunion I don't think either of us is prepared for. When I only hear dishes clinking in the kitchen, I take a deep breath and call out to Elaine. As soon as my voice echoes into the house, I hear a dish clatter in the sink followed by rushed footsteps. Elaine appears in the hallway, faltering only for a second, before she rushes the door.

"Olive! Oh honey." She hugs me the way Gran did in the

airport, and the emotion building in my chest makes its ways to my throat, clogging itself there. I try so hard to keep my emotions at bay, but they open like flood gates and before I know it, I'm sobbing with her the exact same way I did just a few hours ago.

"Elaine, I'm so…I'm so sorry. I never should have lef…" She releases me from the hug and pushes me back so she can look at me with piercing eyes. Eyes that remind me too much of Mitch, another punch to the chest.

"Don't you dare finish that sentence, young lady. I wouldn't have done a damn thing differently if I were in your shoes. Sure I would have loved a goodbye, but after what Mitchell did, keeping secrets like that…" She waves her hand in the air, as if she's swatting the memory away. "I would have taken off too. You were right leavin', doin' something for yourself, and don't ever let yourself or anyone else make you think otherwise. You hear me?"

"Yes ma'am." I say with a weak, watery smile. She hugs me again, even tighter than before and pulls me with her to the kitchen. I glance around nervously, hoping and fearing Mitch will appear at any second. Elaine can sense my thoughts and pats my arm.

"He's on the farm with Collin and his Dad, don't worry." Collin did in fact change his flight, but he wasn't able to get a seat on the same plane as me. As much as I appreciated his offer, I kind of needed the time alone to process everything. I had so many things I wanted to say to Gran, but they just wouldn't come out. It was like all the words in the world wouldn't do what one hug did.

"Elaine, can I ask you something?" I say as she fishes mugs out of the cabinet, and gets to pouring us some coffee.

"Ask me whatever you like, dear."

"Why do people always say follow your heart? How am I supposed to follow something that's in a million pieces?" It's random, but in a lot of ways, it's not. She knows why I'm asking, and she turns to look at me with deep emotion painting her face. Her wispy hair falls lightly around her glasses as she thinks for a moment before responding.

She walks around the counter until she's seated next to me and tucks a stray hair behind my ear, reminding me of when Mitch would do that. "You just have to pick up the first piece and keep going until you feel ready to put them all back together. Sometimes the road is long, but eventually you'll get there. And when you're ready to put the pieces back together, they might make a picture you never even imagined."

A tear slips down my cheek, and I close my eyes to keep more from falling. It's such a simple concept, take things one day at a time, one step at a time and remind yourself you'll get there when you're ready. This is why I missed her so much, I missed her wisdom and her kind demeanor. I needed this in New York more times than I'm willing to admit. I pride myself on getting out there and doing something on my own, with the help of Collin, but I'd be lying if I said I didn't need this comfort still. It's like when Gran gently stroked my hair in the airport as I sobbed into her crisp button down. I never realized how badly I missed home until I was here in the presence of the people that mean the most to me.

It's overwhelming.

"Olive, listen. I won't justify what Mitchell did, he should have been honest with you the second he found out about Drew. But if I've learned anything these past two years that you've been gone, it's that he loves you."

Hearing those words freezes everything in my body. I convinced myself for two years that he didn't care and that he never loved me. He never tried to come see me, and if it weren't for the letters, I'd think he'd forgotten me altogether. But if anyone knows him, it's Elaine. I can't help but wonder if a part of her is disappointed for the way he went about things. As his mother though, she probably just scolded him, whacked him upside the head and told him to fix it. Maybe that's why he sent the letters.

"I'm not so sure that's what people do when they love someone." I confess, my thoughts tumbling out before I can think them over.

"Love clouds our thoughts sometimes, and makes us act in ways we wouldn't normally. You just have to give him, and yourself, some grace, some time and the space to hear him out." She pats my hand, and gets back to fixing the coffee for us.

I'll never truly know what he felt, or how he even feels now, until I talk to him. Having a conversation with him is inevitable, if not for my own understanding, but his as well. It needs to happen while I'm home, but we've waited this long, another day won't hurt. I can't imagine having this conversation before Pop's funeral tomorrow morning. So it'll have to wait until later. All I have to do is avoid him until then.

Shouldn't be too hard.

I open my eyes to the sun streaming in through my curtains, just like the last morning before I left. It's going to be hot today, I can already feel the air thicken as it wafts through the open windows. I slept in my silk two piece pajama set, just like the night I was on the roof with Mitch. I woke up around two in the morning and climbed out onto the roof, like I've done so many times before. My legs brushed against the tiles like sandpaper, resulting in gooseflesh.

The night air was comfortable, warm but not sticky. I could have laid out there all night, I intended to until I felt a presence somewhere off in the field. My skin prickled with awareness, like I was being watched. It didn't unnerve me as much as I thought it would, because in my gut I knew what it was, *who* it was. I wondered how many times he might have come out here over the years to watch this empty roof. Knowing he used to see me star gazing up here. My chest aches at the memory of the last night I sat up here, the night before I left. That's the last time I ever saw Mitch.

It would have been so easy to call him over, which he would have done in a second, but he knew to stay away. He knew I needed space, that I would come to him when I was ready. Tears fall silently down my cheeks as I remember knowing I was leaving the next morning, a fact he was not aware of yet. Had he known, would he have come to the roof that night? Would he have tried convincing me to stay? So many questions swirled around my mind that night, and even still.

I stare at the black dress hanging from my closet door. Sleeveless, lined in delicate lace cutting just above the knee. Summers are scorching here, and I'm already nervous enough as it is. I don't want to be worrying about sweating through a dress that's heavy and uncomfortable. I opted for sandals, something told me wearing high heels outside during a funeral wasn't a smart choice. My luck, I'd trip and fall flat on my ass just as the funeral proceedings began.

As I touch up my makeup, I can hear the faucet in the bathroom down the hall. Gran must be up and getting ready herself. I would offer to help, but I get the feeling she needs this time alone, like I did on the plane here. I pull my hair into a loose ponytail, so that it's off my neck, and slip a pair of earrings in. Standing back, I take in my appearance, clean and simple. I love this black dress, but after the funeral I don't think I'll ever be able to wear it again without thinking of this day.

The stairs squeak beneath my feet as I make my way into the living room to wait for Gran. I take a seat on the settee and stare at the framed photos lining the walls. There's more photos on the wall of people we've lost than are living at this point, and it makes me want to scream. Why is life so fucking hard?

I pull out my phone and check my messages, seeing only one from Elaine about the limo heading our way to pick us up, I put it in my bag and wait by the door for Gran. She comes down, wearing a black jumpsuit, with her hair down and soft makeup. I let her borrow my waterproof mascara, I'm convinced days like today are what it was invented for.

The limo pulls up in front of the house, and we make our way down the steps to get in. Elaine and Mr. Murphy are already there waiting, and to my surprise Collin and Mitch are nowhere to be seen. Elaine must have told them to find another way to the church, I'm not even her flesh and blood and somehow she always has my back.

"Joan, I wish I had the right words to comfort you right now, but just know we're with you every step of the way." Elaine squeezes Gran's hands in her own, and the two sit side by side almost like sisters. Gran leans on her for support and while I'm incredibly happy they have built the friendship they have over the years, jealousy pricks at me that I don't have someone here to lean on in the same way. Sure, I made a few friends in New York, but nothing like this. Nothing like what I had with Mitch. The absence of him is becoming stronger and stronger every second I'm here, and the anticipation of seeing him in just a few minutes has every nerve ending in my body on high alert.

When we pull up in front of the church, I immediately see Collin. He's standing by the front doors, wearing a crisp clean cut navy suit tailored to his body. Sometimes I wish I could feel an ounce of anything romantic towards him, the way I do with Mitch. But it's just not there. He's been there for me in the way a big brother would be for his little sister, and I'll never be able to see him another way.

Mitch isn't with him though, causing my curiosity to grow. I assumed they rode here together, which would be the logical choice. I can't imagine he wouldn't show up at all, but maybe he's keeping his distance so he doesn't have to see me. I almost wish he would just come out from wherever he is right now, not knowing where he might be is distracting me more than it should.

"Ladies." Collin says as he holds out his arm for me to take, leading us to our seats in the front of the church. The congregation is packed, every row filled with towns people and friends, a true testament to how loved Pop was around here. I spot Gwen a few rows behind us, and she just smiles softly with her hand placed over her heart. I'll have to catch up with her after this. I've missed her fiercely, and would love to hear how Raising Hope is doing.

I wasn't at all expecting to see the two people sitting beside Gwen, but to her right is Lucy and *Drew*. My birth father, whom I've never even had a real conversation with. As if today wasn't already gearing up to be an emotional rollercoaster, it sure as shit is now.

Gran whispers in my ear as we sit down, "I invited them here, I'm sorry I didn't tell you. It slipped my mind." Her words sound a little frantic, due to her nerves the services are about to begin, or because she feels guilt for not letting me know they were coming. I don't want her feeling any of that right now, so I smile, squeezing her hand softly, and reassure her it's alright.

"I'm happy they came to support you, Gran. It's a welcome surprise." It might be a stretch seeing Drew, but I am happy Lucy is here. I had just begun getting to know her before I left, and even though we communicated frequently, it wasn't the same as spending time with her on her farm.

Just as the service begins, I hear the door in the back of the church softly click as someone comes in quietly. The hair on my neck rises and I try not to turn around to see who it is, ultimately failing. Slowly, I turn my head to the side and catch a glimpse of tan skin, tall and muscled as always with dark blonde hair and deep green eyes. He looks as good as I remember, if not better. My body's reaction to him is the same as always, and the pull to go to him is commanding. This is why I couldn't see him outside the church, he was waiting off to the side somewhere until I was seated before coming in. His way of avoiding a forced awkward encounter, something I definitely didn't want.

A small reminder that he still gets me.

Elaine and I flank Gran on either side, keeping her upright as the casket is lowered into the ground. Closure is descending over us, bringing no comfort with it. Sometimes closure doesn't bring the answers one needs, all it brings is the finality that the person you loved is no longer physically here. I guess his spirit is still with us, but I don't know how much I believe in all that shit. Until I see some sign that he's with me, I'm calling bullshit. If that were even possible, then where have my parents been all these years.

When the pastor finishes his closing statement, I walk Gran over to where Pop was just lowered, watching as she tosses a white rose on top. She's the strongest woman I know, losing her child and now her husband. I should have been here these last few years, I knew how sick he had been after the heart attack and still, I left. I fucking hate how selfish I can be.

"Gran?" I ask, squeezing her hand in mine. She doesn't say anything, just stares at the hole in the ground where my grandfather now is. What a weird ending, to live a whole life just to end it by being put in the ground like a vegetable. When I go, I want to be cremated. None of this burying the body shit.

"You know..."She starts, then pauses to collect her thoughts. "When I met Henry, I always pictured our life together. I pictured struggles and love, just like anyone else. Life has it's ways of throwing you for a loop, and it surely has." Her small laugh mixes with her soft sniffles as she continues.

"But I never thought of how much could be taken away, how much I could potentially lose for loving him as much as I did. Losing your mother, and Thomas, nearly broke us, but we still had you. We found the important thing in our lives to keep us going." Gran looks away from the spot she's been staring at, and turns to face me. Tears fall silently down my face, matching the ones falling down her face.

"I may not have ever thought about what this day would be like, how hard it would be, and...it *is* hard. But knowing that I got to spend my life with the man I love, the one who provided me with a beautiful family and the serenity of true love. That...well, that's just like winning the lottery. I can't think of anything more valuable."

The tears streaming down my face have doubled as I take in what Gran is saying. People have wandered off, probably heading back to the Murphy's house for the repast. I'm acutely aware that this is the last time it will ever just be my grandparents and I. It makes me want to rewind time and do so many things differently. I'm catapulting down a rabbit hole of regret when Gran shakes my shoulders so that I'm focused on her again.

"Olive, listen to me. I would have given anything to have just one more day with my Henry, but I can't. I miss him and I will always miss him, the way I do your mom. But I still have you. You are the one important thing that keeps me going. And I'll be dammed if you don't go and get what makes you happy. Stop wasting your time being away from your person, Ollie. Go to him, because that boy is madly in love with you and you need to let him tell you. You need to hear him out, not just for his sake, but yours as well. Do you understand me?"

My mouth falls open as I replay her words again and again. Is it clear to everyone else that Mitch loves me? Everyone but me? I never read his letters, so I truly don't know how he's felt since I've been gone. But for the first time, I want to find out. I want to hear what he has to say and *then* I can make the decision that's best for me. Running away only did one thing…Prove that I'm a coward and can't handle the tough things life throws at you. I may have ran away, but those troubles still followed me.

I made it through losing my parents, finding out I was adopted and meeting my birth mom, and now losing Pop. I somehow made it through the biggest challenges in my life, but I haven't been able to face Mitch. He still affects me in such a profound way, a way that can only be described as love.

I'm in love with him, and my soul hasn't been right since I left. That's why New York hasn't been fulfilling the way I always dreamed it would. Only Mitch can do that.

I just fucking hope he feels the same.

I find Mitch leaning up against a tree, just at the opening to the path that leads to the pond. I wonder if he spends a lot of time there still. His back is to me, and he doesn't turn around as I approach. Either he isn't ready to, or he doesn't hear me. Whatever the reason, I take a few seconds to compose myself before having this conversation.

A twig snaps beneath my feet and Mitch startles, turning around quickly to find me frozen in place staring at him. Okay, so I guess he just didn't hear me coming. "Sorry, I wasn't trying to sneak up on you." I say as I look down at my feet, too shy to meet his gaze. I'm nervous, and the shaking in my voice is proof. I slowly lift my eyes slightly, until I'm face to face with his bare forearms. A soft gasp escapes before I'm able to reel it in. "What?" I whisper as my eyes stay focused on the ink.

Before he has a chance to respond, his eyes follow mine to wear they're staring. His sleeves are rolled up, and on his forearm in tiny delicate black ink, is a little butterfly. I look up at him, his eyes locked on mine with equal parts softness and caution. I look back to the tattoo, thoughts swirling around in my head. When I look up at him, so many questions on the tip of my tongue, he just shrugs and rubs the tattoo.

"I missed you. You're etched into my skin, Olive." I can't

breathe, I can't even move as I just stare at him and the little tattoo he got, for *me*. He doesn't move, just watches me with wariness, wondering if I'm about to bolt again. When he takes a step towards me, I stumble backwards on reflex. The pain in his face makes me want to double over. I'm not trying to hurt him, that's the last thing I want to do, but if he tries to touch me right now I might unravel.

He tries again, taking slow steps closer to me until we're about a foot apart. I can practically taste his scent, and it's like a drug I gave up but can never quite quit. His arm slowly reaches out to touch mine lightly. Sparks dance across my skin at the contact, and I have to resist the urge to lean completely into him. "I know I hurt you…But, is there still a part of you that remembers how good it felt to be together? Please tell me you haven't forgotten, even after all this time."

My breathing is labored, I'm so frustrated with my emotions lately, it makes me want to scream and cry until all of it is drained from my tired mind. My body is vibrating with tension, and I want nothing more than to run, or to hit something. Both would be kind of satisfying and totally inappropriate given this moment.

Taking a deep shuddering breath, I focus my eyes on his for the first time. "I remember everything, Mitch. But a part of me doesn't want to. Seeing you is just a painful reminder of what we used to have, I'm at war with myself over it. Because when I look at you I just see secrets, but when I touch you…" I rub his arm absentmindedly, tracing a finger lightly over the tattoo. It's not raised anymore, so he's had it a while.

"Every time I touch you, I feel everything for the first

time again. Do you have any idea what that's like, Mitch?" I pant heavily, years of words tumbling out of me in a rush, the emotions becoming too heavy to remain calm, to heavy to hold onto anymore. I never realized how much they were weighing me down until I got this close to Mitch, all the feelings resurfacing like they never left.

Mitch squares his shoulders, standing taller and furrowing his brows. "Yes, as a matter of fact I do, Butterfly. I can't be away from you any longer than I already have. I wake up and the first thing I see are those dark hazel eyes. Every time I breathe it's like I can taste you on my tongue. So yes, I know what war you're fighting. But don't you think it's time we stop fighting it?" He reaches up and lightly brushes the hair out of my face, allowing his thumb to caress my bottom lip as his fingers tangle with the hair at the base of my neck. "Because every second I spend away from you is one less second I have to worship you. It's already too much."

My mind goes blank, I don't even know how to respond or what words are anymore. I'm staring at him with a dumbfounded expression, willing the words out of me. Willing myself to forgive him and move on. What he did wasn't of malicious intent, he just didn't know how to get the words out. Just like I can't right now.

I finally get it, the desire to be honest, to voice your feelings and get them out there for the other person to hear, but being too afraid to speak. I wish I could have come to this realization two years ago but we've made it to where we are now. Maybe it's time I stop being afraid of abandonment, of being lied to, and appreciate the important things in life. Like

Gran said.

Mitch is watching me carefully, but I still haven't said a word. The hold he has on my neck tightens slightly, and I know he's holding himself back, waiting for me to make the first move. If only I could. "I can taste you past my lips, Olive. You're in my mind, my veins, my very *being*. Every part of me has you flowing through me and I can't turn it off." He steps closer into my space and I don't dare move. Enjoying him close to me once again, having missed it more than I ever realized.

"I was an asshole in the beginning, but you gave me a shot. All I'm asking is for another chance. Because feeling you in me but not being able to have you anymore is like acid burning me from the inside out." He rubs the spot on his chest where his heart is, and my eyes trail to memorize the movements. My hands rest by my sides, itching to cover his with my own, a gesture to make him see that I understand.

With one hand, he lifts my chin, the way he always used to, until I'm looking at him. Tears are brimming my eyes, but I can't close them to keep the tears from falling. I can't look away from Mitch as he opens his mouth one more time. "I love you, and I should have told you that a long time ago."

My body comes alive in ways it never has before, I can finally breathe again. The heavy weight I've been feeling lifts off of me so quickly, I can't be sure it was ever even there. What he did, not telling me about Drew was to protect me, I see that now. He did it in his own way which backfired in both our faces, but I think I've been punishing him longer than he deserved. I am not perfect, I can be selfish and make unfair rash decisions. But standing here with him right now, being given a second chance to *really* see what this could be, is the best decision of my life.

The words I've been unable to speak since I first walked down here, come rushing up from deep within me, finally ready to be spoken. "I love you too, Mitch. There's been no one since you." I wrap my arms around his neck, pulling him close to me until our lips are only millimeters apart. "I'm sorry I never gave you the chance to explain, I shouldn't have run like that."

All the tension in his body releases, I can physically see the relief flood his body and take over. It's like we've both been cleansed in a way, free of our past mistakes, ready to do this *for real.*

A smirk crosses his face, and that playful demeanor of his comes out. He reaches up and tucks a strand of hair behind my ear, caressing my cheek as he lowers his hand to rest on my waist. "I'll just have to find ways to punish you for that, clear your schedule babe…You're mine for the foreseeable future." He chuckles just before he leans down and captures my lips with his. I can taste his laughter along with the sweet and crisp flavor invading every one of my senses. *Finally.*

I still have so many things to figure out, but right now all I care about is the feel of Mitch pressed against my body, molding us together. I've been feeling off since living in New York, this is the sign I needed to show me where I truly belong. *Home.*

Mitch picks me up from under my thighs until I'm cradled around his waist, lips never leaving mine. He walks us down the path towards the pond, and I can practically feel the heat simmer down a tiny bit. I weave my hands through his hair, gripping him closer to me.

As we reach the tree where we had our first time, he sets me down and looks around. "I haven't been here since you left." He confesses, and something about his admission surprises me.

"Why?" I ask, too curious not to.

"Everything about this place was you. I couldn't come back here without thinking of you and how I lost you. It was too hard. But fuck, I've missed it." He pulls me into his arms as he rests us against the white oak tree, sighing in contentment as the water ripples next to us and leaves sway above in the soft breeze. The lights he hung are still up there, and boy do I hope they still work. I plan on spending *a lot* of nights down here with the man I love.

Turning around, I straddle my legs around his waist until we're eye level. I grip his hair in my hands, pulling slightly until I hear a growl. I can feel his hard length pressing up against me, and I've never wanted to rip someone's clothes off faster. It's been two whole years since I've had sex, I wasn't lying when I told Mitch there's been no one since him. No one physically, and no one in my heart.

I plan on taking my time with him, savoring every movement, every sound, until I can't take anymore. But we need to get back to the house, guests will be showing up and I don't want to worry Gran about where I am.

Hell, she probably already knows.

As if sensing my dilemma of wanting to stay in this

bubble, but needing to get back. He caresses my cheek, looks up at the lights then back to me, and whispers deliciously against my ear. "We've got plenty of time, Butterfly."

We kiss for a while before getting up and heading down the path towards the field next to his house. Mitch laces his fingers in mine and looks at me with a sweet smile. My heart beats wildly in my chest at how much I love this man, how much I've missed him. The farm comes into view as we crest the hill, leaving the pond behind us, and already I can't wait to come back here tonight.

I stare down at the tattoo on his arm again, feeling a gush of warmth in my chest that he got this for me, he cared *that* much. I should probably admit I never read his letters, but not right now. I plan on going home and reading every single one before I go to sleep tonight. I smile up at him and he leans in to place a soft kiss on my forehead. "So, what comes next, Butterfly?"

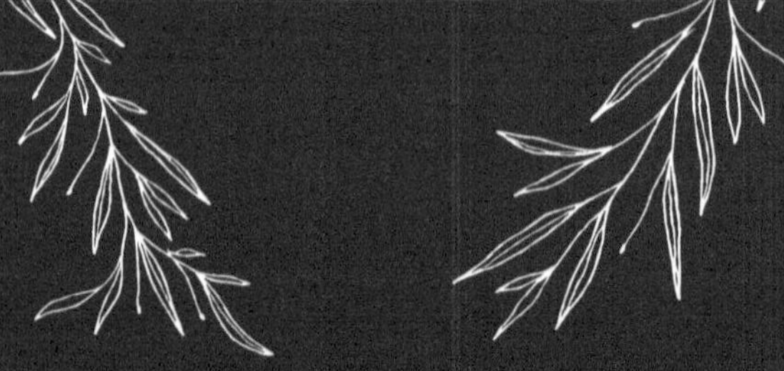

Epilogue
MITCH

"Dude, come on! We're gonna miss the first pitch." I say as we weave through the crowds in New York. The streets are littered with people as we make our way to Yankee Stadium. We finally got to take the trip to the city to visit Collin and catch a baseball game. I had mentioned it to Dad years ago, never expecting we'd actually get the opportunity to go.

Or that Dad would actually agree to leave the farm.

We decided to make it a family trip, rather than just a guys weekend. While my Dad, Collin and I head to the game, the ladies are off sight-seeing and shopping in the city. It took a little arm twisting, but we finally convinced Joan to come. Something I could tell meant a lot to Olive.

Last night she took us to the gallery she'd been working at, and then to her favorite restaurant. The food was delicious, but the prices nearly made Dad choke when he read the menu. We aren't used to fancy like this back home, that's for sure. Places around here make Della's look like a fast food restaurant.

Collin jogs up behind Dad and I, tucking his phone back into his pocket. "Sorry," he breathes in and out heavily a few times, "Just had to check in with Ivy at the office." He falls into step with us, and I give him a knowing look. "Don't look at me like that, asshole."

I lift both hands in surrender, painting a coy look on my face, my attempt at looking innocent is futile though. "I said nothing."

"You didn't have to. I know that look, and before you get ahead of yourself, she's just my new assistant."

"Damn, okay. Don't get your panties in a wad, I've just never heard you mention her is all." Dad looks over with a slight smirk and I know he's thinking the same thing I am. Only difference is, I'm not afraid to call Col on his bullshit. He's the type of guy who will freely talk about someone or something if there's nothing else to it. The fact that he's trying to avoid this topic says it all.

That and the nervous look he's wearing right now.

I decide to drop it, save this information in my back pocket for another day. Something tells me I'll be hearing the name Ivy on more than one occasion. He may think he's brushing us off to prove there's nothing to talk about, but we all know, Collin included, there's *much* to talk about. He's just lucky the women aren't here. They'd be beating him down for details as we speak.

After we scan our tickets and find our seats, we settle in for the game. I've always wanted to come to Yankee Stadium with my Dad and brother, and now that we're here, I can hardly believe it. We didn't travel much as kids, and certainly not this far. Not when my parents had so many responsibilities on the farm. They didn't like leaving employees in charge of things unless it was urgent.

As excited as I am for the game, I'm even more excited for tonight. As a surprise birthday gift for Olive, I got us tickets to Luke Combs tonight at the Madison Square Garden. She told me years ago that she'd always wanted to see him in concert, the night we first danced to his song at the fundraiser for Gwen. That's how this trip went from a guys weekend to a family vacation. Something I'm not mad about in the slightest.

I want to do everything with Olive, now that we have this second shot at a real relationship. Finding ways to make her happy and feel appreciated, is my new hobby. Seeing the look on her face when she sees where I'm taking her tonight, will easily make one of my top five favorite moments.

Olive is demure, never wanting people to make a fuss over her, or attract too much attention to herself. She's thoughtful with everyone else, always putting Joan and others ahead of her needs. It's time she sees how important it is that she comes first. Something I'm more than excited to do.

At the end of the ninth inning, we get ready to head back to Collin's place to meet up with the girls. As we stand we all laugh at the amount of peanut shells under our feet, crunching as we make our way out of the aisle. You can't come to a ball game and not enjoy massive amounts of peanuts and a ball park frank.

When we reach the car, Dad stops and turns to face my brother and I. With no warning, he pulls us both in for a tight hug. It's so out of character for him, that both Collin and I freeze before returning the gesture. Don't get me wrong, Dad has always been there for us and shown us how loved we are. But always in ways much different from Ma and her obsessive need to smother us with affection. This hug says a lot.

"Today was one of the best days I've had in years, thank you boys." And with that, he releases us and gets in the car. I exchange a look with Collin, understanding something words could never quite express, we nod to each other before Col shoves my shoulder and climbs into the drivers seat. Yeah, today was perfect.

"Seriously, Mitch. When are you taking this blindfold off?" Olive is standing in front of me, wearing that soft cotton lace dress she wore the first time I saw her, the same one she wore on our first official date. Sometimes I swear I couldn't love her more, and then I do.

I laugh to myself. This fucking girl.

She still takes my breath away, and I'd gladly give her all of them if I get to be with her just like this for the rest of my life. "It's coming off, just one second." I say as I turn her body until she's facing the Luke Combs SOLD OUT sign outside the venue.

Untying the fabric, I let it slowly fall from her face as she takes in where we are. People are bustling around us, just like earlier today on the way to the game, but I pay them no attention. All I see is Olive, and the beautiful shocked expression she's wearing as she takes in where we are. "You… How?" I love when she's lost for words, it means I've done my job.

I chuckle next to her as I weave my hand through hers, bringing her attention to me. "You told me you've always wanted to see him in concert. So, I got tickets for your birthday. Surprise!" I say, starting to feel a little nervous at her lack of expression.

She stares up at the flashing sign, lights all around us and people crowding the side walk on either side of us. She's immune to it all. Finally, she looks at me, with those soft hazel eyes, and smiles. "You remembered?"

I want to tell her I remember everything about her. That while we were apart I used to quiz myself on things about her so that I'd never forget. I used to find things I knew would smell like her if she were still around, just to catch a glimpse of that paradise I'd been missing so much. I want to tell her that every time I saw a firefly dancing at night, I'd remember that first time we lost ourselves in the tall grass of the field in front of her house. How I still remember how she tastes. The way her body seemed to fit perfectly with mine.

I could tell her everything I remember about her in great detail. The smattering of freckles that line her nose and dip between her breasts. How I used to dream of connecting them like stars in the sky. The way her long auburn hair would blow in the breeze of my truck as we drove around on those summer nights. The look of betrayal on her face when she learned the truth about Drew, and how I kept it from her. Then the look she gave me when she decided I was worth a second chance.

All of it is imbedded so far into my brain, it's become a part of me. My nerve endings buzz for her when she's near.

Like her soul is the other half of me, and my body recognizes her instantly. I look at her, really look at her, and study the expression on her face right now. Saving it to memory, along with all the others I never want to forget.

Her lips are parted, chest rising and falling ever so slightly, and the tiniest bit of moisture lines her eyes almost making her look angelic as the lights illuminate her face. The blush from earlier is gone when I told her how much I loved this dress, how I still remember the first time I saw her in it. She didn't think I would remember, but I did. There is nothing about her too insignificant not to commit to memory. I remember everything.

I smile at her, feeling the warmth spread across her cheeks as I tuck the loose tendrils of hair behind her ear. She dips her head into my hand, enjoying the contact, I kiss her softly, tasting the gasp on her lips as mine capture hers. I pull back as her eyes meet mine once more, "I remember everything, Butterfly."

Bonus
MITCH'S LETTER

Dear Butterfly,

It's apparent to me that you aren't reading my letters. If you had been, I would like to think at least something in one of them would have inclined you to reach out. Since you haven't, I have to assume you've decided against reading them, or you simply don't care anymore. I guess I wouldn't blame you either way.

If you have read them up until this point, first off, thank you. I poured a lot of my heart into those letters, hoping and praying you could see just how sorry I am for betraying your trust. I also want you to know I won't try and convince you to come back to me. If that were something you felt strongly about, you would have by now. But dammit, I wish you'd come home, Olive. Should you ever decide that's what is best for you, know I will be here, always. I guess since this is my last letter to you, I'll just fill you in on some things happening around here. I figured it would be better not to beg you to forgive me like I did in the last five letters.

Your grandparents are doing well, from what I've seen of them. I try not to come around as much anymore because I don't know if I'm a painful reminder for them, I would understand if my presence was. They miss you, we all do, but they're so proud of you. From an outside opinion, I want you to understand that. Joan probably says it to you all the time because that's the kind of selfless person she is, but they truly are.

The lights are still up at the pond, or at least I think they are. We had a big storm a few days ago, so some of them may have fallen. I haven't gone back since you left, everything about that place reminds me of you. If I go there it'll feel like you're with me, and knowing you're not will just feel like another punch to the chest. I do however look at the painting you made for me, I probably stared at it every night for weeks before falling asleep. Sounds creepy I know, but we never took any photos together, so the painting is the only proof I have that you were real, and that at one point, you were mine.

Wherever you are, Olive, I hope you're okay. I hope that one day you find what you're looking for in life, whether that be here or in New York. Only took Ma a month before she broke down and told me you were staying with Collin. I spent a lot of time in the gym that week, not going to lie. The jealous side of me hated that my own brother was the one giving you a safe place, when I no longer could. But the rational side of me was grateful. Collin is a great guy, and as much as I wish he too would move home, I'm glad you have a place to stay.

When we were together, it used to drive me crazy that you couldn't see how incredibly amazing you are, inside and out. I never got to meet your parents, but shit, they did a hell of a job raising you. Then your grandparents after they passed. I'm sure even with the distance, Lucy has been there for you, not taking the place of your parents, but filling the void a little.

As for me, well I'm the same as I have been since the last day I saw you. The hurt in your eyes when you looked at me, the realization that I'd kept something huge from you, haunts me. I wish I could go back and do everything about that situation differently, make you see just how important you are to me. I hate that I hurt you, that the look of betrayal on your face was directly because of my actions. Just know that I never intended to betray your trust, and if you ever give me another chance, I'll spend everyday proving to you I'm worth gaining that trust back.

I also wanted you to know I got a tattoo last week — Ma only mildly freaked out — until I told her what it was for, who it was for. It's a tiny Butterfly, etched into my skin the way you're forever etched into my heart. I look at it everyday as a reminder, a reminder that even the painful parts of life can be worth it, sometimes even beautiful. Pain is a reminder that we're alive, that we feel things so deeply and truly. It hurts not having you here, but I won't ever forget what it felt like to be with you, Olive.

If you've read this far, I want to tell you one final thing. Not for me, or for anyone else, but for you...I want you to do something just for you. Something you feel in your heart is worthwhile, whether it be big or small. Ignore

the rest of the world and it's opinions, and focus on what makes you happy. Follow that feeling, wherever it may take you, and just know I'll always be here for you.
With love,
Mitch

The end